THE BIG BOOK OF
Summer Snogs

THE BIG BOOK OF Summer Snogs

RED FOX

A Red Fox Book

Published by Random House Children's Books
61-63 Uxbridge Road, London W5 5SA

A division of The Random House Group Ltd
London Melbourne Sydney Auckland
Johannesburg and agencies throughout the world

7 9 10 8 6

Playing Away, Girls On Tour and *Too Hot Too Handle*
all first published in Great Britain by Red Fox in 1997

This edition 2001

Printed and bound in Great Britain by Bookmarque Ltd,
Croydon, Surrey

Papers used by The Random House Group Limited are natural,
recyclable products made from wood grown in sustainable forest.
The manufacturing processes conform to the environmental
regulations of the country of origin.

THE RANDOM HOUSE GROUP Limited Reg. No. 954009

www.kidsatrandomhouse.co.uk

ISBN 0 09 940967 4

Contents

Girls on Tour

Alison James

Bon Voyage

Grey skies, an even greyer sea, gale-force winds and a ferry that seemed about as stable and secure as a toy boat in a jacuzzi. It was not, Jodie reflected, clinging to the deck rail and chucking her guts up for what had to be the fifth time in almost as many minutes, supposed to be like this. Not when yesterday she'd forked out a load of dosh on a new 'do' which didn't exactly lend itself to the windswept look. Not when her gorgeous new strappy dress wasn't wind and salt-water resistant. And especially not when she'd done as her mum had suggested and had dosed up on seasick pills which tasted bad enough on the way down, let alone on the way back up again!

A real waste of money they'd been. And the same could be said for the 'all day full English breakfast' she'd scoffed less than half-an-hour ago. A regurgitated £6.99's worth was now adrift somewhere in the English Channel. Mmmmm! Yummy! Lucky fish! That's if there were any fish actually alive in water this murky.

The only consolation was that she wasn't the only one who was suffering. Stella and Ushi, the other two members of their 'girl gang' trio – the 'unholy trinity' as they called themselves – Jodie's absolute best mates with whom she'd come away, had just ralphed up their insides too.

'Oh my God, I think I'm a goner,' moaned Ushi, sinking down onto the deck, her thick hair falling forward across her heart-shaped face while her cut-offs and tiny T-shirt were, like Jodie's dress, completely soaked through. 'Why, oh why didn't we take the flamin' chunnel?'

''Cos it cost too much,' groaned Stella, shakily wiping her mouth with a tissue. 'I'd have gladly paid it if I'd known it was going to be as rough as this, though.'

'No point crying over spilt milk,' Jodie sighed.

'Aw, don't,' muttered Ushi. 'Yeuchh! The thought of off-milk! You'll set me off again!' She took a long, grateful slurp of *eau minerale*. 'Call me a travel dyslexic but I never imagined the crossing between Dover and Boulogne would be this dodgy. It's summer, for crying out loud! I thought we'd be sunning our selves and sipping cocktails, not freezing our butts off and losing our lunch!'

'The mysteries of the sea,' intoned Stella mysteriously. 'Who can predict her tempestuous moods?'

'Eh?' muttered Jodie.

Stella grinned. 'I once wrote a poem about the sea – got an "A" for it, too.'

'Yeah, well . . .' went on Ushi. 'I'm just grateful there'll be no more boats after this one. And no more moody seas, either. We'll be InterRailing, won't we? And who's ever heard of anyone getting train sick?'

'A whole month!' sighed Stella dreamily. 'Can you really believe it yet? I can't. After all those months of planning and talking about it, we're finally doing it. Training our way across Europe for four fantastic weeks. It's going to be a-bloody-mazing. No mardy parents sticking their beaks in where they're not wanted, no college, no boring nights in in front of the telly. But fun, fun, fun! Sightseeing, shopping, scoffing down the local delicacies and . . .'

'Loads-a-lads,' Jodie finished for her. 'Mmmm! Yes please! Foreign fare – and I'm not talking frogs' legs or spag bog, either. It'll be like being let loose in a kind of dream deli. Lean, luscious blonds from Scandanavia, horny *Herren* from Germany, fabulous French men, gorgeous Greeks . . . Ooh yeah, all that hot-blooded totty from the Med. And that's not including the scores of sun-kissed, snog-hungry Brits we're bound to run into, too.'

Easing herself upright, Ushi suddenly looked out to sea. She smiled. 'Forget boys for a mo', me old ship maties! Be it my imagination or has this here vessel stopped rocking n'rolling a tad?'

Jodie hauled herself up and followed Ushi's gaze. Yep, she was right. The wind had dropped and the waves were now lapping gently against the ship's hull rather than threatening to come aboard.

'Affirmative, I'm glad to say.'

'Well hallejuiah for that,' whooped Stella, getting up and tentatively testing out her sea legs. 'I thought we'd be stuck up here for the duration. So little time and so much to see! The games room looked pretty happening and we haven't even touched the duty free yet. My pulse points are just itching to be dabbed with criminally-expensive perfume. Then . . .' she grinned wickedly at the other two, her dark eyes flashing like black diamonds, 'there's the bar . . .'

'Oh yeah?' teased Jodie. 'And what's so special about the bar? As if I didn't know!'

'Posh totty!' Ushi answered excitedly. She held out a hand and Jodie pulled her up. 'That's if they're still there. Three gorge guys. All floppy hair, fresh faces and clipped vowels. Not our usual types, perhaps, but we're on holiday and you know what they say, a change is as good as a rest. Mmmmm . . .' she licked her lips thoughtfully, 'I've never snogged a posh lad before. Wonder what it's like.'

'Absolutely spiffing,' chortled Jodie. 'I bet you can tell a pedigree tongue a mile orf!'

Stella had already started running down the deck. 'What are you waiting for, darlings?' she yelled back over her shoulder. 'If I've got anything to do with it, we're all about to find out!'

'InterRailing round Europe, huh?' the poshest of the three posh-lads smarmed. 'For a month? *Quelle coïncidence, lay-deez. Nous aussi.* My friends and I would be more than happy to accompany *medmoiselles* some of the way.'

Jodie looked at Ushi and Stella, not at all surprised to see that they looked as hacked-off as she felt. What an idiot! Correction. What a trio of idiots! They'd been sitting in the bar with this threesome for the best part of half-an-hour yet Smarm-Features only just seemed to have picked up on the fact that they were InterRailing too. Talk about tedious! He and his mates had been too busy fiddling around with their mobile phones and talking about themselves to absorb information about anyone else. Too busy sounding off about such-and-such a ball and all these 'Taras' and 'Tamaras' who, apparently, found them absolutely irresistable.

'Anyone else noticed that a pack of pigs have just taken flight?' Ushi had quipped at that point.

Jodie and Stella had laughed but not a flicker of mirth had passed across the chaps' mugs. God, they were so arrogant, so up themselves, Jodie considered – not for the first time – that if the interior wasn't up to much, then the exterior – however gorge it might be – didn't count for a whole lot, either. What's more, she was pretty damned sure that the toff-type accents weren't all they seemed. Nobody talked *that* posh – never mind plums, these guys had bricks in their mouths. Not only that, they were way, way, out of date.

'Yuppies,' she wanted to say, 'went out with shoulder pads.'

'Yah,' Smarm-Features brayed on. 'We could act as your knights in shining armour. Real three musketeer stuff. *Mon Dieu*, it is not always safe out there for pretty lay-deez like yourselves.'

'You're right there,' Stella muttered. 'Not with the likes of you on the loose.'

Jodie bit into her hand to stop herself from laughing out loud. So what if they were prime prats? All the better to have some laughs with – or rather at.

'Sorry?' one of them asked Stella. 'I didn't quite catch that.'

'Juice!' Ushi interrupted suddenly. 'She'd like some orange juice. Here Stell, have one of these.'

Trying unsuccessfully not to giggle, Ushi handed Stella one of the cartons that was on the table.

'Actually, they're mine,' piped up one of the posh lads. 'I bought them earlier. You're welcome to buy one off me though, if you like.'

Jodie shook her head in disbelief. Was he for real? Apparently so – God, what a tightarse!'

'Forget it!' muttered Ushi.

'Oh my,' Stella looked at her watch and yawned. 'Doesn't time fly when you're having fun. Not!'

'Know something?' Ushi suddenly announced. 'I feel a bit sick again. In fact,' she got up from the table and lurched towards Smarm-Features, 'I think I'm going to . . .' She made a retching noise in her throat.

'Oh for God's sake!'

Smarm-Features moved his chair away from her. Jodie started to laugh out loud. Ushi could be a real a law unto herself at times.

Staggering around the bar as if the storm really had blown up again, Ushi stumbled out through the door. Jodie and Stella looked at each other then got up to follow her.

'See you, er, Jodie,' Smarm-Features called after them. Stella nudged her. Jodie pulled a face.

'Not if I see you first,' she muttered under her breath and, catching Stella's arm, the two of them walked swiftly out of the bar without a backward glance.

They expected to find Ushi waiting for them but she was nowhere to be seen.

'She'll have gone to the duty free shop,' said Stella. 'She'll be spraying herself like there's no tomorrow.'

But she wasn't. Stella and Jodie spent some time sniffing and sampling the scores of bottles on offer before deciding they'd better look for Ushi. They scoured the loos – on all four decks – the games room, the numerous lounges, restaurants and cafés, the duty free shop (again!) and completely circumnavigated the exterior deck area. But no Ushi. It was weird. In fact two things were weird – the way Ushi had just disappeared and the spooky way the wind had started to blow strongly again. It was almost as if Ushi had prophesied it. Where the hell was she? In the end, they were forced to go back to the bar to ask Smarm-Features and his divvy mates if they'd seen her.

''Fraid not, Jodie m'dear,' he slimed. 'Not that she'd be sitting with us, anyway. Methinks we come from very different places.'

Methinks?!!! Just what was that tosser on?

'Methinks he fancies you, "Jodie m'dear",' chuckled Stella once they were out of his hearing.

'I know – worst luck,' Jodie grimaced.

'You know, it's a shame he wasn't out on deck when it was dead rough,' Stella went on. 'He could have gone for a dip.'

Jodie's face filled with worry. 'Don't say that, Stell. What if that's what's happened to Ushi? She could have gone out on deck when she left the bar. Who knows? Maybe she really did start to feel sick again. Well, the wind *had* just started to blow again, hadn't it? Say she went up to the top deck. Say a sudden gust knocked her off balance. There'd only be one place for her to fall, wouldn't there? And she's not a strong swimmer, is she?'

'Don't be ridiculous, Jodes,' said Stella. 'We'll have one more look around then we'll go see the captain or whoever. Get a message put out over the tannoy.' She put an arm around Jodie. 'Don't get your knickers in a twist – she'll turn up.'

But having circumnavigated the ship a second time and still no Ushi, Jodie had gone into major fret mode and Stella, too, was starting to get a bit niggled.

'What are we going to tell her mum?' Jodie whined. 'We can't just ring up and say, "Sorry, your daughter's fallen off the ferry".'

'Who's fallen off the ferry?' It was Ushi. She grinned. 'Anyone I know?'

Jodie grabbed Ushi and flung her arms around her. 'You're safe! Thank God! We thought you'd fallen overboard.'

'Eh?' Ushi looked bemused.

'We!' Stella exclaimed. 'You, y'mean. Where've you been anyway, Ushi?' Stella scolded. 'We've been looking everywhere for you.'

'Ditto,' replied Ushi. 'When I left the bar, I went to the loo. Then I peeped through the bar door to see if you were still with those creeps. You weren't so I went looking for you. When I couldn't find you, I figured we'd meet up eventually so I decided to chill out and write some postcards until we did.'

She sat down in the nearest chair and threw a couple of cards onto the table.

'Already?' Stella asked. 'We only left home this morning. Who've you been writing to?' She picked one up.

'*Snake Hips*,' she read aloud. '"*It's only been a few hours but I miss you like mad*" ... Blimey, Ush, who the hell's "Snake Hips" when he's at home?'

'Davy,' beamed Ushi. 'You know, that lad I copped off with the other night. He's soooo gorgeous. Call it forward planning but I want to keep him sweet for when we get home. No post-holiday blues for me, girls!'

'So does that mean no holiday romances, either?' enquired Stella. 'If you're keeping yourself sweet for him?'

'Does it hell,' grinned Ushi. 'But what darling Davy doesn't know won't hurt him, will it?'

Jodie shook her head. 'You're what my gran would call a caution, Ushi,' she tutted and sat down at the table with the others. 'It'll all end in tears. Still, never mind about that now. We're all together again so what better time than to work out exactly where we're heading. I mean, we've discussed it often enough but we still have to work out a definite route. Or should that be the definitive route? Well, whatever, either way, we haven't done it yet . . .'

'OK, so where's it going to be?' Ushi reached into her bag, pulled out a map of Europe and spread it across the table. 'Now where did we kind-of agree on last time? Oh yeah . . .' Her fingers started to walk across the map in a westerly direction. 'Once we've arrived in Boulogne, we go to Lille so we can catch a train to Brittany – so that means we're in north west France . . . Then, we move diagonally across country to the Riviera and down into Italy. Yes please!' She shivered deliciously. 'All those divine Latino boys called Carlo and Giovanni. Even their names are sexy. Anyway, where to when we've been there? Is there indeed anywhere worth going after *la bella Italia*.'

'Sure is,' piped up Jodie. 'What about Greece?'

'Mmmm, could be tricky,' mused Ushi. 'I fancy it but it'll mean taking another ferry from – where it is now? – oh yeah, Brindisi. Do we mind about that? What d'you think, Stella? Stell, what's up? You've gone really quiet.'

Jodie looked at Stella. Her usually olivey complexion had turned pink and she looked kind of embarrassed.

'France is OK,' she muttered. 'I mean, it's fine. It's just that . . . when we hit the Riviera we might have to turn right rather than left. In fact . . .' Pink turned to deepest crimson. 'We'd probably do best to skip the Riviera altogether.'

'Why?' asked Jodie and Ushi at the same time.

'Because . . .' Stella shifted uncomfortably in her seat. 'I mean . . . Look, who does this remind you of?' She stood up, slightly stooped her shoulders and pulled on an imaginary cigar. '*You think I mad? I let you go round Europe for a month with just those friends of yours? Nice girls they are but they just girls. Like you. You think you a woman, Stella but you not. You just seventeen. You just a baby. OK, I let you go but on one condition. You go stay with your aunt Maria in España. For one week. I insist. Then I know you all right.*'

Jodie and Ushi stared at her blankly.

'It's my dad,' Stella sighed exasperated. 'I suppose I should have told you before,' Stella started fiddling nervously with her hair. 'But I was just too embarrassed. And a bit ashamed.'

'About what?' Jodie asked, still looking some-what confused. 'Come on, Stell, you can tell us. We're your friends, remember.'

'Your best friends,' added Ushi. '"One For All" and all that.'

Stella smiled gratefully. 'It's just that my parents said they'd only let me come away with you on one condition. Basically, we've got to go to Spain for a bit and stay with my auntie. So she can see for herself that I'm all right and report back to my olds.'

'Well that's OK,' Ushi laughed. 'Blimey, I thought you were going to say something really awful. Going to Spain probably knocks Greece on the head but Spain or Italy? It doesn't really matter, does it? They're both mighty fine places. Yeah! Spain! *Olé*! Thinking about it, I quite like the names Javier and Julio, too. We'll find a happening beach and have ourselves a ball.'

'Er, that's unlikely at Aunt Maria's,' Stella went on. 'It's not exactly the grooviest place on earth. I've been before but not for a good few years now. It's actually inland, high up in the Pyrenees. What I'm trying to say is that it's miles from anywhere. In the middle of nowhere, in fact.'

'High up in the Pyrenees . . .' repeated Jodie dreamily. 'It sounds really romantic.'

'Yeah, it does,' agreed Ushi. 'But is there anyone to be romantic with, I wonder.'

'Dunno,' Stella shrugged. She started to giggle. 'There's Miguel, my cousin, but he's a real jerk. He's a few years older than me but I remember him as being a weedy, little cry baby. He's . . .'

She was suddenly interrupted by an annoucement coming over the tannoy.

'*We will shortly be arriving in Boulogne. Will passengers ensure that they have all their belongings . . .*'

They didn't stop to hear any more but rushed out onto the nearest deck. It was just getting dark and the lights of Boulogne flickered like stars across the water. Instinctively, Jodie grabbed Ushi and Stella and hugged them.

'This is it!' she squealed, her heart pounding with excitement.

They'd arrived! And this was only the beginning. France, Europe, the Continent beckoned. For a whole month, it would belong to them.

Just as was written in Jodie's travel guide, Boulogne train station was literally next to the port. She didn't know why she should be surprised but she was. Excitement, she supposed. And she sure was excited. France – her first time on foreign soil

– and she could hardly contain herself. Running backwards and forwards, pointing at all the signs, straining to hear people speak. In French! Suddenly she was glad that she'd always been pretty good at it. She wanted to see everything, experience everything. A mere hour-and-a-half away from old Blighty yet it was so, so different. It even smelled different – of French cigarettes and strong coffee.

She knew Ushi and Stella were watching her indulgently – she was the novice traveller while they'd both been abroad before – but this was a first for them, too. The first time any of them had been abroad without parents – or parenty-type figures – and it was hugely, fabulously liberating.

'We can do anything we want,' sang Ushi, dancing onto the station platform. 'No "what-time-d'you-call-this", no "you-treat-this-place-like-a-hotel", no "get-off-the-bloody-phone". God it's fantastic!'

Jodie gasped as Stella suddenly pushed her and Ushi behind an advertisement hoarding.

'What the hell's going on?' spluttered Ushi.

'I'm saving you from a fate worse than death, that's what,' hissed Stella. 'Smarm-Features and his slimey mates have just passed by. They're railing-it too, remember. Get stuck on a train with 'em now and the odds are we'll be stuck for the duration. And that I do not want.'

'*Absolument*,' agreed Jodie and Ushi nodded solemnly.

They were momentarily tempted to miss their train and get down to some serious bar-crawling in Boulogne but they figured there'd be plenty of time for that over the next four weeks.

'Miss this train,' Jodie said, squinting at the timetable, 'and we miss our connection from Lille to Brittany – and sun, sand and sea – in the morning.'

Sitting aboard the swank SNCF train as it travelled through the, now dark, French countryside, Jodie reckoned that she'd never been so thrilled about sitting on a train before. She kept touching the blue leather seats and peering out the window – even though she could see nothing but her own reflection. And it was so fast, it made trains at home seem like something out of the dark ages!

'The campsite's about 10 km outside Lille,' said Ushi, reading up in her *Camping Guide to France*. 'In a place called Malée. Even better, apparently it's only a few minutes walk from the station. We'll save on taxi fares and have some decent nosh instead. Don't know about you guys but suddenly I'm starving!'

On leaving Malée station, the three of them followed the directions in Ushi's book. True to its word – thank God, as they were hauling rucksacks on their backs – it was only minutes away. But there was a problem. It had started to rain. Tiny little spits at first which rapidly metamorphosed into puddle-size sploshes.

'Hurrah!' muttered Stella as they stumbled into the campsite reception just as an almighty crash of thunder sounded.

'*Ah bonsoir*,' the woman behind the desk started to say then, suddenly, everything went dark. The three of them screamed.

'*Ah c'est une coupure de courant* – a, how-you-say, power cut,' the woman went on as if it was the most usual thing in the world. Maybe, Jodie thought, it was here. The woman lit one candle and gave another to Ushi.

'Er thanks,' muttered Ushi. 'A candle, eh? For use in the rain. Mmmm – very useful.'

The woman walked over and opened the door.

'Er, p'raps we should stay put till the rain slackens off a bit,' suggested Stella.

'Nice idea,' muttered Ushi, 'but I don't exactly

think that's what she has in mind. Look at her, beckoning us over. She's desperate for us to go. We've got no option, I'm afraid.'

Struggling with her rucksack, Jodie followed Stella and Ushi into the dark, wet night towards their appointed pitch. Detaching their sleeping bags and fiddling around with ground sheets, tent pegs and guide ropes by only the light of a torch during what felt like a mini-monsoon wasn't ideal. Some of Jodie's excitement had started to ebb away. She hadn't imagined this particular scenario when, tucked up in her bed at home, she'd fantasised about their very first night away. She'd imagined a perfectly put-up tent amidst a perfectly beautiful setting with a wonderful café that did a mean veg curry – just what she fancied. But when she mentioned food to Stella, she just laughed.

'You're joking, Jodes,' muttered Stella, attempting – unsucessfully – to slip over the tent's top sheet. 'No power equals no scoff, I reckon. Don't you?'

'Oh don't say that,' moaned Ushi. 'My stomach's about to go on strike if it doesn't get any food.'

'Yeah, you're right,' said Stella. 'Hunger strike. There's no food, Ush. How can there be?'

'Well that's just great!' Ushi threw down a handful of pegs.

'It's not my fault,' Stella snapped back.

'I didn't say it was, did I?' hissed Ushi.

Jodie took a step back and her foot came into contact with something far squashier than grass – however wet. For a second, she couldn't make out exactly what it was but then came the horrible realisation that there was only one – or rather three – things it could be.

'Er, guys,' she said as the others continued to bicker. 'Guys . . .' This time a little louder.

Stella and Ushi looked at her.

'What?' they both snapped.

As gently as she could, Jodie broke it to them that their sleeping bags had been left out in the rain, uncovered, and were now, as indeed, were the three of them, completely drenched. As Jodie attempted to catch some zzzzzzs an hour or so later, shivering with cold, soaked through and starving hungry, she reflected that the feeling of intense excitement she'd been carrying around all day that had reached a crescendo on arriving in France, had disappeared completely. She and Ushi and Stella were barely talking to each other – each blaming the other for forgetting about the sleeping bags, the torrential rain, the lack of food – everything, in fact. No, she thought, it wasn't supposed to be like this at all. It was turning out to be a complete disaster.

Life's A Beach

Hi Davy! ♡
Just had to write to you! Looked
at my watch and realised that
precisely six minutes, twelve
hours and two days ago we were
sitting under that weeping
willow having our farewell snog.
Awww! I don't half miss those
snogsome lips of yours! Stopped
in a disgusting campsite last night -
no food but loads of rain. Yeah, I
know - you're having a heatwave
back home! Don't think I'm a natural
under canvas - only under weeping
willows! Love and kisses xxx
♡ Ushi ♡

'Not *another* postcard!'

Ushi glanced up to see Stella grinning at her from the other side of the train.

'Oh, you're talking to me now, are you?' muttered Ushi.

Stella grinned again. 'I've had a sleep and I feel better. Sorry for being so grumpy this morning but I'm never at my best before about half eleven, especially when I've hardly had any sleep the night before. And I reckon last night was the mother of all sleepless nights.'

'You're not wrong there,' said Ushi and put down her pen. 'Just let's promise ourselves one thing and then forget all about it. Tonight we stay in a hotel. I don't care how much it costs, I just need to get some kip.'

'*Absolument, ma chère,*' agreed Stella.

Ushi yawned and looked out the window. Having picked up their connection at Lille a few hours earlier, they were now en route to Brittany. The rain had stopped, the sun was shining and as they travelled further west, through Normandy into Brittany, the scenery became more and more lush and picturesque.

'This,' thought Ushi, the previous night suddenly becoming little more than a bad dream, 'is the life.'

'Coffee?' Ushi smiled up at Jodie who had just walked into the carriage, carrying a steaming tray.

'You bet!' Ushi murmured and took a cup. 'Oh Jodes, you've bought biccies, too! What a star!'

Jodie gave a mock curtsey and passed the tray to Stella. 'You know, maybe it wasn't such a bright idea to jump on the first train that was leaving Lille station in vaguely the right direction,' said Jodie. 'I asked the girl in the refreshment car where exactly we're going but she started babbling away so quickly, I couldn't keep up with her. I think she said something about a place called St Marion.'

Ushi started flicking through her guide book.

'We're going to Brittany, aren't we?' she said.

'Brittany's a big place,' said Stella. 'A bit like a county.'

'Oh anywhere'll do,' said Ushi airily. 'Just so long as there's a beautiful beach where we can chill out for a day or so, there aren't loads of pesky little kids running around and there's a decent hotel.'

'*Excusez-moi*, but I zink I may be able to 'elp you.'

Ushi looked up and found herself staring up into a pair of sexy brown eyes. The rest of their owner's face wasn't bad, either. A wide, full-lipped mouth, neat aquiline nose and a pair of cheek-bones you could balance a tray on – all topped off with a curly mane of shoulder-length dark hair. Then there was his body – that was amazing! Lean with long, long legs – gift-wrapped in a pair of faded denims and white T-shirt.

Ushi closed her eyes for an instant, thinking she must be dreaming. But when she opened them again, he was still there. Mr Completely Gorgeous – what a result! And, there was an added bonus too – the French accent may be undeniably corny but it was dead horny, too.

'I 'ope you don't mind me interrupting but I over 'ear you,' he said. 'You look for somewhere in Brittany with ze beautiful beach? I zink I can 'elp.'

Ushi glanced at Stella and Jodie. They grinned at her and Jodie gave her a sneaky 'thumbs-up'.

'I am François.' He held out a hand to her. '*Et vous?*'

Ushi told him her name and then introduced him to the others.

'Where's this place . . .' Ushi looked at the guide book again, 'er, St Marion?'

Sitting down to join them, François shook his head. St Marion, he informed them, was too touristy, too commercialised. He apparently knew of an unspoilt seaside village just inside the Brittany border which, apparently, was something of a hot secret.

'It is so very special, so very *naturel*,' he went on. 'You will not find it in any brochure. I go there – I meet some friends. We 'ang out. I camp, but there is a small 'otel there. Small, cheap . . .'

'Sounds great,' enthused Ushi. Fab beach and an even fabber boy-babe she fancied getting to know better. Paradise!

François shrugged. 'I get coffee now. You tell me when I come if you would like . . . You see, it is ze next stop.'

'*Oui, merci*,' giggled Ushi. 'Well . . .' she said to Stella and Jodie when François had left the carriage, 'what do you think?'

'Yeah, sounds ideal,' said Jodie. 'And no wonder *you* fancy it, Ush!'

'What d'*you* reckon Stell?' Ushi turned to her other friend, 'I mean we've all got to want to go there, haven't we? We agreed, remember? Before we came away? We said we'd be democratic. So what d'you think?'

'I'm er . . . I'm not . . .' began Stella doubtfully, but then she smiled. 'Oh, what the hell! Yeah, yeah – let's go for it – it sounds great.'

Ushi grinned. 'Doesn't it just?!!!'

Unspoilt the village certainly was. From what Ushi

could see, there was just one campsite, one hotel, one café/bar and a beach. But what a beach it was! It unfurled like a bright, broad, golden ribbon into the distance and was backed by dunes and lapped by a blue-green sea.

'You stay 'ere? *Oui?*' asked François. 'You like?'

'*Oui, oh oui,*' murmured Ushi, standing so close to him she could smell his cologne – kind of lemony and herby and distinctly foreign-smelling. 'And the resort isn't bad either.' Stella and Jodie, bless 'em, went to book in, leaving Ushi alone for a few minutes with François.

'You want we go to the beach this afternoon?' he asked.

'Sounds good,' said Ushi. 'Be a whole crowd of us, will it? You and your mates plus the three of us? Yeah, we could take picnic!'

'Oh . . .' Francois began hesitantly. 'We go in a crowd? *Je ne sais pas.* My friends . . . they may not be 'ere yet. I go to the campsite and see. I meet you on the beach, *n'est-ce pas?*' He bent forward to kiss her. After a moment's hesitation, Ushi responded. Mmmmm-hmmmm, he certainly knew how to use those pouty lips of his – and his tongue was pretty nifty, too. He obviously didn't believe in wasting any time. This was French kissing for real! His hands moved from her shoulder and started to roam her back – over her shirt – and then suddenly she felt his fingers tugging insistently at her bra strap.

Ushi pulled away. Crikey Moses, he was more than a bit cheeky. She'd only known him a few hours and here he was wanting to explore her underwear! Well, he could forget that. While it was true she fancied him, she rather than he would dictate the pace of things. And at the mo' – hardly knowing him – she wanted to go slow.

François was eyeing her speculatively.

'Down boy!' Ushi grinned.

'*Comment?*' said François.

Ushi shook her head. 'Forget it. We'll see you in an hour or so.'

'Ouch, ooch, ouch!' yelped Jodie as they walked across the sand some time later. 'It's boiling, isn't it? Like walking over burning coals. Oooh, I can't wait to get in the sea.'

'You want to be careful, Jodes, with your fair hair and complexion,' advised Stella. 'The sun really zaps people like you. Are you all oiled-up?'

'Yes Mum,' laughed Jodie. She looked around the beach. There were a few people about but no

François. 'He's not here yet then, Ush?'

Ushi stretched her arms above her head and shook back her hair. 'Doesn't look like it. Come on, let's go for it! Last one in the sea buys the ice creams.'

Yelling like banshees, they dumped their towels and bag full of newly bought French bread, cheese and fruit, and ran down to the sea. In spite of the heat of the day, the water felt freezing. Ushi gasped and squealed as she splashed about. She soon warmed up though. Lying on her back, staring up at the bluer-than-blue sky, she realised she was living the fantasy she'd played out in her mind, over and over again.

Stella nudged her suddenly. 'Hey up, lover boy's just arrived,' she said gesturing with her head towards the beach. She started giggling. 'You can tell he's French, can't you? An English lad would never dare to wear what he's got on. Oooh look at him preening! Fancies himself, doesn't he?'

Ushi stood up in the water and shielded her eyes to look towards the beach. She felt her lips twitching. Stella had a point but then so, it was very, very apparent, did François – dressed as he was in a pair of miniscule trunks. It was a blessing he had such a great body.

Jodie joined them. 'You going over to say hello then?' she asked.

'In a bit,' said Ushi. 'I haven't finished my swim yet.'

'He seems to be on his tod,' Jodie went on. 'What d'you want us to do? Leave you two love-birds alone for a bit?'

Ushi shook her head. 'God, no! We'll run out of stuff to say. And anyway, gorgeous he may be, but he knows it. I don't want be left alone with him. I told you how amorous he was earlier. Blimey! If it was just the two of us I bet he'd be trying to get me bikini off in seconds!'

'You can stay put, love,' hissed Stella out of the corner of her mouth. 'He's just dived in. Looks like the mountain's coming to Mohammed!'

Seconds later, François' sleek head bobbed up beside Ushi. She wanted to laugh. With his hair plastered down on either side of his head, he looked a bit like a sealion!

'Your friends not around then?' said Ushi.

'*Non.*' Francois shook his head. 'But they leave a message for me. They wait a little further up the beach. More – how-you-say – secluded. You want we should go there?'

Ushi quickly glanced at Stella and Jodie. Both

shrugged. They obviously didn't care one way or t'other. It was up to her. Yeah, why not?

'Er, OK,' she said. 'We're up for it.'

They seemed to have walked miles.

'God,' Stella gasped. 'I feel like I'm wandering across the Sahara. Where the hell are your mates, François?'

François, who was walking slightly ahead, turned. 'We find them soon, I'm sure.'

'Yeah, well can't we stop for a bit now?' said Jodie. 'Find 'em later? I'm burning up and I'm starving.'

'Yeah,' Ushi agreed. 'We want to stop.'

'OK,' shrugged François.

They sank down onto the sand. Jodie quickly put up the parasol while Stella and Ushi started sorting out the food.

'Would you like some . . .' The words stuck in Ushi's throat as she turned to François. 'Ohmigod!' she managed to squeak. 'Ohmigod! What *are* you doing?'

Stella's and Jodie's gasps added to Ushi's as François started to take off his trunks! He smiled at Ushi.

'There is a problem? I think not. *C'est une plage*

naturisme. Ze clothes are not allowed 'ere. I zink you will love it, Ushi. Be at one wiz ze nature.'

'Not on your life,' Ushi muttered. 'You do what you like but I'm staying clothed, ta very much.'

François shrugged in a peculiarly Gallic way, stood up and without a backward glance at any of them, strolled leisurely towards the sea. They stared after him. Stella was the first to speak.

'Well . . .' she said. 'Your antennae were spot-on on this occasion Ush. You were right. If you'd been left alone with him, he *would* have tried to get that ikkle old bikini off that beautiful body of yours. What d'you wanna do now? Y'know, I don't know if I like this end of the beach all that much. I certainly don't fancy meeting whatsisface's mates – not here, anyway. I bet they'll all be starkers, too. Call me old-fashioned, but I like to know a person for a bit before they start stripping off in front of me.'

'Me too,' said Ushi.

Jodie suddenly started to giggle. 'There's a bloke and a woman hiding in the sand dunes,' she tittered. 'Neither of 'em have got a stitch on. She's dead skinny and he's a real podge. Ohmigod! It's disgusting!'

'Stop it, Jodes,' murmured Ushi but couldn't help having a sneaky look herself. 'I wanna get out of here. Preferably before François comes back. I don't think I'll be able to look him in the face for a start.'

She started laughing. Stella, too, while Jodie was still tittering away to herself.

'Come on, quick!' Ushi gasped, piling their picnic back into the bag. Next to a bottle of water lay François' discarded trunks. She almost stuffed them into the bag. He'd tricked her. If he'd told her that he was taking her to a naturist beach, she'd never have agreed to go. She should have sussed it when he'd gone on about this place being 'so very *naturel*'. To take or not to take his keks? That was the question. The thing was she much didn't fancy them being in close proximity to their food! And she didn't wish to be accused of theft.

'What are you doing?' asked Jodie as Ushi began to make a hole in the sand. 'It's hardly the right time to start building bloody sandcastles!'

'I'm not,' giggled Ushi. 'I'm hiding François's trunks. Trying to find them will give him something to do when he emerges from the sea. I mean, he won't have us gorgeous girlies to chat to any-more!'

'Ushi!' said Stella. 'Do you really think you should?'

Ushi swiftly piled sand onto the already partially buried garment. She stood up and smiled.

'Too late! I just have.'

Lazing around on the beach in front of their hotel, they kept a look-out for François all afternoon but to their disappointment, he didn't materialise.

'I wonder what he did when he couldn't find his teeny-weeny trunklets?' mused Jodie as they were packing up to leave.

'Made himself a new pair out of seaweed,' laughed Stella. 'Or maybe he found an old banana-skin lying around on the beach.'

'A bit of orange peel would have done just as well,' muttered Ushi.

'OOOO-er,' teased Jodie and Stella. 'Bitchy, bitchy!'

'Well . . .' Ushi grinned. 'It serves him right.'

Jodie suddenly gave a sharp intake of breath. 'Don't look now,' she gulped, 'but he's walking along the beach. With another bloke and a very coupley-looking couple. Must be his mates.'

Ushi froze. 'What's he wearing?' she hissed. 'Not the trunks?'

Jodie shook her head and literally started to shake with laughter.

'He's not still naked?' Stella squealed, not daring to look herself.

Jodie shook her head again. 'Ohmigod, he's leaving his mates and walking towards us . . .'

'Never mind that!' Ushi hissed again. 'Quick, tell us what he's wearing!'

'A . . .' began Jodie but then she stopped suddenly.

'Ushi?' It was François.

Steeling herself, Ushi looked round and literally had to bite her lip. He was wearing a woman's swimsuit pulled down to his waist. This would have looked daft enough in any instance but this particular cozzy just happened to have a fitted bra bit in the top and the underwired 'cups' were on obvious display, bobbing like unfettered buoys around his middle. He looked ridiculous.

'Oh, hi,' Ushi spluttered, trying with difficulty to keep her eyes trained on his face.

'What 'appen to you?' François asked. 'I return to the beach after my swim and you not there . . .'

'I wasn't feeling well,' Ushi replied with sudden inspiration. 'Too much bum, I mean, sun!'

'Oh,' François shrugged. 'I wonder if you see my swimming trouser. They too had gone when I came back from my swim. I wonder if . . .' he grinned, 'you bring them back wiz you. As a joke, *peut-être? Le souvenir, possiblement?*'

Ushi shook her head, not trusting herself to speak.

'Don't flatter yourself, lad!' muttered Stella.

'*Peut-être* a dog nabbed 'em,' piped up Jodie.

François shrugged again. '*Peut-être. Alors* . . . We meet later, Ushi? The two of us this time? *Oui?*'

'*Non!*' Ushi shook her head and linked arms with Jodie and Stella. She wasn't going anywhere without her posse, especially now François had revealed himself – literally – in his true colours. 'I'm a pack animal,' she said. 'Where I go, they go. Sorry, but that's the way it is. Right girls?'

'*Absolument!*' agreed Stella and Jodie in unison.

'Well, girls?' said Ushi once François had gone. 'What's it to be tonight? I don't know about you but after last night, I fancy an early one. 'Specially as we're moving on tomorrow. All this seclusion is fine and dandy but I think we want somewhere a bit more happening, *n'est-ce pas?*'

Coincidentally, the first train out of the village the next morning was going to St Marion. '*St Marion* . . .' Ushi read out from her guide book once they were settled aboard. '*An attractive resort that's had something of a facelift in recent years. As much a favourite with body-boarders and surf enthusiasts as it is with the more traditional holidaymaker, St Marion boasts wide, sandy beaches, chic little pavement cafés and is famed for her seafood.*' Ushi put down her book. 'So what do we think? A hit or a miss?'

'A hit,' said Stella. 'It sounds like the kind of place where there'll be loads going on – not a remote bloody naturist resort – thank God! The kind of place where we'll be happy to stop for a few days. I fancy that – I'm knackered with all this running around.'

'Me too,' said Jodie. 'I say we get to St Marion and completely chill out. I also say a hit! But let's make sure we get there this time. I don't care if some specimen of spunkiness personified gets on this train and tries to talk us into going 'somewhere really special', we're bound for St Marion! Agreed, Ush?'

'Agreed,' Ushi smiled a tad guiltily. 'I sure like the sound of it. Body-boarders and surfers, eh? You know what that means, don't you!'

'Mmm-hmmm . . . !' Jodie and Stella nodded together.

'Totty!' Ushi went on. 'Hoardes of it, too. Groovy-looking guys in tighter-than-tight wetsuits.

So much sexier, in my opinion, than geezers in the altogether!'

'Well hallejuiah for that!' proclaimed Stella.

'Just you wait,' Ushi grinned. 'There'll be plenty of action going in a surf resort like St Marion. I've been to Cornwall, see. I know!'

St Marion station was bathed in sunshine as their train arrived two hours later. They clambered down onto the platform with their rucksacks and staggered out onto the concourse.

'Any ideas, guys?' asked Ushi.

'I guess it'll have to be a campsite, yeah?' said Jodie.

Stella nodded.

'You guys stay here with the bags and I'll go and sort it,' said Ushi. 'Won't be long.'

The tourist information officer recommended a campsite called *La Plage*. It certainly looked nice enough from the brochure he handed Ushi. There was a pool, tennis court, clubhouse, Bar-B-Q area and spotless-looking loos. And, as the name suggested, it was right on the beach. Ushi, after a quick consultation with Jodie and Stella, decided to book them in.

*

Through Ushi's Armani-type shades, the sun was a swirling orange ball set in an infinite purple sky. The sea looked to be practically the same shade – perhaps slightly more violet – tipped with creamy, white crests. And as for the sand? Ushi grabbed a handful. Slipping through her fingers, it felt like powdered silk and looked like powdered gold. She sighed and lay back on her beach towel. She'd already thought it before on this trip but this really was the life. And how could she ever have thought that she hated camping? Today, she loved it. The tent had gone up like a dream and their sleeping bags, now thoroughly dried out, were cosily positioned inside. Jodie, bless her, had even laid out their nighties on top of them and now Ushi was actually looking forward to snuggling down that evening. But that was hours away yet. In the meantime, there was loads more to look forward to. Checking out their fellow campers for a start. True there seemed to be a few fam1lies staying at *La Plage* but luckily most of the clientele seemed to be made up of young, free and single like themselves. She'd already noticed a number of likely-looking lads. No one who, as yet, could quite compare with freaky François in the looks department but, hell, after yesterday, she thought she'd preferred someone not quite so physically fanciable who'd keep their swimming cozzy on!

'I think we should stay here a few days to recharge our batteries,' Jodie piped up suddenly from the beach towel next to Ushi's. 'What d'you two think?'

'I don't want to think about anything,' murmured Ushi. 'I just want to lie back, empty my head of all thoughts and catch some rays.'

'I fancy an ice cream,' Stella announced suddenly and stood up. 'Anyone else?'

'I fancy a willing slave who'll massage me with sun cream,' sighed Ushi. 'But if you can't find one, I guess I'll make do with *une glace*, ta.'

She yawned, suddenly feeling very sleepy. All this lying around doing nothing was exhausting. She must have dropped off then because the next thing Ushi knew, she was being shaken awake by a worried-looking Jodie.

'It's Stella,' she muttered. 'She's gone.'

Ushi yawned and stretched. God, Jodes could be such a worrier at times.

'She'll have gone back to the tent,' said Ushi. 'You know what she's like – brain like a sieve at times. I bet she's forgotten all about our ice creams and gone back for a siesta.'

Jodie shook her head. 'She hasn't – I've looked.

I can't think what's happened to her.'

Ushi rolled onto her tummy and took off her shades to get a better look up the beach. It was filling up and she couldn't see Stella anywhere. She could see loads of talent, though. Just as she'd predicted. Oooooh yes, that guy presently walking up the beach in their direction . . . With his cropped blond hair and tanned, everso taut body, he really was something else. Problem was he was holding the hand of a rather lovely, tall, dark girl dressed in a rather lovely, pale-yellow bikini. Ushi sat up suddenly. She recognised that bikini! She ought to. It was hers. She'd lent it to Stella a few hours earlier. Well, well, well, lucky old Stell! With a lad like that in tow, no wonder she'd forgotten all about their ice creams.

'Here . . .' Ushi nudged Jodie who was busy scanning the sea for anyone who might look like Stella. 'You can stop worrying. Get a load of this! The wanderer has returned. Looks very much like Stella's gone and pulled.'

But before Jodie had chance to say anything, Stella and her new boy-babe were practically on top of them.

'Hi,' murmured Stella in a breathy whisper. 'This is Tomas.'

Love Lines

Day Three

St Marion

Before we came away I promised myself I'd 'do' my diary every day. Great start huh? But we've been having such a ball, putting pen to paper is the last thing I've felt like doing. Been too busy living it up to want to sit down and reflect on it all. The red leather, oh all right, leather-look binding and all these snowy white pages are mocking me now, though, so I'd better get on with it. I want to call me travel tome something clever and timeless but at the moment I guess plain, old Stella's Diary will have to do.

Travelling around like this is just the best fun. I knew it would be, but it's even better than I imagined. Real independence for once – it's fantastic! Independence!!! I was dreading the ferry crossing a bit because I knew I'd chuck up but as we all did, it made it into a group activity somehow. Puking was a bonding experience! Taking the rise out of those stuck-up creeps was a good laugh, too. Hope we don't run into them again. I was dreading telling the girls about the Aunty Maria thing. I was just embarrassed really. I mean, Ushi's mum and stepdad are so cool and liberal about everything and Jodie's mum's quite together, too – though nowhere near as hip 'ngroovy as Ushi's folks. It's like "Hey great! Have a fab time. If it feels good, do it!" with them but mine still treat me like I'm just fresh outta nappies. Old-fashioned mother and old-fashioned, Spanish father? It's not the coolest, most laid-back parenting experience in the world. As it turned out though, Jodes and Ush were fine about it. It was probably a bit silly of me to think they wouldn't be – they're me best mates and know what my olds are like. I'm not quite sure how they'll react when we reach the Pyrenees and they realise that there really is very little to do, that it gets freezing cold at night, even in summer, and that Miguel's tons more nerdy than cute. But I'll worry about that later.

Yep, we're having a brilliant crack. The best ever. Looking back, even that first night at that crap campsite doesn't seem so bad. I keep having flashbacks of the three of us mooching about in the rain, unable to see what we're doing, snapping each other's heads off and I keep laughing to myself. Yesterday was a right laugh too – the 'so special, so naturel' resort. I thought there was something a bit creepy about François – it was why I wasn't exactly gagging to go to his undiscovered paradise. Maybe I'm being unfair. Maybe he genuinely thought we'd be into all that naturist stuff. Well, he got the wrong gals. Buzzy and happenin'; St Marion is much more 'us'. I just lurve it – especially since I met Tomas!

Tomas . . . Ushi's right about foreign names. They're too damned sexy for their own good. Tomas is a world apart, though. The sexiest name out, I reckon – all exotic and romantic. Funny, I always thought German lads had names like Hans or Helmut. A complete turn off. 'Course it helps that this particular Tomas looks a like a bit of a star.

Forgive me dear diary while I totally indulge myself but the way I met him was like something out of a film – and I want to relive it over and over again. There I was, the leading lady, sauntering along the edge of the sea, wondering just when I was going to meet my leading man, when suddenly this surfer appeared from nowhere – on his board – and literally knocked me off my feet! I was none too pleased until it sank in just what this very apologetic surfer looked like – a bit of a sun god in a wet suit, as a matter of fact. I wasn't really hurt but I made out I was shaken up with the shock of it all so that he'd help me up. (I know, I know, but the old ones are always the best.) It worked like a dream! He picked me up – actually scooped me up in his arms, so romantic – and made all these sympathetic noises. Problem was, I couldn't work out what he was saying because it was all in German. He gently put me down and we stood there for ages just grinning at each other. I could tell he fancied me because he didn't let go of my hand and his blue eyes were sooo sparkly. Anyway, I reluctantly started walking back up the beach and he followed me. That was it really. We started walking together and having this weird conversation – unlike the rest of him, his English isn't too hot. It was all very 'me Tarzan, you Jane' sort of stuff but we managed to suss out each other's names. I was so into it all – or rather him – I had no idea where we were going and the next thing I knew, I was back where I'd started and we were practically on top of Ushi and Jodes!

I felt a bit bad 'cos I'd forgotten the ice creams but Jodie and Ushi didn't seem to care and just kept smirking knowingly across at Tomas and me.

I introduced Tomas to the girls but it was a bit difficult because neither of them speak German either. So after I'd given Jodes and Ush a quick rundown on how we'd met and told them that, no, I didn't yet know if he had any nice mates, the four of us sat around just grinning at each other with Ushi and Jodie occasionally giggling and whispering to each other.

Tomas kind of indicated that we go for a drink.

Ushi said to go for it, but I said no. It wasn't as if I thought Tomas was into bathing au naturel *or anything like that, but after yesterday's hoo-haa, I didn't fancy being on my own with him just yet and the girls didn't fancy a drink. So I'm meeting him tonight instead. We all* are – *with Jodes and Ush hoping he's got some cute mates. He's bound to. What top lad like him wouldn't? And* quelle coïncidence! *He just happens to be stopping at our campsite. Major piece-a-luck, eh?*

Tomas – looking hornier than any rhino – is waiting for us in the club house. Some guys have just got it, some guys haven't. Tomas has 'it' in skipfuls. He's an out and out love god as far as I'm concerned!

'Guten Abend,' he says in this deep, gutteral voice which I just know will bring out the animal in me. He takes my hand and I feel like I've just put my fingers in an electric socket. The zzzzzing is sooooo strong!

He seems to be on his own – I'm surprised – but I'll suss out his mate situation later. At the moment, I just too busy gazing into those brilliantly bright eyes.

Once we're sitting down with drinks, I can feel the rest of the world just melting away around me. I just want to be myself and let Tomas get to know the real me. It seems though that Jodes and Ushi are feeling a bit bored and have other plans . . .

'I just lurve this record!' Jodie proclaims as the antiquated juke-box in the corner starts up. 'I've just recorded it actually.'

She starts singing away. Tomas looks seriously confused. Ushi starts laughing and I start blushing. Can't Jodie see how stupid she looks – this is no time for playing alter egos. I know they feel left out of the action, but honestly! Fortunately Jodes gets the hint after a bit and shuts up.

The trouble is, I'd be happy to sit here all night and Tomas seems in no hurry to move. Unfortunately for me and Mr Love, the girls soon start getting restless. Can't blame 'em really. The club house is practically empty and with me and Tomas doing the 'eye-magnet' and pigeon English/ German, they're a bit bored.

'Have you, er, asked him about his mates?' asks Ushi when he's gone to the loo. 'Or who he's here with? Couldn't we, er, join them? I mean there's not much here for me and Jodes to do, is there?'

She's right so when Tomas gets back, I kind of indicate that we want to go.

'Your friends?' I say. 'We go to them?'

'O ja,' Tomas replies after a moment. 'OK.'

Jodie gets up so quickly, her chair goes flying. 'So what are we waiting for?' she grins.

We end up at this little bar called Le Poisson *(The Fish) on the other side of the bay. It takes over half-an-hour to get there and Jodes and Ush start complaining about being knackered. It's different for me. With Tomas's arm snaked around my waist, I feel like I could go on walking forever. In fact, I'm feeling more than just a bit light-headed and* shaky around the knees. We were about halfway there when Tomas stopped me suddenly and kissed me. As far as I'm concerned you can forget French kissing 'cos the Germans have got it licked. This particular German, anyway. He could snog for Germany! It went on for ages – and would probably still be going on now – if Ushi and Jodie hadn't eventually caught up with us and started making irritating kissy-kissy noises behind our backs.

Le Poisson doesn't look much from the outside but inside it's brilliant. The music's good and the crowd look pretty happenin' too. Fairly mixed with the odd semi-trendy wrinkly popping up here and there.

'Better late than never,' I yell to Ush and Jodes as we push our way through the bar, following Tomas. They give me a big smile but their expressions freeze when they see who Tomas has stopped in front of – and I must admit I'm a bit stunned, too.

The two men look fairly well-preserved in their denim shirts and chinos but there's no getting away from the fact that they are seriously ancient. They're old enough to be our dads at least which, looking back, should have given me a clue as to who exactly they are.

'Mein Onkel und mein Vater!' *announces Tomas, looking a bit sheepish. I see Jodie and Ushi exchanging glances and I know what's coming next. I'm right. The two of them start giggling hysterically.*

Tomas and his dad and uncle look at them like they're bonkers so I mutter an apology and drag them over to the other side of the bar.

'Jodes fancies his dad and I'll cop off with his Onkel,' *splutters Ushi.*

'No, I want Onkel!' *snorts Jodie.*

I bit my cheek to stop myself from laughing. If it wasn't for Tomas, I'd be shrieking away with them both. But then if it wasn't for Tomas, we wouldn't be here in the first place. 'Shhhh!' *I hiss.* 'Everyone's looking.'

Still spluttering slightly, Ush and Jodes take deep breaths and calm themselves down. Then Tomas comes over. He looks a bit hurt and I feel really bad. He obviously thinks we've been taking the piss. I look beseechingly at Ush and Jodie.

''SOK,' *says Jodie.* 'Don't you worry yourself, pet. It was just a surprise for us that's all. You know what we're like. We always laugh when we're nervous.'

'Yeah,' *agrees Ush.* 'Take yourselves off into a corner and do the sweet nothings bit.' *She gazes* round the bar. 'There's loads of talent here. We'll be fine.'

I watch them both throw themselves into the fray, then gaze up at Tomas. He kisses me for a nanosecond but that's enough to turn me to jelly. I want to go on kissing him for ever. He smiles and takes my hand and I entwine my fingers with his. It sounds silly because we can't even have a proper conversation with each other but I really think I might be falling for him!

Day Five

Breakfasting Al Fresco at La Plage

There's no might about it! I am one fallen woman! Since that evening at Le Poisson, Tomas and me have been practically inseparable. We spend our days on the beach – Tomas is teaching me to surf and says I look wunderbar in a wetsuit – and most nights there, too. Last night – or rather very, very early this morning – I didn't get back till two. My mum and dad would freak if they knew. But Tomas is just the best kisser! Usually slow and unhurried, even lazy, when we start off but once he gets going, he gets really passionate. Just thinking about his kissing makes me want more. Lots more. He's really demonstrative, too, which makes a real change from the British lads I know, who can be dead off-hand. He's always kissing and hugging me – even when his rellies are about. Normally I'd be dead embarrassed but Tomas's uncle and dad (his parents are divorced) are so cool and continental about it, it doesn't bother me.

Unbelievably, Jodes and Ushi are having just as good a time as me. Actually, I'll adjust that – they're having almost as good a time as me. They've pulled, too. Ushi's hooked up with a lad called Biff – so much for sexy names but then he is a Brit – whom she met at Le Poisson that first night. He's mad about her, absolutely batty, which doesn't exactly displease Ush. She likes having her ego stroked does our Ush, but then don't we all? Facially, Biff's not that fab but being a surfer, he's got the most unbelievable bod on him. He's also dead funny and a nice bloke to boot. Jodie started slowly but she's made up for it over the last few days. She copped off with 'Bernie from Belgium' then she dumped him after a day – she says he stank of chips and mayo – then got together with a hunky French lad called Jean-Louis. They've been together ever since.

Anyway . . . I've decided I want to stay here forever! Oh all right, another week at least. It's just soooo, soooo perfect. There's the beach, great weather, a nice campsite, a happening after-dark scene and for me, of course, Tomas. What more could a girl want?

Day Seven

La Plage *Café-Bar*

It's started to rain today but that's not the only reason I'm feeling like hacked off and as miserable as sin. Funny how quickly things change. Forty-five minutes ago, I was the happiest little soul in St Marion. I was sitting here, at the table I'm still sitting at, having brekkie with Ushi – Tomas had gone off fishing with his dad (I declined cos of my seasickness) – when Jodie walked in, waving this leaflet around in her hand.

'Take a look at this,' she said. 'I've just seen it. It sounds brilliant. Really amazing. I'm desperate to go.'

It was a flyer for a music festival – kind of like a French Glastonbury – with loads of bands including the fantastic 'Divali', performance artists, dance tents, alternative therapies and the like. She was right. I thought it sounded fab, too.

'Count me in,' I said, before I realised that the festival was happening near Bordeaux, miles and miles away down the coast.

''SOK,' Ushi said when I pointed this out. 'Jodes and me were only saying last night that it was about time we moved on. We've been here five days and the weather's gone off on us. We may as well pack up and leave today. Won't take long. In fact, if we want to make this festival at all we're going to have to. It's only on for two days and it starts tomorrow. Plus it's a set price so we want to get our money's worth.'

I was thrown into a complete state of panic. I didn't want to leave Tomas. Not yet.

'What about Biff?' I said to Ushi. 'You can't leave him, Ush.'

She looked at me as if I'd lost my mind. 'Course I can,' she laughed. 'Biff and me have had a good crack but that's all. He's nice enough to have spent a few days with and wile away the time while you've been joined at the hip to Tomas but all good things and all that. Blimey, I probably wouldn't even have looked at Biff at home. He's not really my type.'

I turned to Jodie. 'Jean Louis . . .' I said. 'You've only just met him. Wouldn't you like to spend more time with him?'

Jodie shook her head. 'Not really. Certainly not if it means missing out on this festival, no. And like Ushi, me feet are getting a bit itchy. The old batteries are recharged and it's time we explored pastures new.'

I couldn't help myself. I just burst into tears. 'I don't want to go,' I sobbed. 'I don't want to.'

'You don't want to leave Tomas,' said Ushi gently and put her arm around me. 'But you're going to have to, Stell. You knew you would, at some point. We can't stay here forever – we gotta get going. Hit the road again. There's so much more to see and experience.' She grinned and nudged me. 'Like loads more lads . . .'

'I don't want anyone else,' I muttered.

Jodes and Ushi looked at each other.

'It's time, Stell,' said Jodie. 'Really. In fact I'm, er, going to start taking the tent down. We'd better leave soon – the sooner the better, in fact. We want to get to Bordeaux as early as poss. Then we'll get ourselves a decent camping spot – that's if there's any left.'

As early as poss . . . This gives me hardly any time

to say goodbye – if at all. Tomas probably won't be back from fishing till mid-afternoon. When I mention this to Jodie and Ushi, they say they're real sorry but there's nothing to be done and I'll have to leave him a letter. A letter, for God's sake? I can't say what I want to say in a letter. Can't even kiss him goodbye.

'Stella, we can't hang around till then,' says Ushi. 'I mean, he might not even get back till this evening which will mean us missing a huge chunk of the festival altogether. It finishes tomorrow, remember.'

But suddenly I don't care if I miss it. I just don't care about anything except Tomas.

To The Max

'Where does Ivor the Engine live?' asked Ushi.

'Er . . . dunno,' said Jodie.

'Rails!' Ushi grinned. 'Your turn, Jodes.'

Jodie had one ready. 'What did the big engine say to the little engine?'

Ushi shook her head.

'Time you started training!' Jodie was suddenly inspired. 'You'll like this one too. Why do train drivers wear specs?' She didn't wait for Ushi to even hazard a guess. 'Because they've got tunnel vision!'

Ushi groaned, shaking her head. 'That's terrible!'

Jodie nudged Stella. 'Your go.'

Moving as if she was in slow motion, Stella turned to look at Jodie. She'd been staring morosely out of the window ever since they'd boarded the train.

'Your go, Stella,' Jodie repeated.

Stella shook her head. 'I'm not in the mood,' she muttered and started staring out of the window again.

Jodie started to say something – along the lines that Tomas apart, there was still loads more to look forward to – but she changed her mind. It probably wouldn't do any good anyway. She couldn't help feeling a smidge guilty. Had she and Ushi been out of order about wanting to leave St Marion? OK, it had been a spur-of-the-moment thing but when they'd been discussing the kind of holiday they'd all wanted before they'd come away, all three of them had agreed that spontaneity would be one of the best things about a trip like this.

It would, Jodie decided, have been pretty rough on Stella if she hadn't been able to see Tomas before they'd left. But she had. He'd come back from his fishing trip earlier than expected because of the crap weather and she'd been able to spend a bit of time with him.

'Not long enough to say goodbye properly,' Stella had moaned, but Jodie reckoned she'd have said that even if she and 'Testosterone Tomas', as Jodie and Ushi had secretly christened him, had had a couple of hours to make their fond farewells.

Fair do's, they'd had five days at St Marion.

Fun days they'd been, too. But now it was time to move on – especially for something as exciting as this festival in Bordeaux. Events like this hardly happened every day, and she couldn't wait.

True enough, Jean-Louis had been hot stuff, but Europe, she was delightfully discovering, was full of them. And anyway, what was the point of putting all your eggs in one basket when there were oodles more pebbles on the beach.

Well, if Stella wasn't going to play ball, it was Ush to go again.

'Your joke, I think, Ush,' Jodie said.

'Nah.' Ushi shook her head. 'I can't think of any more.'

Jodie watched as Ushi moved closer to Stella, grabbed hold of her hand and squeezed it. Jodie couldn't help feeling relieved. Yeah, she'd leave the tea-and-sympathy bit to Ushi. Ushi always seemed to know what to say at times like this. Hopefully, she'd make Stella snap out of her depressing mood. It was spoiling the prospect of the festival for all of them. Besides, it wasn't good for Stella to sit and brood over a guy. Life – and in particular this trip – was too short. She'd have a good few days she'd always remember. Time now for something different. Something which promised to be even better!

'It was time to go, Stell,' Ushi said quietly. 'Apart from anything else, I know what you're like. In a day or two, you would have been sick of him, anyway.'

'I wouldn't,' Stella replied, defensively.

'Oh no?' Ushi questioned. 'Come on, you're like it at home. You were wild about Matthew for about a week and then you went off him. It was the same with that Paul lad and that Irish student your mum had to stop last summer. You're hot for 'em one minute but the next . . .' she clicked her fingers, 'you cool right down. You get bored when they're over keen. It would have been the same with Tomas. Go on, admit it. Be honest with yourself.'

'I am being,' Stella insisted. 'I don't think it would have been like that with Tomas. He . . .' She shook her head. 'Oh, I don't know . . . Maybe if I'm totally honest, he was starting to get on my nerves a tiny bit. He was dead clingy at times. I could barely go to the loo without him wanting to come with me.'

'I know what you mean,' Ushi nodded in agreement. 'Biff was a bit like it, too. That kind of attention's nice enough but, boy, can it get claustrophobic! So many boys, when you get to know 'em, are like it, too.' Her eyes went all dreamy.

'Davy's different, though. He seems to be able to tap into my subconscious. It's like telepathy. He knows when I'm in a demonstrative kind of mood and when I want leaving alone. He's sensitive like that.'

'Tomas was sensitive . . .' considered Stella. 'But sometimes he . . .'

Jodie looked out of the window. She wasn't in the mood for this kind of retrospective boy talk. She suddenly felt super-energetic and wanted to get out there. It had stopped drizzling and the flat fields of northern France were eons away from the rolling countryside of western France. It was exciting, dramatic and exhilarating and Jodie immediately had the most fabulous feeling that Bordeaux would be all of those things for her, too.

While she'd been on the train, Jodie had wondered if, once in Bordeaux, it would be hard trying to find out where the festival was happening. The directions on the flyer were pretty sketchy. But she needn't have worried. On leaving the station, they'd simply followed the snake-like procession of like-minded souls, the mile or so out of town to the site.

It was bigger than Jodie had expected and had

a kind of surreal quality. In many ways, this temporary canvas town seemed far more vibrant than the ancient, permanent one it bordered. And it was odd to think that, in another few days, there'd be nothing here but green fields again.

'Life's a pitch!' Ushi quipped, as they put up their tent. She shielded her eyes against the afternoon sunshine and looked around. 'Hey, this site's filling up really quickly. Good job we left when we did or we wouldn't have made it. And thank God we did make it because you know something? I think – no, I can feel – this festival is going to be dead cool.'

Jodie shivered suddenly. She was experiencing it again. The sensation she'd had on the train. A feeling that anything was possible here and that maybe even a life changing experience was in the offing – or at least a seriously life enhancing one. This was her first music festival. In previous years, she'd been desperate to go to one at home but her mum had always said she was too young. No longer, though. Mum was miles away. The shackles of home had been liberated. She could do whatever she wanted and, at this moment, she felt that 'whatever' was more than possible here. It felt almost essential.

Ushi had evidently imbibed the vibe and even Stella looked a smidge more cheerful as Jodie watched her taking it all in.

'Not exactly the Girl Guides, is it?' she muttered as a rather freaky looking couple walked past arm-in-arm.

'And this is only the camping ground!' Jodie laughed. 'Just think what it's like inside the arena.'

Ushi suddenly made a weird howling sound, as her hips gyrated to the bass-heavy music coming from the festival area, proper.

'Into the arena, my darlings!' she announced spookily. 'The hour is nigh!'

The arena was, thought Jodie, in many ways rather how she imagined a medieval village to be – mixed with '60s psychedelia. There were wonderful-smelling food stalls, groovy clothes stalls, artsy craft stalls, palmistry stalls, crystal stalls . . . and all the while, this constant backbeat of thumping, rhythmic music.

She loved it – every part of it. She'd never been anywhere like it before and she wanted to explore every inch of it. Trouble was, there was so much to experience it was hard to know where to start. In the end, Ushi made the decision for her.

'I'm hungry,' she moaned. 'I need sustenance. Breakfast was hours ago and we missed lunch.'

All three of them decided on curry. They were standing next to a stall which was giving off some truly divine, coriander and cumin scented aromas.

'Hey, it's from Bradford,' said Jodie, spotting the sign above the stall. 'Even better. The French may be clever at your fancy foreign stuff but nobody can do a Ruby like we can.'

'Yeah,' agreed Ushi. 'And I bet most of the customers are curry-starved Brits.'

Jodie had just been handed a steaming plate of vegetable korma when she began to wish that they'd opted for some other cuisine-of-the-world instead. Vietnamese, perhaps. Or kebabs. But it had nothing to do with the food. Rather the braying laugh coming from the queue behind them. She gave a furtive glance back before nudging Ushi.

'What did you say about curry-starved Brits? It's only Smarm-Features and mates from the ferry! Ohmigod! What shall we do?'

Ushi glanced back.

'Too late to do anything,' she muttered. 'We've been spotted.'

'Ah, the lovely laydeez we met on the high seas,' Smarm smarmed as he and his two mates caught up with them. 'We meet again. I was hoping we would. Hey, we've been missing ya! *N'est-ce pas mes amis?*'

'Give it a rest, Piers,' said one of his friends. 'Your French is shocking. Hi girls,' he grinned at all of three of them but his eyes were, Jodie noticed, firmly fixed on Ushi. So he fancied Ush! Well, lucky old her. Seeing him close-up, Jodie reflected that he looked a bit like a ferret. 'Didn't get a chance to introduce myself before. I'm Dominic but my friends call me Dom.'

The third member of the trinity then promptly introduced himself. 'The name's Flyte. Richard Flyte.'

'That cockney rhyming slang is it?' Stella suddenly piped up. 'You know – porkpies, lies; apple and pears, stairs; Richard Flyte, Mega-Tight.'

She didn't wait for him to reply but launched another blistering attack.

'Hey, you're not forking out for the scoff, are you? You'd better take care when you open your wallet or the months'll fly out! These curries don't come cheap y'know. Be at least double what those juices on the ferry cost.'

Jodie and Ushi started to laugh. By the sounds of it, Stella was back on form. Her jibe was right on target as Mega-Tight came over all defensive.

'I simply like value for money that's all,' he said. 'I don't like being taken for granted. I'm hardly destitute, sweetheart. I work in the city as a matter of fact. We all do.'

'Fascinating,' breathed Stella in serious sarcasm mode. They needed to get rid of these losers big-time, before anybody saw them with them, put two and two together and decided they were actually with these jerks!

Jodie was just thinking the same thing. As if Dom and Mega-Tight weren't bad enough, it was obvious who had the hots for her . . . Smarm-Features – wouldn't you just know it?

'What do you do?' he asked Jodie, standing so close to her she could smell his non-too-savoury beer breath.

'I'm a dental hygienist,' Jodie came back with, solemnly. 'Specialising in halitosis.'

'Hali . . . ?' Pukey Piers looked confused. Thick as well as seriously smarm-like. Not, Jodie decided, a winning combination.

'Bad breath,' she said pointedly and stared at him.

He looked at her warily then, deciding she had to be joking, started to laugh.

Jodie sighed. It was time, she felt, to take their

leave. This lot were seriously sad and if they didn't put a stop to it now, they'd never be able to shake them off. She glanced quickly at Ushi and Stella who were quick to follow her lead.

'We're off now,' yawned Ushi, pretending to drop off as Dom launched into a fascinating speech on the joys of off-shore investment.

'But we'd like to buy you laydeez a drink,' said Puke-Features. 'Now how about that? A glass of vino, yah?'

'Vino's strictly for toffs, isn't it?' quipped Stella. 'And we hate toffs . . .'

And with that final put-down they turned and started to walk away.

'God what a bunch of jerks,' breathed Stella. 'Do you think they've finally got the message, or what?'

They looked at each other and laughed. This holiday really was the best thing ever, Stella reflected as they walked on in companiable silence. And this festival was amazing, so many sights and sounds assailed her senses she felt almost dizzy with excitement as they lost themselves in the crowd.

'Not still missing old Tomas then, Stell?' Ushi asked eventually.

'No,' Stella sighed. 'In retrospect, I guess I've had

enough of the intensive-eyeball-gazing for a bit,' she laughed. 'So, what's next?'

They looked at each other and the same thought popped into each mind at the same time – shopping!

They browsed around the stalls. Stella bought some patchouli oil, Ushi a hippyish skirt and Jodie a tape. Then they gorged themselves on a bag of cookies from one of the food stalls before having a mad hour in one of the dance tents. It was dark when they emerged but there was still time to kill before 'Divali' came on stage.

'Back to the tent for a quick kip?' suggested Stella. 'I'm knackered now.'

But Jodie knew if they did that, they'd most likely flake out altogether and miss the rest of the evening. She suddenly had a brainwave. 'Massage!' she announced.

The other two looked at her, mystified.

'There's a holistic massage tent here somewhere,' she went on. 'I read about it. I really fancy that. You simply lie down and someone soothes away your aches and pains.'

'Ooo, I hope he's nice,' said Ushi.

'It's not necessarily a "he" who massages you,' said Jodie.

'Don't fancy it then,' shrugged Ushi. 'I'll come and watch, though.'

Shining their torches through the crowds, they eventually found the massage tent – having taken a wrong turning and spent a memorable and smelly five minutes in the gents' loos.

'Aren't you coming in, then?' asked Jodie, seeing Ushi and Stella starting to make themselves comfy on the ground.

'Changed me mind,' yawned Ushi. 'I fancy having a kip, too.'

'Just wake us up when you come out,' sighed Stella. 'Happy massage!'

Not really knowing why, Jodie felt a bit nervous as she walked into the large tent. Softly lit and delicately perfumed from a profusion of oil burners, tinkly new-age music was playing inside the tent giving it a mystical, serene feel. Several comatose-like punters lay spread out on the matting floor, being attended to by the masseures.

'Er, I'd like a massage please,' Jodie muttered in French to one of the off-duty masseuses, a girl who didn't look much older than Jodie.

'*Non, non, je suis étudiante,*' the girl said. '*Un moment, s'il vous plaît.*'

She went behind a screen and a moment later

emerged, now accompanied by a guy of around the same age. 'This is Max,' she said in charming-accented English. 'He is trained masseur. He is very good.'

Jodie didn't know about that, but there was, she decided, something about Max that was very, very sexy. He wasn't chunky like Jean-Louis, wasn't in-yer-face gorgeous either. But he had the most adorable puppy-dog eyes and a fantastic smile that made her feel all gooey inside.

'Hi,' he said. 'You're English, right? Me too.'

Feeling even more nervous – but intensely excited – now she knew just whose fingers would be sooth-ing away her aches and pains, Jodie lay down on the mat.

'Just relax,' Max whispered to her. 'The massage will last almost half-an-hour. OK?'

'OK,' Jodie whispered back and instantly wished it would be the longest half-hour ever. It was absolute bliss as those seemingly magic fingers of his attended to her neck, her shoulders, her head, her lower arms and legs and her feet. Jodie's heart was in her mouth. She'd never felt anything like it before in her life. Every time Max's fingers touched her skin it was like an electric current racing through her body. It had been a half-hour ride to heaven and by the time Max gently touched her on the elbow and told her the time was up she was like putty in his hands

'How was it?' he asked, helping her to her feet. 'Good?'

'Mmmmm.' Jodie smiled dreamily at him. She felt like she was floating. 'It was wonderful.'

'My pleasure.' He smiled back and seemed about to say something, then he hesitated.

'Yes?' asked Jodie. She momentarily wondered if she was being a bit forward but decided she didn't care.

Max smiled again and Jodie's insides did a series of gymnastic moves.

'We're shutting up the massage tent now. "Divali" are due on in a minute,' he said. 'Have you heard of them?'

Jodie laughed. 'Course she had. They just happened to be the best band going right now and one of the reasons she'd been so up for coming to the festival in the first place.

'Yeah, well . . .' Max went on, suddenly looking a bit shy. 'My brother's the singer and I was wondering if you would like to come and watch them with me. Backstage, I mean.'

Jodie literally pinched herself. This couldn't be

happening. It was a dream – it had to be. A gorgeous, sexy boy who just happened to be the brother of the singer in the most happening band in the world had asked her to go backstage with him, in the VIP area no less, where she'd no doubt be rubbing shoulders with no end of glam celebs and stars. This was too much! But, as she'd pinched herself to make sure, this was no dream.

'I'd love to,' she gulped, 'but I'd better tell my friends.'

He nodded. 'Be quick though, won't you? Security's really strict about letting people backstage once the band are on. And,' he looked embarrassed, 'I'm really sorry, but, I've er, only got two passes. Will your mates mind?

'No problem,' gasped Jodie, 'leave it with me,' and she ran out of the massage marquee to find the others. How fantastic that he wanted to give his spare pass to her! Ushi and Stella surely wouldn't mind. How could they? This was a once-in-a-lifetime opportunity.

She circled the area around the tent but couldn't see them anywhere. They'd obviously moved but she knew they couldn't be too far away. Probably gone looking for food, if she knew Ushi. Should she look for them? 'Yes,' said her head. But her excitement gene said no. It might take ages and Max might be forced to go backstage without her. That, she didn't want to risk.

'But what if they worry?' Jodie argued with herself.

'They won't,' she argued back. 'They'll be cool. Stella and Ush aren't the worriers. You are.'

She ran back towards the massage tent, feeling even more like she was floating. When she got there, she couldn't see Max and thought for a moment he'd gone. She felt sick to the stomach. Shit! She'd missed him. But then she spotted him, standing at another entrance, waiting for her.

French Letters

Dear Mum and Mark

Greetings from somewhere in south west France! We've been been gone for nine or ten days now – I'm losing track of time – so I thought I'd better write you to let you know I'm still alive. I actually bought a postcard to send you but I've decided to write a letter because we're having the best time ever and I've just got so much to tell. I'm enclosing the card anyway because I love the picture on the front – three old women in trad French cozzies. Guess who in 30 years time?

Sorry about my scrawl by the way – I've just noticed that my handwriting looks like a spiders' convention. It's not that the train's rickety – this is France after all and one thing the SNCF trains are not, is rickety – rather that I'm absolutely knackered because

I hardly got any sleep the night before last and it's just starting to catch up with me.

Why I didn't catch sufficient z's leads me very nicely into the most sensational thing that's happened to any of us so far on this trip. You'd better get yourself sat down for this, Mum, 'cos it's one helluva story. I could come straight out and tell you the punch line but for maximum dramatic effect – and I know you love a bit of drama – I'll start at the very beginning.

The day before yesterday, we arrived at this amazing music festival in Bordeaux. That's kind of in the last third of France nearest the Med and ... Oh I can't be bothered to explain. Go and get the atlas out of my bedroom. Got it? Found the map of France? Great! Bordeaux's on the Atlantic coast – sort of. Found it? Hurrah! Anyway, there we were at this festival ... Mark, you'd have loved it, you old hippy you. It was all incense, freaky music and loads of Jimi Hendrix looky-likies. Yep, you'd have fitted in well. Anyway, at around 8 pm on the first night, we were standing outside this tent where they do massage 'cos Jodie wanted one. Me and Stella weren't into it so we had a bit of a rest while we were waiting for her. We were starving so we went on a food rekkie after about 20 minutes. We thought we'd only be a few minutes but it took ages – queues everywhere. Anyway, we eventually got back to the tent, having scoffed a revolting burger apiece, and couldn't find Jodie anywhere. Not only that, the massage tent was in darkness. Everyone had gone. We hung around for a bit but still no Jodie. Stella and me were a bit surprised she hadn't waited for us but we figured she must either have gone looking for us or been so relaxed by the massage, she'd drifted back to the tent for a snooze. At this point, we weren't too concerned – she had a torch and knew the way back to the campsite . . . God, Mum, I've just thought. Don't tell Jodie's mum this bit if you happen to bump into her. She'll freak out and say we should have gone looking for her straight away. We didn't think there was any need, though. Not at that stage. Anyway, we watched the main act and then headed back to the campsite, both of us half-thinking that we'd get back to the tent and find Jodie snuggled up inside. But she wasn't.

'Oh well,' we said to each other. 'She'll be here in a minute.' Half-an-hour went by and no Jodie. I started to feel a bit nervous but didn't say as much to Stella 'cos she was still acting like everything's fine and kept saying that Jodie would turn up any minute. But when another 10 minutes went by and she still hadn't showed up, we suddenly confessed to each other that we were worried sick. Anything could have happened to her. I kept imagining all these headlines in the papers at home: 'Young Traveller found Strangled at French Festival'. Stella reckoned Jodie might have gone off with these creeps we initially met on the ferry and bumped into again at the festival. But I doubted that very much.

We rushed back to security in the main arena and had real problems getting in 'cos the gates were locked and the guard spoke very little English. Eventually we managed to make ourselves understood, though. The head security guy, who fortunately did speak English, said the only thing he could do was put out a message on the tannoy. But he was a bit reluctant because he said it was late and, anyway, Jodie would probably be at the tent when we got back. At this point Stella completely lost it. She started screaming that if he didn't put out a message immediately she was going to squat in the HQ. She wasn't going to move until something was done. A message was duly put out, in French and English, appealing for Jodie to return to our tent or to get in touch with security, pronto. All we could do at this stage, old Security Trousers said, was wait for her. If she still wasn't back by morning, they'd put out more messages and, if necessary, organise a search party. Both Stella and I really started to freak when he said this. It was like one of those situations you read about, you dread, but you never think will happen to you. We were just about to leave, having given the most comprehensive description of Jodie we were able to under the circumstances, when his mobile phone suddenly rang. Backstage were calling because they'd heard the message. Apparently, Jodie was in the VIP area at a party!!! Can you believe that? We couldn't. Our ikkle Jodes hanging out with the rich and famous? No way! In fact, we were so sure it was a mistake, we demanded proof.

Security Trousers fiddled about with this close circuit video monitor, and the backstage area where the party was happening came up on screen. All these VIPs – mostly French but a few Brit stars as well – were standing around quaffing champagne. And there, in the middle of it all, stood Jodie and some other bloke – chatting and laughing with the lead singer of the headlining band – 'Divali', no less! Stella and I were so shocked, we literally couldn't speak. I eventually managed to ask if we could go and get her but Security Trousers said 'non'. The party was invite only and we hadn't been invited. There was nothing for me and Stella to do except go back to the tent and wait for the party animal to come back.

Sorry Mum. But I'm going to have to finish this later. I've written so much my hand feels like it's going to drop off. Stay tuned . . .

Ushi looked up from her letter to see Jodie, seated across the aisle of the train, smiling at her slightly quizzically.

'That's a long, long letter,' Jodie said. 'Who's it to?'

Ushi tapped her nose. 'You're not the only secretive one, you know. It's for me to know and you to find out.'

'We'll do a deal with you, Jodie,' said Stella, putting down her book. 'You tell us exactly what you got up to with the divine Max and Ushi'll tell you who she's written to. She'll even let you read the letter. Right, Ushi?'

Ushi nodded. 'Absolutely. If she spills.'

Jodie laughed. 'No thanks. Anyway, I think I probably already know what's in the letter. It's mostly about me, isn't it? You've been giving me furtive little looks all the time you've been writing it, so it must be.'

'Oh all right,' Ushi conceded. 'Yeah, it's mostly about you.'

'Ushi!' Stella scolded her. 'You're crap! You shouldn't have given in so easily.'

'There wasn't much point holding out,' muttered Ushi. 'It's hardly a fair exchange, is it? I let Jodie read my letter which'll tell her nothing new and she tells us all the juicy stuff about her glamorous new boyfriend.'

'He's not my boyfriend – not really,' sighed Jodie. 'It was a . . . a brief "holiday" encounter.'

'But pretty intense, huh?' asked Ushi.

What a dumb question, she thought, as soon as she'd said it. 'Course it had been intense. Intensely intense. Ushi still couldn't believe it. That Jodie had copped off with a geezer whose brother just happened to be the lead singer in 'Divali'. And he'd turned out to be more than just a one – very late – night stand. Jodie had arrived back at the tent at around 2 am that first night and then spent practically the whole of the next day – and night – with Max. They'd met him for a few minutes but that hadn't been nearly long enough to form much of an opinion. It had been fairly obvious that Jodie and he wanted to be alone, though.

She and Stella had started day two of the festival on their tods. The day itself wasn't that eventful – more shopping, more dancing, lots of wondering what Jodie was getting up to – but the evening had more than made up for it. They'd met up with a mad Irish gang – a few girls but mostly boys – shared a few bottles with them and ended up playing a frenzied game of 'Spin the Bottle'. Stella had kissed a couple of the guys but she, Ushi, had gone on a bit of a snog fest. In particular with one bloke, called Rory. It had all kind of fizzled out once the game was over, though, and at the end of the night she and Stella had stumbled back to the campsite to find the tent minus Jodie again. But, unlike last night, they'd both known where she was – or rather who she was with. They'd intended to stay awake so that they could interrogate her when she got back but had fallen asleep within a few minutes. Then Ushi woke up around 5 am to see Jodie climbing into her sleeping bag.

'Dirty stop out!' Ushi had whispered. 'Where've you been you bad lass?'

But Jodie had just put her finger to her lips, closed her eyes, and gone straight to sleep.

Ushi had asked the same question again this morning – several times. Stella too. But Jodie was giving nothing away. Something had happened. Something major. Why else would Jodie be being so secretive about Max? She'd given 'em the lowdown on the showbiz party but she'd hardly mentioned the Max Factor at all besides saying that yes, she had spent the day – and presumably most of the night – with him, too. And why, and this was the most interesting bit as far as Ushi was concerned, why was she going round glowing like a candle that was permanently aflame?

'Lurve,' Stella had said with certainty. 'Our Jodie's been out late a-lovin'.'

And Ushi thought she might be right. They wanted, they demanded, details. Jodie, however, was having none of it. Her lips, it seemed, were sealed. Well not for much longer. Unless Jodes started to dish – and soon – Ushi thought Stella and she would literally go potty. And what better way to wile away the train journey between Bordeaux and Toulouse – their next port of call – than with some extra juicy gossip? The problem was getting her to open up a tad. The best way, Ushi decided, was to be just a bit sneaky.

'You know, we really were worried about you the other night, Jodes,' Ushi began. 'I thought something terrible had happened to you.'

Jodie smiled regretfully, but Ushi could tell she was thinking 'Here we go again'. And Jodie couldn't blame her, she and Stella had really laid into her when she'd eventually arrived back at the tent on that first night, and again the next morning.

'I know,' sighed Jodie. 'And I'm sorry. I should have found you and told you where I was going – especially as I freaked out when each of you went missing for a bit. But don't you think I've said sorry enough now? Surely I'm forgiven.'

'You might be,' said Ushi. 'It depends.'

'On what?' Jodie began. Suddenly her eyes narrowed and she started to laugh. 'Oh I get it. This another of your "deals", is it? I'm only forgiven, you'll only stop going on about it, if I dish on Max and me. Am I right?'

Neither Stella nor Ushi spoke.

'I am,' Jodie went on. 'Aren't I?'

- 'Might be,' muttered Ushi eventually. There was no way Jodie would reveal anything now.

'Well, he first kissed me while we were at the party backstage,' said Jodie, quite conversationally – she could have been talking about the weather. 'I'd being dying for him to – all the time we were watching the band – but, I dunno, it was just a bit funny. It was worth the wait, though. He's a fantastic kisser. I tell you, it's not just his hands he's talented with . . .'

Stella screamed and clapped her hands. 'Yes, yes, yes . . . tell us more!'

'Wait a bit,' gasped Ushi. 'Can you hear yourself, Jodie? You're telling us about him! Intimate details!'

'Yeah,' grinned Jodie. 'Well, I thought it was about time. The two of you have suffered enough.' She was laughing so much, she'd started to shake. 'Oh my God, it's been brilliant watching the two of you trying to worm all the gory details out of me. Best laugh I've had in ages.'

'You mean you've been winding us up?' asked Ushi.

Jodie managed to squeak out a 'Yes'.

'You cow,' Ushi exclaimed, wagging her finger at Jodie. 'But you can just make up for it by telling us everything. The works.'

Jodie was just getting to the exciting bit. Stella and Ushi had barely moved, barely spoken for the past twenty minutes. Glorious countryside was speeding past them but they couldn't have cared less. They were too wrapped up in 'The Max and Jodie Story'.

'So last night, there we were inside his tent after our final supper,' said Jodie. 'Max starts giving me this massage – but practically all-over-body this time instead of the routine stuff . . .'

'What does "practically" mean in this context?' interrupted Ushi. 'Details! We want details!'

'You know,' muttered Jodie, looking embarrassed in case any of the other passengers could hear.

'What do you think "practically" means?' Stella nudged Ushi. 'I'd say it meant pretty much everywhere. Am I right?' she asked Jodie.

Jodie gave a secret little smile. 'Not quite but, yeah, pretty much.'

'Jodie Parker!' Ushi exclaimed. 'Blimey, you're a sly one. What was it like?'

The secret smile grew into a wicked grin.

'Amazing but a bit scary, too. I mean, I've never had that kind of immediate reaction before. It was so strong. I really wanted to . . . I mean, really wanted to, well, . . . Oh, you know . . .'

'And did you?' Ushi and Stella asked at the same time.

Ushi held her breath. She could hardly bear to listen.

Jodie looked at them both for a moment.

'We . . .' she began hesitantly.

'*Excusez-moi mesdemoiselles, vos billets s'il vous plaît!*'

Ushi glared at the railway official who'd just interrupted them. Talk about bad timing!

'Well?' she whispered to Jodie, purposely ignoring him. 'You can't just leave it like this.'

'I bet that's what Max said,' giggled Stella.

'*Vos billets, mesdemoiselles!*' The official was getting a bit stroppy.

Jodie opened her bag, took out her ticket and handed it to him.

'Now's not the right time,' she muttered to Ushi. 'For God's sake show the man your tickets and I'll tell you the rest when he's gone.'

Reluctantly, Stella and Ushi did as she asked. Ushi watched the official with growing impatience. What the hell was he looking so closely at their tickets for? Trust their luck to have landed a 'jobsworth'.

'*Parlez-vous Français?*' he finally asked them.

'*Oui,*' said Jodie. '*Avez-vous un problème?*'

The official immediately launched into quick-fire French of which Ushi couldn't understand a word. She looked at Jodie. She seemed to be having problems, too. She certainly looked confused enough.

'Well?' Stella asked Jodie when the official finally paused for breath.

'It's ridiculous,' said Jodie. 'He says these tickets – our passes – aren't valid for this journey. He says unless we pay the supplement, we've got to get off at the next station.'

'How much is it?' Ushi asked.

'That's the real problem,' said Jodie. 'More than we can afford at the moment. We've hardly any cash, have we? We were going to go to the bank in Toulouse.'

They each scrabbled around in their packs to see

how much they could raise. It came to a grand total of 20F.

'That's nowhere near enough,' moaned Jodie. 'Not even enough to pay for one supplement – let alone three.'

'Can't we just explain our situation?' asked Stella. 'Tell him we'll send the money when we've got it?'

Ushi laughed. 'Oh yeah, he's really going to believe that.'

'Well, I'll try,' said Jodie.

She cleared her throat and started to talk but the official just shook his head.

'It's no good,' she said. 'He's not having any of it. He says we've got to get off. We've no option.'

'Can't we hide in the loos or something?' asked Ushi, getting desperate.

'What, and risk getting into even more trouble?' said Jodie. 'It's not worth it. Besides, –' she glanced up at the official who seemed in no hurry to check the other passengers' tickets. 'I reckon he's hanging around to make sure we do get off.'

The train began to slow down. The next station was obviously approaching.

'But we don't have a clue where we are,' wailed

Stella and started delving around in her pack for her map.

'Somewhere between Bordeaux and Toulouse?' offered Ushi.

'Yeah but where?' said Stella, flicking madly through pages. The train stopped. Ushi peered out of the window and saw nothing but miles and miles of fields. This couldn't be the next proper stop. This place – wherever it was – didn't even have a station. But then she noticed what looked like a tiny platform attached to what looked like an even tinier house.

'*Condom*,' proclaimed a sign on the platform.

They were so hacked off, they couldn't even raise a smile at the name.

'Looks like we're here,' said Ushi. 'Well, *quel* cock-up!'

They ended up sitting on the platform. On their backpacks as the station wasn't large enough to even warrant a bench. It was fryingly hot in the late afternoon sun and there was no shade.

'We've got to get out of here,' said Stella.

'Full marks for observation,' muttered Ushi. 'But just how exactly do we do that? There don't seem to be any taxis or buses. Even if there were, we wouldn't be able to stump up a fare. I've got a credit card but that hardly helps. Who's ever heard of a bus driver saying, 'Oh yes, that'll do nicely!' Oh God, why didn't we go to the bank in Bordeaux before we left?'

'Because we thought we were going to Toulouse,' said Stella. 'And we were going to get cash there.'

'We're going to have to ask someone for help,' said Jodie. 'Maybe there's a campsite near here or a small hotel. We could pay by credit card or maybe cash some travellers cheques there. Well, there's no one around here, is there? I'll go out on a rekkie.'

'Oh no you don't,' said Ushi. 'Look what happened the last time you were let loose on your own! You . . .' She smiled. 'Or did you? That was what you were just about to tell us before we got chucked off that train.'

Jodie shook her head. 'Sorry to disappoint you girls – especially as we find ourselves in such an aptly-named place – but no I didn't. Or rather we didn't. We kissed some more and spent the rest of the time in each others' arms but that was all. It wasn't the right time and we decided we hadn't known each other long enough.'

'I think you did the right thing,' said Stella smiling at Jodie. 'Good for you.'

98

Ushi nodded but didn't say anymore either. Normally she would have wanted to know loads more – like just how far Jodie had been tempted to go and if she'd made plans to stay in touch with Max. But the moment had passed. Their present predicament had taken precedence over everything else.

'Let's all go on a rekkie,' said Ushi, standing up. 'It's pointless staying here. We're acting like three eccentric old ladies waiting for a non-existent train.'

Half-an-hour later they found themselves in the back of a tractor trailer, chugging down the narrowest road Ushi had ever seen. They'd hailed down the tractor about ten minutes after they'd left the station. They'd never normally be stupid enough to hitch-hike but their luck was in as the driver happened to be a girl around their own age. She told Jodie that there was a campsite a few kilometres away and that they were welcome to a lift.

'Don't know what this place'll be like,' said Jodie, waving goodbye to Lucienne, their chauffeuse, as she deposited them outside the campsite. 'According to Lucienne, most of the clientele are in their forties with a passion for bird watching. Apparently, they get loads of rare breeds in these parts.'

'Fascinating,' said Ushi. 'Not! Who cares, though? It's somewhere to pitch our humble square of canvas.'

'I was rather hoping for a bed for the night,' complained Stella. 'My back's killing me.'

'Ungrateful cow!' exclaimed Ushi. 'You very nearly spent the night on that station. You still might if this campsite doesn't take credit cards.'

'They do!' sighed Jodie in relief as the tractor shuddered to a halt outside reception. 'There's a sign on the door.'

While Ushi sorted out the paperwork for payment, Jodie and Stella went off to start putting up the tent. Ushi gave the reception area a quick once over while her card was being authorised. It was obvious that the clientele were of a more mature nature. There was no blaring music rather softly playing supermarket muzac. And the cards on the noticeboard offered up caravans for sale rather than beat-up combi-vans. Oh well, it was only for a night. There was no way they were going to stay any longer in a place where the three of them were the youngest by about twenty years.

'I retract that,' Ushi said to herself as she caught a quick flash of faded cut offs and a red top – highly un-forty plus wear – flash pass the glass door. She decided to take a closer look. The wearer of the cut-offs and top was ambling across the car park. He turned his head – not for long – but long enough for Ushi to recognise who it was. Jee-zus! Stella was in for a surprise. What the hell was Tomas doing here?

Kiss 'n' Break Up, Kiss 'n' Make Up!

Week Two

Condom Campsite in South West France

We're in this elephant's graveyard of a campsite in the middle of gawd knows where, when we're supposed to be in 'France's student capital – Toulouse', at least that's what my trusty travel guide reckons to the place. This backwater isn't even in 'old trusty'. The only vaguely exciting thing about it is its name, which suggests a bit of a raunchy past. By the looks of it and the clientele, it sure as hell doesn't have a raunchy present.

At the moment, me and Jodes are having a bit of a sunbathe while Ushi sorts out all the boring paperwork stuff. Hope she remembers to buy a few postcards with 'Greetings from Condom' emblazoned across 'em. Not that I'd dare send one to my folks. Thank heavens for that girl's credit card! If we didn't have it, we'd be right down the Dordogne – or whatever the nearest river to here is called. Tent's up, bags are in! All that girl guide stuff's a cinch now, we've done it so often. Anyway, seeing as though I seem to have a few spare minutes, I decided it was time I gave dear diary a bit of an outing.

I've decided to give up writing in days 'cos I just haven't bothered filling in it – not since St Marion, anyway. So much to see, so much to do and so little time. Blimey, it's scary how time flies – it's no wonder that these clichés catch on. Far as I can work out they're all true!

It's a bit cringy reading back over my last entry written on our last day in St Marion. There I was sitting alone in the campsite caff, swearing undying love for Tomas and all that. Practically willing to sacrifice the rest of the trip for him. Dumb or what? But that's what a touch of the lurve-thang can do for you. And it's me all over to meet someone, decide it's the real thing within hours and then just a few days later, go off 'em. Ushi's right – I go from one extreme to the other. It's like a crush mentality, I guess. A real flash pash. I place lads up on a pedestal then bring the whole contraption crashing down. Tomas and me had fun but I'm glad now we left St Marion when we did. It was over between us before it could start going wrong. And now he's just a lovely, sexy memory – which is what he should be. Hopefully, I'll have a few more of those before this trip's over.

Bordeaux was a gas! I'd have hated to have missed it. It got a bit scary when Jodie went AWOL for those few hours of course but, wow, talk about an unexpected outcome. Her revelations on the train were a real eye-opener and dead thrilling. And to think before we left that I wondered – not for long admittedly – whether we might not meet any lads!

I didn't see much bloke action in Bordeaux but I wasn't that bothered. It was good chilling out on my own after all that intensive stuff with Tomas. I don't know what's in store for tonight. Probably zilch in a place like this. I don't mind though. I could do with an uneventful night after Bordeaux.

The Next Morning

Under Canvas

It's spooky! As soon as I get out my diary, things

start to happen. What was I saying about an uneventful night? I must have tempted fate. Last night was like a night of back-to-back soaps. Just thinking about it now makes my head spin.

It started pretty soon after I'd stopped writing. Ushi came back from reception and announced she'd just seen Tomas! I didn't believe her and thought she was taking the mick but she kept saying 'honestly, honestly'. Then I thought she must have seen someone who looked a bit like him. Tomas was a surf dude so what on earth would he be doing here? In bird watchers' paradise?

'Think Stella,' Ushi said. 'Who's he on holiday with?'

'His dad and his uncle,' I said. 'So?'

'And they just happen to be on the crinkly side, right?' she said. 'There something else, too. Didn't I once hear Tomas say that his Onkel Willy liked birds?'

'Yeah, you're right, he did!' said Jodie.

Uh-oh – this was disaster with a capital D for me. I didn't want to know. It made everything slot into place. It made sense that Tomas should be here but I still didn't really believe it.

Then Ushi said that she swore on her own life that it was him and I knew I had to believe her.

Even Ushi wouldn't do things like that as a joke.

'Oh God!' I wailed. 'What am I going to do?' I was so confused. I didn't know whether I wanted to see Tomas again or not. In my mind, I'd ended it. I couldn't see the point in starting the whole thing up again, especially as we were moving on tomorrow. I decided I'd hole up in the tent for the night.

'Don't be daft,' said Jodie. 'What if you go to the loo or something and he sees you? You'd be better facing up to him and telling him how you feel.'

Admirable sentiments perhaps, but I didn't know if I was brave enough for that.

'What do you think?' I asked Ushi.

Ushi shrugged. 'Well you can hide away if you want but I'm not going to – and if Tomas sees me and Jodie then he's automatically going to know you're here too.'

'I could pretend I'm ill,' I said.

'And if he thinks that, what's the first thing he's going to do?' said Ushi. 'Come over all nursey, dash over here with choccies and grapes and the next thing you know he'll be angling to get into your sleeping bag with you!'

'Not if I made out it was something very contagious,' I argued.

Ushi shook her head. 'You're really complicating

things, Stell. I reckon your best policy is to act normal and see what happens. No big explanations or anything like that. Just go with it.'

So that's what I did.

I was all nerves walking into the club house a few hours later. Ushi and Jodie were hungry so we went first into the restaurant, although I didn't feel like eating a thing. Thankfully, Tomas wasn't in there but my eyes never left the door. I kept thinking he'd walk in at any minute.

We went into the bar after that. There was a kind of disco going on. I was convinced Tomas would be there, too, but he wasn't. When half-an-hour went by, I started to relax a bit. Maybe he wasn't coming at all. Maybe he'd been struck down by some contagious disease.

Some '70s disco started to play and Ushi, emboldened by a couple of glasses of the local brew, got up and started strutting her stuff on the handkerchief-sized dance floor. Everyone started looking at her and she really played up to it. As soon as the record finished, this well-preserved wrinkly rushed over and asked her to dance. Being Ushi, she said yes.

Jodie and I were watching her and laughing about it when I suddenly saw Tomas walk in with his dad – Onkel Willy was no doubt hanging out up a nearby tree studying the habits of the lesser spotted nocturnal sparrow-tit thing. Thankfully, Tomas didn't see me immediately which gave me a bit of time to gather my thoughts and give him a secret once-over. It was strange – he didn't look half so gorge as I remembered. I'd expected his appearance to jump up and sock me between the eyes – like it had on the beach that first time – but there was barely a pat. He looked a bit scruffy – not cool-scruffy but scruffy-scruffy – his hair seemed to have grown and he looked really tired. I looked at his lips but didn't even feel much like snogging him. Weird, eh?

I was tempted to run – in fact, I nearly did – but then he turned and saw me. This incredulous look came over his face and he rushed over to us. He was talking really fast, only stopping to kiss me all over my face. Isn't it odd? One week you can want that more than anything and the next it makes you feel a bit queasy. I pulled away and said a quick hello. He noticed my coolness immediately. That wasn't surprising I guess, the last time I'd seen him I'd been all over him, making a tearful farewell.

Tomas reached for my hand, I pulled away again. Prolonging the agony like this was awful. Maybe

Jodie was right – I should try to tell him how I felt. I decided to go for the jugular.

Entschuldigung, *I stammered*, hoping I'd got the right German expression for sorry. But I couldn't for the life of me think how to say 'It-was-wonderful-while-it-lasted-but-it-was-just-a-holiday-thing-and-there's-no-point-carrying-on' in his lingo, so I just said, 'Auf Wiedersehen', grabbed Jodie and we ran like the clappers, hoping he wouldn't follow us.

Neither of us expected to find Ushi in the tent. We'd been so wrapped up in the Tomas thing, we hadn't noticed what had been going down on the dance floor. She said she was hiding from the wrinkly she'd been dancing with.

'He came over a bit fruity so I said I was going to the loo and I legged it,' she laughed. 'What did you say to Tomas?'

I quickly told her then decided to change the subject. I wanted Tomas to be history and anyway, I wasn't feeling all that proud of the rather un-brilliant way I'd handled the situation, I hadn't exactly been very nice. Where, I asked the girls, were we heading next? We'd thankfully been able to cash some travellers cheques at the camp office so we were alright for dosh but where to go now?

That was the question. Although we'd originally planned to go to Toulouse, I no longer fancied it. In fact, I was a bit bored with France, period. I wanted to move on. Luckily the others seemed to feel the same.

'Where to though?' said Ushi. 'Not your aunt Maria's. Not yet. And I don't feel like beach-bumming just now either. Know what I really fancy? I'd love to hit a city – but not just any old one. I want somewhere that's really buzzy and happening.'

She spread out her map on her sleeping bag and shone the torch on it. One place jumped out at us and I was annoyed that I hadn't thought of it before. Barcelona – it wasn't that far away – just over the border, in fact. More to the point, as cities went, you couldn't get much more happening, more buzzy than that.

'Barcelona?' I enquired.

'Olé!' came the reply. 'Viva España!'

Day 13

Barcelona

For the first time I appreciate my Spanish roots!

And I'm not talking onions, either. I felt at ease as soon as we changed trains at the French/Spanish border, and railing into Barcelona, I felt like I'd come home, I love it here! I love the amazing buildings, the rambling streets, the feel of the place. I love the fact that I look like I could easily come from here. And it's great being able to speak the language.

The first day in town, we arrived early evening. We'd already decided we deserved a bit of a treat so we booked ourselves into a small hotel in the centre of town. Right up in the attic we were, but it was fine 'cos the room had three little beds which meant we could share. It was dead dinky actually – like something out of a fairy tale – and the view out of the window was incredible. The three of us stood at that window for ages when we first got there – just looking down at the city sprawled out below, absorbing the atmosphere. It seemed to us like a giant fun fair. I think we were all a bit stunned, too. The sounds of the city after camping out on the coast and in the country sounded outrageously loud to our delicate little lugholes and took some getting used to.

A quick shower and change, and we went out to explore. To be honest, Barcelona seemed a bit dead at first, then I remembered that the Spanish don't go out till really late – 10 or 11 at least. We were about three hours too early but it didn't matter. We walked and walked, taking in the sights. Ushi, fancying herself as a bit of culture-vulture, got totally into it and went off on one of her artsy-farsty rants about the 'fabulously surreal architecture' as she called it.

The shops were something else, too. We gawped in some of the windows of the seriously fashionable stores, swooned over the designer clothes and completely freaked out when we clocked the prices. Those items that had prices on them, that is. Jodie reckoned if we pooled all the money we'd laid out on this trip, including the price of our tickets, we'd just about be able to afford a dress between us!

The fashions weren't the only thing we gawped at. The Barcelonian lads were something else, too. All black hair, flashing eyes and general all-over-pouty loveliness. But then the Barcelonian girls were pretty hot, as well. They looked so well-groomed and chic. There we were, dolled up in our best togs – Ushi in a pair of fake Versace jeans and little denim jacket, me in a floaty white number and Jodie in a little lycra dress – yet we felt scuzzy and scruffy next to them.

Had something to eat around 10ish – yummy, scrummy tapas – then we hit a couple of bars and ended up in a sweaty, packed-to capacity, neon-lit club. We danced a bit, chatted to a few guys – or at least I did – but I didn't pull. Neither did Jodie. Ushi did of course but then she practically always does. She says she just can't help herself at times and, for her, walking into a club full of tasty-looking lads is the same as walking into a gorgeous-smelling bakery. You always fancy a little something even when you're not particularly hungry! This time she copped off with this Rasta guy with the most amazingly long dreads. He wanted her to go back to his flat. She politely declined! Thank Gawd. Me and Jodes had to kick our heels for a bit while she snogged him goodnight but we eventually got back to the hotel around 3 am, knackered but gagging for more. We'd taken to this town. We decided we wanted to stay.

Day 15

Barcelona

It's unanimous! We love Barcelona which is why we're still here. There's just so much to do in this city, I reckon you could be here forever and still not see it all. We've changed location because we couldn't afford more than one night in a hotel – especially as for most of that night we were out partying. So we're in a youth hostel now and it's fine. It's cheapish, we've hooked up with a good crowd and you don't feel embarrassed if you slurp your coffee at breakfast time like we did at the hotel.

Not that we've seen too many breakfast times. Getting in during the early hours like we do after a night's clubbing, we usually sleep in till 10 or 11. We have a lazy-type brunch at one of the cafés near the hostel, do the culture or shopping bit – OK, the window-shopping bit – in the afternoon then back to the hostel for a quick kip and spruce up for the night ahead. I reckon it's the perfect way to live.

Boy talk? Ushi's seen her Rasta again – once. But he came over all heavy and muttered something about wanting her to have his babies! After that, she told him, less-than-politely, to sling his hook. Since then she's been hanging out with the crowd we've met up with at the youth hostel. She quite fancies this sweetie of a Swedish lad called Bjorn and he seems to like her. They've danced together a few times but no proper lip action, yet. Knowing Ushi, though, that won't be long in coming.

Jodes seems happy enough just to chill out to the music and have a laugh at the moment. I think the Max Factor's still big with her and she's not interested in anyone else right now. As for moi – or should I say moy? Well, I've had a few dances and the occasional snog with Italian Guido, another lad from our hostel but that's all. He's nice, but not that nice.

Day 17
Barcelona

Sadly our last day in this top, top city. Just time to squeeze in a final bout of sight-seeing and then we're off. A regretful decision we came to over breakfast (we made it for once!) as the three of us worked out just how much money we had left. Basically, we're going through the dosh in this town like there's no tomorrow and we just can't afford to stay here any longer. It's tempting to run up a bill on Ushi's credit card. Ushi says she doesn't mind and neither would her mum, but the thing is, money's not the only commodity we're running short of. It's scary how quickly the time's passing too. We've been gone over two weeks already yet it seems like only a matter of hours ago since we were on that ferry heaving our guts up. We've still got to go to Aunt Maria's and then we all fancy a chill-out spell on a beach to soak up a final ray blast before we take the express train back up through France to Boulogne. Lloret de Mar on the Costa Brava sounds like it was put there with us in mind. The guide book describes it as being a haven for those who like their nightlife 'loud, late and libidinous'. After an oh-so-quiet spell at Auntie's mountain home, I just know we'll be gagging for all of that! So y'see, we gotta go now 'else we won't fit it all in. It feels like we've done miles and miles but looking at the map of Europe makes you realise just how much more there is to see.

'Next year . . .' says Jodie.

Yes please! I feel like booking my ticket now!

After brekkie, I go and phone Auntie – thinking about it, I'm amazed she's on the phone – to tell her to expect us in the evening. She's almost beside herself with excitement at the prospect of our visit. I guess in the backwater she lives in, it's like she's expecting the second coming!

'And such luck,' she babbles just before I put down the phone. 'Your timing could not be better.'

'Why?' I ask, momentarily excited myself. What's going down up there? A festival perhaps? Like the one in Bordeaux?

I cross my fingers, but by the time Aunt Maria's told me what it's all about, I feel like shoving them down my throat.

'Your cousin, Miguel, is due home from university,' she chuckles. 'He comes tomorrow and will be so pleased to see you.'

I ring off feeling completely devoid of excitement and anticipation at that prospect. She calls that lucky? Well, that kind of luck I reckon we can do without.

Love 'n' War

'Miles from anywhere,' Stella had said on the ferry crossing. 'In the middle of nowhere . . .' Arriving in the Valle d'Aran, the area of the Pyrenees where Aunt Maria's village was situated, Jodie could see what Stella had meant. It sure was remote. The train, the smallest one they'd travelled on so far, seemed to have taken ages from Barcelona and had literally chugged its way up mountains, down valleys and back up the otherside again. But there was no doubting that it was pretty. With the majestic Pyrenean mountains as a backdrop, it was, Jodie thought, one of the most picturesque places she'd been to. And the air was so fresh, she wanted to drink it.

Aunt Maria's three-storey house had a definite Alpine feel to it. Once again, she, Stella and Ushi were sharing an attic room – like they'd done that first night in Barcelona. But the view from this window couldn't have been more different. Taking in the mountain air and marvelling at how green the valleys were the morning after they'd arrived, Jodie had felt a bit like Heidi – the heroine of her favourite childhood story.

Mmmmm, mmmm, Jodie reflected, it would no doubt be numb-skullingly boring to stay here for any length of time. But four or five days sleeping in a comfy, cosy bed, eating home-cooked food and being thoroughly spoilt wasn't to be sniffed at. While she'd hardly have come here out of choice, now she was here it made sense to make the best of it. She was sure they'd be able to find something to do. Like, er, swimming, for instance. They could go for a dip – or ten – in one of the lakes nearby.

Yeah, thinking about it, some kind of energetic, sporting activity would be a good idea. Exhaust their minds and bodies so they'd be too knackered to imagine what might have been going down in this oh-so-romantic setting if only the right lads were around. She kept seeing herself and Max walking arm-in-arm through the countryside and lying down together in the lush, green meadows. The sweet smell of newly cut grass and the even sweeter smell of Max's skin, the feel of his lips on hers and those magic hands of his massaging her into a state of pure bliss. Oooooooooh, if only he were here now, she'd . . . But then in another way, Jodie was glad he wasn't. They'd had a fab couple of days in Bordeaux but it had been a one off – they'd both known that. She'd never forget Max but, hey let's get real, holiday romances didn't travel well. Look at Stella and Tomas, for instance. When they'd met up again, it had been a disaster and now – and in the future – when Stella thought about Tomas, she'd remember their unhappy last meeting in Condom rather than all the lovely, luv'd-up stuff in St Marion.

After lunch, Jodie and Ushi had offered to go down to the nearest village and do some shopping for Aunt Maria's special celebration supper which she'd planned to welcome both them and the returning Miguel to the mountain homestead. Jodie and Ushi's offer hadn't been made entirely unselfishly. Following a morning of Spanish family gossip, they'd both wanted to get out of the house while Stella and her auntie caught up on more news.

'What are you thinking about?' Ushi went on as they walked down the steep pathway leading to the village. 'Wondering just what we're going to do with ourselves in this mountain retreat?'

'Kind-of,' mumured Jodie. 'And thinking about life, love and the universe.'

'Oh Gawd, don't go all philosophical on me,' muttered Ushi. 'You know, you haven't been the same since you had that massage in Bordeaux!'

'You're right there,' sighed Jodie dreamily.

They turned a corner, and a few shops and some village folk came into view.

'At last! Provisions!' exclaimed Ushi. 'Hey up, Jodes, have we come out with our knickers at half-mast or something? Have we got porridge all over our faces? Because we seem to be attracting quite a few stares.'

'Hardly surprising, is it?' Jodie commented. 'I mean we're strangers in these here parts.'

Ushi giggled as two young girls of around ten stared at her in amazement and obvious admiration.

'Y'know, I quite like it. Must be what being a celeb feels like.'

'Well, cast your mind back to . . . what is it?' Jodie peered at Aunt Maria's shopping list. '*Cebollas* rather than celebs. That's onions to you!' She opened the door to the first shop they came across – a kind of deli-cum-greengrocers. 'Now this should be fun – neither of us speaks a word of Spanish nor the local dialect, either. Aunt Maria must be bonkers trusting us to do her shopping for her. I reckon we should hand the shopkeeper the list. And hand over the money. Yeh?'

'Absolutely!' Ushi agreed.

The shopkeeper was just wrapping up their purchases when Jodie spotted what looked like a large loaf of bread entirely covered in sugar. On impulse, she gestured to the owner that she wanted to buy a loaf.

'Eh?' piped-up Ushi. 'Is that on Auntie's list?'

Jodie shook her head. 'I want to contribute to supper, though. I think we should – as a kind of thanks to Aunt Maria for having us.'

'Nice idea, Jodes,' said Ushi as they left the shop. 'It is sweet of her to put all three of us up. But I just wish . . .' She paused suddenly. 'Ohmigod!' Her voice had become a squeak. 'Ohmigod – take at look at that! Ohmigod! Forget what I just said. Suddenly I love it here. I think I must be in heaven!'

Jodie looked at what, or rather who, Ushi was staring at and immediately felt herself being unfaithful to the memory of Max. Sitting across the street, sipping coffee at a dinky pavement café, was, quite simply, one of the best-looking lads Jodie reckoned she'd ever seen. Movie stars, pop stars, world famous sports stars ... they had nothing on this bloke. He was utterly, utterly droolsome! Black, black hair which flopped silkily across his forehead, flawless olivey skin, perfectly chiselled nose and a full, sensuous mouth – he was a veritible portrait of gorgeousness.

Sensing he was being gawped at, he looked up suddenly and Jodie felt like her heart was in her mouth – or the other way round. His eyes – languid and golden hazelly-green – stared straight into hers. Jodie couldn't tear her eyes away. It was as if they'd been artificially fixed in one position and were unable to move. Finally, he smiled at her, raised his coffee cup to her, got up from the table and walked away. Jodie shuddered with excitement – he fancied her! She knew he did. That look he'd just given her had been a definite I-want-to-snog-the-lips-off-you kind of look. And my God was it mutual! She watched him walk down the street. He had to be at least six foot and he swaggered slightly – like a sexy cowboy.

'Ooooooh!' murmured Ushi in her ear. 'Oooooh, oooooh, oooooh! Did you see him? More importantly, did you see the way he was eyeing me up?

That lad's got the hots for me and he's left me all of a sizzle! Ahhhhh! I'm not going to let him get away. Let's follow him.'

Jodie was too shocked to reply. Ushi thought he'd been staring at her? Well, she was wrong about that. One hundred and ten per cent wrong. He'd been looking at *her* not Ushi. She just knew it! Could feel it deep, deep down inside.

'But . . .' Jodie started to say, then she changed her mind. If Ushi was convinced that this lad fancied her, there's no way she'd just say, 'Yes, OK, Jodes – you're right' when Jodie informed her that she'd merely been thinking wishfully. It was far more likely, she'd storm up the street after him, stop him and demand to know exactly for whose benefit the flirty eye action had been for. And that, for embarrassment and cringe-making value, just didn't bear thinking about. Much better to play dumb – for now.

'We can't follow him, Ush,' said Jodie. 'We've still got stuff to buy and Auntie's expecting us back. We'll have to let him go.'

Making whimpering noises like an injured puppy, Ushi followed Jodie into the butcher's. Once again, Jodie handed over a list but they could have given her back pig swill ingredients for all she cared.

She kept seeing golden-green eyes looking at her. At *her*, she was positive they'd been looking at her. Inwardly, she started to panic. Oh God, she might never see him again. She should have tried to make some excuse to Ushi and gone after him. But suddenly she felt calm again. They were here for the best part of a week, weren't they? In a tiny place like this, she was bound to run into him again. In fact, Jodie decided with a sudden burst of determination, she was going to do everything in her power to make sure of it.

Dear Davy - Why haven't you written? I arrived at Stella's aunty's expecting to find a lovely, long letter from you. I wrote the address on that postcard I sent you from contraceptive campsite in France so you've no excuse, my lad!! Spain's great - Barcelona especially. After we've taken the mountain air, we're off to Lloret for a bit more sun-soaking and cool camping...

Ushi threw down her pen. She couldn't be bothered to write to Davy at the moment. Couldn't give him her full attention. But then that seemed to be true of everything. It was early evening now but since spotting that gorgeous guy at the shops, she'd spent practically the whole afternoon thinking about him. There'd been something dead fascinating about him. So many unanswered questions about him, too. Questions she was desperate to know the answers to. Like what, for instance, was somebody who looked like him doing in a place like this?

'You'd better get changed, Ushi,' said Stella who'd just walked into their room, fresh from the shower. 'You too, Jodie.'

'What for?' Ushi muttered. 'We're not going anywhere, are we?'

'No but my auntie's been slaving over a hot stove all afternoon.' Stella started drying her hair. 'She doesn't get that many visitors so our being here is a big thing for her. And she wants it to be special.'

'I know, I know,' sighed Ushi and slowly got up from her bed. 'I was thinking, Stell . . .' she said, her voice momentarily muffled as she riffled through her rucksack looking for something to wear. 'After supper, d'you think your aunt would mind if we, er, schlepped down to the village for a bit?'

'What for?' Stella asked. 'There's nothing to do and nowhere to go apart from sitting sipping coffees with the locals and watching a very tiny corner of the world go by.' She grinned suddenly. 'Oh I get it! You want to go down to the village to see if this apparently gorgeous lad's there, yeah?'

Ushi looked at her sheepishly.

'Might do,' she said.

Stella shook her head. 'I've already told you, Ush. He must have been a figment of your imagination. There aren't any lads like the one you described living up here. You must be suffering from altitude sickness and be hallucinating with it. Either that – or he's a wind-up. You and Jodes having me on about some amazing bloke who doesn't even exist.'

'Oh he exists alright, doesn't he, Jodie?' said Ushi.

Jodie nodded. 'He sure does but, er, you're right about one thing Stella . . .' It was time, Jodie suddenly decided, that Ushi faced up to reality – that it had been *her* he'd eyed up, not Ushi – if only because Ushi had been going on about him all afternoon like he was her private property, and Jodie was sick of it. 'I reckon Ush's imagination must be playing a few tricks on her 'cos, er, sorry Ush . . . I don't exactly know how to put this so I may as well come straight out with it . . . I'm pretty sure he was looking at me, eyeing me up rather than you. In fact, I'm positive.'

'What?' Ushi exclaimed, puzzled. 'You don't think . . . ?' She shook her head. 'Oh Jodes, I'm sorry but . . . I mean you were standing next to me so I can understand the mistake but no, really, he was eyeing me up. I'm absolutely sure of that.'

'Yeah, well I'm just as sure it was me,' said Jodie, resolutely.

'I saw him first,' Ushi came back with. 'You'd never have noticed him if I hadn't pointed him out.'

'So?' Jodie shrugged. 'What's that got to do with anything? You . . .'

'Girls, girls, girls . . .' interrupted Stella. 'I can't believe I'm hearing this. Fighting over a lad, for God's sake! A lad, by the way, whom I still don't really believes exists. I know what you two are like, especially if you're a bit bored. Wind-up

128

merchants, the pair of you. This little scenario might all be for my benefit. But if it's not, well . . . you should just hear yourselves! I thought we'd agreed eons ago that no bloke's worth arguing about – however gorge he might be.'

'You didn't see him,' muttered Jodie. 'Anyway, that's not the point.'

'What is the point?' asked Ushi.

'That you've got the wrong end of the stick, Ush. I don't want to fall out about this but you have. It was . . .'

'Oh not again!' Stella yelled. 'Enough! Can't we just leave it for now? Maybe he was eyeing up the pair of you.'

'No way,' Jodie hit back with.

'That we do agree on,' said Ushi.

'I'll tell you what,' suggested Stella. 'OK, we will go into the village after supper. If he's there, I'll act as ref and decide which of the two of you he fancies.' She started to laugh. ''Course we might be able to solve it a whole lot easier than that. He might just fancy me!' Ushi joined in the laughter but she felt deadly serious inside. She'd never felt so determined. He was hers and if any of them was going to pull him, she was.

Just then Aunt Maria called up the stairs.

'What did she say?' asked Jodie.

Stella sighed. 'Oh to hurry up and come down because Miguel's just arrived. My oh-so-dreary cousin. That's all we need.'

Ushi quickly slipped off her wrap and pulled on her fake Versaces and a silk shirt. She'd forgotten all about Stella's cousin, too wrapped up in her thoughts and fantasies about 'lurve-stuff-on-legs', as she'd named him. She sincerely hoped that Miguel was a fast eater who had very little to say. 'Cos the sooner this supper was over, the sooner she could run down to the village and the sooner she might see L.S.O.L.

*

'So where is he then?' asked Ushi as the three of them sat down at the dining-room table. 'The "magnetic" Miguel. Not!'

'Just getting changed, apparently,' replied Stella. 'He'll be down in a minute. God, I hope he's improved since the last time I saw him. We didn't exactly part on good terms. I put melted choccie in his Action Man's trousers which seemed to upset him no end and . . .'

'So I hang up your Barbie by her hair,' a lightly-accented voice called down the stairs. Miguel, obviously. Well, thought Ushi just before she turned round to take a look at him, his voice sure didn't sound wussy. It was a little bit sexy actually. It would be interesting to see what the rest of him was like.

She was sitting with her back to the doorway and didn't see him walk in. But what she did see was a look of total amazment of Stella's face while Jodie's expression . . . well, there was no other word for it, was totally rapt.

Ushi slowly turned her head and found herself gazing into a pair of sleepy-green eyes. She'd been here before. It was him – Mr Gorgeous was standing right here in Auntie Maria's dining-room! She didn't understand. This dish was 'manky' Miguel? Stella's dweeb of a cousin? It didn't make sense.

'You've changed,' Ushi heard Stella say, in a kind of cross between a gulp and a gasp.

'You too,' murmured Miguel. 'You're . . . you're really pretty, *chicita!*'

He kissed her soundly on both cheeks which by now were glowing. Stella had come over all preeny. So she fancied him, too. That much was already clear from the ga-ga look on her face, the sound of her voice and the way she'd suddenly kicked into major, hair-flinging flirtation mode.

Were cousins allowed to fancy each other? Ushi didn't know.

'Introduce us!' Ushi hissed.

'Oh yes,' gushed Stella. 'Jodie and Ushi, this is my cousin, er, Miguel.'

'*Hola*,' Miguel smiled first at Ushi and then Jodie.

Ushi was just about to mention their kind-of meeting earlier when Aunt Maria bustled in, carrying a steaming pot of delicious-smelling food and beaming all over her face. She said something and then burst out laughing.

'What did she say?' Ushi asked Stella but Miguel answered for her.

'That never before has she prepared such a welcome for me,' he said, smiling at Ushi and revealing a set of perfect white teeth. 'I have to say, yes, that is true.'

Oh wow! thought Ushi. He is just so gorgeous! She suddenly felt all light-headed. This was too good to be true. All afternoon, she'd been brooding on how she might find him again and now here he was – sleeping under the very same roof! She hadn't particularly been looking forward to this part of the trip but now, against all the odds, it had the potential to turn into the best bit!

Ushi spent the rest of the meal in a bit of a daze. The food was delicious but she'd hardly tasted a thing. She was too busy at first watching Miguel and then too busy trying to make him laugh – not exactly easy when she was having to compete with full-on flirt attacks from Stella and Jodie. One point in her favour was that, to her delight, she'd discovered that Miguel was studying art and design at college like she was. But whenever she'd try and engage him in some relevant conversation, Stella would produce another 'Action Man' type reminiscence from up her sleeve.

Then Jodie leapt up, disappeared into the kitchen and returned bearing the sugar loaf.

'I bought it as a surprise,' she said, suddenly blushing up. 'To say thanks to Aunt Maria for having us.'

'That is so sweet of you,' murmured Miguel and briefly stroked Jodie's hand which made her blush even more.

'*Er, excuse me!*' Ushi had wanted to yell across the table. '*I was there when she bought it. I thought it was a sweet idea, too. So don't I deserve a hand-stroke, too?*'

'It's sugar loaf,' Jodie said smiling at Miguel.

'No, no,' he responded. 'This is *Sal Pan* – salt

bread – not *Azucar Pan*. You're so funny . . .' He started to laugh. 'It's lucky you didn't put some honey on it to eat too . . . Very delicious,' he was really laughing now.

'I . . . I . . . I . . .' Jodie started to stammer.

Quite unexpectedly, Stella started to giggle too. She licked her finger, tentatively touched her piece of bread, then licked her finger again. She grimaced. 'Good choice, Jodes!'

Ushi started to laugh too. She expected Jodie to start tittering too but she didn't. Her emotions were obviously running high because she started to blub.

Aunt Maria immediately started fussing round her while Miguel did even more. This time, in addition to Jodie's hand, her stroked her hair and put his arm round her! Aghhhhhhhh!

'*Er, excuse me,*' Ushi wanted to yell again. '*I was there when she bought it. It was my fault too. So don't I deserve a bit of a hug, as well?*'

After supper Stella, Ushi and Jodie cleared away the dishes, leaving Aunt Maria and Miguel to have a bit of a chinwag.

'You'll be glad to know that Auntie's cool about us going down the village, Ush,' said Stella. 'She wants to spend some time alone with Miguel. She's a bit narked because he didn't come straight home when he arrived. He went to an old school-friend's instead.'

Ushi grinned. 'Oh I, er, don't think I want to go to the village any more . . . Come on Stella! As if I need to tell you why! He's here – the gorgeous creature I was telling you about. He's only your cousin! The cousin you've been slagging ever since we came away. Blimey, if I'd known he what he was really like . . .'

'How was I to know? His metamorphosis has come as a real shock to me, too,' Stella admitted. 'Auntie neglected to tell me just how gorgeous he'd got – although she did mention he'd changed a bit.'

'He's simply beautiful,' Jodie piped up suddenly.

'Isn't he?' beamed Stella, sounding very territorial. 'Totally droolsome.'

'He's just stunning,' breathed Ushi.

She looked at the other two. They looked at her. And she knew they were all thinking the same thing. This was weird! In all the years they'd been mates, they'd never gone after, or really been attracted to, the same lad. Whenever it had got close to happening before, one or two of them would always back down without argument. Or they'd all decide that none of them fancied him, anyway. But this time, Ushi sensed, was different. There was a definite whiff of war in the air. They all fancied the cute little bum off him and not one of them was going to give in without a fight. Maybe they should go down to the village after all. They had things to discuss. Miguel.

Day 19

Aunt Maria's
I'm dog-tired but I'm making myself write this because I feel tonight has been a night of momentous importance. First up, I discover that my cousin's no longer a weedy little caterpillar but a fabulous, totally amazing butterfly. Second-up, within about a nanosecond of seeing him again after all these years I realise I fancy him like crazy and third up, it takes me about another nanosecond to clock that Ush and Jodie are feeling exactly the same as me. Our little post-supper chat definitely confirmed this. We all fancy Miguel, we all want him and not one of us is willing to back down. It would be a damned sight easier if (a) he had

a steady girlfriend but one bit of family gossip I absorbed today was that there's no one special in his life. When Aunt Maria told me this, I presumed it was because he couldn't get anyone to go out with him but now I realise the reverse is true. He must have so many girlies gagging for him, he must have a ball playing the field. And (b)? Well, it would also make things easier for us three gals if Mig made it clear just who he likes best. I'm usually pretty hot at picking up pheromones but tonight, I wasn't. I can see why Ush and Jodes were arguing about which of them he'd been looking at when they saw him in the village because he's got this way with him. He's a complete charmer who probably gives every girl he meets the impression that he's really into them.

Anyway after supper, Ush, Jodes and me go down to the village for a coffee. It's like any other night since we've been away except it's not. We're laughing and joking with each other as usual, but tonight there's a definite undercurrent of tension as well. It's about Miguel. We're just getting stuck in to our cappucinos when I decide I can't stand it any longer. Something has to be said.

'We all fancy him, right?' I blurt out.

We're actually in the middle of talking about something else but Ush and Jodie are onto the wave-length immediately.

'Yep,' says Ush while Jodie just nods.

There's silence. Stalemate. Each of us waiting for the other to say 'OK – forget it. Forget him. Count me out.' It doesn't happen. 'Then we've no choice,' I say eventually. 'It has to be a three-girl contest.'

'But you're his cousin,' Jodie says.

'So?' I shrug. 'That's got nothing to do with it. It's not illegal to marry your cousin, let alone snog 'em. Anyway, it's not the matrimony bit I'm interested in.'

'Yeah, yeah, alright . . .' says Jodie.

'Open combat then,' muses Ushi. 'Is this wise?' A competitive gleam comes into her eye. 'Yes, why not? If nothing else it'll give us something interesting to do while we're here. A new project to wile away the time. It'll be a laugh. But I'm warning you both, you don't stand a chance.'

Jodie and I smirk at this. 'Ush,' I say. 'You're just too modest!'

'You may mock,' says Ushi. 'But I mean it.'

'Yeah, well,' says Jodie, lowering her voice, licking her lips and running her fingers through her hair. 'You've never really been in competition with me before, have you, darling?'

'Me neither,' I say.

'You two don't worry me, darlings!' Ushi comes back with.

We're all laughing but underneath it all, we're serious. We've never had this kind of conversation before, never been love rivals before – not properly anyway – and I'm not sure that I like it.

'A nice, clean fight then?' says Jodie. 'We're all agreed? We all go for it – or rather him? And no hard feelings?'

'Absolutely,' says Ushi. 'I think we're mature enough to handle it – or rather him – whatever the outcome!'

For a moment, I feel panicky. But it passes. Yeah, it'll be fine. Like Ushi says, we're sensible enough to cope with it. And we're best mates. The best ever. Nothing can alter that. I raise my coffee cup. 'To us!' I announce. 'And to Miguel, God help him and may the best girl win!'

Babes In Battle!

Instead of a free-for-all where the three of them would constantly be vying for Miguel's attention, they decided – before going down for breakfast the next morning – on a structured game, or rather pulling, plan.

'A kind of Miguel mesh,' giggled Ushi.

'I guess,' said Stella.

'There's a "do" down in the village the night after next,' said Jodie. 'We saw that poster in the café, remember? Well, I reckon we should aim to have the sitch sorted by then. Yeah?' Both Stella and Ushi nodded.

'So how do we divide the time up before then?' asked Stella. 'God, it's complicated isn't it? Not to mention calculated!'

'Well sometimes you have to be,' Jodie went on briskly. 'This is a competition and you have to be organised in competitions else they don't work.

Alright then, who's going first?'

'Eh?' asked Ushi.

'. . . And I suppose we should discuss exactly what we each intend to do with him,' Jodie continued.

'Isn't that a bit personal?' giggled Stella.

Jodie shook her head. 'Not like that. I'm talking about specific plans of attack.'

'Oh I get it,' said Ushi suddenly. 'Like, Miguel and me obviously have art 'n stuff in common so I ask him to show me round the nearest gallery or something?'

'Right!' smiled Jodie. 'And I love swimming so I'll ask him to come for a dip with me in the nearest lake.'

'Oh great!' Stella pouted. 'Ush gets to be all artsy and romantic with him, you get to swim with him – which means you'll get to see each other nearly naked – and I get to . . . what? Reminisce about Action Man, "Kerplunk" and the Spanish version of "Mousetrap" some more?'

'Well you seemed more than happy with that last night,' muttered Ushi. 'On and on and on, you went.'

'Yeah, well, I reckon I've pretty much mined that vein now,' said Stella. 'And besides, that kind of thing's hardly going to get him in a smoochy-moochy frame of mind, is it? I want him to see me as I am now, not as some brat of a kid who constantly fought with him.'

'Stell . . .' Ushi wagged a finger at her. 'He only has to look at you to see that. What did he call you last night? A *chicita*? I don't know what it means but it sounds dead nice.'

'Plus you have a joint history,' said Jodie. '*And* you speak his language. There'll be no awkward silences for you, will there?'

'I guess not,' said Stella, looking marginally happier. 'What else then, Jodes? What's next? You seem to have this whole crazy thing worked out.'

'We work out who goes when,' said Jodie. 'For instance – me this afternoon, Ush tomorrow and you, Stell, the next day. I reckon we've got to space it a bit – poor lad will be confused if we don't allow him a rest between each of us. Basically, we each go out and give it our best shot.'

'And rules . . .' mused Ushi. 'We must have rules.'

'Like what?' asked Jodie, surprised.

'Like we don't give each other any kind of bad press,' said Ushi. 'You know . . . like mentioning other squeezes – holiday or otherwise – in order to

142

score extra points ourselves.'

'Oh come on!' replied Jodie. "As if.'

'Ush, honestly . . .' tutted Stella.

'We might,' said Ushi. 'You never know, we just might. I'm only being realistic. I can get pretty competitive when I'm roused – we all can. We all like winning, don't we? And if the going gets tough, I bet we'll be tempted to, too. So we're fair about each other. Like if Mig says something like, 'I'm really into you but what about your friends?' we come back with something like, 'Oh that's fine. Don't worry. We're all pretty cool about this sort of thing'. She paused to take a breath. 'And another thing – we don't butt in on each other's time, we stay out of the way, plus . . . we keep schtum on what occurs on each of our dates. We don't want to put each other off. That, I think, will be the hardest thing of all . . .'

'And . . .' Stella added finally. 'We don't wind each other up. However tempting it might be.'

'Absolutely,' said Ushi and Jodie together.

Suddenly they heard the man himself calling to his mum. He was already downstairs. 'Go on then, Jodes!' Ushi gave her a nudge. 'There's no time like the present. Off you jolly well go!'

*

143

Splash!

Perched on a rock like the little mermaid, Jodie admired the spectacle of a tanned, tautly-lean Miguel diving into the mirror-like surface of the lake. In spite of the confident exterior she'd shown to Ush and Stella, and in spite of the fact she was truly confident that he fancied her, she'd been pretty damned nervous about asking Mig out.

'I was wondering . . .' she'd said to him. 'Is there anywhere to go for a swim round here? It's such a gorgeous day.'

'Sure,' he'd replied with a lazy smile. 'There is *La Panta de la Torcassa*. There is wonderful swimming there.'

'Where is it, exactly?' she'd said, although having read up on the area she already had a pretty good idea.

He'd started to explain but then he'd said, just as she'd hoped he would, 'I think it would be easier if I showed you. You'd mind . . . if I came along? Stella and Ushi . . .'

'Oh it's just me,' she'd come back with. 'The others are, er, busy. OK?'

Miguel smiled again and said, 'Fine, no problem' and if he had any notions that the whole thing might be a set-up, he sure wasn't letting on.

Jodie glanced at her watch. She was trying terribly hard not to be but she couldn't help feeling just the weeniest bit impatient. They'd been here for almost two hours. They'd shared a picnic in a deserted spot, chatted at length about their respective colleges and courses, read a little, swam a little and sunbathed a little. But in spite of all this, and the not inconsiderable fact that she happened to be wearing her grooviest swimsuit, which made her stomach look really flat and her legs look almost as long as Ushi's, if she was honest with herself, she didn't feel she'd made much progress. Certainly nowhere as much as she'd hoped. It wasn't that Miguel was being 'off' with her, he just wasn't being especially 'on'. True, he smiled a lot and seemed quite interested in what she had to say but, well, nothing else. Nothing very intimate. It was as if he was holding back. Maybe she'd imagined that he'd been eyeing her up in the first place. Maybe – and this was the rub – he really did fancy Ush – or even cousin Stella. Well that had to be nipped in the bud, pronto.

Now battle had commenced, she wanted, but really, wanted to win. In many ways, the 'prize' had become immaterial.

Watching Miguel climb out of the water, Jodie

got up and quickly walked back to the grassy area of shore where they'd been previously. It was now or never. When he came and laid back down next to her, she'd take some seriously decisive action.

'Good swim?' she asked as he sat down.

He nodded, his teeth chattering loudly. Jodie lightly touched his arm. 'OOOOOh, you're freezing. Here . . . borrow my towel.' She made to put her towel round his shoulders and suddenly found her face just centimetres away from his. Jodie moved closer until her lips brushed his. She started to kiss him, expecting his mouth to be as eager as hers but he seemed completely frozen, and she couldn't help feeling disappointed.

'I think we should go soon,' mumbled Miguel hurridly as soon as Jodie had pulled away. 'It will be late by the time we get back.' Jodie decided to go for the jugular. Despite the embarrassment of the failed kiss, the way she saw it, she didn't have much to lose.

'The village bash on Thursday . . .' she began. 'What d'you think it will be like?'

Miguel grinned. 'Much as you would expect. Why? Will you be going?'

Jodie felt suddenly encouraged. Maybe it was just that Miguel wanted to take things slowly. Not exactly a prime consideration of hers at the moment with the ever-present spectre of a predatory Ushi and Stella hovering at the back of her mind. This was her one chance at trying to get Miguel in her camp and she wasn't doing too brilliantly thus far.

'Yeah, probably,' she grinned back. 'How about you?'

'Maybe . . . Will Stella and Ushi want to go also, do you think?'

Rats! Now why had he suddenly brought them up? Just when relations between them – despite the mediocre snog – had seemed on the up again. There was only one possible reason. Because he fancied them, that's why.

'Oh I doubt it,' Jodie heard herself saying. 'It's not really their scene. They'll probably prefer to spend the night writing to their boyfriends. Ushi's got this heavy thing with a lad at home while Stella met Tomas in France and she's mad about him.'

Ohmigod, she'd gone and done it! Brought up the other lads in Ushi's and Stella's lives. She'd snitched, she'd fibbed, she'd blabbed. She hadn't meant to – honest she hadn't. It had just slipped out – like a reflex action, a defence mechanism. She felt terrible but not that terrible as she saw Miguel nodding with obvious understanding at what she'd just said.

'I see,' he murmured. 'Well, certainly I will be going. It wouldn't do for you to be alone. Apart from Aunt Maria, you do not know anyone here.'

Yes!!!!!! Yes!!!!!! Yes!!!!!! Jodie just restrained herself from punching the air. She'd done it. She was sure she had. It, or rather he, was in the bag!

'Well?' Ushi and Stella demanded to know once they'd gone to bed that night – the first chance they'd had to talk properly since Jodie and Miguel had returned. 'How did it go?'

Jodie allowed herself a superior little smile although deep down, now, she didn't feel quite so confident. Over supper, Miguel hadn't paid her any special attention. He'd been just as into Stella and Ushi, and had seemed positively keen when Ush had suggested making a trip to the nearest art gallery. Still, maybe she was reading too much into it. He *had* snogged her and even more importantly, he'd more-or-less promised to hang out with her at the festival.

'Fine,' Jodie had smiled mysteriously. 'But of course, I'm not at liberty to tell you any more. We agreed, didn't we?'

'Awwwww,' groaned Ushi. 'Just a few of the

juiciest bits! Go on – like did you pull?' Jodie shook her head and tapped her nose. 'That's for me to know and you to find out!'

Ushi couldn't quite work out where she was going wrong. On the surface, it was all going swimmingly. Showing her around the gallery, Miguel was being as charming as ever – pointing out specific paintings he thought she'd be interested in, laughing with her at the patently awful ones, taking time to give her the lowdown on local painters . . . It was all undoubtedly interesting but not exactly what she wanted to hear. She'd been hoping for something more on the lines of '*You're gorgeous Ushi! How can I concentrate on still-life when the real life I'm presently experiencing is far more appealing . . .*' At which point, Miguel would insist on leading her out of the gallery to some quiet, private place where they could be alone and get to experience a little more than each other's opinions on brush techniques.

There was, Ushi decided, a definite – albeit invisible – barrier between Miguel and herself. A barrier she was pretty sure would answer to the name of Jodie. Despite the fact that Miguel hadn't seemed particularly into Jodes over supper last night, that had evidently been a ploy. No doubt dreamt up by Jodie to make it seem all the more interesting. On the other hand, though, he didn't react in the slightest whenever she mentioned Jodie. What she needed was some definite way of knowing exactly how he felt about her. Stella she wasn't too worried about. She was his cousin, for God's sake! And although they hadn't seen each other for years, Ushi felt sure that their old brother–sister type relationship would make it impossible for them to suddenly form a new romantic type one. No, Jodie was definitely the one to be watched.

'Did, er, Jodie tell you anything about the music festival we went to in France?' Ushi began, innocently enough.

Miguel shook his head. Aha! thought Ushi.

'We had the best time,' Ushi went on. 'Jodie especially.'

'Why Jodie?' asked Miguel.

'Oh she hooked up with a celeb's brother,' said Ushi. 'Got backstage passes – the lot. Oh yes, Max *was* gorgeous – no doubt about that. I still think she's really into him.'

Oooops! She hadn't meant to mention Max – at least, not consciously. He'd just kind of slipped out kind of naturally. She couldn't have mentioned

Bordeaux and not mentioned Max. Ushi felt guilty but then decided such an emotion was pointless. To hell with it! This was each girl for herself.

Now was it her imagination or was Miguel now looking at her in a different light. He seemed to be looking *at* her for a start, rather than beyond her.

'No music festivals happening around here, then?' Ushi said, hoping this particular line of questioning might lead somewhere.

Miguel smiled and shook his head.

'Just the same village party that happens every year,' he said. 'You think you will go?'

'I think I might,' Ushi said. 'And you?'

Miguel shrugged. 'Of course – as always.'

Ushi smiled. Mig smiled back. It didn't tell her everything she wanted to know but it would do. For now.

That evening there were opportunities aplenty to discuss tactics as Miguel took Aunt Maria out to visit a friend. Ushi, however, despite pleadings from Stella and Jodie was keeping schtum, as agreed.

'You next, Stell,' said Jodie. 'Any ideas? You must have. You've been going on about it all day.'

Stella shook her head. 'I've decided it's best to keep it simple,' she said. 'I'm not making any plans. I'll see what occurs tomorrow and take it from there.'

'Oooo, you little risk-taker, you,' said Ushi. 'Playing the spontaneity card, eh?'

'I think it's best,' said Stella.

The next morning, however, she'd changed her mind. She'd got up and gone downstairs early in order to nab Miguel. She had it all worked out. It would be simple but effective. They'd walk into the next village for lunch and then walk back again – hopefully with one or two detours on the way back.

'That would have been nice, *chicita*,' Miguel smiled regretfully when Stella mentioned her plans. 'But I am already busy today. A previous arrangement, I'm afraid.'

'But it's really important,' said Stella. Talk about unfair! She felt she was at a disadvantage anyway, and now this!

'Sorry,' shrugged Miguel. 'It'll have to wait. But I'll see you tonight, won't I? Down in the village?'

Stella watched Miguel go out the door. OK, so she didn't get to spend her allotted time with him but it wasn't the end of the world and certainly not the end of things between Mig and herself. He said he'd see her tonight, hadn't he? Which suggested he didn't have plans to spend exclusive time with either Jodie and Ushi. Yeah, to hell with today. It was this evening that was all-important! Stella smiled to herself. She'd make herself look so sexy and gorgeous, he simply wouldn't be able to resist her.

With Miguel out of the way, the girls spent the day preparing themselves for their big night out and indulged themselves in a mammoth make-over-and-make-up fest. They decided to ban any chat about Miguel but it was inevitable that little snippets would slip through.

'I don't think I'll wear that much slap,' considered Jodie, after some deliberation. 'I think Miguel will prefer a more natural look.'

'Oh do you?' said Ushi, applying another layer of lippy. 'Well that's not the impression I get. I reckon he wants a glam girl who'll really stand out from the crowd.'

'And you reckon you're her, do you?' muttered Jodie. 'Well you're wrong. So very wrong. You see . . .'

Jodie broke off suddenly as Stella walked proudly into the room. Dressed in a tight crimson number with her dark hair pinned up high, she looked stunning. There was no other word for it.

'Aunt Maria lent it to me,' Stella trilled, whirling herself around and around. 'It used to belong to her. What do you think?'

Normally, Jodie and Ushi would have been wowing all over her, telling her the truth – that she looked truly a-mazing. But this wasn't 'normally'. This was tantamount to war! And seeing Stella standing there in such a fabulous dress caused the competitive juices to start flowing even more.

'Uhmmm, not bad,' muttered Jodie and furiously started applying lipstick while Ushi didn't say anything but suddenly deciding that her favourite jeans weren't quite the thing after all, promptly changed into a mini skirt.

'Well I think I look fab,' said Stella huffily. 'And d'know what? I'm pretty damed sure that Miguel will, too. When he sees me in this, he just won't be able to keep his eyes – or his hands – off me. I'd throw the towel in if I were you, girls. You'll see . . .'

She preened herself in the mirror. 'Quality will out!'

'Yeah?' muttered Ushi, elbowing her out of the way. 'Well if that's the case, you may as well forget all about it, right now!'

Before a shocked Stella could think of a sufficiently cutting reply, Jodie had her say.

'I'd both forget it, if I were you,' she said. 'There's only one winner around here. And you're both looking at her!'

Ushi tapped her foot impatiently and looked around the village square. They'd been here for ages and still no Miguel. Just where had he got to? She glanced at Jodie whose eyes seemed permanently fixed on the door. Momentarily they flickered towards Ushi. Ushi looked away. They'd barely spoken since leaving the house while Stella seemed to have well and truly disappeared into the bosom of her family! She'd hardly left Aunt Maria's side.

Suddenly Ushi heard Jodie sigh with obvious relief. Ushi looked around the room. About time! Miguel had finally arrived and was talking to his mum and Stella by the buffet table on the other side of the room. Thinking that she just might be a bit hungry, Ushi sidled over there – followed at a discreet distance by Jodie.

Purposefully hovering next to the plates of *tortilla* while sneaking little glances at the Rodriguez family group, suddenly she saw Aunt Maria's hands fly up to her face while Stella's usually olivey complexion took on a definite chalky hue. Ushi was intrigued. Just what the hell was going on? The next thing she knew, a slight dark girl had joined their group. Ushi felt rooted to the spot as she watched Miguel put his arm around her, undeniably protectively. She heard Jodie give a slight yell and only just managed to stifle one herself. Then, unbelievably, Miguel was beckoning them both over.

'Hi Ushi, Jodie . . .' he said, with a smile. 'There's someone I'd like you to meet. This is Juanita, my fiancée. We've just got engaged!'

If the train from Barcelona to Valle d'Aran had seemed to have taken forever, then the train from Valle d'Aran to Lloret seemed to take an eternity – and then some! Of course it didn't help that Ushi, Jodie and Stella just happened to be travelling in silence.

After Miguel's announcement, they'd called a truce. But it had proved to only be temporary. Once back at Aunt Maria's, they'd discussed 'the Miguel madness' in more detail and it had all come out. How Jodie had just happened to mention Davy and Tomas to Miguel and how Ushi had let slip about Max.

Stella, who felt herself to be the innocent party in all this, had declared herself shocked and very hurt.

'How could you both?' she'd asked. 'After all we said at the beginning . . . The rules we made.'

'Sorry,' Ushi had muttered. 'I guess it was a really dumb thing to do.'

Jodie had also apologised but Stella hadn't been moved. They had, however, agreed on one thing. It was time to leave Valle d'Aran.

Staring out of the window as the train chugged its way down a steep hillside, Jodie felt she had to say something. She had to clear the air. They had little more than a week left but the bad atmosphere that had grown up between them was threatening to ruin it all.

'Look,' she began, turning towards Stella. 'Can't we forget all about it? Put it behind us? It was a mistake. Ushi and I have apologised. What else can we do?'

Stella eventually returned her gaze. 'I dunno . . . I know I should forgive you but it's hard. I feel kind of betrayed.'

'You're right,' Ushi suddenly piped up. 'But we all betrayed ourselves, really, didn't we? All that guff we spoke about it not spoiling our friendship – whatever the outcome. And what was the outcome, for God's sake? *None* of us ended up with him, yet we're still scrapping about it. I can't believe we've let a lad come between us like this.'

'It got completely out of hand,' agreed Jodie. 'And so competitive. Now you were guilty of that, too, Stell. You have to admit that.'

Stella looked at them both. 'Oh alright,' she said. 'It's just that . . . Oh, I don't know. I feel such a fool. I mean what d'you think Miguel thinks of us now?'

'Who cares?' shrugged Ushi. 'It doesn't really matter, though does it? None of us did anything with him we need to regret. Just said a few daft things, that's all. To be honest, he seemed pretty bemused by the whole situation. Maybe he thought it was a giant wind-up.'

'I, er, snogged him,' said Jodie in a quiet little voice.

'What???!!!!' exclaimed Ushi. 'You never told us that!'

Jodie grinned. 'I wasn't allowed to, was I? One of our daft rules, remember?'

'What was it like?' Stella couldn't stop herself asking.

Jodie started to laugh. 'Not that great, actually. Max was tons more talented. And I bet Tomas was too! You know, Stell, you cousin's looks promised a lot more than they were actually able to deliver.'

Stella nodded. 'You know something else? Thinking about it, I don't think he was that great after all. It's probably just 'cos we were bored and didn't fancy the prospect of a few flirt free days.'

'Yeah,' added Ushi. 'Well, it's about time all that changed. I've had enough of lads! From now on, I say we do exactly what *we* want to do. The male sex can take a running jump!'

'What, even old Snake Hips?' asked Stella. 'What would happen if your insurance policy suddenly matured and darlin' Davy appeared?'

Ushi shuddered. 'Don't even think about it! I don't want to know. Us girlies – that's the only thing I'm interested in now – and sod the post-holiday blues. We come first with each other, right?'

Stella and Jodie grinned. 'Absolutely!'

They found a happening little campsite on the outskirts of Lloret which was directly on the beach. Eager to hit the sand and surf, they decided to put the tent up later rather than straight away. They were just strolling through the Bar-B-Q and recreation area when Ushi stopped dead in her tracks.

'What's wrong, Ush?' asked Stella. 'You look like you've just seen a ghost.'

Ushi couldn't speak but managed to point to the tennis courts.

'Ohmigod!' muttered Jodie. 'Talk about Smarm Features and tempting fate!'

Absorbed in a game of doubles were the ferry-nerds and another equally geeky-looking bloke.

'Look, look over there,' Ushi eventually managed to squeak.

'Ohmigod,' muttered Stella. 'Let's get the hell out of here. And quick!'

Rushing back to their pitch, they were laughing so much they could hardly stand. They picked up their tent and legged it out of the site.

'So what now?' Jodie said once they were back on the road. 'Do we wait for a bus?'

'No fear!' replied Ushi. 'No, we get a cab back into town. And hey, we'll book into a hotel. Let's live a little!'

Stella stood in the road and hailed a passing taxi.

'Let's get the hell out of here – like, NOW!'

A Card From The Heart

✱ Dear Ushi, Jodie and Stella ✱
Sending ourselves a postcard?
Great idea - eh? But it's just
a little something to cheer us
all up when the post-holiday
blues have kicked in with a
vengeance. What larks! What
laughs! And what lads! It
wasn't all plain sailing, but
what the hell? We had fun,
we learnt a lot, and most
important of all - after
everything we've been through -
we're still mates. The best of.
So here's to next year!
Lots of love ♡xxx♡

Stella, Jodie and Ushi
   xx   xx   xx

Playing Away

Jenni Linden

Left In The Lurch

C'mon, Damian, Nia whispered. C'mon, *please*.

He wasn't really late – she'd got to the cinema much too early – but she could hardly wait.

Any minute now he'd be crossing the road and strolling languidly towards her. Nia was so excited she couldn't stop herself from performing a few little dance movements up and down the steps of the Carlton cinema.

A group of guys streaming in for the movie grinned at her and one even gave a loud wolf whistle. Nia's face flamed. It wasn't surprising that Damian, two years older and the original Mr Cool, found her a pain sometimes. He'd often asked her not to show him up with her immature behaviour. She was lucky he hadn't seen her.

Nia didn't mind if he *was* late. He was worth

waiting for. She thought of his cool grey eyes, his lazy smile, the way he never hurried anywhere. He was drop-dead gorgeous, and he was HERS! How had she done it? How had she nabbed a dishy, art student type like Damian? Compared with Damian, all the other guys seemed so crass and unsophisticated. No wonder he didn't have many friends – Nia couldn't have named *one*. They just couldn't handle his fantastic good looks, his brilliant dress sense and his laid-back personality.

Nia wrapped her arms around her new orange jacket and hopped up and down. She glanced at the church clock opposite. The time they'd agreed to meet had come and gone. Damian was ten minutes late. So what? Ten minutes was nothing for Damian. He spent so long choosing the right gear from his extensive designer collection that the minutes slipped by without his realising. He'd been known to take half an hour to select a pair of trainers.

Nia understood that he wanted to look good, even if her mates didn't. Sometimes she wondered if Damian was right and she was beginning to outgrow Ravvy and Maxine. He'd even hinted that

Ravvy's loud-mouthed behaviour might be rubbing off on her. Nia cringed. She wished her friends could get on better with Damian . . . they just didn't really know him like she did.

'Do you two ever fight about who gets to use the mirror first?' Ravvy had asked sarkily when she'd seen Damian moving Nia out of the way so he could check his hair in a shop window. She was jealous, Nia told herself. Ravvy would probably kill for a supercool, sophisticated boyfriend like Damian.

Nia certainly wasn't going to confess that she'd given up trying to compete with Damian while he organised his hairstyle. She usually went and had a chat with his mum in the kitchen until he'd finished.

There was a splash of wetness on her cheeks. Nia looked up to the dark sky and a whole lot more descended on her face. Should she wait for Damian inside, instead of on the steps?

Nah – he'll be here soon, she reassured herself. He promised. He promised he'd never stand me up again. Not after the last time. Any minute now he'll be here. She strained her eyes across the dusky road. But the excited, bubbly feeling inside her chest was beginning to fade away and she didn't feel like dancing any more. A cold, sick feeling was taking its place.

Nia glanced at the moody-looking posters behind her. It looked like another Japanese film season. The Carlton was an art-house cinema. Some of its films were so long and deep and dark that Nia spent the whole time trying not to yawn or wriggle. So far, however, she'd managed to conceal her true feelings from Damian. She didn't want him thinking she was shallow as well as immature.

That was another thing her mates had gone on at her about.

'You should assert yourself with that guy,' Ravvy had told her. 'He's so up himself it isn't true. Why shouldn't you see something *you* enjoy for a change?'

Before Nia could point out it was nobody's business but hers, Max had seized the opportunity to stick her oar in.

'Yeah, and you shouldn't let him put you down so much,' she said. 'Why d'you let him treat you like that? You're gorgeous, Nia, any bloke ought to be *proud* to have you as a girlfriend. Perfect skin, lovely eyes and hair . . .' Max had paused for breath, her green eyes indignant.

It was *pouring* down now. Nia put her hand up protectively to her dark hair. Her sister, who had ambitions to be a hairdresser, had styled it for her. Up to now, it had been looking really good. She tried to brush the raindrops off the sleeves of her new jacket. If she stood here much longer, it'd be *ruined*.

Nia walked down the steps and pressed herself against the wall, hoping it would shelter her from the worst of the downpour. She forced herself not to look at the church clock again. If Damian didn't come soon, her lovely hairstyle would turn into a mass of frizz before she even got to the ticket office.

There was a loud chime and Nia jumped. Her eyes flew to the clock. Half an hour! He was half an hour late! She pictured him running frantically through the streets towards her. No – not running. Damian never ran. It wasn't exactly cool to break into a sweat, was it? Even for me? Nia thought before she could help herself.

He – he *couldn't* be leaving her in the lurch again! Could he? Have faith, Nia told herself, shivering. That was what Damian had said – she had to trust him. He hadn't *wanted* to let her down all those other times. Either he'd been unavoidably detained or it was her fault, she'd got the time or the place wrong.

Yeah, that was it – she'd got it wrong again. What a wuss. Nia bit her lip. Her heart was jumping. What should she do?

It was getting darker, colder and wetter by the minute. People were brushing by Nia, their heads down. As they passed, they snapped their brollies shut and shook them. The raindrops jumped off and sprayed all over Nia.

'Sorry,' some of them muttered. Most didn't bother. Nia didn't protest. She was too demoralised. Her hair was ruined anyway. It had soaked up all the wet it could and the water was trickling down her neck.

Had she got the wrong night or the wrong place or – had something happened to Damian? Something to stop him coming? An *accident*. Nia caught her breath. *Anything* could have happened.

'Yeah, like he didn't want to risk his hairdo,' she could hear Ravvy snorting. And too bad about yours, Nia finished for her.

Nia closed her eyes in misery. The clock chimed another quarter of an hour and she opened them again. It had suddenly struck her how totally stupid she was. As soon as Damian had realised he wasn't going to make it, he'd have phoned her at home. She'd been so keen to get here on time that she'd left early and he'd missed her. What an idiot!

She'd better get back straight away. Nia took a step away from the wall and stopped. Suppose – just suppose – he *hadn't* phoned? What was she going to tell them at home?

Like most of her friends' parents, Nia's mum and dad took a keen interest in who she went out with and where. Particularly her dad. Nia was quite sure that if she and her sister had been boys it would have been totally different. Ravvy's elder brother Saj had gone where and with whom he wanted for a long time now and practically no questions were asked.

'Isn't he coming to pick you up?' Nia's dad had started when he'd finally got out of her that she was going to the cinema with Damian. 'Why have we never met him?' he complained to her mum.

'I'm SIXTEEN! I – CAN – LOOK – AFTER – MYSELF! *Will you get out of my life!*' Nia had wanted to scream at him. But the last thing she needed when she was brimming over with the excitement of meeting Damian was a run-in with her dad. She didn't want to arrive all hot and flustered – and she didn't want to be late.

'She's meeting him there,' her mum had said quickly. 'Hadn't you better go, Nia? You look lovely.' Nia could have hugged her. Her dad had made a snorting sound and buried his face in the sports pages. Five seconds later Nia had been out of the house and hotfooting it towards Damian and the cinema.

How could she go back now and confess that Damian simply hadn't turned up? But what was she going to do? Where could she go? She couldn't stay *here* all night.

'Been stood up, darling?'

Nia had vaguely noticed the creepy looking guy hovering on the top of the steps staring at her. One thing was certain. She had to go *somewhere*. Nia pulled her soaking wet jacket around her, put down her head and fled.

I'll go to Ravvy's place, she thought wildly. In

spite of all the disloyal thoughts she'd been having about them, she knew Ravvy and Max would have died rather than mutter 'told you so'. They were great mates, the best in the world.

Then she remembered. To everyone's amazement except her own, Ravvy had passed her driving test first time. She and Max had plans to celebrate tonight by driving to a new club in another town. They'd invited Nia, of course, but she'd turned them down for Damian.

Nia turned round and started walking homewards. There was nothing else for it. Anyway, Damian was almost a hundred per cent certain to have phoned. He was probably wondering why she hadn't rung back yet. So why wasn't the cold, sick feeling in her stomach getting better instead of worse?

Luckily Nia's dad had gone to visit her uncle, so at least she was spared his comments.

'Has anyone phoned?' she asked breathlessly, bursting in just as her mum had settled down to her regular hospital soap viewing.

Her heart leapt when her mum nodded.

'Aunty Pritti rang,' she said. 'She wanted us to be the first to know. Cherry's finally got engaged. Isn't that wonderful?'

'Great,' said Nia dully. Her cousin Cherry, a few years older, was a huge success, with an adoring boyfriend and her sights set on a high-flying career in banking. Good old Cherry.

Nia's mum waited for more, but when it didn't come she took in Nia's soaking wet jacket and skirt, her shoes leaking water at every step, the pathetic ruin of her hairdo.

'What's happened? Why are you back so early? Who were you expecting to phone?' she asked. She even leant forward and switched off a riveting organ transplant operation that had started going spectacularly wrong.

'Nothing, no one,' said Nia. 'I'm going to my room, OK, Mum? If anyone phones . . .'

Nia's mum was obviously dying to find out what had happened. But after one look at Nia's tragic face all she said was, 'Take off your jacket, love, and I'll put it on a hanger. And leave your shoes in the kitchen.'

Nia nodded, squelched into the kitchen and kicked off her shoes, then rushed upstairs. Another minute and she'd have broken down and started blubbing in front of her mum. Never had she been so glad to reach the sanctuary of her room. She closed the door, threw herself on the bed and buried her face in the pillow.

The *relief* of finally being able to howl in private – even though she had to do it in silence. Her mum hadn't switched the telly on yet. She was probably prowling up and down the hall, listening like a hawk. Any sound of blubbing and she'd be upstairs in a minute.

After it seemed she'd cried more tears than raindrops had fallen on her, Nia sat up, reached for a tissue and blew her nose. If she couldn't have Damian tonight, she *could* have a hot shower. And afterwards she'd get herself together and compose a letter to him. A seed of hope sprouted in her heart. If she could only find the right words, she was sure she could make everything alright again. She changed into her dressing gown and padded into the bathroom.

When Nia returned, towelling her hair, she felt

a lot calmer. She slotted in a slushy tape and rummaged for her best writing paper. It was thick and grey and totally plain and it had long, crisp envelopes to go with it. It had also cost a bomb – Nia's dad would have gone ballistic if he'd known how much.

Damian had introduced her to this stylish stationery after she'd sent him a love note on the pink paper with little flowers round the edges that Aunty Pritti had bought her. Nia blushed every time she thought of it now. She hadn't realised its true naffness until Damian explained it to her and pointed her in the direction of the grey variety. Now she'd seen the light, she wouldn't dream of using anything else.

When Ravvy had seen it, she'd muttered something along the lines of 'pretentious git', but then Ravvy was hardly the neighbourhood style queen . . .

Hunched up on the bed, Nia stared at the blank surface of the elegant grey paper. If only she could find the words that would bring Damian back to her. They'd got to be right, and they'd better be good . . .

A big, fat tear plopped onto the top piece of writing paper. It was followed quickly by another.

Nia tried to wipe the tear stains off but the paper went all wrinkly. She crumpled it up and threw it on the floor.

'Damian . . .' she started on the next piece. She stopped and nibbled her pen. 'I can understand if you didn't feel like meeting me tonight, but please give me another chance. Perhaps we could . . .'

Nia examined her writing. Propped up against her ancient teddy-bear wasn't exactly the best position for composing an important letter. The words swooped into a kind of dip in the middle of the page and then straggled up again. The whole thing looked ridiculous.

Nia screwed up the sheet of paper and sent it to join the first one. She made herself sit up straighter. What a slob she was. Concentrating really hard, she wrote it out again.

Was her handwriting too large and loopy? Damian was always telling her it looked childish, but Nia didn't know what she could do about it. She'd tried making the loops smaller, but Damian said the result was even worse.

'At least you could *read* it before,' he'd complained. Then he'd laughed and said it matched the pink, flowery paper – perhaps she'd better go back to that. He'd obviously no idea how much his remark had hurt her.

Yeah, it's really babyish, Nia decided in despair. She tore the third piece of paper in half and scattered it over the others by the side of the bed.

Perhaps capital letters were the answer? 'PLEASE GIVE ME ANOTHER CHANCE, DAMIAN', Nia printed carefully. 'PLEASE' she added and under-lined it.

It looks *pathetic* now, thought Nia, dropping it over the side of the bed to join the other three pieces. No wonder Damian's realised he's totally out of my league. He's absolutely right. I can't even manage joined-up writing. I can't do *anything*.

Nia rolled over onto her pillow again. Oh, what was the use – how could she have fooled herself she had any chance of keeping a cool and gorgeous guy like Damian? She didn't know why he'd ever agreed to go out with her anyway. There were probably hundreds of girls at the art college all waiting for the opportunity to move in on him. Dumping her tonight was probably his way of making it clear he never wanted to see her again.

The rain and the crying had totally exhausted Nia. Perhaps if she slept on it, she'd wake refreshed and reinspired. But there was something she had to do first.

Nia rolled off her duvet, tiptoed downstairs, picked up the phone and left a message with Ravvy's mum for Ravvy to phone first thing in the morning. She needed Ravvy and she needed Max. Ravvy would tell her not to be so stupid – her writing hadn't stopped her getting top grades in English, had it? And Max would remind her that lads were always eyeing her up, what about that curly-haired guy in the class above them, she could get anyone she wanted . . .

They'd probably also attempt to tell her a few things she didn't want to hear – about Damian, for instance – but she didn't have to listen to that part of it.

Pretending not to hear her mum calling to ask who she'd been on the phone to, Nia returned to her room.

She needed her mates and she needed them SOON.

Operation Sunnyvale

Ravvy woke early.

She hadn't meant to, she'd intended to sleep in,
but her brother was on his mobile phone again.
When Saj was using his mobile, his voice volume
went up several decibels and he paced backwards
and forwards, in and out of the kitchen, up and
down the stairs. Ravvy had wanted to exile him
and his mobile to the garden, but her parents had
been horrified at the suggestion. Saj had to make
his business calls, hadn't he?

'He's only phoning his *mates*,' Ravvy pointed
out, but they'd laughed and shaken their heads
as if Saj's business affairs were way beyond her
comprehension. Ravvy's ma and pa thought the
sun shone out of Saj's backside.

Ravvy wasn't really narked about being dragged

out of her beauty sleep. Her mind was still full of the great club she and Max had visited and she also wanted to plan for the day ahead. Ravvy was a great one for planning and organising. It made her feel powerful and in control.

It was brilliant having her own car, even though it was only an old banger. She was lucky to get that. Ravvy had a suspicion that her dad had only promised her a car if she passed her test because he and Saj were quietly confident she wouldn't. It had taken Saj three attempts. Ravvy grinned. Well, she'd shown them all . . .

Ravvy stretched, and wiggled her toes happily. What a fantastic difference driving was going to make to her life! She'd be able to spread her wings even further. The world was hers – and her mates' – for the taking.

More clubs, thought Ravvy, more outings, and more . . . boys. Wow! Having a car practically *quadrupled* your opportunities on the boy front. The possibilities were infinite.

When she'd brought this to her mates' attention, Max's green eyes had widened and an unmistakeable gleam of excitement had come into them.

Max was constantly falling for one guy or another, but she had a habit of turning strangely shy when she got within actual breathing distance of a bloke.

Nia had been a bit snooty, a habit that had been growing on her ever since she'd started going around with Damian.

'I don't know,' she'd muttered. 'Damian' – Ravvy had groaned – 'Damian says the clubs around here are hardly worth visiting. Compared with the amazing London clubs he's been to . . .'

Ravvy had managed to bite back her suggestion about what Damian could do with himself and his top London clubs. For some weird reason, Nia was crazy about the big-headed git. There was nothing she and Max could do about it. They'd just have to bide their time and hope it wouldn't be too long before she came to her senses.

She and Max had had a brilliant time at the Snake Club but they'd missed Nia, even though she'd been such a pain recently. They'd always worked better as a threesome. Nia apparently had had a date with God's gift to girldom.

Nia! Ravvy shot up in bed and threw off her duvet. She'd remembered there was a message about Nia on her dressing-table, her mum had left it there. Why was Nia leaving messages when she was supposed to be on a hot night out with Damian?

Ravvy padded over, retrieved the note and peered at it. All it said was, 'RAVINDA. Phone Nia as soon as poss. URGENT'.

Urgent? Was that just her mum being dramatic, or did it mean what it said? Was Nia in dire need of their help? She'd take no chances, Ravvy decided. She'd call her straight away.

Halfway down the stairs she stopped. What an idiot she was. It was blindingly obvious what had happened. Nia's git of a boyfriend had stood her up again.

Ravvy stood in the hall, absent-mindedly picking at the trailing ivy, while Nia explained how it was all her fault that Damian had left her standing outside the cinema in the pouring rain.

I've heard everything now, she thought, as Nia dreamed up more and more pathetic excuses for the low-life creep not bothering to turn out. I don't *believe* this girl. Nia had always had a confidence problem, but this was something else. This was rampant paranoia.

Something needed to be done. And soon.

'I thought, if I could write to him, tell him I understand why he didn't turn up, he . . . he might give me another chance. What d'you think?' Nia ended hopefully. 'I tried last night, but I couldn't . . . will you help me, Rav?'

Ravvy took a deep breath. She was proud of herself for keeping her mouth buttoned for so long, but a girl could only take so much. She thought of Nia's delicate face, her cloud of dark hair, her enormous brown eyes. She was *gorgeous*. Just who did that creep Damian think he was? He ought to be over the moon having a girlfriend like Nia instead of treating her like a doormat and wiping his feet all over her.

Yeah, it was up to Nia's friends to remedy the situation pronto.

'Listen,' she said, as Nia paused for breath. 'Never mind all that. What you need right now is a good, healthy dose of self-confidence. A change of scene and a fabulous, fun weekend in excellent company. It'll do wonders for that self-esteem I keep telling you about. And fortunately, your mate Ravvy is in a position to provide it.'

'What . . . ?' squawked Nia. 'I can't go *away*, Ravvy, not now – I can't *leave* him. Don't you understand, if I leave him now he's so gorgeous some other girl is going to leap in and nab him.'

Again, Ravvy refrained from pointing out that she didn't know one single girl who, given a choice, would touch Nia's Damian with the wet end of a barge-pole.

'Don't ask any questions,' she commanded. 'Just get over here *now*. I'll get Max to come as well. We've got plans to make.'

It had dawned on Ravvy, while she was bending an ear to Nia's pathetic witterings, that, for once in his life, her brother Saj might come in useful.

Saj was employed in a large leisure corporation. Ravvy suspected he wasn't quite the high-powered Mr Big he made out to her mum and dad, but if it made the olds happy, so what?

Saj spent a lot of time boring on about his totally-heavy work schedule and his incredibly influential clients. Ravvy had developed a method for filtering most of this rubbish out of her hearing while her parents listened enraptured. Two or three nights ago, though, a few of Saj's words had bypassed the filter system and lodged themselves in her brain.

Saj had been boasting about the amazingly cheap deals his firm was offering. There were some fantastic bargains about, he informed them. Out-of-season weekend breaks at Sunnyvale Holiday Centre, for example. They were practically *giving* these away.

His mum and dad listened smiling, while Ravvy flipped through her favourite mag. '*Giving* them away' wove itself in and out of the pictures of the models in the latest cool autumn colours.

'Holiday camps?' enquired his mum. 'Won't it be rather cold this time of the year, dear?'

'That's why they're cheap, mum,' said Saj. 'And we don't call them camps any more. We in the trade' – what a poser, thought Ravvy, scanning the problem pages and waiting for her favourite programme of the week to roll on the telly – 'we refer to them as holiday centres, or parks, or . . . worlds.'

Ravvy's parents nodded respectfully.

'But it doesn't matter about the weather,' continued Saj, ''cause there's loads of indoor entertainments – swimming, cabaret acts, snooker, sauna, Jacuzzi . . . There's the all-weather sports facilities, discos, crazy golf, everything you can think of for an exciting, fun-packed holiday.'

He sounded like one of the glossy brochures he left about the place. The words 'sauna', 'discos' and 'fun-packed' floated into Ravvy's ears and took up residence in her brain cells. She started reading the feature on the best togs for snogs.

Saj was well away now.

'Sunnyvale are running some theme weekends at the moment,' he continued. 'Tap dancing, murder mystery, Seventies Glam Party Weekend. Suitable for all tastes and ages. A perfect winter-time pick-me-up.'

Ravvy, Max and Nia had been to a seventies party recently. They'd had a great time, dressing up in their flares and platforms and dancing to seventies disco music. Max's mum had dug out a kaftan for her and a Biba bag. It had been one of their best parties ever.

'They're so cheap,' Saj finally wound up, 'they're

virtually *free*. Especially if you've got a staff discount like me, and the right sort of contacts. And if you take advantage of our special low-rate economy accommodation . . .'

He'd got so carried away with his sales spiel he'd forgotten it was only his family he was pitching it at. His parents were staring at him gobsmacked by the brilliant picture he'd painted. Even Ravvy, who had put down her magazine, had to admit he'd shown them a far better world than the one currently outside their living-room window. It was more interesting than Saj's usual ravings, anyway.

Saj's mobile had bleeped and he'd come down to earth.

'I'll take it in my room,' he said after listening for a minute.

Must be his girlfriend, thought Ravvy, dismissing, as she'd thought, the whole episode from her mind. However, certain key words had obviously seeped into her subconscious without her realising it. They surfaced now as she pondered the Nia problem. Chief among them were 'parties', 'discos' and 'virtually free'.

'See you soon,' she said, putting the phone down

on Nia's protests, then picking it up again and calling Max's number.

'A Seventies Glam Party Weekend,' she told them impressively when she'd got them assembled in her room. 'And virtually *free*. If we take the economy package they'll be practically *paying* us to go. And discos, parties, saunas – what have we got to lose? Can you think of a better winter-time pick-me-up?'

She was amazed how much of Saj's spiel she'd remembered. Perhaps she'd underestimated him.

Max and Nia, though, seemed less than impressed.

'A holiday camp?' said Nia slowly. 'Won't it be a bit . . . well, naff?' She could imagine very well Damian's look of cool disdain when he heard where she was bound.

Ravvy squashed a feeling of uneasiness.

'They're not called holiday camps in the trade,' she said. 'They call them parks and centres. And worlds.'

'Oh,' said Nia. She had to admit, it did *sound* better.

'What shall we do there?' demanded Max. 'And who goes there, anyway? Aren't they all wrinklies? I've seen pictures of them, sitting around wearing funny hats or doing ballroom dancing.' She shuddered.

'All sorts of people go there,' said Ravvy. 'Boys go there. There are photos of them in Saj's brochures, dancing, playing pool, chilling out in the clubs, having a great time.' She couldn't believe she was selling Saj's holidays for him like this. 'You remember *boys*, Max? Those things you were drooling over at the club last night.'

'Yeah,' said Max dreamily. 'D'you remember that cool guy with the fringe, Ravvy? You were right – I should have just gone up to him and started dancing. Shall we go again next week?'

'You'll have all the lads you've ever dreamt of queueing up at the Sunnyvale discos,' said Ravvy firmly. 'And this is a Seventies Glam Party Weekend. How many grannies d'you think'll be coming to that?' she demanded.

'I don't know . . .' muttered Nia. 'I don't know if I want to go away. Not at the moment.' She'd had another shot at her letter to Damian before she'd come out, but the only result had been a binful of the rest of the grey paper.

'Now is exactly the time you want to go,' said Ravvy. 'Trust me. It's the best thing you could do. It'll give you a new perspective on . . . everything.'

She could be right, thought Nia. Perhaps all I need is some time to get myself together. Then I can get down to writing that letter to Damian.

'Okay,' she said slowly. 'Okay. Why not?'

She didn't sound as thrilled at the prospect of Sunnyvale Holiday Centre as Ravvy would have liked, but at least she'd agreed. It was better than nothing.

'Max?' asked Ravvy.

Max was a tad more enthusiastic.

'I don't mind,' she said. 'You're *sure* it won't cost much?' Max was permanently short of dosh.

'A fabulous, fun-packed weekend for practically nothing,' Ravvy assured her. I could take up writing holiday brochures as a career, she thought. 'I'll get my dad to fill up my car, so we'll get free transport too.'

It was brilliant to be able to say 'my car' in that throwaway manner.

'We're going in your car?' asked Nia. A slight frown had appeared between her eyebrows.

'Great!' said Max. 'Ravvy's a fantastic driver,' she informed Nia. 'She never lets anyone overtake her. And she always gets away first at the lights.'

Nia brooded for a moment. Damian had expressed his opinion of Ravvy's car several times. 'A load of junk' had been one of his kindest remarks. Damian didn't own a car himself, but, as he said, it was better to wait and get a proper one than a pathetic heap like Ravvy's.

'My dad and Saj have been over it,' Ravvy told her coldly. 'And it passed its MOT – easily.' In the end, she added silently.

'We could put it through the car-wash before we go, I suppose,' Nia said. 'And clear away all that rubbish inside.'

'Or you could come round and clean it if you're so worried about being seen in it,' snapped Ravvy. Nia had been having a bad time lately, but she couldn't take much more of this. Then she laughed. This was supposed to be a *fun* break for them all. She didn't intend to start a quarrel before they'd even set out.

'Aww, c'mon, Nia,' she said. 'We'll have a fab time. We're going to really enjoy ourselves. Let's look at Saj's brochure. We'll go to the nearest camp, shall we?'

'Where's that?' said Max. They pored over the brightly coloured brochure, with its pictures of people swimming, dancing, hurtling down water chutes, sipping exotic-looking drinks in softly lit bars or relaxing in their luxurious apartments. They were all smiling and waving happily. Even Nia felt a stir of excitement.

The nearest Sunnyvale Centre seemed to be on the east coast.

'Easy-peasy,' said Ravvy. 'We'll be there in no time. Plenty of time for a good nosh-up and then – we can take our pick of what's on offer.'

'Hey, check it out, Ravvy,' Max gasped. She pointed to a picture of several severely fit guys grinning at them from an intimate corner of a candlelit restaurant.

'*Well* tasty,' said Ravvy. 'And there'll be many, many more, I promise you. It'll be great.'

'Just *great*,' she repeated, to reassure them. And, more to the point, herself.

We're Off!

They'd never be able to fit all their bags into Ravvy's tiny car. Something would have to go.

They'd done some serious shopping and after a few sessions browsing through the nail varnishes and iridescent eyeshadows, the perfumes, glitter gels and fake jewellery, even Nia had perked up.

When they added the seventies gear they'd borrowed or discovered lurking at the back of their mums' wardrobes, they were amazed at the clobber they'd accumulated.

'Are you taking all that just for the weekend?' Max's mum had asked when she'd staggered out of the house with her holdall, several carrier-bags and her fun-fur back pack. 'I thought you were hard up. You were moaning about having no clothes. Take care, Maxine,' she'd added.

'Yeah, yeah, right, bye, Mum,' Max had panted, putting on a spurt for the bus to Ravvy's place.

The others were equally lumbered.

Ravvy looked at the heap of bags occupying the pavement outside her house.

'No problem,' she said. She started pushing things into the minute boot and then they leaned on it to force it shut. There was loads of stuff still on the pavement. Ravvy kicked a holdall towards her car.

'We'll stuff the rest in the back,' she said. 'Plenty of space – it's amazing what these cars can hold.'

'I'll go in the back,' Nia said quickly. She clambered into the back seat. Max and Ravvy arranged stuff around her, behind her and under her feet.

'That's fine,' said Nia. Soon Ravvy's stereo would be blasting in her ears, but for the moment she could tuck her feet under her, lean on Max's fluffy rucksack and let her thoughts drift back to Damian.

She'd reminded her mum several times to take a message if anyone phoned, but could she trust her? Or her dad? Nia bit her lip. Perhaps she'd made a big mistake. Yeah, she should have stayed at home so Damian could contact her. It'd be *terrible* if he phoned and she wasn't in. He'd probably get discouraged and never ring again.

Nia uncurled herself and tried to fight her way out of the mound of luggage imprisoning her. Max and Ravvy would throw a wobbly when she told them she'd changed her mind, but tough. How could she possibly abandon Damian for a cheapy theme break halfway across the country?

There were two thumps, one after the other, and the car rocked. The assorted baggage on the back seat swayed and Nia clutched at it for support. Max and Ravvy had flung themselves into their seats and were fastening their safety belts.

'We're off!' Ravvy shouted out of the window. 'Bye, Mum! See ya, Saj!'

Saj had joined his mum on the pavement and was waiting for Ravvy to crash into gear and roar the engine so he could shake his head and smile pityingly.

'Bye, everybody!' shouted Ravvy again. She moved the car smoothly into gear, took off the hand-brake and glided away. Through the mirror she could see Saj's mortified face. It was a great start to what was going to be a fab weekend.

Nia slumped back. Too late to escape now – fate had decided for her. Ravvy drove to the bottom of the road, turned right and pushed a map at Max.

'That's where we are,' she said, jabbing her finger at it, 'and there's the Sunnyvale Holiday Centre. It's about a hundred and thirty miles. What do I do next, Max?'

'*What*?' screamed Max. 'Don't you know where we're going?'

'To the East!' said Ravvy grandly. It sounded really exotic. 'Yeah, 'course I know. It's dead easy. Same road nearly all the way. I'll just need you to remind me sometimes, Max. Okay?'

Nia closed her eyes and sank back, thanking her lucky stars she hadn't got Ravvy rabbiting on in her ear. Max took the map with the tips of her fingers as if it was a dangerous snake that might sink its fangs into her arm if it wasn't handled properly. She shook it out and stared at it in horror. Like all the maps she'd ever seen, it was totally incomprehensible.

Max had always been hopeless with maps. It was the reason she'd wanted to drop geography. Nothing on them tied up with the world she saw around her. She held Ravvy's map away from her to get a general idea of the direction they were going in, then brought it closer to see which lines they were supposed to be following.

There was a jumpy feeling in Max's chest and she was getting hot. Even if, by some miracle, she hit on the right road, how would she know if they were *on* it or not? She looked up. Where were they now? Ravvy had guided the car out of the town and was speeding confidently into the open countryside.

Max turned the map round and peered at it. She turned it round again. It looked completely different. That was another thing about maps. How could you tell which was the right *direction*? Now all the right-hand turns had become left-hand ones. If she'd known this trip would involve *maps*, she'd have stayed at home. They could have gone back to the Snake Club . . .

Nia was slumped on the back seat like one of the living dead. She'd certainly chosen the right place to be, thought Max. She started tracing a promising-looking black curve that turned out to be a railway line.

The one location it *was* easy to pinpoint was the Sunnyvale Holiday Centre. Ravvy had highlighted it in yellow. It was on a stretch of the east coast that even on the map managed to look cold and bleak. Max could almost hear the sea-wind howling and the icy waves crashing on the shore. She shivered. Why had she let Ravvy talk her into believing she might actually *enjoy* a weekend on what looked like the coastline of Alaska?

Ravvy seemed blissfully unaware of the dark thoughts occupying Max's brain and the corpse-like figure at the back. She was humming happily as she skilfully negotiated the roads. So far, she seemed to know exactly where she was going. Quickly and quietly, Max stuffed the map under her seat. With any luck, she might never have to set eyes on the thing again.

'Music!' said Ravvy suddenly. 'I've got loadsa tunes to put us in the mood.'

She slotted in a cassette and some thumping disco started up. In the back seat, Nia stirred and almost smiled. The music lifted her mood slightly. She laid her head on Ravvy's toilet-bag, closed her eyes and nodded along to the rhythm.

Ravvy upped the volume and wound the windows right down. The music belted out into the tranquil countryside. A few cows peacefully feeding their faces looked up startled. Their jaws went on chewing mechanically as their heads swivelled round to watch Ravvy bombing past.

'And now for something a *leetle* more recent,' shouted Ravvy. She slotted in some bouncy boypop. The wind rushing through the car blew the music in and out and round about and tangled Ravvy's thick, dark hair.

'Isn't this *great*?' screamed Max. She was feeling on top of the world now the map was well and truly disposed of. The sun-roof was open now and she bounced up and down, waving her arms.

There was a parp-parping sound as a van came up beside them and then overtook. The two scuzzy-looking lads inside were leaning out, grinning and waving at them. Max and Ravvy waved back.

'Omigod!' groaned Ravvy, as the guys in the van, taking this as encouragement, waved even more enthusiasticaly and started pointing at the road ahead. One of them raised a pretend mug invitingly to his mouth several times. A large and grotty caff was looming up. He jabbed his finger at it and gave a thumbs-up sign.

'In your *dreams*, mate,' muttered Ravvi. She smiled and nodded vigorously. Nia had sat up and was looking at her in alarm. The van screeched into the forecourt of the caff and the two lads jumped out grinning.

Ravvy slowed down as she neared the caff, then suddenly accelerated. As they shot past, she clenched her teeth and smiled sweetly. The guys' expressions turned from smug to bewildered to total disbelief.

'What a pair of wusses!' said Ravvy. 'They really thought their luck was in.'

'The one driving was quite cute,' said Max. 'That's if you like the scruffy type.' She laughed.

'And if you're desperate enough,' said Ravvy. 'Which we're not. But hey, coffee's not a bad idea. And I wouldn't mind a jam doughnut. All this fresh air is making me hungry.'

Four or five miles further, on the other side of the road, was a small coffee-shop. Ravvy pulled expertly across and parked the car round the back to avoid the blokes from the van. Ten minutes in the toilets with their make-up bags and they were ready to face whatever the café put in front of them.

'I feel so *free*,' said Max, shaking back her hair and

reaching for the menu. 'Getting away for a break was a great idea. It makes you feel so, well . . . *free*. I'm going to have a doughnut as well,' she announced.

'Yeah,' said Nia thoughtfully. 'I know what you mean. Things don't seem quite so . . . heavy. If you two are having a doughnut, I'll have one too.'

She still hadn't composed her letter to Damian. The swank grey writing paper had long since gone and she couldn't afford any more. Unbeknown to the others, though, she'd brought a plain white writing pad. Perhaps the weekend would inspire her.

Ravvy nodded.

'We'll be alright if we remember one thing,' she said. 'The only thing we have to do this weekend is enjoy ourselves. No work – there'll be enough of that after half-term – and no parents on our backs. We're here to have FUN. Got that, girls? *Fun!*'

The doughnuts had arrived and she sank her teeth into the crisp, sugary coating, then licked the jam from her fingers.

'Got that?' she repeated indistinctly. 'Two and a half days of total, undiluted ENJOYMENT!'

*　　*　　*

'We'll stop for a fry-up in about an hour,' said Ravvy as they re-inserted themselves in the car. 'We should be nearly halfway there by then. And after that – Fun City, here we come!'

'Chips,' said Max. 'Big, fat, golden ones or thin, crispy ones, it doesn't matter. I don't care. Whatever they throw at me, I can take it.' Some sugar from the doughnuts had stuck to her T-shirt and she brushed it off. 'What about you, Nia?'

'Yeah, I don't mind,' said Nia. 'Try and stop at somewhere halfway decent, though, Rav. Damian says the ambience of a place is just as important as the food one eats. They should both be in total harmony.'

Damian's evil influence had raised its ugly head again. It's lucky Ravvy's so good-natured, thought Max. Things just roll off her, thank God.

The huge roadside restaurant that Ravvy eventually pulled into would have satisfied even Damian's good taste test. There were plants with polished, gleaming leaves, pine tables with tasteful bunches of flowers on them and loads of temptingly displayed food. There wasn't a stray Coke can or empty crisp packet to be seen. To a girl, they made straight for the all-day breakfast section.

'Sunnyvale is probably swimming in this kind of nosh,' said Ravvy. 'I'll have that and that and that, please. With chips.'

'How strange,' said Max happily. 'Just what I was about to order. Plus a Diet Coke.'

'Me too,' admitted Nia.

It was a total mystery how they managed to end up at a table next to a bunch of good-looking guys sitting by a massive palm tree. Max had suggested sitting a few tables away, where she could take a sneaky peek at the dark one with navy blue – yes, *navy* – eyes. But Ravvy had simply gone straight to the nearest table and plonked herself down. Nia drifted beside her, her lips slightly parted and her eyes far away.

The guys nudged each other and whispered. Then one of them got up and strolled over.

'Mind if we borrow your ketchup, girls?' he asked. Max had taken the opportunity to sneak a quick look at the boy with navy eyes. When he looked back and grinned, she lowered her head, speared a chip with her fork then put it down again. She was incapable of doing anything as gross as eating while this guy was looking at her. Nia ignored the whole bunch of them.

Ravvy picked up the ketchup and handed it over. 'Nah,' she said coolly. 'Here. Take it.'

'Ta,' said the boy. 'Erm . . . ta.'

He returned to his mates, put it down carefully in the middle of the table and they all stared at it. It was obvious none of them had a clue what to do next. One of them reached out and started absent-mindedly picking at the fronds of the palm tree.

Lads! They can be so *pathetic*, thought Ravvy. She'd like to have taken matters into her own hands, but there was still a fair way to go and she wanted to check the route. She lowered her head and started chomping into her chips. The others did the same.

'Where's the map, Max?' she asked when they'd finished.

Max's eyes flickered.

'Might be under the seat,' she said shiftily. 'Erm, shall I go and get it?'

'Yeah, then you can tell us where we're going,' said Ravvy.

Max rose reluctantly. As she brushed past the boys'

table they looked up hopefully. Max ducked her head, blushing, and walked on. When she returned she handed the map to Ravvy, who glanced at it then handed it back.

'We should be about here on the A47. We've just passed King's Lynn.'

Max swallowed and scanned the map. A bubble of excitement began to grow inside her chest. She could see it! She could see that the road Ravvy had pointed to led to the place she'd highlighted – Sunnyvale Holiday Centre! Max traced it with her finger. She couldn't believe it.

'It's quite easy,' she said. She measured the scale with her thumbnail. 'It's about seventy miles.' She was amazed and delighted by her efficiency. She bent over it, studying it carefully. 'Or I could take you a different, more scenic route, by some minor roads.'

The lads were still staring at them. Then the dark one that Max had fancied picked up the ketchup bottle determinedly and advanced towards them.

'Er, thanks for this,' he said. He looked at Max, who was still gazing enraptured at her beautiful map. 'Need any help with directions, girls? Where are you going?'

'It's OK, I can manage,' said Max. She spread her hand possessively over the map.

Ravvy grinned. Was Max turning into a serious map anorak, or what.

'Where . . . ?' he started again, but Ravvy was getting to her feet.

'Gotta get on, I'm afraid,' she said, smiling kindly at him. 'Sorry.'

She nodded as they passed the tableful of disappointed faces. 'Bye, guys.'

'Did you see that dark one's eyes?' said Max after they'd closed the door on the downcast-looking lads. 'Amazing,' she murmured.

'Plenty more where they came from,' Ravvy assured her.

They were on the final leg of the journey now, and excitement was building up.

'I wonder what'll be on offer at the camp tonight,' said Max.

'Every night is a glittering explosion of brilliant music, dance and entertainment,' said Ravvy absently, quoting from Saj's brochure. 'We'll be able to take our pick, girls.'

'It'll be good to get to the apartment and unpack. I hope it'll be OK,' said Nia. Ravvy had been hoping the same thing. When she'd asked Saj what economy accommodation was, he'd muttered something about basic facilities and bunk beds. He'd also used the words 'scheduled for refurbishment'. They came back to her now, as she wondered exactly what they meant.

''Course it will,' she said. 'Anyway, we'll be out enjoying ourselves too much to bother about the accommodation. We'll be hardly there. Have a look at the map again, Max.'

Max unfolded it eagerly. This time she was able to pinpoint almost exactly where they were.

'We're practically there,' she said. They were all peering out of the windows now, ready for the first sighting of Sunnyvale Holiday Centre. Who knew what excitements awaited them? *Anything* might happen, thought Max. Some of the brochure's more colourful promises returned to her. 'Fantastically exciting atmosphere', 'stunning live music', 'spectacular entertainment' . . .

They'd reached the crest of a hill now. They gasped as they saw the sea spread out below them, steel-blue and with little lines of waves running across it. Set back from the coast was a cluster of low buildings surrounded by a high fence. Near it was a little town.

'Yeeeha!' shrieked Ravvy, and even Nia's eyes shone with excitement. 'Sunnyvale, here we come!'

They descended the hill and Ravvy aimed her car towards a massive entrance in the middle of the fence. Above it was a huge arch. On it were displayed the words, 'Welcome to Sunnyvale Holiday Centre'.

They stopped and peered inside. A colourful sight met their eyes. A long, straggling line of old people, attired in bulgy, brightly coloured trackies or gruesome shorts, puffed and panted past. Beyond them, on a patch of grass, a further selection of senior citizens jumped up and down while a hatchet-faced instructor barked keep-fit instructions at them.

Ravvy, Max and Nia stared at them in silence. Words were unnecessary. The situation was crystal clear.

They had set out for Fun City and arrived in Granny Heaven.

A Room With A View...

'And this is your big-value, budget accommodation,' said Vince proudly. He turned the key
in the battered-looking door and threw it open.
'There you are, girls, clean, tidy' – he bent to
pick up a stray thread and realised it was part of
the carpet – 'and' – a desperate note had entered
his voice – 'wonderful value for money. All yours
for the duration of your glittering, fun-packed
holiday.'

Vince had been their first human contact at
Sunnyvale Holiday Centre. He had bounded up
to meet them as they were standing uncertainly
by their car, afraid to proceed any further in case
they knocked down a wandering senior citizen.
There were more of them here than in the local
old folks' home.

Vince was wearing the same loud, rainbow-coloured jacket as the guy in charge of the jogging geriatrics. His pale hair was smarmed back and his smile seemed permanently superglued to his face.

His eyes had lit up when he'd clocked the girls – Max's shiny blonde hair falling over her face, Nia's slim figure and Ravvy's infectious, thousand-watt grin and bouncy hair.

'Hi, girls!' he'd cried. 'Looking for some fabulous, thrill-a-minute holiday action? Well, I'm Vince, one of the famous Eurocoats, and I'm here to see you get it. Don't tell me – you're here for the Seventies Glam Party! I knew you were party girls the minute I set eyes on you.'

'Are there any others our age?' Max asked him. 'Or are they all . . . ?' She indicated the line of puffing pensioners, now disappearing round the corner of a large, gaily decorated building with a sign saying 'Launderette and Ironing Facilities'.

'Room for all ages, shapes and sizes at Sunnyvale,' Vince reassured her. 'Whatever you girls have come looking for, I can guarantee you'll find it.' He twinkled his eyes at her. 'Now, allow me to escort you to your top-value economy apartment.'

They passed many buildings on their journey through the complex. All were gaily decorated along the lines of Vince's Eurocoat, in bright and clashing colours. There was also a crazy golf course, several sports courts and an enormous funfair in full swing, with shrieks and shouts of laughter coming from it.

Some of the chalets and apartments overlooking the sports field and the lakes looked rather nice.

'Is our apartment near here?' asked Ravvy.

'Not exactly,' said Vince thoughtfully. 'This is one of the most favoured areas of the site, containing our top-class luxury accommodation.' He looked quickly at them. 'The economy accommodation is round the back.'

It was. Right round the back, just past the dustbin area. Instead of the sports field and the lakes, there was a good view from the tiny window of the car park and the fence.

Ravvy, Max and Nia surveyed what was to be their home for the next two days. Apart from themselves and their luggage, there wasn't all that much to see. One wall was taken up by two bunk beds, there was a minute wardrobe against another, and in the middle of the room was a small, plastic-topped table with chairs even grottier than the ones in their college refectory.

In one way, it was a good thing the room was so simply furnished. With themselves and their luggage, there wasn't space for anything else.

Suddenly, Nia turned on Vince.

'There's *three* of us,' she said. 'Three of us – and there's only two beds!' Her voice was rising hysterically, and the others looked at her in alarm.

Vince's smile remained firmly in place. He waved towards a sad-looking heap of metal huddled in the tiny space between the wardrobe and the window.

'Our economy accommodation offers the flexibility of a camp bed, which can be folded away during daylight hours, thus allowing more room for . . . social activities,' he said smoothly. He wheeled round and pushed open a door they hadn't noticed before.

'Your very own private bathroom and toilet,' he said, shutting it again hastily. 'As a gesture of goodwill, Sunnyvale Holiday Centre has provided you with an economy-sized bar of soap and one toilet roll.'

'Ta,' said Ravvy, as the others remained silent.

Nia was still looking around as if she couldn't believe what she was seeing.

'It smells!' she said. 'What's that smell?'

'Only disinfectant,' said Vince haughtily. His smile was beginning to slip. He was clearly beginning to tire of their whingeing.

Max reached over and pulled open the teeny wardrobe. She peered inside and sniffed.

'I think I'll keep my things in my holdall,' she said.

Vince didn't seem inclined to linger in their big-value economy apartment. Ravvy didn't blame him. She'd already decided the only time it would be seeing her would be when she hit her pillow at night.

'I have to visit some guests in one of our high-quality luxury suites,' Vince said. He gave a final look round. 'Our economy accommodation hasn't been through our renovation process yet. That's why it's so . . . so . . . cheap. Anything you girls want, you know where to find me. Or any of our fun-loving, highly trained Eurocoats. "Ready to help and willing to please", that's our motto.

Au revoir, girls.' He closed the door firmly behind him.

There was silence after Vince's departure. Even Ravvy was too depressed to speak. All three had secretly suspected the accommodation might be on the naff side, but this was worse than their very worst fears.

Max was the first to break the silence.

'We're here for the whole weekend,' she said. She looked at the ratty chairs. 'I don't even feel like sitting down. The weekend! Two whole days! Three nights!'

Nia dragged her holdall over to the bottom bunk-bed and lay down, carefully folding her jacket and putting it beneath her head.

'I could have been at home,' she whinged. 'I very nearly didn't come anyway. I'll miss all the phone calls . . .'

'To think we've *paid*,' moaned Max. 'We've actually *paid* to stay in this dump!'

'Not much,' said Ravvy.

'Whatever it was, it was too much,' came Nia's muffled voice from the bed. 'If we'd paid *nothing*, it'd have been too much.'

'We'll only be in here to sleep,' Ravvy attempted to comfort them. 'We'll be letting our hair down in the rest of the complex most of the time. Did you see that fantastic glass-roofed leisure suite?'

'Yeah, it did look good,' Max admitted. At least she was trying. She pushed Nia's feet out of the way and sat at the end of the bunk bed. 'Vince said the swimming facilities are fantastic, and there's a sauna and Jacuzzi in the health section.'

'So we'll be able to get in loads of pampering after we've been clubbing,' said Ravvy.

'The crazy golf looked fun,' said the voice from the bed. 'And they weren't *all* wrinklies playing there.'

'Yeah, there's obviously plenty of fun to be had in this place if we dig deep enough,' said Ravvy. 'And remember, now we're here it's all free! So we can pick and choose exactly what we like.'

'Including the grub,' said Max. 'Does anybody else feel a craving for nosh coming on? Shall we head over to the dining hall soon?'

The idea of abandoning the grungy apartment for a warm, food-filled dining hall was an instant morale-booster. A little of the excitement they'd felt on the journey was beginning to creep back. Even Nia crawled off the bed and started trawling through her holdall. Before long the tiny wardrobe was bursting at the seams.

'Let's get out those new nail varnishes,' said Max, after they'd finished dodging in and out of the mini bathroom. They squatted on the bottom bunk bed and spread out the range of translucent, glittery and coloured varnishes.

'I feel in a yellow nail mood,' said Max. She picked up a zingy, canary-coloured bottle. 'How about you, Nia?'

Nia selected a deep violet varnish and Ravvy a hot pink one. By the time they'd painted their nails and flapped them dry, they were well in the mood for a night of action.

On the way out, Ravvy prodded the camp bed with the toe of her shoe.

'We'll take turns to sleep on that,' she said. 'One night each.'

'Food looks good,' said Max, when they reached their table in the dining hall. 'Let's get our trays and head for the queue. Hey, I wonder if anybody luscious'll be joining us?' As well as their own places, there were three empty seats.

'Like two grannies and a grandad?' asked Nia.

'Yeah, well, we won't be stopping long,' said Ravvy, as they piled up their plates from the self-service selection. 'Cause after we've filled our faces we'll be checking out what's on offer at Planet Sunnyvale.'

But when they turned round to make for their table again, the three seats were no longer vacant. They were occupied by three eager-looking blokes in identical sad-brown trackie bottoms. They were wearing orange T-shirts with 'Sunnyvale Centre' printed on the front.

'O – mi – god, clock The Ugly Blokes,' whispered Ravvy.

As Ravvy, Max and Nia approached with their trays, weaving in and out of the other tables, the eyes of The Ugly Blokes grew large as saucers. Their mouths fell open and a deep red blush swept like a crimson tide across their faces, clashing wildly with their T-shirts.

They'd been rising to join the queue of diners,

but now they sank back in their seats. As the girls started unloading their trays and sorting out the cutlery, they leaned forward.

Ravvy, Max and Nia hadn't been especially bothered by The Ugly Blokes' reactions. In their experience, guys like these three anoraks were capable of little more than speechless admiration. They picked up their knives and forks and prepared to plunge them in their pizzas.

But The Ugly Blokes were different. As soon as the girls sat down they broke into speech. Once started, there was no stemming the flow. It didn't faze them that Ravvy, Max and Nia said not a word in reply. They didn't even seem to notice. They just went wittering on.

'When did you arrive?' asked First Ugly Bloke. He continued without a pause, 'Must've been today, or we'd have noticed you. Wouldn't we, guys?'

'Yeah, yeah, we would,' breathed Second and Third Ugly Blokes. They were practically *drooling*.

Nia cut a dainty triangle of pizza, speared it on her fork, then put it down again. She gazed far over the heads of The Ugly Blokes across the room. Ravvy could practically see the words, 'What else d'you expect of a dump like this?' forming in her brain.

'We've been here all week,' Second Ugly Bloke cut in. 'Pity you didn't come earlier or we could've teamed up. If we hadn't been leaving tomorrow, we could've shown you the ropes.'

Ravvy, whose hand had tightened on her knife, relaxed her grip. So they were going home tomorrow!

'We've had a *great* time,' gushed Third Ugly Bloke. His eyes had been swivelling from one to the other, but they had finally settled on Max. Max twitched her shoulders as if bothered by a mosquito and stared down at her salad.

'We've got to know every inch of the camp,' he dribbled on.

'Every inch!' repeated the Other Ugly Blokes, nodding their heads.

'Yup, been everywhere, done everything. From the Big Names Lookalike Show to the Champion Scrabble Contest. Pity you missed that.' He craned forward, trying to peer under Max's fringe as she twirled a piece of lettuce on her fork. 'We found some really great words. We were almost runners-up.'

Some really great words were seething inside Ravvy's brain, but she managed to swallow them down together with a fragment of bread roll. When would this end? Hadn't they suffered enough?

It was First Ugly Bloke's turn again.

'Yeah, we could've shown you round, given you a good time. You don't know what you've missed.'

NO THANKS. Ravvy picked up the ketchup bottle, weighed it in her hand for a moment, then reluctantly put it down again.

'We haven't been off the camp all week,' Second Ugly Bloke informed them.

FASCINATING. How much more of this could they take?

Suddenly, Third Ugly Bloke's face lit up.

'Hey!' he said excitedly. 'Hey!'

Ravvy regarded him coldly.

'D'you know where we're going tonight?' he demanded. 'We're going to see Lee Dean and his Sparkling Starlets! In the Cabaret Palace! At least you'll be able to come with us to that.' His eyes were still fixed yearningly on Max.

The Other Ugly Blokes gawped at him admiringly, astounded by his quick thinking. They probably had one brain cell they passed around between them and it was his turn tonight, Ravvy decided.

But enough was enough. They could take no more. Ravvy, Max and Nia looked at each other and came to a silent decision.

Laying her cutlery carefully on the top of her pizza, Ravvy spoke for the first time since they'd sat down at the table.

'Hadn't you guys better go and get your dinner?' she asked. 'The cheese and tomato pizzas are just about running out.'

A look of alarm came over the eager faces of The Ugly Blokes. They tore their eyes from the girls and rose to their feet.

'Back in a minute,' First Ugly Bloke reassured them. 'Then we'll sort out the times, girls.' They shambled off to join the queue.

Swiftly and efficiently, Ravvy, Max and Nia pushed their plates away, stood up and headed for the door. There was a kind of bleating sound behind them as one of The Ugly Blokes turned his head and realised what was happening, but they ignored it.

There was nothing for it but to cut their losses and head elsewhere.

'Where shall we go?' asked Nia, as they stood outside the dining hall, inhaling huge gulps of fresh, Ugly Blokeless air. 'It's just the sort of thing that would happen in a place like this. What else could you expect?' she moaned.

'I dunno, I've gone off the entertainment here,' said Max. 'Tonight, anyway. We don't want to run into' – she jerked her head towards the dining-hall – 'those blokes again.'

'They'll probably *all* be like that,' sniffed Nia. 'I wish I'd never . . .'

'Hey, girls, let's think positive here,' urged Ravvy. 'Don't let The Ugly Blokes get us down. We don't have to stay in the camp. We can head for the town. There'll be plenty of action there.'

'Yeah, course, there *is* life outside Sunnyvale,' agreed Max. 'Did anybody manage to eat anything in there?'

Everyone shook their heads.

'Right, first we'll track down a good eaterie,'

said Ravvy, 'and then we'll investigate the night life. And tomorrow The Ugly Blokes'll have gone. Excellent!'

They moved off towards the car park.

'It's quite a big-sized town,' said Ravvy. 'There'll be a massive choice of clubs. We'll be spoilt for choice.'

'It'll probably be even worse than this dump,' said Nia.

A Night On The Town

'We should've put our pizzas in a doggy bag,' said Max.

They'd trawled the town for cheap places to eat in vain. Even the humblest burger or pasta joint was way out of their league. There was only one place left.

They walked down the High Street, past a church, a grayeyard, a few posh restaurants with big, expensive cars parked outside and two garages. Just round the corner from the last garage they saw it. The local chippy.

'I'm not all that hungry now,' said Ravvy as they joined the queue.

'I'll just have a bag of chips,' said Max, taking out her purse and counting her money.

'Me too,' said Nia. What am I *doing* here, she

asked herself for the millionth time. She'd sneaked a look at Ravvy's map on the way into town and tried to work out exactly how many miles apart she and Damian were. It was far, far too many. Nia stared gloomily at her violet-coloured fingertips. What had Damian been doing while The Ugly Blokes were trying to get off with them in the dining-hall? What was he doing now? He certainly wasn't standing in a queue waiting for a chip dinner at what felt like the edge of the universe, thought Nia bitterly.

The aroma of freshly fried chips drifted towards her. Nia lifted her head and sniffed. She edged forward in the queue.

The chippy was obviously the top meeting-place for the town's teen population. It was seething with groups of lads and girls – there were more of them crammed into this tiny space than they'd seen in the whole of the Sunnyvale Centre. It was warm and noisy, and the sizzling fish and crackling chips smelled really appetising.

Standing in a queue in the chippy would probably turn out to be the high spot of the holiday, thought Nia.

Just in front of them was a bunch of likely-looking lads chatting and arguing and jostling for position at the counter.

Ravvy was eyeing them with interest. They were obviously regular patrons.

'Hey, they're local!' she hissed.

Nia raised her eyebrows.

'So?' Admittedly they were several giant steps up from The Ugly Blokes on the evolutionary scale, but then so were ninety-nine per cent of the world's population.

'So they'll be a mine of information on the local hot spots.' Ravvy tapped a broad-shouldered, curly haired bod on the shoulder.

'Know any good clubs, lads? We're here for the weekend – we've just liberated ourselves from Chateau Sunnyvale.'

Max looked at Ravvy admiringly. If only she possessed just a shred of Ravvy's total self-confidence around the opposite sex.

Behind her, Nia was whingeing on again.

'As if there'd be *anything* good around here,' she grumbled. Ravvy took a deep breath but ignored her.

'So you're from Sunnyvale, girls?' asked the guy that Ravvy had accosted.

'Yeah, worse luck,' muttered Nia. Ravvy felt her temper rising, then she remembered that Nia had had a hard time and managed to control herself.

'Most of the guys hang out at the Pier Club,' he said. He had a cheeky grin and was rather cute. 'I'm Dan – this is Dave, Sean, Elia. We're going to the Pier later, might see you there.' His mates turned round and nodded.

'Ravvy, Max and Nia,' said Ravvy. Nia had almost turned her back on them and was staring intently at a mural of a mermaid. Max had gone all shy. She backed away a few steps, lowered her head and took refuge behind her fringe.

There was a shout from behind the chip counter. Dan and his mates were being called on to collect their bags of chips. After they'd sprinkled them with salt and doused them with vinegar, they turned to go.

'Catch you later, girls?' Dan repeated, looking at Ravvy. It was hard to look anywhere else. Max, still frozen with shyness, had her gaze glued to the tiled floor. Nia was muttering something about getting grease on her trousers.

'Yeah, maybe,' said Ravvy, with a big smile. She liked the look of Dan. She waved as the lads went out of the door, then moved up to the counter. The bod with the chip-basket ladled out three lots of crisp brown chips, wrapped them up and handed them over. Taking them, Ravvy, Max and Nia went in search of somewhere to park themselves while they chomped through them.

The bus stop faced the sea front, and currents of cold air curled around their legs and stirred their hair.

'It's *much* colder here than at home,' moped Nia.

'The wind comes straight across from Russia, you know,' said Max. 'I saw it on the map,' she added proudly.

Ravvy swallowed her last chip and rose.

'Right,' she said. 'This is where the good times really start. I haven't been wasting my time while we've been sitting here. I've been scanning the scene.'

She pointed across the road.

'There's a great-looking pub over there. Let's get in it.'

'It looks a bit – old,' said Max uncertainly, peering at the low grey building. 'And quiet.' There wasn't, in fact, a sound coming from it and the door was firmly shut.

'Yeah, 'course it's old, that means it'll have loads of atmosphere,' said Ravvy impatiently. 'And it won't be quiet for long – it'll liven up as soon as we get in it.'

'It'll be *warm* at least,' said Nia, huddled in her jacket. 'That wind from Russia . . .'

'Come *on*,' said Ravvy, and they raced across the road.

When they reached the pub, Ravvy pulled back the heavy oak door and they all fell in together.

Ravvy, Max and Nia and the inmates of the pub gazed at each other. There'd been only a low buzz of sound before, but now there was complete silence. The tablefuls of old men lifting their pints remained frozen, their glasses raised halfway to their lips. The ancients leaning on the bar, their equally ancient pooches snoring at their feet, stared at them bug-eyed. The aged geezers aiming their feeble darts at the board stopped in mid-throw. A dart clattered to the floor.

They made the Sunnyvale joggers look like a toddlers' playgroup.

'Umm . . .' Ravvy started. You could have heard a pin drop. Then slowly, very slowly, she backed out, waving one hand to the old men and pushing Max and Nia with the other. As she closed the door, an excited cackling broke out.

'*What*?' demanded Ravvy, as the others stood in the cold street and glared at her. 'How was I to know it'd be full of geriatrics?' she defended herself.

'What else would you expect around here? It's worse than the camp,' moaned Nia.

'God, you're so *negative*,' snapped Ravvy.

It had been a long day.

'What'll we do now?' asked Max. The uplifting effect of the lovely crunchy chips had begun to wear off and she was beginning to tot up the calories. Two lots of chips in one day . . . That was *seriously* unhealthy.

In the distance, the cold waves crashed and boomed against the shore. A bus drew up across the road, waited a few minutes and then set off again. Nobody got off and nobody got on. They watched as its lights disappeared around the corner.

'I smell of chips!' said Nia disgustedly. She sniffed at her sleeve. 'So does my jacket.'

'Right!' said Ravvy. 'I'll tell you what we can do now. We can stand around moaning and bitching' – she couldn't resist a meaningful look at Nia – 'or we can just give up and go back . . .'

'To our fantastic, high-value apartment,' said Max. 'By the way, who gets to have the camp-bed tonight?'

'Or,' continued Ravvy, 'we can hit that club the lads told us about. The Pier Club. And have a good bop. Enjoy ourselves.'

'Yeah,' Max nodded. 'They did say it was good – and they seemed like sussed up guys.'

'Especially Dan. That's what I'm going to do, anyway,' said Ravvy. 'I'm going clubbing and I'm going to have a great time. Just watch me hit that dance-floor!'

'Well, the rest of us don't have much choice then, do we?' Nia pointed out. 'Since you've got the car.'

'There's always the bus,' said Ravvy. She wanted to say they wouldn't be here at all if it wasn't for her, but decided it might be wiser not to.

'Ravvy's right,' Max declared. 'Let's find the club and make the most of it. Let's start *enjoying* ourselves!'

'As if,' said Nia. She sniffed her sleeve again. 'Okay – at least we'll be able to wash our hands.'

Luckily, the Pier Club was surprisingly near. Their spirits rose as they joined the groups of lads and girls streaming towards it. Inside, it was even better. Ravvy gave a sigh of satisfaction as she looked around. There was a fantastic atmosphere and the floor was packed with fit guys and good looking girls dancing to the loud music.

After a quick makeover in the cloakroom, the girls hotfooted it back to the dance-floor.

'This is great!' shouted Ravvy. 'Let's get out there and *dance*!' She moved onto the floor and started gyrating and shaking her hands in the air. A few people looked over at her and grinned.

'Brilliant!' she said breathlessly when she returned. 'What did I tell you? Things are gonna get better and better.'

'They could hardly get worse,' said Nia.

'*Nia*!' started Ravvy, then she raised herself on tiptoe and waved across the room. 'Hey, look who's here!'

'Well, whaddya know, the guys from the chippy,' said Nia flatly. 'Great. Is that supposed to make our evening, Ravvy?'

Suddenly Ravvy snapped. She'd had enough of Nia's moods. She'd thought she was coming round when they'd left the grungy apartment, but she was worse than ever now. Why couldn't she just make an effort, let her hair down, *enjoy* herself for pity's sake?

As Dan, Sean, Dave and Elia threaded their way across the floor towards them, she turned on her.

'Look, Nia,' she said. 'D'you *have* to be so snooty about everything? I know you've had a bad time recently, but you needn't take it out on the rest of us. This is meant to be a holiday, whatever you think of it, there's no need to spoil it for everybody else.' The boys had reached them now and Dan was standing grinning in front of her. 'C'mon, Dan.' She grabbed hold of him and stomped off onto the dance-floor.

Nia was shattered. She'd never seen Ravvy like this before. She watched as Dan and Ravvy flung themselves about on the floor. Ravvy's a right show-off, thought Nia, but there was a nasty, guilty feeling beginning to grow inside her. Had she really been such a pain?

She turned to Max, who'd been listening wide-eyed.

'Did you hear that, Max? What's *her* problem? I only asked . . .'

'I heard it,' said Max. There was a table nearby and she led Nia to it. It was time for a heart to heart.

'Look,' she said, when they'd parked themselves. 'You know what Ravvy's like, Nia. Okay, she can be a bit over the top, but she's a great mate and all she wants is for us to enjoy ourselves. So this holiday hasn't exactly turned out as planned – but it's hardly Ravvy's fault, is it? She's been trying really hard. And you have been a bit of a whingy cow recently, Nia.'

A whingy cow?

At first Nia didn't recognise herself at all in this description. Then she made herself step back and look at how she'd been behaving tonight. And at the camp. And in the car. She'd been *awful*. She'd been taking out her misery on her pals, who'd just been trying to help her. It wasn't surprising Ravvy had finally cracked.

She swallowed.

'You're right,' she said. 'I s'pose I *have* been a bit moody lately. I – I don't know how you've both put up with me. I'm sorry.'

Max grinned at her.

'We've *got* to put up with you, haven't we?' she said. 'We're your mates. And like I said, we only want you to have a good time. Hey, Ravvy's right, this is a great club. Let's get on that floor, shall we?'

'C'mon you two,' shouted Ravvy. Her spat with Nia seemed totally forgotten. 'Get bopping!' She hopped onto a nearby chair and waved her hands in the air.

Like a werewolf when the darkness falls, Dan, the curly-haired lad from the chippy, had finally emerged in his true colours. Ravvy had found herself a soul-mate. He was a truly mad lad.

He was leaping around Ravvy now as she stood on her chair and making 'Yeeeha!' noises. Finally he made an extra high leap and joined her on the chair. They clung to each other, swaying dangerously. They'll be on the table next, thought Max.

Ravvy and Dan wobbled precariously on the chair within a hair's-breadth of falling and Max and Nia breathed a sigh of relief as Ravvy finally saw sense and descended to floor level. Dan jumped after her, grinning.

'I think they're closing now, Ravvy,' said Max.

'Yeah, just as it was really hotting up,' grumbled Ravvy. The others were ever so slightly beginning to wilt, but she was still on top form.

'I suppose we'd better get back to Fort Sunnyvale,' she said reluctantly. 'The lads can walk us to the car.'

It took forever to get back to the car. Dan, Sean, Dave and Elia pointed out local landmarks on the way and they lingered to chat. By the time they got there, Max and Ravvy were more than ready to get their heads down – even the apartment from hell had begun to seem attractive. They leaned on the bonnet, exchanging goodbyes with the guys and waiting for Ravvy, who was standing a little way apart and chatting with Dan.

What's the *point*? thought Max. We'll probably never see them again. She yawned loudly in Ravvy's direction, but Ravvy ignored her. What on earth was she rabbiting about?

'Are you *coming*, Rav?' called Nia. She was getting desperate. Any more of this and she'd be frozen to the bonnet of Ravvy's car.

Ravvy muttered something to Dan, then finally headed off to join the others. She gave them a brilliant smile.

'Let's go then,' she said. 'What are we waiting for?'

'It's a pity you won't see Dan again,' said Nia as she squashed herself thankfully in the car. 'You two seemed to be getting on really well.' Both as mad as each other, she thought.

'That's the way it goes,' said Ravvy vaguely. She gave a little secret smile at her reflection in the mirror before she switched on the ignition.

The way back to the camp seemed much longer than when they'd come.

'It's two o' clock!' said Max when they finally arrived at the entrance. 'Come on, Rav, what're you waiting for? Drive in. I can't wait to hit that bunk-bed.'

'Or camp-bed,' said Nia gloomily.

'Yeah, um, well there's just one teeny problem,' said Ravvy. 'The – well, everything seems closed. It's all locked up.'

'*What*?' screamed Nia.

'You can't be serious,' said Max. 'How are we going to get in?'

'It'll be okay, don't panic, just keep your cool,' said Ravvy, but she was frowning. 'I'll park the car and . . . we'll think what to do.'

'We'll have to sleep in the *car*,' groaned Nia. 'It'll be even worse than the apartment.'

They got out and inspected the entrance gate.

It was large and solid-looking. Ravvy shook it experimentally.

'Yup,' she said, 'Definitely closed. The security arrangements here are excellent, girls.'

'Who *cares* about the security arrangements?' shrieked Max. 'What're we going to do?'

Ravvi thought for a moment, chewing her finger. She would have died rather than admit it, but she was getting slightly rattled.

'There are no problems, only solutions,' she said automatically. It was one of Saj's pet phrases. She lifted her eyes to the fence towering above them. Her face lit up. 'It's obvious. All we have to do is hop over that thing. Come on.'

'Climb the fence?' said Nia slowly.

'Got it in one, Nia,' said Ravvy briskly. 'Okay, girls, there's a tree. An oak, I think. We can scramble up, launch ourselves across and kind of slither down the other side.'

The others stared at her.

'Like a snake, you mean?' asked Max sarcastically. 'You're *mad*, Rav,' she said flatly.

'We can do it,' urged Ravvy. 'Come on. We've got to. We'll *throw* ourselves at it.'

She broke into a run, launched herself at the tree and scrabbled up to a branch overlooking the fence. Pausing only to stash their purses in their pockets, Max and Nia followed her. Pushing, scrambling and pulling, just as Ravvy had instructed, they hauled themselves over the fence and dropped neatly on the other side. They looked at each other, laughing in amazement.

'We've done it!' said Max. 'Ravvy, you're fantastic!'

'I've ripped my trousers,' said Nia. 'But it doesn't matter,' she added hastily. 'Yeah, you're a genius, Rav.'

'I know,' said Ravvy, as they ran giggling back to the apartment. 'Sometimes I feel I can do *anything*. Hey, who gets to have the top bunk – that's the big question.'

'You can have it, Ravvy,' said Max. 'For tonight anyway. You deserve it after getting us in.'

Nia looked at the camp-bed and swallowed. 'I'll have that thing,' she said nobly. 'Might as well get it over with.'

'Right, that's sorted,' said Ravvy. She gave a big yawn. The day seemed to have got to her at last.

'It was a good night, wasn't it?' she said. 'In the end.'

'It wasn't a total dead loss,' Max admitted. 'And it'll be better tomorrow. The party should be good.'

'*And* The Ugly Blokes will have gone,' said Nia, who had dragged the camp-bed out and started wrestling with it. 'Plus most of the grannies. In fact, by tomorrow, this place might be halfway civilised.'

The others looked at her in relief. It seemed as though Nia might be actually turning the corner and coming out of her depression. Ravvy squatted down to help and together they shook and pummelled the camp-bed into submission.

'Yup,' said Ravvy. 'It's our turn now.' She looked up and grinned. 'The olds and The Ugly Blokes have had their day. Tomorrow – the world is ours!'

A Steamy Situation

Carefully, very, very carefully, Nia turned over. The camp-bed gave a nasty creak.

Nia glanced over at the others. Ravvy, curled up on the top bunk, remained totally motionless. Once Ravvy got her head down, it took a small earthquake to dislodge her. Max stirred, mumbled something and snuggled into her duvet. Her breathing became deep and even again.

It was the camp-bed from hell, and Nia's duvet had kept slipping off all night, but somehow things didn't look quite as black as when they'd set out on their holiday. There'd even been times last night when she'd managed to forget how miserable she was, and how much she missed Damian.

Nia raised herself slightly off the pillow, then

sank down again. After their late night yesterday, she was knackered.

She turned her head to where a load of her stuff was piled beside the bed, the ripped trousers on top. She reached out and pulled the writing pad from the bottom of the heap, then scrabbled in her bag for her pen.

Sometimes things seemed clearer halfway between sleeping and waking. She'd have another shot at the letter to Damian.

'Dear Damian,' she wrote very quickly. 'Please give me another chance.' Nia stopped writing and shook her head. No, that wasn't right. She put a big black cross through it, flipped it over and started a fresh page.

'Dear Damian, I know I can be a pain . . .' Nia screwed up her eyes. She gave a little squeak of agony, remembering all her sad attempts at trying to match up to Damian's coolness – some of them were really blush-making. In the bottom bunk, Max flung out an arm, turned over and stuck her head under the pillow

'BUT,' Nia wrote slowly, then paused. *But*, why did Damian put her down so much? Why did he criticise everything she did, and most of her clothes? Her whole life was dedicated to living up to his impossibly high standards, but he never gave her credit for it. Most of the time he just *laughed* at her efforts.

Nia chewed the end of her pen. OK, she wasn't perfect, but was anybody? WAS DAMIAN? Perhaps even Damian might have a few faults . . .

Nia grasped her pen firmly and bent over the writing pad again.

'BUT you could be a bit more understanding.'

Nia stared at her words gobsmacked. The writing looked clear and confident. A thrill of excitement ran through her. It was the first time she'd even thought of criticising Damian. She hadn't felt so strong for ages. Not since she'd met him . . .

The top bunk was heaving and stirring. Ravvy had flung off her duvet and was sitting up. Quickly Nia closed the writing pad and slid it back into the heap.

Ravvy always woke up quickly. She grinned at Nia and reached down and poked the figure in the bunk below.

'Stoppit, go 'way, not getting up yet.' Max

huddled down into her duvet. *'Tired ...'* she mumbled.

Ravvy swung her legs over her bed and descended to the floor. She yawned and stretched. Then, kicking away a pair of trainers, she squatted down by Nia.

'Hey – we had a good time last night, didn't we?' she said.

'What?' said Nia. She was still thinking about her letter to Damian. If Ravvy hadn't interrupted her, she might have thought of a lot more to say.

'Good, wasn't it? At – the – club,' Ravvy repeated patiently. 'With – the – lads. Then abseiling over the fence. One of our greatest triumphs, I'd say.'

Her eyes were shining, her hair was crackling with vitality. There were no half measures with Ravvy. Asleep, she was dead to the world. Once on her feet, she was one hundred per cent alive. She sent out waves of positive energy that flooded the whole apartment.

The letter to Damian slid straight to the back of Nia's mind. Yeah, dancing in the club had been good. It had been *fun*. Even the horror of finding the camp gates closed had been exciting in a heart-lurching kind of way. And then the impossible challenge of outwitting Sunnyvale's security arrangements, the fantastic exhilaration when they'd actually climbed the fence.

Nia grinned at Ravvy.

'Yeah, I enjoyed it,' she said. 'It was a good laugh.' When had she last had a good laugh? Not to mention fun. That also went back to the time before she'd met Damian.

Max was sitting up in bed now, her arms clasped around her knees.

'Wasn't it *amazing* how we all got over that fence?' she marvelled. 'I still don't know how we did it.'

'The power of positive thought,' said Ravvy grandly. 'We can do *anything* if we put our minds to it.'

She looked around the apartment, half-buried now in the clothes they'd flung off last night. 'We can even rise above this dump if if we really want to.'

'Yeah,' said Max, her eyes greener than ever in the half-light. 'And I really really want to. We can do *anything*,' she repeated, then flopped back on her pillow. 'We'll start with a late brekkie, shall we?' she suggested.

'Yeah, give The Ugly Blokes and the grannies time to get away,' nodded Ravvy.

'Then we can spend the morning slobbing about,' said Max sleepily.

She lay with her eyes closed for a moment then opened them again.

'I'm going to have a very *healthy* breakfast,' she announced. 'After all those chips yesterday. Orange juice, muesli, p'raps a piece of wholemeal toast . . .'

'The Uglies said there was a great buffet selection in the breakfast hall,' said Ravvy. She moved over to the window, pushed aside the curtain and peered out. 'Yep, just time for a quick shower, and then I think I might be ready for a little refreshment.'

'God,' Max groaned, 'In a minute . . .'

The Ugly Blokes had been spot on about the break-fast hall. There was a *massive* selection of food. When they came to unload their trays, Ravvy, Max and Nia were surprised to find them overflowing.

Most people had scoffed their breakfast and departed. A quick scan of the room showed The Ugly Blokes had obviously been among them. Not a single specimen remained.

On their way over, Ravvy, Max and Nia had already spotted Vince loading the oldies into their special coaches ready for departure. Still reeling from the excitements of the Glamorous Granny Competition, they had waved and beamed at the girls, opening the windows to shout goodbyes and wish them as much fun as they'd had.

Vince had closed the coach doors firmly on them and waved them off. He was perspiring slightly.

'Alright, girls?' he'd asked. 'Enjoying your comfortable, high-value accommodation?'

Ravvy, Max and Nia had exchanged glances.

'The bathroom . . .'

'That wardrobe . . .'

'The camp-bed . . .' they'd started. But already Vince was gliding away, muttering, 'Ready to help, and willing to please. Any time you need me . . .'

Now, as they surveyed the almost empty breakfast hall, they felt a thrill of excitement. Who knew what the fresh intake at Sunnyvale might consist of? It might even contain some recognisable members of the human race. *Anyone* might come.

'What next?' asked Max, buttering her toast and reaching for the honey. 'Shall we go over to the leisure suite?'

'Yeah, we could have a swim, go in the Jacuzzi, have a sauna,' said Ravvy. 'We deserve a bit of pampering this morning, girls. We owe it to ourselves. A reward for our enterprise and daring last night.'

'Slobbing out time,' Max agreed happily. 'This is meant to be a *holiday* after all.' She looked at the remains of their breakfast. 'Good breakfast, wasn't it – God, I'm stuffed. I suppose we could always have a workout in the fitness room later.'

'All things are possible,' said Ravvy. 'And we can do a bit of thigh-slapping in the sauna. That'll get yesterday's chips moving, Max. Right,' she rose from her seat. 'Let's get our gear and go. Today is offical pampering day. Then we'll be all set for the party.'

* * *

250

'I could've stayed in the Jacuzzi all morning,' said Max as they sprawled in the hot, steamy sauna. 'I could feel it toning me up *all over*.'

She leant back on the bench and stuck out her legs. 'They *do* look kind of firm and toned up, don't they?' she asked. 'Watch.' She slapped her hands against her thighs. 'See – no wobbling! Well, hardly any.'

Ravvy leant forward and peered at Max's thigh.

'Just a few surface ripples,' she said. She started slapping at her own legs and then at Nia's. 'This'll get those toxins running for cover!'

'Hey!' protested Nia. She drew her legs away and began smacking Max and Ravvy's legs. In a few minutes they were all reaching out and smacking at each other's legs and giggling.

'Aargh – that's enough!' gasped Max, waving the others away. 'I'm going to *melt* in a minute in this heat.'

She examined her thighs. 'Eek! They've gone all *red*. I'll probably get masses of *broken veins* now.'

'They'll be alright if you massage them,' said Ravvy

soothingly. She leant back and started kneading her own thighs.

'That pool attendant looked rather dishy, didn't he?' she said thoughtfully.

'Um, yes,' agreed Max. She looked towards the window, hoping to catch a glimpse of the tanned up guy who'd been striding around the pool. 'I wonder if he's going to the party tonight.'

'There's only one way to find out,' said Ravvy. 'Ask him.' The sauna room door was being pushed open and the pool attendant was coming in. As Max watched wide-eyed, he began to fiddle with the heating and reached to replace the wooden bucket that sat beside the hot coals.

Ravvy leaned forward.

'You going to the party tonight by any chance? Only my friend here'd really like to know,' she informed him.

'Stoppit!' hissed Max desperately. Sometimes Ravvy went way too far. The pool attendant wiped his hand across his forehead and turned and grinned at them.

'Nah, I usually keep clear of those events,' he said. He looked at Max and she curled her toes and stared down at her feet. 'Too much temptation. My girlfriend doesn't like it. But have a great time anyway, girls.' He gave them a final grin and departed.

'He was *hot*,' said Ravvy approvingly. 'Pity he's not available, Max. Never mind, we'll find you someone tonight.'

'Ravvy, just *don't*,' said Max. 'I was *cringing*. Just – just leave things, why can't you?'

Nia had been sitting apart while this interaction had been going on. Like the others, she'd pulled her hair right back and she could feel the perspiration trickling down her face. She'd been trying to imagine Damian having a slobout in a sauna. It had been totally impossible.

'We're turning into real greasespots,' she said. 'What *do* we look like?'

Ravvy fanned her face with her hand, ineffectually.

'Don't know how much more of this I can stand,' she said. 'I think it's time to move on to the shower soon. We can always come back later.' She glanced towards the door then froze.

'O-mi-god!' she said slowly. Then, 'Omigod!

Will you look at *that*!' Her voice had risen to an incredulous shriek.

Max and Nia followed her gaze and their mouths fell open. For a truly amazing thing had happened. A face had appeared in the window of the door. It was not any old face, though. It was one of the most gobsmackingly gorgeous they'd ever clapped eyes on.

And then it disappeared. Max and Ravvy gave a moan of disappointment and sagged back against the wall. But an instant later the door was thrown open. In strode the owner of the face at the window, and – it was almost too much – the rest of him more than lived up to that first tantalising peek. He was tanned, fit, and totally gorgeous.

Ravvy nudged Max, who appeared to have entered into a trance-like state.

'Clock those legs!' she hissed. 'Firm and muscley! Fwoaar!'

Max blinked. Then her eyes widened and she shook her head in disbelief.

For there was more! The gorgeous one was not alone. Following close on his heels were five – *five* – more lads, all of the same superb quality.

Every single one of them top specimens of delicious boyhood totty.

In one single second, Max and Ravvy forgave the gruesome apartment, smarmy Vince, the killer grannies, even The Ugly Blokes. After sending them these godlike creatures, Sunnyvale could do no wrong. Even Nia stared transfixed.

The sauna wasn't all that big anyway, and now it was filled with all this gorgeous male flesh they could hardly breathe. There were brown, muscley legs and firm, defined chests everywhere. Where were they going to *sit*?

The same problem had obviously occurred to the lads, who seemed as gobsmacked as the girls. They muttered and shuffled among themselves and then the guy who had come in first manoeuvred himself casually in the direction of Max and sat down next to her. His dark, glowing eyes interlocked with her green ones then they both looked away.

'Well, that's Rael sorted,' laughed a boy in blue stripey shorts. He wasn't quite in the same league of gorgeousness as the others, but he had nice twinkly eyes. He flopped next to Ravvy, and gave her a friendly grin. Ravvy grinned back. Ravvy had an instinct about these things, and she'd sized him up almost immediately as potential soul mate.

'Hope we're not squashing you,' he said. 'Must be quite a shock having an entire footie team descend on you when you're trying to relax.'

Ravvy shook her head. A footie team? Aha – that was the reason for their total tonedness and fitness.

'Aw, I think we can stand it,' she said. 'Can't we girls?' Max dipped her head and smiled coyly, while Nia blinked and looked into the distance.

'Hey, lads,' she called out to the three remaining guys, who were still looking around uncertainly. 'There's a space at the end – move up, Nia.'

Nia squashed herself into the corner and two of the lads made for the few inches next to her. The one in white shorts that showed off his gorgeous brown legs got there first.

'Sorry, Rob,' he said. 'You'll just have to go and hold the mirror for James while he organises his hairdo.' The fifth guy was leaning against a wall.

He had withdrawn a small mirror from somewhere about his person and was examining his face and combing his tresses.

The boy next to Nia turned towards her.

'Am I squashing you?' he asked politely. He had warm hazel eyes which he gently held her gaze with.

'S'alright,' she muttered. She hunched herself together and managed to move an inch further away. He'd been looking at her with obvious admiration but now his hazel eyes showed his disappointment.

Further down the bench, the most amazing thigh was pressing against Max's leg. She sneaked a peek sideways and met the dark lad's eyes again. Rael, she thought, her heart was hammering, what a lovely name. Her thigh felt *glued* to his – how would she ever get it unstuck? She'd quickly shaken out her hair when the gorgeous bunch had entered and now she lowered her head and peered at them through her fringe. Her stomach was in chaos.

'I'm Bill,' the guy next to Ravvy was saying. 'And that's Perry at the end, next to your friend.'

Ravvy nodded. She could see – anybody could

– that Perry had taken a bit of a fancy to Nia, but she was doing her level best to blank him out completely. She seemed to have lost all interest in the opposite sex, thought Ravvy with concern.

'Hey,' Bill continued. 'Can I interest any of you girls in the knobbly knees contest this afternoon? Would you believe, these guys are too shy to display their gorgeous limbs to the world. Can't get 'em on the dodgems either.'

'You're on, Bill,' said Ravvy immediately. She didn't even have to stop and think. Here, as she'd instinctively sussed, was a lad with exactly the sort of attitude she went for.

'Great!' said Bill. 'Hey James,' he called over to the tall languid-looking guy, who was rubbing the steam impatiently off his mirror. 'Want to borrow a hairband from the girls?'

James looked up. 'I have my own supplier, thank you,' he said. He returning to studying his hairdo. 'I'm still not sure whether to move into dreads,' he mused.

Bill winked at Ravvy.

'They'd look good in the portfolio,' he said. 'Our

258

James has his sights set on a career in modelling. He'll be a great loss to footie, though.'

'Yeah, right,' said Ravvy. 'Like the face of D&G or Calvin Klein, you mean, James?'

'I haven't decided yet,' said James. 'It depends what they're prepared to offer.' He turned his head the better to admire his cheekbones. Ravvy grinned at Bill. This guy was unbelievable.

'That's Rob with him,' said Bill. 'Sure you don't want to go in for the knobbly knees contest, Rob?'

Rob grinned shyly, shook his head and looked down interestedly at his feet. He studied the big toe on his right foot then looked up again.

Ravvy leaned forward, her eyes sparkling.

'Aw, go on, Rob,' she said. 'You've got a great pair of pins there. Flaunt them, why don't you?'

'No, I, no . . .' Rob leapt to his feet and swathed himself in his towel. Looking sideways at Ravvy, he pulled it down over his knees.

Ravvy grinned at him then looked around. The sauna seemed twice as steamy and even hotter than when the lads had entered. She could see that Max and Rael obviously fancied each other like crazy, but little progress was being made. Max was totally paralysed with shyness. Rael's dangerous nearness and his overall lusciousness had taken away her powers of speech.

A few metres away, Perry was getting desperate. Nia was gorgeous, and when he'd found himself sitting next to her he couldn't believe his luck. But she seemed so remote and distant. She wasn't exactly giving him the cold shoulder – she just wasn't interested. He looked at her in bewilderment as she stared into space.

'What time's the knobbly knees thing?' asked Ravvy.

'Later this afternoon. What were you girls planning on doing?' said Bill.

'Mmm, we thought we might go over to the funfair,' said Ravvy. 'Try out the Big Dipper and the Octopus.'

Rael continued to gaze at Max. 'It's good fun racing on the Go-Karts,' he said.

'Yeah, great!' Max managed. Her face was radiant.

'The crazy golf's good,' said Rob eagerly. He unwound his towel and mopped at his face.

'D'you like crazy golf?' Perry asked Nia softly.

'What? Oh, yeah.' She actually glanced at him. Her face was flushed, but she didn't look the greasepot she'd imagined. Her pinned back hair showed off her delicate face and emphasised her cheekbones. Perry was entranced.

'I like the Big Wheel as well,' she told him flatly, and gazed into the distance again.

'We could meet up at the crazy golf course later if you like,' proposed Rael.

'Yeah – and take it from there,' agreed Ravvy. 'That'd be good. Right!' She picked up her towel. All these half-naked boys in such a small, steamy space was making her feel dizzy. 'I think we've perspired enough now, lads. We were just off for a shower when you came in. So, seeya at the crazy golf place later, yeah?'

'I can't *wait*,' said Max, hugging herself as they flip-flopped to the showers. It had required all the will power she possessed to pull herself away from Rael's side 'What a fantastic piece of luck meeting those guys!' She only hoped her throat would unlock itself before this afternoon so she could actually talk to Rael.

Ravvy looked over at Nia. That was one delicious

dish she'd had sitting beside her. Shame she was obviously too Damian-blind to see it . . . Would nothing make her see sense about the pretentious git . . . ?

Nia glanced back over her shoulder at the door of the sauna.

'Might be quite fun, I s'pose,' she admitted tentatively.

And the three of them went, smiling, for a freezing cold shower . . .

All The Fun Of The Fair

There was a breeze blowing over the crazy golf course, making the red flags flutter. The guys were messing about with their clubs, tripping each other up and trickling the ball under and over a little bridge type thing.

They'd changed into jeans, but that had done nothing to lessen their appeal.

Nia had turned difficult again on the way over.

'Why do we have to meet up with all those guys?' she complained. 'Why can't we just go to the funfair on our own?'

Max and Ravvy stared at her as if she was crazy.

'Cause it's more *fun* with the lads,' said Max. 'They're really nice.'

'Just because you've fallen for that Rael,' said Nia.

263

'Yeah, well what about Perry, he obviously fancies you,' Max teased. 'He couldn't take his eyes off you at the sauna. And he seems like a lovely guy, Nia. Not in the same league of gorgesomeness as Rael, of course.' She laughed.

'Yeah, well, I don't want him getting the wrong idea,' said Nia. 'I've got a boyfriend, remember?' She was still trying to work out how to finish her letter to Damian.

'Mr Very-Much-Up-Himself', Ravvy muttered, but the guys were waving and calling to them now, so luckily it was lost on Nia.

Perry had almost decided there wasn't much point pursuing Nia since she so obviously wasn't interested. But when he saw her walking towards them, the wind lifting her dark, soft hair, his heart melted and he was knocked out all over again. So far, it seemed the feeling definitely wasn't mutual, but he didn't care, she was worth making an effort for. He went to meet her.

'Hi, Nia,' he said, offering her a club. 'D'you want to start?'

'Yeah, okay,' said Nia. The others were right, Perry *was* a nice guy, it was just a shame she was already spoken for. She'd just have to act cool and hope he got the message. She took the club and knocked the ball with amazing accuracy towards the first hole.

'Hey, that was great, Nia,' said Perry warmly. In spite of herself Nia glowed at his praise. She couldn't help thinking of the one time she'd played crazy golf with Damian. He'd said her efforts were so pathetic it'd be better if she played with her little cousins in future. When it had come to his turn and he'd done even worse, he'd pointed out it was a kids' game anyway. They'd never played again.

Because he couldn't keep his eyes off Nia, Perry was hitting the ball all over the place. He couldn't believe he was making such a fool of himself in front of this gorgeous girl. He grinned sheepishly at Nia.

'I don't seem much good at this,' he said, as he hit the ball over instead of through a kind of drainpipe thing. 'But you're a natural, Nia.'

Nia shrugged. Flattery will get you nowhere, she thought to herself.

Max had just come to an impossibly steep slope.

She tapped the ball up a couple of times and it trickled miserably down again. She was about to take a third swipe when Rael came up and put his arms around her. She felt all the breath leave her body.

'Here, like this,' he said, smiling down at her. His muscular brown arms held her tightly as he guided her aim. It was an amazing moment. Not only was Max speechless, she also felt faint. It was the very same trembly feeling as when she'd felt his thigh pressing against hers in the sauna and it nearly knocked her off her feet.

Rael's hold lingered even after she'd hit the ball, then he gave her a little hug before finally letting go.

Max swayed slightly. Rael was amazing. Her throat felt dry. She tried to get a grip on herself and made herself smile directly into Rael's meltingly dark eyes. He smiled back at her. They stood looking at each other for a few moments while Nia, Ravvy and the rest of the footie guys faded into the distance. Max went round the rest of the course floating on cloud nine.

The others had turned things into a kind of race,

and were rushing around the course screaming with laughter. Balls were bouncing and and criss-crossing everywhere. Rob won easily. He was so excited he even forgot his shyness.

'Let's go and race on the Go-Karts,' he said. He was obviously dying to repeat his success.

'Good idea, Rob,' said Perry, grinning. Watching Nia's slim figure being buffeted by the wind, he'd knocked his ball straight into a patch of pebbles and had spent the last ten minutes trying to fish it out again. Nia had watched him in silence, trying not to smile sympathetically. It had been amazingly difficult.

They'd had a fantastic time roaring around the Go-Karting circuit. They'd had a Kart each and the girls had found themselves screaming hysterically as they raced for the line. The boys were great. Really easy to get on with and really up for a laugh. Max felt so happy, she thought she might burst and even Nia seemed to be letting herself go for a change. She'd nearly crashed straight into the side barrier in her rush to overtake anyone that got in her way. Damian definitely wouldn't approve!

Then when they'd finished racing the Go-Karts against each other, the guys took on a bunch of kids. The kids won every time.

'Perry could have won if he'd wanted,' said Nia, watching him with interest. She shook back her hair, which was blowing all over the place. 'He just hung back and let them overtake him.'

'Yeah, dummy, cause he's a nice guy,' said Max. She was glowing with happiness. She and Rael had been getting on really well. The power of speech had been miraculously restored to her. She'd just taken a deep breath, turned to him and started chatting. No problem! She longed for him to put his arm around her again. She wondered how soon she could get him over to the dodgem cars.

Nia was frowning.

'Well no matter how nice he is,' she said, 'I'm not interested.'

'Aw, lighten up, Nia,' started Ravvy, then she shrugged. If Nia really wasn't interested in Perry there was nothing she could do about it. Oh well, it's her loss, she mused.

'Anyway, it *was* fun on the Go-Karts, wasn't it?' she said firmly.

'Yeah, it was really good,' Nia agreed before she could help herself.

'*Brilliant*,' said Max. She turned to Rael, who had just reappeared at her side, a grin already spreading across his face. 'Shall we go to the funfair? We could go on the dodgems.' She didn't think she could wait much longer to feel his arm around her again.

'Sounds good,' smiled Rael. She could see exactly the same idea reflected in his eyes.

It had been the best afternoon of her life, Max decided, as Rael put one arm around her and guided the dodgem car with the other. In fact it was almost *too* perfect. Max gave a little shiver and Rael glanced down at her in surprise and tightened his brown hand around her shoulder.

Nia was beginning to find it more and more difficult to act standoffish with Perry. She gasped and shrieked with excitement as they careered around bumping into Max and Rael. They'd lost Bill and Ravvy to the knobbly knees contest on the way over and Rob and James had stayed to support them.

'Like to go on the Big Wheel?' Perry asked when

they climbed out. He remembered Nia had told him it was one of her favourites.

Nia shook her head. She'd been enjoying herself almost too much with Perry, she told herself sternly – but it had been good to let her hair down for a change. Everything was usually so tense and uptight with Damian. She suddenly felt guilty. Why should I, she thought firmly, I'm only having a bit of fun . . .

'We ought to go back and change,' she told Perry, quickly.

'See you at the party then, Nia,' said Perry, a look of disappointment and confusion clouding his deep hazel eyes.

'D'you know how many points me and Bill got in the knobbly knees thing?' Ravvy asked. She looked at her smooth brown legs with satisfaction. 'Nil! We were joint bottom!'

She giggled. 'It wasn't really fair. Some old grandad in the most amazing baggy shorts got the prize. We never stood a chance.'

'Yeah, you were way out of your league there,'

said Max. She picked up a pink curly wig from the flares and the platforms, the wing-collar blouses, the kaftans and Ravvy's ruffly shirt spread out on the bed. They'd decided to really go for the seventies look tonight.

'It was a great afternoon,' she said. 'Rael is s-o-o-o *sexy*. I can't *wait* for tonight.' She twirled the wig round and round on her finger then laid it down on top of a psychedelic pink and yellow kaftan. She picked up a pair of banana yellow platforms.

'These platforms are *wicked*,' she said. 'How did your mum ever walk in them, Nia?'

'Bill and I went wild on the trampoline after the knobbly knees,' continued Ravvy. 'That guy's *mad*. Then, when they made us get off, we went on the Octopus and the roller-coaster. What a laugh!'

'So it *was* you we heard screaming,' said Nia.

'Probably,' said Ravvy. 'Not much point in riding a roller-coaster if you don't holler a bit. Hey, things are really looking up, aren't they, girls? Didn't I promise you fun?'

The others nodded and grinned at her. Their grungy apartment hardly mattered now. Everything had changed. Even Nia seemed to have withdrawn her objections to having a good time. She pulled out some white flares.

'I think I'll wear these,' she said. 'With that blue sequinned top. Oh – and I'll put some blue nail varnish on.' She rummaged through the heap on the bed. 'There's some white platforms with daisies on them somewhere.'

'I've made Bill promise to stick on some black sideburns,' said Ravvy. 'And he says he's got a wing-collar shirt somewhere. Hey, have you seen these?' She pulled out a pair of black and silver platform boots. 'Watch me hit the floor in these!'

They were already on the dance-floor when the lads arrived. Max's throat went dry again when she saw Rael. She waved and went over to him. Oooh, he was lovely! She was so *happy* . . .

'You look *great*, Max,' said Rael, taking in her figure-hugging outfit and her shiny golden hair.

Max's green eyes sparkled as she smiled at him. Everything was just so perfect . . .

Perry had eyes only for Nia.

'You look lovely,' he said softly.

'Thanks,' said Nia looking away, the nervous feeling she'd felt earlier threatening to return. She scanned the room. It looked really good. Everyone had made an effort to dress up, and the flashing lights and beat of the music gave her a warm, exciting feeling. It was Saturday Night Fever out there now, the dance-floor was really beginning to fill up.

She was determined not to be a drag tonight. Max and Ravvy's words yesterday had really hit home. She probably hadn't been very nice to Perry either this afternoon, she thought guiltily. Most of the time she'd been blanking him. It wasn't his fault she'd already got a boyfriend. It wouldn't do any harm to open up to him a bit, she reasoned. Without giving him the wrong idea, of course.

He was watching her uncertainly now, his hazel eyes puzzled. When she smiled at him, his face lit up in relief.

'I wouldn't mind a dance,' she said to him. 'I love this music, don't you?'

'Yeah,' said Perry eagerly. 'Right, Nia, let's get out there then.' And they moved out on to the dance-floor closely followed by Ravvy and the rest of their mates.

Later, when they'd all stopped for a drink and to get their breath, Ravvy looked at her watch.

'Oops!' she said. 'Nearly forgot.' She put down her drink and rose swiftly to her feet.

'Off to powder my nose. Back soon.'

She plunged across the room and was lost to view.

'Ravvy's a long time in the cloakroom,' Max commented when she and Nia stopped for another breather. 'Must be at least half an hour since she disappeared. Where *is* she?'

They looked around for Ravvy. Not a sign.

'I shouldn't worry,' said Nia. 'Ravvy usually knows what she's doing. I bet . . .' Her mouth fell open and she caught hold of Max's arm. 'Look! There she is! And look who's with her. It's . . .'

Striding towards them in her black and silver boots was Ravvy. There was a big, triumphant grin on her face. Close behind, and looking a tad sheepish, was mad Dan from the chippy.

'Hi,' he said. He gestured towards Ravvy's platform boots. 'Check out the footwear.'

'Hi, what – Ravvy, what's *he* doing here?' spluttered Max.

'We organised it last night,' said Ravvy smugly. 'Just another of my brainwaves, girls.'

'But – how'd he get *in*?' asked Nia. 'You didn't make him climb over the fence, did you, Rav?'

'Nah, I just distracted the guy at the gate's attention and Dan slipped in when his back was turned,' said Ravvy smugly. ''Seasy!'

'I hope it'll be alright,' worried Nia. 'You know they're very strict here about letting non-guests in.'

Dan stood there grinning and swaying in time to the music. The situation didn't seem to bother him one way or the other. He'd handed over total responsibility for his presence to Ravvy.

''Course it'll be alright,' said Ravvy. 'Why shouldn't it be? You two are such worry-guts. Don't worry about it, everything'll be fine.'

The lads had left the floor and were clustering

round. When Dan learned they were a visiting footie team, a gleam came into his eyes.

'I play for the local team,' he told Bill.

'Yeah?' said Bill. 'Where d'you play?' But before they could move on to an in-depth analysis of the Newcastle–Manchester match, Ravvy had broken in.

'No, no, no,' she said, shaking her head. 'No footie chat here, guys – save that for the daylight hours. It's Planet Party now. So let's get back on that floor. It'll be *fine*,' she repeated impatiently to Max and Nia. 'Don't worry!'

And for a couple of hours it *was* fine.

'Great music,' Dan told Ravvy. 'And great atmosphere. And great guys. You look great too.' Dan's vocabulary didn't exactly have the colour and variety of his dancing. He executed a neat foot twirl and jerked his head towards the side.

'Hey, Rav, who's that guy leaning against the wall and staring at us? I'm sure I know him from somewhere.'

A large, bald man, in some kind of uniform,

was watching them and frowning, his arms folded. Ravvy recognised him immediately. He was one of the security guards and she happened to know he was a stickler for rules and regulations.

'Let's move over there,' she said, laying hold of Dan and attempting to drag him in the opposite direction. They hadn't progressed more than a few metres, though, before the bald bod was tapping Dan on the shoulder. For a heavy guy, he was a swift mover.

'I've seen you before, son,' he said. 'But not in here. You're a local lad, aren't you? – in fact, I think I know your dad.'

Dan mumbled something and twitched his shoulders.

'All right, son,' the security man continued. 'You've had your fun, it's time to go. You know the rules – and so does the young . . . er, lady. Out you go,' he repeated.

'Right, OK,' said Dan. 'I'll go then.' He turned to Ravvy. 'Bye Rav, great rave-up.'

Ravvy had been getting more and more narked as she was forced to listen to this rubbish. Now she lost it altogether.

'You're not really going to take that, are you, Dan?' she stormed. 'Why should you go, just 'cause he says so? What *harm* are we doing? You're not actually *leaving*?'

'We . . . ell,' said Dan uncomfortably, 'I thought I would. He knows my dad,' he pointed out.

'Just keep out of this, missy,' said the security man. 'Now we don't want any trouble, do we? So out you go, son. Now.'

Ravvy was like a raging tornado now.

'God, that is so *pathetic*,' she shouted. She put her hands on her hips and glared. 'Just what is your problem?' she demanded. 'We're not *doing* anything. What are you, a control freak?'

'Missy, you're barred,' said the security guy. His tone was flat and final.

'Oh, for God's sake, that is just so typical . . .'

'You're barred, and that's that.' He looked at Dan, who was hesitating, not knowing whether to hang around or go. 'On your way, lad.' Dan slipped thankfully away. 'And I should watch your step, missy. I saw what you and your friend did to that trampoline this afternoon.'

* * *

278

Far across the room, in a dark, quiet corner, Max and Rael had found themselves a table. Rael had put his arm around Max and her head was resting on his shoulder. Max didn't feel tongue-tied and her throat wasn't dry. She felt all dreamy, soft and wonderful. She could stay here, leaning against Rael's solid chest, until the millennium. She gave a little sigh and stirred in his arms.

Rael looked down at her and smiled. He ran his finger down her cheek and it felt like an electric shock. Then slowly, very slowly, he cupped her face in his hand and bent towards her. He was going to kiss her! It was going to be like no other kiss she'd ever had. Unbelievable! Max's heart missed a beat and she tipped her face up towards him. She closed her eyes and waited, all her senses alive with anticipation.

And then, from the other end of the room, she heard the commotion. Someone was throwing a wobbly. Max's eyes shot open. She tried to tell herself she was mistaken, but it was no use. She'd recognised that voice immediately. It was Ravvy, and she was going into one again.

Rael raised his head in amazement.

'What's going on?' he asked. He let go of Max and craned his head across the room. 'Who's that?'

'I know – I know who it is,' said Max bitterly. It was the last thing in the world she wanted to do, but she slid out of his arms. 'I'll go and see what's going on.'

'Don't be long,' said Rael. He grinned and raised an eyebrow.

'I'll be right back,' Max promised. She really really meant it . . .

Max was furious. This time Ravvy had gone too far. Max and Nia reached Ravvy and the security guy at the same time.

'She gets a bit carried away sometimes,' Nia told him. 'Just cool it, Rav,' she muttered.

'We were *enjoying* ourselves!' cried Ravvy. 'What's wrong with that? It isn't a *crime*, is it? God, you people are so *petty*. Aren't they?' she demanded of Max and Nia.

'And you can take your friends with you,' said the security man. 'You're *all* barred.' He started making flapping movements towards the door. The music had stopped and everyone was staring.

'Alright, alright, we're going!' screamed Ravvy. She turned to the others. 'We wouldn't stop a minute longer in this pathetic dump if you *paid* us, would we, girls?' The others said nothing. People leapt aside to let her pass as she stormed out.

Max and Nia skulked behind her, trying to make themselves invisible and ready to die of mortification. Max thought she might cry.

'Can you *believe* that bloke?' cried Ravvy once they were out in the open air. She reached back and slammed the door behind them. They could hear the music starting up again inside. '*What*? Why are you looking at me like that?'

'It's *you* we can't believe, Ravvy,' said Max. She spoke in a low, deadly voice. 'Of all the . . . *We* were enjoying the evening as well, we were having a *fantastic* time. And now you've ruined it for all of us with your big mouth. I *knew* it,' she cried, 'I *knew* it was too good to last.'

'Why d'you always have to make a scene?' asked Nia. 'It was a brilliant party. I was having a really

good time. And now – God, you were so embarrassing, Ravvy, why d'you have to do it?'

'Aw, c'mon, girls, I couldn't let that security guy
get away with it, could I?' asked Ravvy. 'You've
got to stand up to these people. And it wasn't
as if anyone really noticed . . .' Her voice tailed
away as she remembered the total silence that had
accompanied them as they'd left the party.

'Of *course* everyone noticed,' snarled Max. 'And
I was, I was just . . . I don't want to *speak* to you,
Ravvy.'

'Nor do I,' said Nia.

'You were just what, Max?' asked Ravvy interestedly. 'Aw, you're losing your sense of proportion,
girls. Look, I'm sorry if I broke up the evening, OK?
And your wonderful romance, Max. I'm sorry,' she
repeated as they remained silent.

I'll never speak to her again, vowed Max as,
silently apart from Ravvy's bleatings of 'C'mon,
girls', they walked out of the leisure complex, past
the crazy golf course, round by the dustbin area and
back to their apartment. She ruined it. The most
important moment of my entire life, and Ravvy
ruined it.

She hadn't even had time to explain things to Rael. What would he think? Ordered out by a security guard in front of everybody. *Barred!* He'll probably never want anything to do with me again, she thought miserably to herself. She could *strangle* Ravvy.

They'd reached the apartment now. Ravvy had given up protesting and was walking silently behind the others. When they'd got inside and Max and Nia had flung themselves on their beds without speaking, she tried again.

'I'm sorry, I'm *really* sorry you got caught up in that. Give me a break, girls, please,' she pleaded.

Max and Nia sat up.

'Just leave it, Ravvy,' said Nia wearily. 'We're going to bed now.'

'Yeah, we've got nothing more to say to you,' Max added.

She kicked off the yellow platforms and threw them viciously across the room.

'And it's your turn for the camp-bed.'

The Morning After

Rael and Max looked into each other's eyes for a long, dreamy moment.

Then Rael drew Max gently to him. The pounding music echoed the beat of Max's heart. Rael's arms tightened around her, he bent his head and their lips met in a long, warm, tingly kiss. It was every bit as wonderful as she'd imagined.

Max woke from her lovely dream, sighed happily and stretched her toes under the duvet. Life was great. Life was total bliss.

And then she remembered. She sat bolt upright, nearly knocking her head against the ceiling. She gave a little moan. It hadn't been like that at all. Life sucked.

It *could* have been like that, it could have been perfect. Her first kiss with the loveliest bloke in the entire universe. And it *would* have been like that if Rav hadn't gone and got them chucked out. Max cringed into her T-shirt as she remembered their humiliating exit.

'Max,' said a gloomy voice below her.

Max peered over the edge of her bunk-bed.

'Max, wasn't it *awful*?' whispered Nia. 'As soon as I woke up I remembered. *Everyone* saw what happened.' She pulled her duvet up to her chin. 'I don't even want to get out of bed. I don't think I can face it.'

'We'll be the laughing-stock of the camp.'

'Just imagine walking into breakfast.'

'Everyone watching and sniggering about last night.'

'They all saw us being thrown out. *Everyone.*'

'What – what'll the guys think, Nia? Rael – and Perry and the others?'

'They'll probably keep well away now. You should've seen Perry's face when Ravvy was yelling at that security geezer. He couldn't *believe* it.'

'Yeah, and Rael ... Rael couldn't believe it either.' Max gulped. 'It was all going so *well*,' she wailed.

'Oh God, are you two still in a state about last night?' came from the camp-bed. 'Look, I've said I'm sorry. What else could I do? I couldn't let Attila the Hun get away with it, could I? Now can you both shut it? I'd like a bit more shut-eye before brekkie.'

'*Breakfast*? You're not going to breakfast, are you? Everyone'll be looking at us and laughing. You've got no *idea* what you've done, have you, Rav?'

Abandoning the idea of sleep, Ravvy sat up.

'Look, girls, aren't you over-reacting here? It really wasn't that big a deal. I bet it happens all the time with that security freak. Anyway, it livened things up a bit, didn't it?'

She grinned and reached out for her toilet-bag. Max and Nia could have killed her.

'We didn't *want* them livened up!' screeched Max. 'Things were fine as they were. They were *perfect*. And then you – you went and *destroyed* them.'

'I *can't* go into breakfast,' moaned Nia.

'No one will even remember it this morning,' said Ravvy firmly. 'It'll be the last thing on their minds. Trust me. I can hardly remember it myself. I suppose I'll have to get up now.' She started to extricate herself from the camp-bed.

'I can remember every *detail*,' said Nia. She closed her eyes and flopped over on her stomach.

'Well you and Max are the only ones who will,' said Ravvy. She was standing up now. 'You're too sensitive. Now let's have a shower and get over to breakfast. You wouldn't want to miss Rael, would you, Max? And you and Perry seemed to be getting very friendly last night, Nia.'

'Oh, for God's sake, Ravvy!' Nia protested.

But already Max and Nia were pushing back their duvets and climbing out of bed. Ravvy was probably right, they told themselves hopefully. Most people would have totally forgotten the events of last night. Just because they remembered every mortifying detail didn't mean the rest of the world had them imprinted on their brain circuits.

Things had started to look better already. Like Ravvy had said, the footie lads were probably even now sitting in the dining-hall, scoffing their breakfast and waiting impatiently for their arrival. She might have been cheated of her kiss with Rael last night, thought Max, but there was still the rest of today. And the evening.

Ah, *Rael* . . . Max put on a spurt and leapt past the others into the tiny bathroom. All of a sudden she couldn't wait to get over to the breakfast hall.

'Our last day,' mused Ravvy as they walked across the complex. 'It'll be great to spend it with the lads, won't it? We were lucky they turned up here weren't we?'

'Umm,' said Max. Although she kept reminding herself that nobody would remember last night, she was beginning to get cold feet. She decided to sneak unobtrusively through the swing doors, keep her head down and peer through the protection of her fringe for Rael's whereabouts. She hoped Ravvy wouldn't make her usual loud-mouth entrance.

'Right, here we are,' said Ravvy, banging back the door and sending a gust of cold air through the breakfast hall so everyone looked up. She stood in the doorway and scanned the room. 'Now, where are those boys?'

There was silence for a moment as everyone

gawped at them. Ravvy grinned and waved to a few people while Max and Nia tried to look cool and unconcerned.

'Get *inside*!' muttered Max, giving Ravvy a big shove from behind.

A storm of clapping and cheering broke out. As they looked around in surprise, shouts of 'Nice one, girls!' filled the hall. It was unbelievably embarrassing.

'Isn't this *fantastic*!' screamed Ravvy above the uproar. 'We're heroes, girls! What did I tell you?'

'You told us they would all have forgotten by morning,' said Max through gritted teeth. 'You said they hardly *noticed*.' She wanted to die on the spot, but at the same time she wanted to kill Ravvy.

'Yeah, well, they did notice,' said Ravvy impatiently. 'And like I said, to the inmates of Sunnyvale Holiday Centre we three are heroes. So relax and enjoy it, why don't you?'

'This is so *embarrassing*,' muttered Nia. 'Let's get our trays and find a table. Come *on*, Ravvy – move.' She looked around and frowned. 'Can't see the guys anywhere, can you, Max?'

'No,' said Max bleakly. She'd looked at every single occupant of every single table and scanned the food queue twice. Just to make sure, she checked them all again. 'They're not here. They probably came early so they wouldn't have to see us.' Her voice quivered.

'Oh, they'll be in here somewhere,' said Ravvy. She gave a final wave and grin and reluctantly quitted the limelight to join the queue. 'Or if they're not they soon will be. Why shouldn't they?' She was still high from her tremendous reception.

'It's obvious why,' said Nia. 'Obvious to everybody except you, Ravvy. They're too embarrassed to be seen with us. Ravvy, you've really blown it this time.'

'Nah, they'll turn up in a minute.' said Ravvy. 'They're probably on their way now. We'll bag a table and save some seats for them.'

'They *won't*!' Max burst out. 'They wouldn't be seen *dead* with us. You've ruined everything, Ravvy. Why d'you have to keep making these big scenes?'

'Oh, it's have a go at Ravvy time again, is it?' said Ravvy. She led the way to an empty table and started unloading her orange juice and cereals. 'Well, when the lads come panting up to tell us how great we – I – was last night it'll be a different story. I shall expect a full apology. Now – if you can stop whinging at me for just a moment we can get down to planning the programme for today. Honestly, why do I always have to take the blame for everything?' she muttered.

'That's long enough,' decided Ravvy after they'd sat in the dining-hall for about three-quarters of an hour. She started getting to her feet. 'The guys'll just have to come and find us. They've obviously overslept.'

'Yeah, we might as well go,' said Nia. 'There's no point in hanging around here any more.' There was a flat, cold feeling inside her. She'd drunk too much chilled fruit juice, she told herself.

'They're deliberately avoiding us,' said Max. 'Satisfied now, Ravvy?'

Ravvy ignored her. 'I've got a great idea!' she said desperately. 'Let's – let's go *bowling*!'

Anything to lighten the atmosphere. Max and

Nia's black looks were really starting to get to her.

'I suppose we might as well do *something*,' said Max heavily. 'We've got the whole day to get through before we go home tomorrow.'

'Yeah, I don't mind,' said Nia. She was amazed at the dark cloud of disappointment that had descended on her. It must be Max's influence. She'd gone massively overboard for Rael. She was still scanning the breakfast hall as though, if she looked hard enough, he might crawl out from under a table or pop up in the middle of the flower arrangement.

'Right!' Ravvy sprang up doing her best to remain cheerful despite the circumstances. 'All set for another morning of FUN?'

Max and Nia shrugged.

From the first, the bowling was a bit of a disaster. Nobody's heart was really in it.

While they were changing their shoes, several people nudged each other and pointed. Max and Nia kept their heads down and concentrated on tying their laces, but Ravvy always had to bound over for a quick word.

She came back grinning all over her face.

'Mustn't disappoint my fans,' she said. 'Right – you first, Max.'

Max selected a ball, bent down and aimed it vaguely at the pins. She knew for certain now that Rael had gone right off her, and after last night she didn't blame him. That meant she'd have to spend the rest of her life imagining his kisses, since she was obviously destined never to experience them. She'd lost her chance with him for ever.

Ravvy was jumping up and down, trying to act excited.

'Strike! D'you realise you've made a strike, Max!' she shouted.

'It was an accident,' said Max gloomily.

She went to the window and peered out at the landscape. Perhaps by some miracle she'd see Rael walking towards her. A good-looking, dark-haired figure came into view and her heart leapt, then flopped again. Only your averagely tasty bloke, not her super-gorgeous, brown-eyed footie genius Rael. She returned reluctantly to the others.

Max continued to aim the balls almost without looking. She was having a phenomenal success. The others watched gobsmacked as she knocked down all the middle pins, leaving only the end pins standing.

In the middle of bowling her second ball, a shadow passed the window. Max glanced at it hopefully. The ball left her hand with a crafty swerve. It knocked one of the end pins down then trickled across to dispose of the other.

'That was *unbelievable*, Max,' said Ravvy. She'd never seen anything like it.

Max shrugged. She peered through the window again. Not even a glimpse of Rael. Why was she even bothering? He was obviously keeping as far away as possible. She glanced without interest at her score. It was astronomical.

Compared with Max's throwaway brilliance, Ravvy and Nia were pathetic. Their minds too were far away from the bowling alley. Ravvy, although doing her best to hide it, had been more than slightly shaken by the non-appearance of the footie lads. There couldn't be any truth in Max and Nia's accusations, could there?

Where *were* those boys?

Nia was still wondering why she felt so disappointed and anxious. She followed Max's longing gaze towards the window. She knew exactly how Max felt, first a blip of hope followed by a swift plunge into a black pit of despair. Like when she'd waited all those times for Damian – and strangely like the way she was feeling now.

Nia picked up a ball and glanced automatically out of the window. Her heart jumped into her mouth. Her knees went weak and the ball fell from her fingers.

'What's the matter, Nia?' asked Max.

Nia didn't answer. She couldn't. She'd just seen Perry.

Perry! While the others stared, Nia rushed over to the window for a closer view. She could hardly breathe. She watched him advance towards her. There was a kind of glow around him, and suddenly everything became a zillion times more bright. The grass beneath his feet had changed from dusty green to emerald, the sky was brilliant blue. Even the sparrows had become as bright as parakeets.

What was going on?

Perry! Her heart was doing backflips now. He was lovely, he was gorgeous, he was *wonderful*! And she realized with a lightning-like shock she fancied him like crazy!

Omigod, this is *awful*, thought Nia in anguish. I've only just realised what I really feel about him and I've probably already blown it! He thinks I'm just not interested. Her mind was in turmoil.

And what about Damian? Funny how that thought had come so low on the list.

The world was spinning around Nia. Then her vision cleared. The glow faded. She peered more closely at the guy striding towards her. He'd seen Nia goggling like a goldfish through the window and he gave a friendly grin. He wasn't Perry.

Nia's heart took a fast dive into her bowling shoes then slowly returned to normal. She felt almost sick with disappointment. She wasn't quite sure what was happening to her, but one thing was certain. Whatever it was, it was extremely serious.

'Your turn, Nia,' called Ravvy.

Nia suddenly felt very depressed. 'I'm sick of bowling,' she said.

'How's your score, Max?' Ravvy tried.

'Who cares?' said Max. 'I'm sick of bowling too. Let's do something else.'

'We could always head for the sauna again,' suggested Ravvy.

They considered the suggestion carefully. The sauna was where they'd first encountered the footie lads, so it would be packed with bitter-sweet memories. On the other hand, though no one wanted to actually say it, there was always the chance the boys might take it into their heads to return there.

It would be nice to wallow in the baking heat and try to make sense of all the emotions scrambling through her brain, thought Nia. And if Perry chanced to drop in . . .

Max had been thinking along the same lines.

'Yeah,' they said together. 'Yeah, alright. Why not?'

They were walking in the direction of the sauna when Ravvy gave a sudden scream.

'Hey, girls, look what's coming!'

She pointed in the direction of the sports field. Emerging from it at a fast jog, grinning and waving, were the lads. All five of them. Their shirts were sticking to their muscular torsos, their hair was rumpled and they looked unbelievably good.

Stunned all over again by their amazing gorgeousness, uncertain what to say, Ravvy, Max and Nia stood rooted to the spot. Even Ravvy seemed stuck for words.

As the boys came up, breathless and laughing, Rael ran straight to Max. It was as though no one else existed. He gave her a little hug, then ruffled her hair and dropped a kiss on the top of her head.

Max thought her legs were going to give way beneath her. It was alright! She could hardly dare to believe it. Everything was going to be alright! Aw, what a guy! *What an unbelievably great guy!* She was so blown away all she could do was smile and smile with happiness.

But it was Bill who spoke first.

'Last night,' he said, 'Last night – what a laugh! Ravvy, you were *great*!'

Get It Together

'We've been out since early, training,' Bill explained. 'We've only just finished. We thought we'd missed you.' He looked round at them all and grinned. 'Great night, wasn't it?' he repeated.

'Was it?' asked Ravvy cautiously.

'One of the best,' Bill told her.

Ravvy threw a look of triumph at the others.

'You weren't . . . embarrassed?' she asked.

'Embarrassed? Nah – why should we be? The way you took on that security bloke . . . Fantastic!'

He turned to Max and Nia.

'Isn't she the greatest?' he demanded.

'Er, yes, she is,' said Nia. She was trying to catch Perry's eye without actually looking at him. 'Unbelievable.'

'Ravvy always livens things up,' said Max, though

she wasn't really concentrating. Rael was fantastic! He'd had no problem showing his mates just how much he really liked her. She wondered if the others had noticed how her voice had gone from husky to squeaky.

Neither of them looked at Ravvy, but they knew exactly what expression she'd be wearing. Smug. At least she hadn't said anything to the boys. They didn't know how she'd managed to restrain herself.

Shy Rob was gazing adoringly at Ravvy. His eyes were shining.

'I – I don't know how you had the bottle to stand up to that guy, Ravvy,' he blurted out. He'd turned bright red with the effort.

'Oh, Ravvy's full of bottle,' said Nia. 'Isn't she Max?'

Max nodded.

'Why, thank you, girls,' said Ravvy. 'You can always rely on your friends for appreciation,' she told the boys.

'You were *brilliant*!' Rob managed. His hands were obviously bothering him. He put them behind his back, then brought them forward and folded them, then unfolded them and let them just dangle. It was clear he was developing a major crush on Ravvy.

Max's heart was soaring and fluttering like a bird. She took a sideways peek at Rael's arm casually draped around her shoulders. The spot on the top of her head where he'd kissed her was still tingling. Rael's eyes were dancing. He gave her a little squeeze.

'What're we doing today then?' he asked.

A little of Max's shyness had returned and she choked for a moment. Before she could reply, Bill had broken in.

'We could go back to the funfair,' he said. 'We haven't tried the Big Wheel yet. Or the Octopus. And there's the flume ride in the leisure pool.'

'Whatever we do, it'll be great,' said Ravvy. She was well back on form now. She grinned. 'Though I can't guarantee it'll be up to the standard of last night,' she added modestly.

Nia continued to sneak looks at Perry, but whenever he happened to return her gaze, she looked quickly away.

The moment she'd seen his broad shoulders and

warm hazel eyes she'd been overwhelmed by the same heart-lurching symptoms as before.

How *could* she have fallen for him? Perhaps it was just – she glanced at him again and caught his puzzled look – that he was so kind and thoughtful and so easy to get on with. And sooo gorgeous . . .

But a guy could be all that and you could enjoy his company without coming over all trembly when you saw him. You didn't have to fall in *love* with him. Did you . . . ? Or did you?

Although they all set out together that afternoon, it wasn't long before they became mysteriously separated.

They had met up at the Go-Karts. Rob wanted to race with Ravvy again. Driven to desperation by the sudden passion that had descended on him, he inserted himself in the next Go-Kart to her. Within seconds, though, Ravvy had leapt away and left him far behind. They were racing with Bill and James, and Ravvy was determined to win. She did, overtaking with a speed and flair that left Rob stunned with admiration.

'Rob's a great driver too,' said Ravvy, accepting the congratulations modestly. 'When he gets going.'

She was beginning to like Rob more and more. Sure he was shy, but he'd swerved out of her way immediately when she'd shouted instructions to him from her Kart. Also, when you really looked at him, he was just as delectable as the others – even more so, perhaps. He was the tallest of the bunch, with gorgeous deep blue eyes and nice, muscley legs.

'Ravvy was great,' he mumbled, leaning on the side of the Kart for support. Seeing Ravvy in action clearly bowled him over.

'We'll go on the Cup "n" Saucer next,' Ravvy told him. 'Hey, where are the others?'

Max and Rael had completely vanished from the scene. Nia and Perry were two disappearing dots in the distance, walking towards the funfair.

'We'll see them all there,' said Ravvy, unconcerned.

But Max and Rael had no intention of revisiting

the funfair. They'd made off in exactly the opposite direction. To the boating lake.

After they'd watched Ravvy's victory, Rael had turned to Max.

'D'you think there's any chance of getting away from this lot?' he murmured, grinning. She smiled back at him and he ruffled her hair again.

'Yes, that would be nice,' she replied, once she'd got her breath back.

But where? It might be out of season, but it was still amazingly difficult to be on your own. Max scanned the hordes of people milling around.

'Where shall we go then?' she asked.

Rael grinned teasingly. 'Follow me!' he said.

'Anywhere . . .' Max laughed.

'Here we are . . .' said Rael.

The cold, grey boating lake panned out in front of them. To most people it probably looked like the least appealing place to be in the whole camp. But to Max it looked like paradise.

Rael held her hand and helped her into a rowing boat.

They laughed together as it rocked dangerously from side to side in the cold water and Max clutched on to Rael's arms for support. She breathed deeply, relishing the fresh autumn air and settled down in the back of the boat. She watched admiringly as Rael's strong arms took the strain of the oars as he rowed them expertly out into the middle of the lake.

'It's – it's lovely,' she told Rael. 'I could just stay floating here for ever. It's just so . . . peaceful . . .'

'Yeah, it's great, isn't it . . .' he smiled gently at Max.

'Let's go to the island,' she said quietly. It was small, round and covered in trees. 'Can we get out on it, d'you think?'

'Yeah, I should think so,' said Rael, pulling towards the shore.

Max trailed her hand in the water. It was colder than it looked, but she didn't mind. It was perfect, like the rest of this magical afternoon. It completely made up for the terrible traumas of the morning.

'We'd better make sure it doesn't drift away,' she said to Rael, when they scrambled off the boat.

'Let it,' Rael said recklessly, 'I wouldn't mind if it did . . .'

Max beamed. He was sooo nice . . .

'Come on,' he said, taking her hand, 'let's have a look around.'

They started walking towards the centre of the island, through a clump of tall, mottled trees.

'Aargh!' Max gasped. 'My hair!'

It had caught against some of the branches and had gone all tangly.

Rael stopped, looked deeply into her eyes and smoothed it down with his firm hands. Little shivers ran up and down Max's spine.

She leant back against a tree and Rael gently pulled her close to him. Max blinked at the sunbeams dazzling through the leaves. We could be the only people in the world right now, she thought. She turned her face to Rael and now, at last, their lips met in a long, gentle kiss.

In a way, it was better because she'd had to wait so long. It was even better than her dreams. And this time there was no Ravvy to interrupt them. She was far, far away . . .

Perry was amazed when Nia asked him in a slightly

squeaky voice if he'd like to go on the Big Wheel. He'd been on the point of giving up on the whole Nia thing. It was obviously going nowhere. Sometimes it seemed as if she liked him, sometimes he thought she couldn't care less.

This morning, he'd been really looking forward to seeing her again. But then all she'd done was flick him a couple of quick glances and turn away. She was gorgeous, and they'd got on really well at the party, but it was clear she wasn't really interested. So what was the point?

Nia hadn't been able to help herself. She'd been waiting for Perry to suggest a ride on the Big Wheel, but although he'd smiled and said hallo, he'd seemed quite happy to hang around with the others. In the end, she'd decided she'd have to get up her courage and go for it.

At least he'd accepted, even though he didn't seem as pleased as she'd expected. She'd obviously blown it, totally.

They walked along in silence. Nia tried desperately to think of something to say. Perry seemed to have deliberately distanced himself from her.

'I like the Big Wheel,' she said in the end.

Perry smiled at her kindly, a bit like he'd smiled at the kids yesterday.

'I know you do,' he said.

'Do you like it?' said Nia desperately. It was agonising to remember how easily they'd chatted the night before.

'Yeah, it's good,' Perry told her. They'd come to the funfair now. 'Let's get our tickets.' Even if she didn't fancy him back, he was still looking forward to sitting next to Nia.

As they swung slowly into the air, Nia gasped. One of the reasons why she loved the Big Wheel was the way everything below just faded away while you soared right up into the freedom of the sky.

She looked down. This was the most shivery part of the ride. It was a long way to the ground, but even further to the top.

'You're not frightened, are you, Nia?' Perry asked as he followed her glance.

Nia wasn't, it was the best part of the ride, but if Perry didn't hold her hand or put his arm around her soon she'd die. And once back on the ground, it could be goodbye to her chances with him for ever.

It was completely silent up here, except for the occasional cry of a sea-bird and the creaking of their seat. She might never get another opportunity.

'I'm not frightened with you,' she murmured and smiled straight at him. He stared at her gobsmacked.

'It's great being on our own at last, isn't it?' she continued desperately. 'Away from the others.'

Perry nodded. He looked totally amazed, and Nia didn't blame him. Oh God, wasn't he going to say something?

The seat reached the top, swayed slightly, then started to descend.

Nia clutched Perry's arm.

He looked at her and smiled, then finally, at *last*, he put his arm around her. It was hard and muscular and warm and comforting and *lovely*.

'Better?' he asked. He sounded like a big brother. 'Don't worry, we'll be down again in no time.' Nia could have stayed suspended on the Big Wheel, rocking gently backwards and forwards, for ever.

She leant back and let his arms encircle her. She felt shivery and her heart was thudding, but it wasn't the Big Wheel's fault. It was Perry's delicious nearness.

Perry too longed to remain on the Big Wheel with Nia in his arms. He didn't know what to think. She's one strange female, he thought to himself.

He decided to find out once and for all just what was going on, when they got back on solid ground.

'Alright?' he asked, after he'd helped her carefully off.

'Yeah, I'm okay now, thanks,' said Nia. 'Shall – shall we go for a coffee?'

Perry grinned at her. She'd gone from the sublime to the ridiculous, not that he was complaining.

'Just what I was thinking,' he said. His arm was still around her shoulders and he kept it there as they walked along.

The coffee-bar was packed, but there was an empty table near the window. They were making their way towards it when a familiar voice made Nia jump.

'If it isn't one of my mad-for-it party girls!' said Vince. 'Now, are you and your boyfriend having a fantastic, fun-filled time at Sunnyvale?'

'He isn't . . .' started Nia, but Perry interrupted her.

'Yeah, we are,' he said. 'The party last night was brilliant.'

'Good, good,' said Vince. 'That's what we like to hear. Pity about that little upset – we don't usually have that type of person here,' he apologised. 'Still, there's a few rotten apples in every barrel. I hope you and your partner weren't too distressed.'

'We're not . . .' Nia tried again, but her voice faded away. She'd felt such a shiver of delight when Vince had taken them for a couple.

'It didn't bother us,' said Perry. 'We just ignored it.'

'Good, good,' said Vince, rubbing his hands. 'Well, I'll leave you two young lovers in peace. Anytime you need me . . .'

Perry grinned and nodded. Nia was staring at the floor.

When they sat down, neither of them knew quite what to say. Perry had felt so good when Vince had assumed he was Nia's boyfriend he hadn't wanted to deny it. He hoped she didn't mind too much.

He decided to make one last attempt. Nia had

been behaving so strangely this afternoon, he had to know how she really felt about him.

'Nia, he said awkwardly, 'There's something I have to ask you.'

Nia waited.

'It – it – I – well, I think you're great, Nia. I don't know how else to put it.' He picked up his coffee-spoon then put it down again.

Nia stared at him over her coffee. Her heart had gone into orbit and her mouth was dry. He still fancied her!!

'But,' Perry continued, 'But, if you don't . . . I mean . . .'

Nia said nothing. Her heart was singing.

'What I'm trying to say is,' continued Perry, 'do you already have a boyfriend back home, Nia?' He seemed relieved to have finally got the sentence out, but anxious about her reply.

'Yeah, I do – did,' she said slowly.

Perry's face dropped. 'I should've known, someone as lovely as you would have,' he said sadly. 'I just hope he realises what a lucky guy he is.' His voice was so kind it brought tears to Nia's eyes. 'Hey – what's the matter, Nia?'

'He doesn't think he's lucky,' she said flatly. 'He – doesn't think I'm good enough for him. He's always telling me how stupid I am.'

Perry looked angry 'He shouldn't treat you like that. You deserve the best, Nia. I mean, what d'you see in him anyway?'

The coffee-shop faded into a gaping silence as Perry waited for Nia to reply.

'I don't see anything in him,' she told him finally. 'Not now I've met you.'

Their eyes locked. Then, very deliberately, Perry leaned forward and, in front of everyone, he kissed her. It was sweeter and sexier than anything Nia could have imagined. It had never been like this with Damian.

They drew apart and smiled at each other. Then Nia leaned forward and kissed Perry right back.

'We'll do our packing tomorrow, shall we?' asked Max. The long, lovely day was over and they were back in their grungy, clothes-strewn apartment.

'Oh God, yes,' said Ravvy. She gave an enormous yawn. 'Great weekend, wasn't it, girls?'

'It was *brilliant*,' said Max. 'Only two days and three nights – I can't *believe* so much happened.'

'Yeah,' said Ravvy. 'Hey, Nia, absence didn't make the heart grow fonder for you, then, did it?'

Nia shook her head.

'It just made me see . . . things properly.'

'And change them,' said Ravvy approvingly. 'Perry's a great guy, Nia. Not that a *rattlesnake* wouldn't be an improvement on that self-centred git Damian.'

It was a relief to be able to come clean about her true opinion of Nia's ex-boyfriend.

'I take it you two have been organising future fixtures with your footie boys?' she continued.

'*Naturellement*,' said Max. Nia blushed and nodded.

'You were right when you said it'd be a great pick-me-up, Ravvy,' giggled Max. 'Just look what we picked up – a whole footie team!'

'Whose turn is it for that thing?' asked Nia, pointing at the camp-bed.

'All mine tonight, I think,' said Max. She gave it a kick. 'Then we've finished with it for ever.'

'So it's me on the top bunk,' said Nia. 'D'you

mind if I keep the light on a bit? There's something I want to do.'

'Nah, tattoo your fingernails if you want,' yawned Ravvy. 'You're still on your hols.'

'I'll just get this,' muttered Nia, retrieving the writing pad from her heap on the floor.

High up on her bunk-bed, Nia propped her writing pad on her knee. Below her, Ravvy plotted future meetings with the footie lads. Rob was so *cute*, was her last waking thought. The camp-bed squeaked as Max tossed and smiled in her dreams. With the aid of the map tucked under her pillow she'd worked out several convenient ways of meeting up with Rael. She was looking forward to presenting him with them tomorrow.

Nia poised her pen, thought for a moment and began to write.

See Ya – Wouldn't Want To Be Ya!

Dear Damian

I have never met anyone as up themselves as you.

[Yes! About to punch the air, Nia remembered the ceiling a few inches above her head.]

Just *who* do you think you are, leaving me standing in the pouring rain? You didn't even bother to let me know you weren't coming. But then you wouldn't, would you? Ever since I've met you, you've thought of no one except yourself.

I expect you thought I'd come back for more. Well, this is the end. I've had enough of being undermined and humiliated by a total prat like you.

I'm worth much more than that and I deserve

a lot better. I can't think what I ever saw in you.

    IF I NEVER SEE YOU AGAIN IT WILL BE A MILLION YEARS TOO SOON.

    Yours (NOT!)

    Nia

Too Hot to Handle

Kate Cann

Anticipation With A Capital A

Free, free, FREE. It was in the air, all around us. Everyone gathered round in a group, wailing about the awfulness of the last exam paper, and kissing and chatting and promising to stay in touch. Then, shouting 'See you in college!', we all grabbed our stuff and headed out through the doors.

'No more *school*!' squealed Zoë.

'No more uniform,' I gloated, undoing my tie and flinging it into a nearby bush.

'We're *adults* now.'

'Too right we are.'

We celebrated by legging it into the newsagents and buying a huge bag of Fizzy Fish each. Then we went into the park and hung upside down on the swings and swung slowly to and fro, letting our hair drag across the ground. We felt so fantastic it was unreal.

'My brain feels like it's been liquidised,' I said. 'What we need to do now is some serious relaxing.'

'Mmm – chill out . . .'

I turned to grin at her. 'And think about our holiday in Greece.'

We both let out a long, blissful sigh. For the last few weeks, neither of us had allowed even the *thought* of

Greece to enter our scrambled little brains. It would have been like dwelling on steak and chips when you were hooked up to a saline drip feed. But *now* – now we could.

Greece. Blue skies, hot sun, water sports, beach cafés, crystal seas, night life and best of all – fabulous holiday-making *boys*. It was only two weeks away now. We started to discuss it, how it would be, savouring every word, every thought. This was Anticipation with a capital A.

'I can't believe your parents agreed to this holiday,' I said dreamily. 'It is just too brilliant to be real. I mean – it's not really their thing, a flat in Greece, is it?'

'No,' Zoë agreed. 'Dad wanted to do an organised tour round the Scottish castles, complete with hill walking. They get you up 7am, apparently.'

I shrieked with laughter. 'And you changed their minds. You have power, Zoë Chester. Real power.'

She grinned. Zoë has no brothers or sisters, and over the years she's brought her only-child, spoilt-princess act to perfection. She knows just how to use it – like using a weapon. And like a lot of weapons it's really ugly to watch in action but it sure gives results.

When the Chester family annual two-week break came up for discussion, she'd turned her act on full force. 'I feel so *stressed* with these exams,' she'd wailed, wringing her hands and rolling her eyes. 'It would make it all less awful if I had something good to look forward to, something *relaxed*, somewhere hot.'

They'd bought it. Anything to help the Princess through her exams. A relaxed, hot holiday it was.

And when she'd said she wanted to bring a friend, they'd bought that too. 'Someone your own age, of course we understand, darling. We know what you girls are like.' Actually, I reckon they wanted a break from the Princess as much as she wanted a break from them.

It caused a few problems, though, because Zoë has *two* friends. Me, and Pandora. Yes, she is really called Pandora, and in my opinion she should never have been let out of her Box.

'Did Pandora really not mind about you taking me to Greece instead of her?' I asked, tipping the last of the Fizzy Fish in my mouth.

'No. Well – not really. Not after I told her it was only fair because you didn't ever get to go away on good holidays.'

'Oh, so I'm a charity case, am I?' I grumbled.

'Oh, don't be sensitive. It worked. I described just how awful your brothers were and how you only ever go on camping holidays and she ended up feeling really sorry for you.'

'How *nice*,' I snarled. 'Anyway, it's not always camping.'

'Yes it is. It has to be because no sane hotel would let you lot through its doors.'

I shoved her backwards onto the grass, but she had a point. I reckon the only way to cope with the horrors of my home is to wear a virtual reality mask permanently clamped to your face. That way it will at least *seem* as if you're somewhere else.

'Come on, Brianna, don't be sour,' said Zoë. 'You

know I'd sooner go with you. You know you're a lot
more fun than Pandora.'

'Well, that's not exactly hard,' I said. 'An empty
egg box is more fun than Pandora.'

'Oh, shut up. She's OK, really. I promised her I'd
send her lots of postcards. So she won't feel left out.'

I laughed. 'Zoë, you won't be able write what we'll
be getting up to in Greece on a *postcard*. And if you
could – it would make her feel so *completely* left out
she'd never speak to you again.'

'Oh, Bri, I hope it's that good,' Zoë said dreamily.
'I really hope so.'

Shop 'Til You Drop

And now – two weeks of glorious anticipation before we went off on the holiday of a lifetime. And two weeks of hard work. Shopping! We had an awful lot to get through. The next day, incredibly early – before 11 am, anyway – we hit the shops, and started the long trawl.

'Brianna, it makes me look *fat*!'

'Nothing makes you look fat. Being *fat* wouldn't make you look fat. Get it.'

'But I like the greeny-blue one, too . . .'

'Get both.'

'Oh – you're right. I mean – beachwear is all-important, right?'

'And nightwear. We should do nightwear next.'

'*Nighties?*'

'No, idiot. Party stuff. Club stuff.'

'Oh, *right*! I think we should go – minimalist.'

At that we both went into high-pitched cackles that got the assistant bearing down on us grimly, asking 'Can I help you?' and meaning 'Shut up or get out.' So Zoë paid for her bikinis and we left the shop.

Shopping that day was pure pleasure. It helped that, for once, we were *loaded*. This was because:

1. we'd been such slaves to revision that our allowances had been left neglected and mounting up in our piggy banks; and
2. both sets of parents had come over all proud and indulgent at all the hard work we'd done and pressed loads of loot on us.

It was great, touring the shops. People getting out of prison must feel just like this. Suddenly everything is there for you again. We ran around, picking stuff up, putting it down, grabbing, trying, buying. It was ace.

'What you've got to remember,' said Zoë as we riffled through a rack of very short, very sheer dresses, 'is just how *incredibly hot* it's going to be.'

'Mmmmm,' I agreed happily.

'I mean – in the day, obviously. But at night too. Those crowded little bars. Clubs, with everyone dancing . . .'

'Pavement cafés under the moonlight . . .'

'I mean – you need to wear the right things.'

'We will,' I said, holding a scrap of purple up against me, 'we will.'

After two hours, we'd bought three short, thin dresses between us. We'd also agreed to swap clothes around on holiday, although I wasn't too sure about letting Zoë wear my new red shift dress.

'It needs my hair to set it off,' I said. 'Your light brown . . .'

'Blonde.'

'It's not.'

'It will be.'

'Oh – OK, then. But I'm wearing it first. Now – nail varnishes.'

I love nail varnish counters – those rows of gorgeous little bright bottles bring out serious greed in me – I want them all, and I can never choose. Luckily, Zoë doesn't have this problem. She grabbed my hand and dobbed some 'Sizzling Cinnamon' on my fingernail.

'H'mm,' she said. 'Hard to tell. I mean – it's a bit too brownish. But it'll look great with *very brown* skin.'

'I'll get it,' I said. 'Now – sun tan lotion.'

By the end of the day we were so weighed down by goodies we could barely walk. 'This is not just indulgence,' Zoë was saying. 'I mean – we're not sad I-shop-therefore-I-am merchants. This is preparation.'

'Yup,' I answered happily. 'Preparation for the best holiday in the history of the world.'

'We have to have some ground rules,' Zoë said as we collapsed exhausted on her bedroom floor. We'd just tried on all the new dresses, swimsuits, bras, makeup and nail varnish we'd bought and had a stand-up fight in the bathroom with some 'scientifically proven' depilatory cream that didn't so much remove the hair on our legs as spread it around a bit.

'Rules?' I moaned. 'Zoë, I never want to hear about another rule as long as I live . . .'

'Some rules are necessary,' said Zoë piously. 'Without them there would be chaos.'

'Great. I love chaos – I worship chaos.'

'Brianna, shut up. Rule 1: no going to bed before 2am.'

'Three am.'

'Rule 2: No reading serious books. Only trash allowed.'

'Agreed!'

'Rule 3: Minimal time spent with my parents.'

'Zoë, that is not a *rule*. That is a requirement for basic *survival*.'

'And Rule 4 – boys.'

'Right! We *have* to get off with at least . . .'

'Brianna! Calm down. This is serious. Holiday romances are . . .'

'*FABULOUS* great wonderful wanna *have one*!'

'Shut *up*, Brianna. Holiday romances are famous for their transitory nature.'

'Y'wha'?'

'They don't last.'

'Yeah – but they're great while they do.'

'Maybe. But the point I'm trying to make *is* – if we *do* have a holiday fling . . .'

'*If*?!'

'. . . we should keep it in perspective. Don't go letting it get all out of hand. Remember boys are just part of the fun. They are *part* of the holiday not the *point* of the holiday. OK?'

'OK,' I said, not really believing it, and we started trying on all our new clothes for the second time.

Organisational Nightmare

Departure Day arrived. I was packed, I had my passport and my purse-load of Greek money, and I was so excited I felt faint. I even felt a bit tearful as I said goodbye to Mum and Dad, and promised to send a postcard express mail as soon as I got there.

Steve, my oldest brother, gave me a lift over to Zoë's house. He usually has to be bribed or bullied into giving me lifts but he has a thing about Zoë and I suppose he thought he'd get another crack at pulling her if he drove me over there.

Some hope. As far as Steve is concerned, Zoë is the original glacial maiden. Her constant rejection just gets him moonier, of course. Boys can be so masochistic.

We drew to a jerky halt outside the Chesters' place, and Steve said, 'I'll see you in, shall I?'

'No need,' I replied firmly, opening my door and clambering out.

'Well, have a great time,' he called after me. 'You lucky cow. God, I wish I was going with you.'

Pulling a face over that horrific thought, I heaved my case out of the boot and staggered up the front path, through the door and smack into Zoë.

We hugged each other, both squealing. Me with excitement, her because I'd dropped my case on her foot.

'Girls, PLEASE!' said a voice. 'Settle down, PLEASE.'

Mr Chester. The only downers to this bliss-trip were Zoë's parents. But as they were also the Organisers, we were stuck.

Organisation – that's the problem. The Chesters organise everything in their lives down to the last tiny detail. They have an antipathy to any kind of spontaneity. And they *worry*. I mean, you'd have thought we were heading for a six year trip to Mars the fuss they were making.

All the cases were lined up in the hall with military precision, and Mr Chester stood over them with his 'last-minute' check list.

'SNORKELS!' he rapped out.

'Blue bag, dear,' Mrs Chester said.

'Anti-diarrhoea tablets.'

'Medical kit, dear. Big suitcase, right hand side.'

And so it went on. He's a dentist, and his approach to everything in life is neat, clinical and preferably with an assistant in attendance, usually Mrs Chester. Or if she's not around, his daughter. So you can't blame Zoë for pulling her appalling Princess act occasionally. It's basic survival.

Mr Chester loaded the cases in the boot, made two final phonecalls, triple-checked the lock-up procedure and the burglar alarm, and we were off. They'd allowed about three hours to get to the airport and it only took forty minutes so Zoë and I had lots of nice hanging around time once we'd got there. Airports are a bit like shopping centres, only with fewer shops and more buzz. I love them.

'Check out the totty in the line,' Zoë hissed, tossing back her newly blonde hair, as we queued up to check in our baggage. 'Anyone on the same flight as us might be with the same Tour company going to the same place.'

'Jeez, I hope not,' I muttered. All I could see ahead of us was a party of shell-suited grannies and two families with about ten whining kids each.

'Eyes behind,' said Zoë, grinning.

Behind us in the queue were about seven lads. Half a footie team. One of them had a ghetto-blaster balanced on his shoulder, blaring out thumping rhythms, and the rest were talking and laughing loudly and moving to the beat.

I swivelled my eyes round and did my best to check them out. And one of them was really special, one of them was . . .

Uh-oh. The music was definitely beginning to get to Mr Chester, and he has a strong sense of citizens' rights. His rights, anyway. He turned towards the boys, frowning.

'Zoë,' I muttered, in panic, 'don't say your dad's going to . . .'

'Would you MIND turning that thing DOWN?' Mr Chester barked, glaring at Ghetto-blaster-boy.

Ghetto-blaster-boy smirked. 'What thing, mate?' he asked.

'You know perfectly well what THING. That

infernal machine you have perched on your shoulder. Why do you imagine the rest of the airport wants to listen to your APPALLING taste in music?'

Zoë had wandered off to stare fixedly in the window of a nearby Knickerbox shop. I joined her. Knickers had never seemed quite so interesting. Meanwhile, Ghetto-blaster-boy had just about worked out that he was being insulted but didn't seem quite sure what to do about it.

'You saying you don't like my music?' he said.

'Oh, you've GRASPED that, have you? Excellent. Now perhaps you'd mind turning it DOWN?'

'On whose orders, mate?' asked one of the bigger ones.

'No one's orders, young man. A polite and civilised REQUEST. That I strongly advise you to FOLLOW.'

A burly uniformed official was heading towards us, attracted by Mr Chester's raised voice. The lads, who had started to edge rather alarmingly towards Zoë's dad, moved back.

'Everything all right, here, sir?' the official asked.

'Perfectly, thank you,' said Mr Chester, smugly. 'These young men were just responding to a request from me to turn their music down.'

'Well done, lads,' said the huge official, swinging round towards them rather like a bull turning on some young goats. The boy with the ghetto-blaster reached up and twiddled with his dial. He would've had to have been made of steel not to.

As everyone moved away, Zoë glared even harder at the window display of knickers and let out a strangled kind of whimper. '*I hate* it when Dad does that. He thinks he's in charge of *everyone*. One day, someone's going to turn on him and *do him over*.'

'Roll on that day,' I thought, as we slunk back to join the Chesters. Mr Chester was smirking in a really irritating way, and saying things to Mrs Chester like, 'A firm hand, you see, Marjorie. All it needs is for a few more people to take a stand against that sort of behaviour and we'd soon have this country back on its feet', and she was agreeing with everything he said. I actually think she was a bit proud of him.

Old couples can be dead weird.

Up, Up And Away

After what felt like months of waiting we were at the head of the queue and checking in our suitcases. Mr Chester only found it necessary to confirm our seating arrangements – two sets of two window seats, non-smoking – three times, and then we headed into the Departure Lounge.

'Well – there's still over an hour to wait until our flight,' said Mr Chester complainingly, as though it wasn't all down to *him* that we'd got to the airport so early.

'Let's go and get a drink, shall we?' said Zoe, brightly. 'I could murder a cappuccino.'

'Cappuccino!' scoffed Mr Chester. 'You two go. Mother and I have bought a flask of tea.' And he sat down on a vacant bench. Mrs Chester pulled a tartan flask from her bag and began pouring. They take flasks everywhere – Mrs Chester hates cafés. That's because two years ago she discovered a lipstick smear on a café cup she was drinking from. Honestly, you'd have thought it was a pair of false teeth clamped to the rim the fuss she made. I know, I was there.

Still, it meant Zoë and I were off the hook. We

escaped gratefully, and found a really sweet little café next to a newsagent's stand.

'Dad does my *head* in,' snapped Zoë. 'I bet those blokes will be on our flight, and that'll be seriously embarrassing.'

'They *knew* we were with him,' I agreed glumly. 'Nobody's that interested in knickers. We were looking in that window for like – half an hour.'

'A couple of them were OK, did you see?' said Zoë, thoughtfully.

'Yes,' I said. 'And they must be going to Rhodes Island if they're on our flight. I really liked the one in the black T-shirt.'

'Didn't notice him,' Zoë lied. Anyone would've noticed him.

'He had brown hair,' I said pointedly. 'And *gorgeous eyes*. And he was tall, and *extremely* fit . . .'

'Boys in a big group are bad news, Brianna,' Zoë broke in, knowledgeably. 'They behave like morons to impress each other.'

'Well – maybe. But they're not going to spend the whole holiday superglued together, are they?'

'Don't you believe it. They're only here to get pissed and go on the pull.'

'Well, aren't we?' I said.

Zoë raised her eyes heavenward. 'Honestly, Brianna, d'you have to be so . . .'

'You're wishing you'd brought Pandora on holiday instead, aren't you?'

Zoë looked at me, grinned, and said 'No way.'

Suddenly, Mrs Chester appeared beside us at the table, looking panic stricken. 'Oh, thank goodness I've found you!' she breathed. 'They've been calling our flight!'

We jumped up guiltily, and ran after her to the departure desk.

'Come ON, girls!' barked Mr Chester. 'It would hardly be an auspicious start to the holiday if we missed the FLIGHT!'

'*God*, I wish we were going away on our own,' hissed Zoë. A group of three very glamorous girls pushed past us, all long legs and expensive haircuts and very much free of adult supervision.

'When we're on the plane let's pretend we're not with your parents,' I whispered back.

'I do that a lot,' replied Zoë, ruefully. 'It doesn't usually work.'

Once on board we edged down the narrow gangway towards our seats. Zoë – typically – grabbed the window seat. Only after I'd told her I didn't care because I expected someone totally lush would take the seat next to me did she promise to swap with me half way through the flight. Some friend.

Mr and Mrs Chester were in the seats in front of us. Mr Chester only made a brief fuss about the overhead locker being too full for his hand luggage, and summoned the air hostess a mere three times to:

1. complain about the proximity of the smoking area;
2. enquire about the exact timing of the serving of lunch; and

3. ask for a pillow for Mrs Chester.

'We're not with them,' said Zoë through gritted teeth. 'We're *not*.'

Then the occupant of the seat next to me arrived – a huge, bald man with too much aftershave on. I pinched Zoë's arm hard to stop her gloating and said, 'I'm holding you to that promise to swap, *friend*.'

Soon we were on our way and we settled down to enjoy the flight. Magazines, boiled sweets to stop our ears popping, bags of honey-sweetened peanuts and a chinking drinks trolley.

'Don't have more than one glass of wine, will you, Zoë dear?' came Mr Chester's voice from the seat in front. 'High altitudes accelerate the effects of alcohol.'

'Sounds great,' grinned Zoë.

Mr Big beside me seemed to think so, too. He'd ordered a succession of brandies, and fallen noisily asleep. And I realised I needed to go to the loo. Badly.

Avoiding Mr Big

There was no way I could squeeze past him. He took up all of his seat, half of my seat and most of the space in front.

'Oh no,' I muttered. 'I'm *desperate*.'

'Wake him up then,' said Zoë calmly.

'I *can't*. He'll go mad.'

'Well, you can't wet the seat,' said Zoë, practically. 'Go on – he'll be asleep again in no time, the amount of booze he's put away.'

So I took a deep breath, and prodded him. Nothing happened, so I shook his arm. Then I said '*excuse me*,' loudly in his ear.

He still slept like the dead.

'I'm going to climb over him,' I announced. 'He's so out of it he won't notice.'

'Oh, *Brianna* . . .' wailed Zoë. '*Don't!*'

As soon as I'd stood up and put one foot on his armrest I regretted it, but I wasn't going to chicken out. I heaved myself up, holding onto the headrest for balance. Slowly, carefully, I reached out across his sleeping form with my other foot and put that on the far armrest. Then I put my other hand on the other side of his head.

It was a dodgy position to be in. I was – to put it bluntly – straddling him. If the plane chose that moment to heave about with turbulence I'd land straight on top of him. I tried to let go and jump sideways, but for some reason I couldn't move.

'*Jump!*' hissed Zoe. 'Brianna – quick! You look like some kind of pervert!'

'I'm . . . I . . . I'm . . .' I whimpered.

'Bri, for heaven's sake *go on!* You'll get arrested! What are you waiting for?'

'I can't!' I wailed. 'I'm *stuck!*'

People had started to turn and look at us. Some of them were laughing, and I could see several disapproving faces. Then I heard: 'They really shouldn't serve so much alcohol on these tourist flights.' I could feel my face getting hotter and hotter, and my limbs getting more and more rigid and unable to move.

Beneath me, Mr Big snored on, breathing brandy up into my face.

'Zoë – help me!' I wailed.

'How?' bleated Zoë, sounding as panicked as I was.

Then a pair of large hands gripped me round the waist, and I heard, 'It's all right, Brianna, I've got you, just let yourself fall towards me.'

I never thought I'd be glad to throw myself into Mr Chester's arms, but I threw myself towards him then as if he was the love of my life.

'Are you all right?' he said sternly, as he set me on my feet in the aisle.

I couldn't even begin to meet his gaze. 'I couldn't

wake that guy,' I said, indicating Mr Big, 'and I *had* to get out . . .'

'Well, get along then,' said Mr Chester.

And I went.

Chronically embarrassing things never happen singly, do they? You never get time to recover from one before the next dumps on you. I rounded the corner to the toilets praying there wasn't a queue – and ran smack into half of the boys from the airport queue.

Apparently they even had to go to the loo in a group.

'Well, look who it is,' said Ghetto-blaster grinning.

I felt myself going bright red. 'Can I get past?' I was *desperate* by this time.

'There's a queue,' said Ghetto-blaster-boy, standing right in front of me.

'Where?'

'Here. We're the queue.'

'Well – that one's empty . . .'

'Is it? You sure?'

If he didn't stop making stupid comments I was going to pee myself. Desperately, I looked behind him, straight at the really gorgeous one.

And he looked back at me.

'Look . . .' I began.

'Oh, stop messing around, Reg,' said the completely gorgeous one, still in riveting eye contact with me. 'Let her through.'

'Get lost, Karl,' Reg laughed. 'Don't you recognise a chat up line when you hear one?'

'Call that a chat-up line?' said Karl, 'You're really sad, mate, you know that?' Then he kind of pushed Reg against the wall, and in the confusion I scrambled into the cubicle, slammed the door shut and locked it. I wasn't planning to come out in a hurry.

Arrival

When I finally emerged from the loo, the lads had gone. Of course I was relieved (in both senses) but I had a good look round for Karl as I swayed back to my seat. He really was a stunner. Shame about his mates. There was no sign of him, though. They must all have been over on the other side of the plane.

When I got back to my seat I found that Mr Big had woken up and was trying to engage a frosty Zoë in conversation.

'Oh, Brianna – hi!' she said, in obvious relief. 'Look – could you let me out, please? I need to . . .'

Mr Big muttered 'Of course, of course' and, after much straining, managed to heave himself out of his chair. Then he let Zoë out, and me in. Smiling, I thanked him – and slid into the window seat.

Well, it *was* my turn.

Another hour, and we arrived. There was a blast of incredible heat as we stepped off the plane and headed into the terminal. There, we collected our luggage, went through passport control, and walked out once again into the wonderful, exotic, scorching heat of Rhodes.

'Oh, my goodness,' whimpered Mrs Chester, fanning herself frantically. 'Oh, my *goodness*. Oh, this is dreadful.'

'Now, Marjorie,' said Mr Chester soothingly. 'You will acclimatise, you know.'

'Oh, I won't,' she wailed. 'Not to this. Oh, it's *awful*!'

A plump, official-looking tour rep bustled over, obviously fully trained in the art of spotting potential panic-situations.

'Chester party?' she said brightly. 'This is your coach – it's fully air conditioned.'

Mrs Chester's feet barely touched the ground as Mr Chester propelled her towards the coach. Zoë and I were picking up two suitcases to follow when we heard uproar behind us. We swivelled round to look. It was the lads from the plane, going crazy with excitement from the sudden blast of heat. As one, they dropped their bags and began ripping off their T-shirts.

'God, and they say *we're* the vain sex,' muttered Zoë, staring hard. 'They can't bear to waste a second's tanning time.'

I was trying to look indifferent while I craned frantically to see Karl. He always seemed to be behind the others.

'Stuart party?' called the tour rep, heading towards them.

'Yep! That's us!' Reg shouted. 'Let's go, guys!'

343

'This coach,' she said, indicating ours. 'And look lads – I don't want sweat all over my seat backs. Put your T-shirts back on.'

'Spoilsport,' hissed Zoë, then we turned and hurried onto the coach ahead of them.

Mr Chester waved to us from a seat near the back so we more or less had to go and join him. The boys got on and filled up the seats at the front. I suppose the last thing they wanted to do was sit near Mr Chester.

Soon we were off, driving through sun-bleached countryside. Fig trees and cactus plants grew by the roadside, with goats grazing in among them. It was all so different from home I felt shivery with excitement. And when I wasn't staring out of the window, I was staring at the back of Karl's head. He'd looked round at me a couple of times when the journey had started, but that was it. I felt quite disappointed until I realised he'd fallen asleep. Most of his mates had, too. They were all sagging at the necks and sprawling into the aisle.

'Too much lager on the plane,' snorted Mr Chester.

The tour rep picked up a microphone and began to lecture us on avoiding mosquitoes and not getting sunburned. Every now and then, the coach would stop and she'd escort a few people off and into their holiday flats, then come trotting back.

Then we stopped outside a line of huge concrete tower-block hotels, and she announced, 'Faliraki!' And the lads all came to, dragged their bags off the racks and staggered off the coach. As they left, Ghetto-blaster-boy turned round and shouted, 'See ya girls!'

Mr Chester snorted, again. He had an amazing repertoire of snorts. 'Thank goodness we won't be seeing those louts again,' he said.

Lindos was the last stop, and I noticed with interest that it wasn't that far from Faliraki. We dismounted, and the tour rep explained we'd have to walk to the apartment and the cases would be delivered by motorbike-pulled trailer later on. No cars were allowed in the ancient centre of Lindos. Mainly because they wouldn't fit.

We started to follow her into the tiny town, along the steep, narrow lanes, past the gleaming white houses. Zoë and I had gone all giggly with excitement. The sun was just starting to set and this strange, hot wind was blowing – it felt like a jacuzzi with air instead of water.

As we got closer to the centre, the streets got more crowded. There were groups of people with lilos and beach-bags staggering back late from the beach, and groups of early-evening revellers, all dolled up, heading for the bars. In among the seriously glamorous people were some great-looking lads, unfortunately all with girls velcroed to their sides. We wove our way through everyone, trying not to feel intimidated, trying to look relaxed.

'Oh, this is *brilliant*!' said Zoë at my side. 'It's like – so *exotic*.'

'Don't you feel really – "first day here", though?' I murmured.

345

'Yes,' she agreed. 'And incredibly *white*.'

'In a couple of days,' I whispered, 'we'll have this place sussed. It's going to be ace.'

We stared into seductive looking bars and tiny shops full of souvenirs as we passed. Old ladies in black sitting outside the shops stared back.

Mr and Mrs Chester were looking grim faced. 'Have you seen the pictures on some of those T-shirts?' peeped Mrs Chester, pointing to the lines strung between the shops like washing.

'Pornographic!' growled Mr Chester. 'Keep up, girls!'

'Here we are!' said the tour rep, coming to a stop beside a flight of worn stone steps. 'This is one of my favourite apartments. It's very old.'

'Oh, dear,' murmured Mrs Chester.

We followed the rep up the steps and she opened a dark wooden door, like the door to a chapel. Then we were inside, only we were still outside. The late sun streamed down on us, and a soft wind blew.

'This is the terrace,' said the rep. 'The rooms all lead off this.'

The terrace was crammed with masses of lush plants. Some grew tall against the walls, some tumbled out of their pots across the ground; all dripped and sparkled from a recent watering. A thick vine canopy swayed above a table and four chairs. Along the open side of the terrace ran a low stone wall; beyond it, in the distance, you could see the sea.

'It's *fabulous*!' breathed Zoë, eyes huge.

'*Wonderful*,' I added fervently.

It was a dream place. But you could tell Mrs Chester was having enormous difficulty getting her head around a room that didn't have a ceiling over it. Or curtains.

'Is there a living room?' she asked faintly.

'Well, this is it,' said the rep. 'Bit hot in the day, but then everywhere is, isn't it? That vine gives a good shade, though. Just watch the bugs don't fall in your gazpacho!'

'Can I see the bedrooms?' Mrs Chester said, fainter still.

As the rep showed her towards the main bedroom, Zoë and I dashed into the other one. It was great. One window, onto the terrace; two plain beds, all crisp cotton sheets; white washed walls, a washbasin and a cool, tiled floor.

'Which bed d'you want?' Zoë asked.

'You're giving me first choice?' I said, amazed.

'No, but if you don't want mine, we won't have to fight, will we?'

'Typical. Well, I like being near the door.'

'Great! I don't. Now – how big's the wardrobe?' She wrenched the door open. 'Brilliant. Huge. And look – that stone windowsill. Perfect makeup station.'

Laughing excitedly, we began to unpack, hanging up all our gorgeous new clothes, laying out our gear. Then there was a thin wail from outside: 'De – rek! There's no *shower* curtain!'

Giggling, we pushed past a stricken-looking Mrs

347

Chester into the bathroom. It was a plain, tiled cell with a shower hose on the wall, a basin and a loo.

'It's great!' said Zoë. 'No one can tell me off for flooding the floor.' She pointed to the central drain. 'You're *meant* to flood it.'

Mrs Chester had moved into the kitchen. 'I'll never be able to cook proper meals in that oven,' she said, piteously.

'Oh, Mum,' said Zoë. 'You're on holiday. You're not supposed to *cook*. We can eat out. There're loads of little bistros and bars and places.'

'Well, your father won't like that. Not every night. He likes a proper dinner.' And she started to unpack a bag she'd brought. It was full of packets of tea and All Bran and J-cloths and disinfectant.

'How depressing,' murmured Zoë, and we escaped.

Mr Chester was seated at the terrace table, determinedly opening the complementary bottle of wine. 'Drink, girls?' he said. 'First night of the holiday, after all. Then I thought we'd go out to eat. The tour representative recommended a fish restaurant down on the local beach.'

'Blimey, what's got into him?' muttered Zoë.

'He's decided to have a good time,' I answered. 'Let's get ready!'

Newbies

We swapped our flight-worn gear for shorts and
T-shirts – no point wearing the good stuff until
we'd got the tans to go with it – and followed
Mr and Mrs Chester down the steep path to the
beach.

'As soon as we get our bearings, we'll ditch them,'
whispered Zoë. 'But right now I'm starving.'

The restaurant was under a huge, coloured canopy;
sand from the beach drifted across the sun-bleached
planks of its floor. It was buzzing with life. Waiters
carrying bottles and plates of seafood whirled between
tables packed with brown, confident people.

'Cross your fingers,' hissed Zoë.

'Hoping what?'

'That Dad doesn't completely embarrass us.'

I crossed them on both hands.

Mr Chester strode into the centre of the restaurant
and looked around him challengingly. A dark-haired
waitress approached us. 'Do you speak English?' he
demanded.

'Yes, love,' she replied. 'I'm from Bradford.'

'Ah. Well – a table for four, please. Next to the
beach if possible, and on the left side.' He turned to

Mrs Chester. 'They're furthest from the toilets, dear,' he explained.

Cringing, Zoë and I followed him to our table. I knew Zoë was a bit in awe of everything, a bit unsure, just like me. But it would have been taboo to discuss it. What we had to do now was keep a low profile, and watch what was going on, and in a few days – well, we'd really be on holiday then.

Mr Chester laid down his menu. 'Full Seafood Platter for me,' he pronounced. 'After all, when in Rome, do as the Romans do. Or in this case, when in Greece, do as the Grecians do, eh? Ha, ha.'

And Mrs Chester actually laughed with him. 'You're brave, Derek,' she peeped. 'Just pasta for me. I don't want a funny tummy.'

'I'd like pizza,' Zoë muttered.

'Me too, please,' I said.

'Oh, you girls. So unadventurous, eh?' Mr Chester smirked.

Once we'd ordered, the waitress brought the drinks and cutlery. She laid out a whole array of instruments by Mr Chester's plate, and he picked them up one by one and examined them, smiling. It was like he was back in his dental surgery again.

When the food arrived, I could hardly bear to watch him in action. He kept this running commentary up, too. 'Ah, this is efficient. You hold the shell SO – and then you prise the flesh out with this – and then . . .'

'*Dad*,' broke in Zoë. 'We're finished. We're going for a stroll along the beach, OK?'

Mr and Mrs Chester exchanged glances. 'OK,' Mr Chester said. 'But not too far.'

We got to our feet thankfully.

'Sure you don't want a pudding?' he bellowed, as we wove our way through the tables. 'Watching those waistlines, are we?'

It was a relief to escape onto the dark beach. As we walked away from the bright lights of the restaurant, we could hear the waves, loud and rhythmic, in front of us. We reached the shoreline and sat side by side, throwing pebbles into the water.

'It's still so *hot*,' murmured Zoë.

'That sea looks wonderful,' I said. 'I can't wait to get in it.'

Zoë looked at me, grinning, and I looked back, and then we both looked all around us, to see if there was anyone nearby. Then we stripped down to our underwear and ran into the water.

We splashed and swam around blissfully in the warm waves, then floated on our backs and looked up at the sky and its amazing stars, until Zoë started banging on about squids and jellyfish, so we both ran out, shrieking.

'Wurr,' Zoë grumbled. 'Not so warm now!'

'And we've got no towels.'

'Never mind. Shake it off. Oh, Bri – look!'

A little blunt head was looking over the top of one of Zoë's sandals. It watched us for a second, then with a whisk of green tail, it was gone.

'A lizard!' said Zoë, in such awe that we both laughed.

We walked back to the restaurant to meet the Chesters, and Zoë bought a couple of postcards from a stand there. Then, when we got back to our room, I scribbled a postcard to Mum and Dad to tell them I was fine, and Zoë wrote to Pandora. She wondered aloud about me signing it too, but we thought that would be a bit tactless.

Hi Pandora! Well, we're here! The apartment is really sweet, and right near the beach. Mum and Dad are being _pitiful_ as usual, but Brianna and I don't plan to spend too much time around them. Want to get some serious tanning in over the next few days because I KNOW the tan you bring back from Nice is going to be _fantastic_! Lotsa l♥ve, Zoë xxx

Greek-God Watch

We were woken early next day by shouting and
clattering from the street outside. We ran to lean
over the wall, and stood staring down at a line of
donkeys, each with a tourist astride.

'Poor *things*,' muttered Zoë. 'Look at that guy on
the little brown one – he must weigh fifteen stone!'

I cupped my hands to my mouth like a loudhailer
and boomed, 'WALK – you lazy scumbags! Get off
and WALK!' Then we both dropped giggling out of
sight behind the wall.

'What are you girls up to?' said Mrs Chester,
emerging from the kitchen. 'Come on – breakfast's
ready.'

'Oh, *Mum*,' wailed Zoë. '*Muffins*? This is *Greece*!'

'I don't care,' said Mrs Chester stubbornly. 'You still
need a good breakfast inside you. And I'm packing up
a picnic for the beach.'

'Oh, terrific,' groaned Zoë, as we both grabbed a
muffin and went to get ready.

We followed the Chesters down to the beach,
pretending we weren't with them. Mr Chester was
carrying about six bags, three lilos and two sun
umbrellas, and he was wearing this little beanie hat
that was too naff to be true. Then, when we got there,

we found you had to *hire* the sunbeds and umbrellas, so most of his stuff wasn't needed anyway.

'Now – you be VERY careful in the sun at first,' he lectured us loudly as we peeled off. 'Lots of cream. You don't want to burn on your FIRST DAY.'

'Does he have to point out to *every single person* on the beach how *white* we are?' snarled Zoë, as we spread cream on our legs.

'Just – ignore him. Come on – fifteen minutes each side, then let's go for a swim.'

As we settled back on our sunbeds, we noticed something. Just about everyone else who was sunbathing was doing it bareback. I mean everyone.

'Jesus,' muttered Zoë, looking round. Girls were strolling along the beach topless, playing in the waves topless, sitting and chatting to *men* topless. Mrs Chester took off her robe to reveal a huge floral costume with serious bust underpinning, and sat there looking scandalised. Mr Chester sat next to her very obviously *not* looking at anyone.

'No way,' said Zoë, shaking her head in disbelief. 'No *way*.' And – for the moment at least – I agreed.

We lay down and let the sun flay us. It was easy remembering all the warnings about the dangers of sunburn. That heat felt savage. It was only good for a very short time.

It's weird, switching to beach mode. You have to get used to functioning with barely any clothes on, and you have to get used to that laid-back, loping style of walking along the sand. But as the day gradually unwound, so did we. Once we'd been in the sea a couple of times, and sussed out how to use the freshwater shower by the café, and bought a couple of ice-creams using real, Greek money – we felt we belonged.

'Bri, do you notice anything depressing about this beach?' asked Zoë, as we lay down for another spot of sun-worshipping.

'Everyone has bigger tits than us?'

'That's not true! No – the good-looking guys are all with girls.'

'I know. Just like last night.'

There was a couple a metre or so away from us who were so in love it made you ill just to watch them, but you found yourself watching them all the same. They kept rubbing oil over each other, and stopping to smooch. Then they'd prance out into the waves and play this pat-ball game with little bats and a ball. Then they'd come back in and rub in more oil and have another torrid smooch.

'I reckon it's honeymoon beach, Brianna,' said Zoë, glumly.

'Well . . .' I began, 'it's not the *only* beach on the island . . .' and I was just about to launch into my little plan for a day-trip out to Faliraki in search of Karl when she jabbed me with her elbow, hard.

Two guys were sauntering along towards us, just where the sea met the sand. They were both tall, and slim, and very tanned. They had their heads tipped back and these very, very expensive shades on.

They caused a distinct ripple as they walked by. Even Ms Totally in Love nearby had a quick lech before going back to massaging loverboy's shoulders.

'Forget it, Zoë,' I hissed.

'Your problem, Brianna,' she hissed back, 'is that you always set your sights too low.'

We watched them promenade in slow motion to the end of the beach, then swing round and start back again. They exuded this incredible elegance, and this scary, but altogether desirable, confidence. Unlike most blokes, they had no need to show off. Just being what they were was enough.

'Stop drooling, Zoë,' I whispered. 'It doesn't look nice.'

'Shut up. Oh, *God*, they're gorgeous.'

And then the miracle happened. They stopped right near us, and began wading slowly out to sea.

'Let's go for a swim!' I said brightly.

'You are so *obvious*!' snapped Zoë. 'Wait!'

We watched as their beautiful brown backs slowly sank from sight, and they began swimming. Then, as casually as we could, we set out after them.

They were doing a type of lazy breast stroke out to the rocks at the side of the bay, barely splashing their sun-specs. When they reached the rocks they clambered out onto them. For a few moments, they were stunningly framed against the blinding, blue sky. Then one of them took off his sunglasses, put them down, stepped to the edge of the rock, and dived in.

'Ooo – oooh!' gurgled Zoë. 'Serious heroics!'

We were both frantically treading water, so we could stay in the best ogling spot. We watched as Greek God Number Two stepped to the edge and dived. He actually flipped up into the air for a second, before coming down and entering the water like a spear.

'Ooo – oooh!' moaned Zoë again. She has an exaggerated respect for male physical prowess. To be honest I'm not exactly indifferent to it myself.

We watched them climb out and dive in two more times before we felt we really had to swim off – we were beginning to look too obvious. No one treads water for that long, even if they are having the kind of animated conversation that we were faking at the time. We swam slowly back to the beach, trying to decide which of the two was the most fantastic and discussing how things on the beach scene had taken a clear turn for the better.

When we got back to shore, things improved even more. Mr Chester was standing there, all packed up. 'Mother's not feeling too good,' he said to Zoë. 'She's had enough of this heat. I thought we'd take the picnic back up to the apartment, and then maybe we can all have a little nap.'

Woooow. Exciting.

'Oh, Dad,' said Zoë. 'We love it here. You go on, and we'll meet you later.'

'But what about your lunch? Mother's made some lovely egg sandwiches. Look – I'll get yours out . . .'

Zoë put a hand on his arm. 'Don't Dad. They'll spoil in the heat. We'll grab something at one of these cafés, and then have the sarnies later, eh?'

Mr Chester looked resigned. 'Have you got enough money?' he said. 'Here – take this.' And he handed a couple of notes to Zoë. Then the Chesters tottered off and we were on our own. Parentless at last.

Classy Guys!

The first thing we did was go and buy two flimsy sarong cover-ups. We'd sussed that these were what you put on when you went to get lunch. You tied them round your waist and they kind of floated round you, not really covering you up at all, but making you look all gone-native and sexy. Then we toured the outside of all the cafés, checking the menus and (more importantly) the clientele.

'Come on, Zoë,' I moaned. 'This is the third time we've schlepped along here. Let's *choose*.'

'Oh, OK. Well – those two guys aren't in any of them. That first one has three blokes on their own but crap food. This one has the best – *ambience*.'

'Y'wha?'

'Ambience, you peasant. You know – atmosphere. And that one has a lot of life but a lot of çouples.'

Finally, after more discussion, we settled on the last one. Truth was, we were a bit scared about going in on our own. This wasn't exactly Pizza Hut on the High Street any more. I made Zoë promise to do the ordering and she kept checking with me how many drachmas there were to the pound. Then we went in.

It was really lively inside. Zoë ordered two Cokes at the bar and we asked for a table. Then we sat down, trying not to look all excited, as though we'd pulled off something big.

'Don't have pizza,' Zoe hissed at me. 'Have shellfish.'

'But I hate shellfish!'

'I don't care. It's cool.'

'I won't look cool if I start gagging on it. I'm having a baguette. Avocado and bacon. Yum.'

'Oh – OK,' she agreed, sulkily, as the waiter appeared beside us.

'Two lovely ladies all alone?' he gushed mechanically. No, I thought, we're with each other.

'What can I get you?' he went on.

We ordered, and relaxed back, gazing about us.

'This is *great*,' said Zoë. 'I love eating with hardly any clothes on. D'you think I'm getting brown already?' We both gazed mutely down at the pink forearm she'd shoved forward.

'Give it another few days, Zoë, you can't expect . . .' then I broke off and gawped at the bar. The guys had come in. I mean – The Guys.

'Oh, *wow*,' I hissed. 'D'you reckon they saw us come in here?'

Zoë had gone kind of rigid, like a pointer dog when it spots a duck in the reeds. 'Go and get some more *drinks*,' she murmured.

'Me?' I wailed, softly. 'You go. You're the sophisticated one.'

'Yeah, but you're the funny one. Go on Brianna

359

– it's your *turn*.' And she kicked me hard under the table.

As casually as I could, I stood up, briefly rearranged my cutlery and sauntered over to the bar. As I got there, the guys were just being served. I stood close enough to them to be noticed, but not enough to look obvious, and waved my drachmas at the barman.

'What's the food like here?' came a voice to my left. Oh, this was too good to be *true*. One of them was *talking* to me.

'Er – OK, I think. I mean – we've not eaten yet. But it looks OK.'

Killer. Why do I always witter like that?

The barman whirled across to take my order, and while I gave it I racked my brains for a way of continuing the conversation. But there was no need.

'So – on holiday?' the voice said, which was a monumentally stupid remark to make, but I reacted with as much delighted surprise as if he'd just guessed my name, age and telephone number.

'Well – *yeah*! Yeah, we are! You?'

'Yes. Just a short break. We're off to do the Inca Trail next. In the Andes. You know, Peru. We wanted a few days relaxing in the sun first.'

I made myself turn to look at him, hanging onto the bar in case his sheer gorgeousness caused my legs to give way. 'Wow!' I bleated, not really knowing what I was saying. 'The Inca Trail! You must be so *fit*!'

Fit – I actually called him fit! AAGH! Great, Brianna, just great.

But he was laughing suggestively. 'Well – thank

you. Hey – if you haven't eaten yet, why don't we join you? That's your friend over there, isn't it? At a table for four?'

Oh, this was so smooth it was scary. Some demon was going to pop up any minute now and demand my soul if I wanted this scene to continue. I choked out, 'Sure – great – why not . . .' picked up our drinks, and headed over.

Zoë is some actress. I mean, someone really should give her an Oscar. As we walked over she pretended to be studying the menu, and then she looked up all cool, and said, 'Hi?' slightly frostily, as though she was marginally miffed at having her girly lunch interrupted.

'Hi,' came the reply. 'I'm Jason, and this is Mark. OK if we join you for lunch? Your friend just invited us.' Which wasn't exactly true and also made me sound like a right pushy tart, but never mind.

Zoë waved a languid hand. 'Sure. Help yourselves.'

And they did.

It was weird having these two icons sitting opposite. Unreal. They looked so polished, so perfect – everybody's ideal holiday romance.

The conversation that followed was smooth as olive oil – on Mark and Jason's part, anyway. They told us about the island, where the best beaches were, and what other parts of it were worth visiting. It turned out Jason's folks owned a 'little house' in Lindos, so they came here quite a lot.

'Have you been into old Lindos at night yet?' asked Mark.

'No,' replied Zoë. 'We've only just got here. It looks great though.'

'Oh, it *used* to be great,' said Jason. 'But it's got so tacky and commercial over the years. Half the restaurants serve up pizza and chips now. Still, there are a few good places left if you know how to find them.' Then he leaned dizzyingly across the table towards me. 'Maybe we could show you one or two.'

I left the reply to Zoë, because my throat seemed to have seized up. 'Oh, that would be lovely,' she said calmly. 'It did all look a little – confusing.'

'Are you booked up tonight?'

'No – no we're not. We were just going to wander around, take a look, you know . . .'

'Well, why don't we meet you? And then we can all eat together. I know a fantastic seafood restaurant.'

'That would be great,' said Zoë. 'We adore seafood.'

They found out where our apartment was, and said they'd call for us at eight. Then Jason beckoned to the waiter for the bill. 'This is on us, girls,' he said.

'Oh, we couldn't . . .' began Zoe:.

'Sure you could.' He chucked some plastic down, and we stood up to go.

When we got outside I was hoping we'd all go and sunbathe and swim together, but Jason and Mark said they had something on that afternoon. 'You enjoy the rest of the day,' said Mark. 'And we'll see you at eight. Don't get sunburned, OK?' Then they sauntered off.

Zoë and I headed for our sunbeds. We were both nearly passing out with excitement.

'I can't *believe* how easy that was,' squeaked Zoë. 'They even paid for lunch.'

'This place must be enchanted,' I said moonily. 'Where dreams come true. We were handed them on a *plate*.'

'Which one d'you like best? Come on, Bri, tell me.'

'Not sure. Mark, I think. Or maybe – well, they're sort of similar, aren't they?'

'Both absolutely fabulous.'

'That Jason bloke must be seriously loaded,' I added.

'I know. I felt a bit – I mean, those guys seemed to know it *all*. I had a chronic inadequacy attack during lunch.'

'Zoë – you didn't find them a bit – stuck up, did you?'

'All that stuff about Lindos going downhill? Dunno. They've probably got a point.'

'Anyway, who cares. We're only on the second day of our holiday and we're going out tonight with two of the classiest lads on the island!' And we both lurched into the sea, splashing like maniacs.

Leave Dad To Me...

We decided to leave the beach quite early that day, while the late afternoon sun was still hot. We had to put in some serious glamorisation time. As we plodded up the hill to the apartment, a sudden awful thought hit me. 'Zoë,' I squeaked, 'how are you going to handle your dad? I mean – what's he going to think? We've picked up a couple of blokes on the beach and we're meeting them tonight?'

'Well – that's what's happened,' she said, calmly.

'Yes, but he'll –'

'Oh, leave him to me. Don't worry about it, Brianna.'

So I didn't. As soon as we got in I headed for the shower. It's lovely, feeling all the sand and sea-salt wash away, and your skin just a little bit sore from the sun – then you lather in gallons of moisturiser to repair any damage. We both had distinct marks where our cozzies stopped, which we compared jealously.

It took us only half an hour to agree which clothes we'd wear. We had to get the right balance between looking completely wonderful and not trying too hard. Then we moved on to hair, makeup, nails . . .

'What about your egg sandwiches, dears?' called Mrs Chester from the terrace.

Zoë pulled a face. But I was hungry. For some reason, I'd only been able to swallow half my lunch. 'It's a good idea to line your stomach,' I explained, as I left the room. 'Come on – and you'd better tell your dad what we're doing tonight.'

I leaned up against the terrace wall, chewing egg sarnie, listening to Zoë explain. What a con artist. It was an education just to listen to her. She didn't lie outright, but she knew just which bits to embellish to convince Mr Chester that what we were up to was fine, even educational. She said that Mark and Jason knew all about the island, and might take us sightseeing later on (go for it, Zoë!), and we were meeting them tonight to go to a restaurant 'that a friend of Jason's father runs'. The final decider was the fact that the lads were coming here to pick us up. I'd hoped to avoid them meeting the Chesters – to maybe dash outside when we saw them coming – but I trusted Zoë's instinct to know what was needed.

Then we went back to our room to carry on getting ready. I redid my nails, while Zoë tried to lecture me on how to act that evening. She seemed really wound up about it. When I told her to get lost, she stomped out to the terrace with her writing things.

Dear Pandora 88 Droolsome
news. We have met two of
the most _amazing_ lads!
They're about twenty, and
so cool, so laid back -
seriously sophisticated!
We're going out to eat with
them tonight. I just can't
believe it. I hope this is IT
for the holiday. I just hope
Brianna doesn't BLOW IT!
Wish YOU were here ♡ Zoëxx

Mark and Jason turned up at 8.05 pm, and were
so unbelievably charming to Mrs Chester that she
practically asked them to forget the restaurant and
stay on to dinner. As it was, we all had sparkling
wine and cashew nuts forced on us while Mr Chester
cross-examined the lads.

'Now I'm trusting you two young men to get the
girls back no later than midnight, all right?' said Mr
Chester in a jovial, men-together way as we inched
our way to the door.

'Oh, absolutely, Mr Chester,' said Jason. 'No
problem.'

'*Sorry* about Dad,' Zoë blurted, as we went down
the steps.

'Why? He's just protective,' answered Mark urbanely.
'So shall I be, when I have daughters.'

Together, we strolled into the centre of Lindos. What a glam group we must look, I thought, proudly. I just wished I could think of something to say.

Zoë was stricken with the same silence affliction. But Jason and Mark didn't seem bothered. They kept up a running commentary as we wandered along, which bar did the best cocktails, which restaurant brought in the best profit, who was running which scam. Then we stopped outside an exclusive-looking little place with wrought iron bars at the windows, and Jason began to speak to the doorman.

In Greek.

Those two were so suave, it was unreal. I was feeling completely out of my depth by this time, and I knew Zoë was too, although she'd have had her toenails pulled out before admitting it.

Within minutes we'd been whisked inside to a table in the corner, half-hidden by an enormous potted palm, and leather-bound menus had been placed in our hands.

'Well, girls, what's it going to be?' asked Mark. 'I'm having the lobster. It's excellent here.'

Zoë asked for braised swordfish, while I scanned the menu in desperation. 'I'll have the kalimari,' I said, wildly.

Then the wine waiter came over, and Mark and Jason got stuck into a deep conversation with him, all about vintages and stuff.

'D'you know what kalimari is?' Zoë hissed at me.

'No – what?'

'Squid.'

'Oh, Jesus.' I could feel myself going green already, and the plate hadn't been put in front of me yet. I'll relax soon, I told myself, as the waiter filled our glasses and the starters arrived. This is amazing, being here with them. This is what a holiday is all about.

Then Mark and Jason started to talk about their Andean trek. They went into great detail about the route they planned to take, stopping for a brief argument about whether to take the longer trail all the way up to the mountains, despite the freezing conditions at night. They told us all about how perilous the Dead Women's Pass (*great* name) was going to be, and, by implication, how brave they were to tackle it. They recounted in exact detail the training they'd been putting in over the last six months, to bring them to their obvious present peak of physical fitness.

After a while, Zoë and I gave up making little admiring noises and asking little interested questions, but it didn't put them off their stride. They worked out in front of us how they would keep a check on average mileage per day, and how much allowance they would make for weather and altitude. They practically gave us an inventory of the gear they were taking along with them, and then spent a good ten minutes discussing the relative virtues of each others' trekking boots.

It was all so disappointing. Mark and Jason made being boring into an art form. They droned on through both courses and up until the waiter wheeled the dessert trolley over to us. I hadn't enjoyed the meal one bit, and not mainly because I'd had to eat wriggly disgusting squid tentacles, either. Mark and Jason were so up themselves it was appalling. I'd even stopped fancying them.

'No one keen on dessert?' murmured Mark. 'Why don't we wander back to the house for coffee? I'd love you to see it – it has a stunning view of the Acropolis.'

I wished Zoë and I had had the guts to behave like complete girlies and gone to the bog together. That way we could've worked out a tactful way to escape. But we didn't so we found ourselves towed along the crowded streets and up the steps to their 'little house'.

Everything ran as smoothly as clockwork once we were inside – it was sinister. The wine was chilling, the smoochy music all lined up, the door to the balcony open. Mark invited Zoë out to 'look at the view', and as soon as they'd gone, Jason put his arms round me, and steered me towards the spiral staircase.

'Let's leave them alone,' he whispered.

I pushed him away. There was no way I even wanted to *kiss* him, at this stage. 'I wouldn't mind seeing the view from the balcony myself,' I said, stalling.

'Oh, but four's a crowd, don't you think?' he said, and put his arms round me again.

'Look,' I said, disentangling myself. 'This is – ridiculous. What did you do – draw lots to see who ended up with who? I mean – it's not as though we've made any sort of – connection together.'

'Well,' he murmured, like some phoney film character, 'that's what I'd like to put right, Zo – Brianna.'

'You *see*!' I squawked in triumph. 'You nearly got my name wrong. I'm out of here. Thanks for the dinner and everything, but no thanks.'

Zoë appeared at the door to the living room, looking pink. 'You coming, Brianna?' she choked out. And we fled into the night.

Beach Vampires

Outside, we had a fit of hysterical giggles.

'What a pair of *creeps*,' I shrieked.

'They thought they could bore us half to death . . .'

'And then get off with us!'

'On the balcony – I felt I was being watched by a lizard – a real reptile.'

'Urgh – the mechanical men. Urgh, they were revolting.'

'They must try it on with every girl they meet. Same old routine. That's why it felt so – *tired*.'

'They didn't want to talk to us. They didn't really like us. They didn't really *see* us.'

'They're beach vampires,' Zoë said, inspired. 'Attracted by our white skin. That meant we were new and out of our depth and . . .'

'Easy prey.'

'Yeah. And you know what was the most insulting bit of all?'

'What?' I asked.

'That they didn't try very hard. I mean – they couldn't even be bothered to *talk* to us properly. They didn't really care one way or the other.'

'Creeps,' I agreed.

'Patronising gits,' she added.

'Boring, boring jerks.'

'Stuck-up sleazebags.'

This heartfelt exchange went on for quite a while. It really made us feel better, as we hurried through the narrow lanes.

Then, after a while, it dawned on us that we weren't exactly sure where we were hurrying *to*. In fact, we were lost.

'Oh, save us' muttered Zoe, checking her watch. 'It's ten to twelve. We'll get the "If-I-can't-trust-you-to-get-back-on-time-how-can-I-trust-you-out-so-late-and-in-a-foreign-country-too" routine.'

'Zoë, I'm beginning to feel worried about getting back *at all*, never mind late. All these streets look the same. It's like a maze.'

'I'm sure it was this way. Down here, past this church.'

'Wurgh. It looks all dark and spooky along there.'

'But I'm sure it leads into – *AAAAAGH!*'

A figure draped from head to foot in black cloth had stepped out in front of us, blocking the path. I was about to echo Zoë's scream when I realised it was a priest.

'Holiday maker?' he said, in a thick Greek accent.

'Y-yes,' I stuttered.

'I know. Santa Maria. You lost?'

'Y-yes,' Zoë admitted.

'Follow me.'

'Santa Maria,' whispered Zoë. 'That's what our

apartment's called. He must be going to take us there.'

'Either that or lock us up in a nunnery,' I muttered, as we started off after him. We followed the trailing black cloak further into the dark maze of streets, recognising none of them. But within five minutes, we were heaving a joint sigh of relief on the familiar steps outside our apartment. The priest pointed to the tiny chapel opposite. 'Mine,' he said simply, then he bowed and glided silently away.

'Thank you *so* much,' gushed Zoë after him. Then she carried on loudly: 'Wonderful evening – it was really great! Bye, Jason – Bye, Mark! Thanks! Byeee!'

'What,' I snorted, as we ran up the steps, 'was all *that* about?'

'No point letting the 'rents know how it all turned out,' she muttered.

The following day, we were both rather subdued when we crawled out of bed. Mr Chester wanted to try out St Paul's Bay beach, which he said was very quiet and secluded. Normally, of course, we would have been dead against anything quiet or secluded, but today it suited us just fine.

We set off in the same embarrassing cavalcade as before, only minus the sun umbrellas, and plus the snorkelling gear. Mr Chester seemingly had no feelings of embarrassment at plonking along the beach in flippers.

The bay was beautiful: a great horseshoe of beach, surrounded by cliffs. Zoë and I hired a couple of sunbeds and an umbrella as far away from the Chesters as we could without being really insulting, then we settled down to sunbathe. We didn't talk much. It was as though the disappointment of last night was still taking time to settle. When we got hot, we swam underwater to the rocks with the snorkels on, and watched bright shoals of fish weave past us, in and out of the sun shadows. It had quite a therapeutic effect on us, somehow.

Lunchtime approached, but the Chesters hadn't brought the picnic hamper this time. They'd got into the idea of lunch at the apartment, followed by a 'siesta', as they now called it. Well, being left alone on the beach suited us fine.

I nudged Zoë as we watched their solid figures head off up the steep path to the road. 'You don't think they're going back to – you know, do you?'

'You know what?'

'Well – back to the flat for a siesta – you know what that usually . . .'

'Oh, *Brianna*! That is just too gross for *words*!' snapped Zoë, as she stalked into the waves for another swim.

There was only one café on the beach: a tiny ramshackle affair, with a sizzling griddle that the owner made the most amazing fried egg and ham sarnies on. As we sat at a table made of crates, swigging Coke and munching, we began to feel a lot better.

374

'I don't care about last night any more,' announced
Zoë.

'Me neither. Put it down to experience.'

'We should have guessed it, though. They were too
smooth. They looked like Next adverts. Actually – I
didn't really fancy them.'

'Oh yes you *did*!'

'Well – only kind of. Look – let's go back early and
get dolled up and go out – *on our own*.'

So that is what we did. And as we swaggered into
town that night arm-in-arm we realised something.
We no longer felt like newcomers. We no longer felt
as though everyone else knew more than we did. We
felt like we could take the place on.

'There's nothing quite like surviving smarmy seducers
and getting lost and meeting spooky priests to make
you feel confident you can handle things,' I said. 'I
mean – what else can happen, right?'

We toured the bars. We danced to music from
the '60s, we flirted with any bloke who made eye
contact, and we had a real laugh. We were chatted
up by some lads from Birmingham but decided to
escape while it was still at the chat-up stage. We
ordered huge ice-creams at a pavement cafe and
were asked by no less than three different blokes
'if they could have a lick' (someone should do a
survey on the sad lack of male originality). Then
we went to another bar, danced to '70s music, and
reeled home in the early hours, chewing pitta and
lamb we'd brought from a stall, and vowing to do
it all again tomorrow.

Dear Pandora❀❀ It didn't work
out with the two guys. Don't
ask! What a pair of creeps.
It's great here, though. I'm
really beginning to get into
this lifestyle. Lots of sun
in the day and partying at
night. Who needs boys   ❀❀
anyway?!?!* Tons of   ❀❀
          Love,   ❀❀
        xx Zoë   ❀❀

Alexander The Great

The next morning, obscenely early, Zoë's parents stuck their heads round our bedroom door and announced that two beach days were enough for them; today they wanted to go sight seeing, and they thought we'd like to come, too.

'This island has a formidable history,' began Mr Chester. 'I've been reading all about the Turkish invasion, and it's –'

'*Dad!*' groaned Zoë, head half under her pillow. '*History* is an *exam* subject! History – as far as I'm concerned – is history!'

'Now, Zoë –'

'You and Mum go. Brianna and I need to go to the beach. After we've had some more *sleep*, Dad!'

'Well – if you're sure,' Mr Chester said. 'As long as you stick together, and be careful in the water, and watch the midday sun, and . . .'

Why didn't he just code all his nags? A is for 'stick together', B is for 'don't be late' and so on. Then he could just shout A-F-C-L or whatever at us, and save an awful lot of time.

'And shall we see you back tonight for a Proper Dinner?' Mrs Chester was saying. 'You shouldn't just exist on snacks, you know. I'm doing Shepherd's Pie tonight.'

'Shepherd's . . . ?! Oh, *Mum*. OK. We'll see you tonight.'

The next three days followed the same lovely pattern, with the Chesters leaving before we even woke up. Our tans were getting really impressive, and we told ourselves that the swimming we did was burning off all the ice-creams we were eating. In the scorching heat of midday we'd don our flimsy sarongs and retire into a beach café for shade, ice-cold drinks and lunch, then head back to the shoreline for the afternoon. We were getting on brilliantly together, too. We had such a laugh the whole time.

We went mostly to the beach that was nearest the apartment, partly out of laziness and partly because we'd got to know a few of the people there. We'd done a survey of the beach talent and had several possibilities lined up, but we were in no hurry to take it further than just chatting and flirting and the odd, splashy swim. As the sun went down we'd head back to the apartment to switch off and eat while Zoë's parents wittered on about all the historical sights they'd seen that day. Then we'd have a creative hour or so glamming ourselves up, and hit the island nightlife.

We'd moved on to the Discos now. They had excruciating names like 'Apollo's Wings' and 'Hera's Dive'; they were loud, crude and dated and we loved them. On the fifth night we arranged to meet up with some people from the beach, but it hemmed us in a bit, so the next night we didn't.

We went from dance partner to dance partner – we got bought drinks – we had the odd snog under the star-filled sky and that was enough. I guess Jason and Mark, the beach vampires, had made us wary of getting sucked in by anyone.

I only acted like a real idiot once. I saw Karl, the gorgeous guy from the plane, on the other side of the dance floor. And my stomach did this high-jump up into my throat, and without even saying a word to Zoë and the two lads we were dancing around with, I skirted round the floor towards him, heart pounding. Then when I got to his side I realised it wasn't Karl at all. He just had Karl's loping way of moving, and his hair, and his height. And he also had a ferocious looking girlfriend, who turned and lasered her eyes at me until I'd scuttled away again.

When I got back to Zoë the other two guys had gone but Zoë was very philosophical about it. She just said it was time to move on.

Zoë and I made a brilliant team; we worked together. We'd even worked out a code. We knew what meant 'Clear off – I'm enjoying this' and we understood 'Help – rescue me!'

It was fabulous – the best fun – I could have carried on doing it for ever.

*

379

We were wandering back to the flat after a riotous, flirtatious Friday night when Zoë announced, 'Tomorrow, Brianna, we take our life in our hands. We do Beach Sports.'

'Oh, no. Oh, please. Not that horrific banana thing.' I'd seen tourists being tortured on it. A speedboat towed a great blown-up banana along at about 100mph, while the poor mugs who'd actually paid to get on it got thrown in the water at every sharp turn.

'Yup,' insisted Zoë. 'I met someone tonight who told me which beach does the best sports. They have parascending, and speedboats with rings, and the banana – the works.'

'Oh, GOODY,' I said, sarcastically. Truth is, I'm a chronic coward when it comes to anything like that. Zoë loves all the scary stuff – upside down, 80mph, sheer drops into water – but I'm the original Theme Park drop-out. Nevertheless, the next morning saw me on the coastline bus with her, heading for the Beach-Sports Beach, determined to go through with it.

'This is on the way to Faliraki, isn't it?' I asked casually, as we rattled along, holding onto the bus rails which were already blistering in the heat.

'Yes. The beach is just before you get there. Brianna, you aren't still on about that lad from the plane, are you?'

'Might be,' I muttered. 'He was gorgeous.'

'Oh come on Bri, you know what his mates and he'll be doing now don't you? They'll be holding

380

burping competitions and seeing who can pee the furthest.'

'Yeah, I know you're right. It's just you have to admit that Karl was pretty cute.'

'God, Brianna, you're obsessed! Hey – quick – this must be our stop. He said it was by the Vista Hotel.'

We clambered off the bus and headed along the scorching pavement. White tower-block hotels loomed over us. Unlike ancient Lindos, this place had been slapped up in the last few years, with profit in mind. It made a nice change. We peered in all the flashy, tacky restaurants and casinos as we went along, wondering if we'd dare go in any of them.

Then Zoë spotted a signpost: *WATERWORLD*. 'That's it!' she cried triumphantly.

'Original name,' I sneered, as my stomach churned in nervous anticipation.

'Oh, come on, misery. It must be over there – that little landing stage.'

We climbed up some steps and along a rickety boardwalk over the rocks. Basking lizards scattered as we approached; there was no shade anywhere. Emerging onto the landing stage, we looked about us. Two incredibly brown girls were stretched out like cats at one side, silent and unmoving. An equally brown man appeared from a little hut with a palm leaf roof.

'Want a ride, darlin's?' he said, in a Geordie accent.

'Er – yes, please,' said Zoë.

'What's the least scary?' I piped up. 'To start with?'

He grinned at me. 'Got a bad 'ead for heights, 'ave you, luv?'

'No – not for heights. Just for anything too fast.'

'You want to try parascending. It's really – like – restful and nice.' And he pointed across the bay, to where someone was hanging in the vivid blue sky under a little parachute, being towed gently along.

'That looks all right,' I said, relieved. 'Zoë – I'm going first. Before I lose my nerve.'

'OK,' she said, grudgingly. 'Then it's the banana, right?'

The man laughed, and banged on the side of the hut. 'Out here, Alexander, you lazy sod.' And the vision that was Alexander materialised in the doorway of the hut. Tall, browner even than the sleeping girls, with short, curly black hair, and wearing not much more than a thong. I could sense Zoë's jaw practically hit the deck beside me. He had the kind of romantic look that Zoë loves. I'm not that keen on it, myself. His nose could have been a girl's.

'So,' he said, picking up a couple of life jackets, 'parascending, yes? You girls want to fly?'

He helped us into the jackets. He took a very long time buckling up Zoë's. Meanwhile, I'd paid the fee and stepped into a waiting motorboat; the Geordie was already in the driver's seat, fiddling with the controls. Then Alexander stepped into the boat and made a great show of gallantly handing Zoë into her seat.

The boat started up, moving out into the bay. Oh, Lord, I thought. No going back now.

'So,' said Alexander, showing all his white teeth, 'you're English, yes?'

'Yes,' simpered Zoë. 'What about you?'

'My mother was Greek, my father Australian,' he announced solemnly, as though this was the most stunning genetic combination in the Western World. And you had to admit, it was a pretty winning mixture. His mum must have passed on the melting dark eyes and smouldering expression, while his dad let him have the height and broad shoulders. Some parents can be OK.

'That's . . . amazing,' Zoë breathed.

I stared over at her, concerned. She didn't usually talk in that breathy-husky voice. One look at her face told me the truth – she was gone – hooked. This was far worse than the beach vampires, this was for real. But I didn't have time to worry about it, because the Geordie had slowed the boat right down and was saying, 'Right then. Lift-off.'

Alexander wrestled me into this little seat with a harness, and then pushed me gently towards the back of the boat. 'Now,' he said, 'the boat speeds up a little – and you just step backwards, yes?'

'Step off the boat?' I squeaked. 'You're joking!'

'No. I don't joke. You step off and then you – float. It will be fine.' He smiled meltingly at me. 'Trust me.'

I wouldn't trust *you* further than I could *throw* you, I thought grimly, as the boat started to gain speed.

'Go on,' he repeated. 'One little step back.'

So I shut my eyes, and stepped, and to my amazement, my feet stayed perfectly dry. I just floated out behind the boat, climbing higher and higher. Gradually, the boat gained speed, and as it did Alexander let the rope out, and I went higher still. Then I just hung there, swaying slightly, looking at the amazing scene below, all the tiny people and the bright, dolls' umbrellas, and the little boat, attached to me by its long line. It was fabulous. I'm not brilliant at heights, but this was different. I felt exhilarated, uplifted.

After the boat had circled the bay once, with me floating behind, it began to slow down, and I could see Alexander reeling me in. That was a short trip, I thought, disappointed. Lower and lower I drifted, until I came right down to the level of the boat and my feet splashed into the sea. 'Oh, God, I'm going *under*,' I wailed, as I ploughed deeper into the waves, then suddenly the boat shot forward again and I rose out of the water and up into the air, like a seabird taking flight. It was thrilling.

After another tour of the bay, they reeled me in for good. 'That was *unbelievable*!' I jabbered to Zoë, as I struggled out of the harness. 'When you're up there, the view is just stunning, and the breeze . . .'

She hadn't heard a word I was saying. Her eyes were fixed on Alexander's face as he took the harness off me and turned towards her. It took him about five months to fit her into it, doing all the buckles up in slow motion, then triple-checking them. 'Now move to the back, like your friend did,' he said. 'I'm with you.' And he was, too. You couldn't have slid a sheet of paper between them.

'OK, step back. Be brave,' he whispered to her. 'Be as brave as you are beautiful.'

I was hoping Zoë would come to her senses and burst out laughing when she heard this, but no; she gazed at him as if she might learn the secret of existence from his eyes, then she stepped back, off the boat, and floated off into the blue. He waved at her in slow motion as she rose higher; every wave was packed with emotion. You didn't wave me off, did you, I thought grumpily. He turned to me. 'Your friend,' he said simply, 'is exquisite.' Then he sat at the end of the boat and watched her, as if anything else would hurt his eyes.

Caught Between Friendship And Lust

I could hardly bear to witness the reeling in and unbuckling procedure. It was like Zoë was an incredibly precious gift being unwrapped. Alexander kept congratulating her, as though she'd pulled off something unique. Then they sat together in the prow, murmuring together, so the only space left for me was in the front next to the Geordie, whose one topic of conversation was the havoc that barnacles wreaked on his boat bottom. We chugged slowly back to shore, and came to a stop alongside the landing stage. It had suddenly filled up; there were about six boys crowded onto it, jostling each other and messing about. The two cat-girls had rolled right to the edge of the wooden platform in fastidious disgust.

'I *told* you it was them,' came a loud, cocky voice. 'Hi girls! It's us!'

And I realised to my delight that the crowd of lads was none other than Reg and friends from the airport. Eagerly, I craned my neck to look for Karl. He was at the back looking even more lush with a tan and shorts. Suddenly, I felt incredibly excited.

I clambered up onto the landing stage, making it

more crowded still. Alexander half-lifted Zoë up from the boat, and very slowly set her down.

'Been up, have you?' demanded Reg. 'Parascending? What d'you reckon to it?'

'Great,' I said. 'Lovely.'

'How's the holiday been so far, then?' he asked, moving in closer and grinning right at me. His sudden friendliness took me slightly aback. I guess he felt sharing a plane gave us a real link.

'Er – OK. Great. Terrific.' I moved sideways, a bit further from him, and a bit nearer to Karl.

He followed me. 'Your tan looks good. Hey – they browner than us, lads? What d'you reckon?' He got hold of my arm, and compared it to his. He seemed strangely reluctant to let go.

'I reckon the girls look better,' said a tall blond boy, stepping forward and standing practically nose to nose with Zoë. 'A lot better. You look kind of roasted, Reg mate.'

'Yeah, well, at least I go brown,' Reg retorted. 'You blond-boys don't tan at all.'

'We were just going out on the banana,' said the blond guy, talking straight at Zoë. 'Have you tried it yet? It's wicked.'

'No,' said Zoë, distractedly. She was watching Alexander help secure the boat.

'Why don't we all go out? It takes eight. If we leave Reg behind, there'd be room for the rest of us.'

'No-one's leaving me behind, Mike, you prat,' roared Reg, shoving him good-naturedly into Zoë.

Zoë stepped back, and gave Mike her best glacial-maiden stare. 'Do you *mind*?' she spat.

'Not in the slightest,' said Mike. 'Come on, let's go for a whirl on the banana.'

'No thank you,' she said, icily.

'I thought you wanted to go out on the banana?' I put in. Dammit, this was my chance to legitimately squeeze up close to Karl, and she was just chucking it away!

She turned to glare at me. 'I've just changed my mind.'

'Oh, change it back again, go on,' said Mike. 'Your friend wants to go.'

'Yeah, let's do it,' said Karl, looking straight at me.

'Have you tried it yet?' I asked him, looking straight back.

'Yeah – once,' he answered, smiling. 'I came off twice.'

'Let's go, shall we?' broke in Reg, beckoning to the Geordie.

'Count me out,' said Zoë, in a super-snotty voice.

'Oh, go on,' said Mike. 'I'll make sure you don't drown.'

Reg jeered, and gave Mike another shove, so that he collided into Zoë once more. Zoë staggered backwards, swore violently, teetered for one heart-stopping moment on the extreme edge of the landing stage, then fell into the water with a huge splash.

There was a horrified pause. Then we turned as one to see Alexander executing a perfect dive off the side of his boat. Seconds later, he broke the surface of the water, clutching Zoë in a full-blown life-saver's hold. Three pairs of hands reached over the side to haul Zoë to safety. She lay gasping like a mermaid on the wooden planks of the landing stage. Alexander clambered out of the water, pushed me out of the way, and threw himself down beside her. 'Are you all right?' he breathed into her ear.

Zoë turned to him, weakly. 'Yes,' she whispered. 'Thank you.'

Alexander sprang to his feet, all wet and heroic-looking. '*WHICH ONE OF YOU ANIMALS THREW HER IN??*' he roared.

'Nobody threw her in, mate, she fell,' said Reg.

'*SOMEBODY PUSHED HER!*'

'Oh, for God's sake. It was an accident.'

Meanwhile, Zoë had staggered to her feet. 'You *idiots*,' she wailed. 'I could have hit my head on the side, I could've . . .'

'Oh, come on,' broke in Mike. 'I mean – I'm really sorry that it happened, but . . .'

'I grazed my *knee*!' screeched Zoë. 'You gits, you pathetic . . . God, it's just so typical . . .'

Alexander put a protective arm round her, murmuring, 'It's OK, it's OK.'

'Look, it was my fault,' admitted Reg, diplomatically. 'But there's not exactly a lot of room on this platform to mess around on . . .'

'No, there isn't,' said Alexander, fiercely. 'And now you can go and mess around somewhere else. You're banned. Go on, get out.'

'*Banned?* What the hell for?'

'We were just having a laugh and . . .'

'You saw it,' said Karl, turning to me. 'Can't you tell him it wasn't deliberate?'

Oh, great. Caught between friendship and lust. Zoë stopped coughing out seawater to glare at me. Friendship – I supposed – had to win.

'Look, they were stupid,' I said to Alexander, 'but there's no need to . . .'

'They were stupid. That's all I need to know,' interrupted Alexander grandly, tightening his protective arm round Zoë. 'Go on, get out, and don't come back.'

The boys knew there was no point in arguing. Alexander probably had a panic button in his hut with a direct link to the local police heavies. It was quite pitiful, watching them all swear bad-temperedly and troop off the landing stage, deprived of their trips on the banana for the rest of the holiday. It was especially pitiful seeing Karl disappear. In fact, I could have cried.

It would have been pretty crass to get angry with Zoë, all dripping wet and shaken as she was. But it was hard to feel nice about her, either. Alexander and she carried on whispering together for a bit, then he came over to me, and told me to get her back to the apartment safely. 'She's very shaken up,' he said, tenderly. 'You be good to her.'

So I carried our beach-bag all the way to the bus-stop and not very graciously gave Zoë the one empty seat when the bus finally arrived. As the bus pulled away, she appeared to make a total recovery.

'Did Alexander say anything about me when I was up in the air?' she asked urgently.

'Yeah,' I replied, sulkily. 'He said you were a real sucker to get taken in by all the corn he was spieling out.'

Zoë pinched my arm viciously. '*Brianna! Tell* me.'

'*OUCH*! Gerroff. He said you were exquisite. Then he went off into a kind of trance. Maybe he's a Buddhist or something . . .' But Zoë had gone off into her own kind of trance, and stopped hearing me. We bumped along for a bit, and then the unfairness of the whole situation got hold of me again.

'You didn't have to be so fierce with those guys,' I said, loudly. 'You knew I really liked Karl.'

'Oh, for *heaven's sake*, Brianna,' she snapped. 'He's an idiot. They're all idiots.'

'Maybe,' I replied. 'You didn't give me a chance to find out, did you?'

'Find out? What more proof d'you need? I could have *drowned* if Alexander hadn't rescued me.' And she glowed at the memory.

'It wasn't Karl who pushed you off,' I muttered, then I gave up, and stared out of the grimy bus window at the cacti and the goats.

Give Me A Break

Zoë and I arrived back at the apartment in almost total silence. In fact there was a distinct rift between us. Though I'm not sure Zoë cared – or even knew – about it, she was off in fantasy land, thinking about Alexander.

Mr and Mrs Chester were already there. Mrs Chester was seated at the terrace table doing something painstaking with a pile of red peppers, and Mr Chester was polishing his sandals. Seriously, he was.

'Oh, good,' beamed Mrs Chester as we wandered in. 'In good time for dinner! Look – I've gone all Mediterranean!'

Well, wow, I thought grumpily. Shepherd's pie with peppers in it.

'Had a nice day, girls?' asked Mr Chester.

'Great thanks,' said Zoë, absently. 'Er – Mum? What time's dinner? Only I'm going out at eight . . .'

I'm going out. Oh, terrific. And no prizes for guessing who with.

'Oh, seven-ish, dear. You've got plenty of time.'

But Zoë looked panic stricken. 'I'd better get ready first then,' she cried, and made a rush for the bathroom.

She was in there for hours. As I sat on the terrace wall waiting bad-temperedly, I swear I could feel the salt drying on my skin and my tan flaking off. When she finally came out, she barely glanced at me as she rushed by, let alone apologised for using up all the hot water. Which, when I went for my shower, I discovered she had done.

And I *hate* washing my hair in cold water. It never rinses properly. I stomped back to our bedroom, grumpier still. Zoë stood there transfixed in front of the mirror, blow-drying her hair as though her life depended on it.

'So,' I began, 'you're meeting your Greek god tonight, are you?'

She turned to me, pleadingly. 'Oh, Brianna, you don't mind, do you? He said he'd pick me up at eight. On his bike.'

'And will Daddy swallow that?' I said a bit nastily. 'He'll come out with his "you girls stick together" routine, won't he?'

Her face fell. 'Oh, God, I hadn't thought of that. What shall I do?'

'Drag Alexander up to meet them, I suppose,' I said, softening. 'He's such a charmer, he'll win them round. Then maybe you could just walk into Lindos, if they're worried about the bike.' Boy, was I magnanimous and helpful or what?

Zoë rushed over and hugged me. 'Oh, Brianna, you're *great!* Thank you. And maybe you can say we spent the day together, all three of us, and how nice he is . . .'

Don't push your luck, I thought sourly.

'And look – can I borrow your red dress tonight?'

Dinner was not brilliant. Mrs Chester's Mediterranean effort was pretty dried up and unappetising. Zoë hardly ate or spoke. Her eyes were fixed on some distant plain, far away from us. Mr and Mrs Chester just about wrung it out of her that she was going out tonight with someone called Alexander who ran a beach sports centre. Then they turned their attention to me, in a really irritating, consoling sort of way.

'Oh, well, Brianna,' said Mr Chester kindly. 'Never mind. I'm sure you could do with an early night. You girls have been burning the candle at both ends, you have.'

'And we're staying in too,' added Mrs Chester, 'so you'll have company.'

Oh, terrific.

'We had a grand game of Scrabble last night. Do you like Scrabble, Brianna?'

Oh, *terrific*.

I glared at Zoë as she sailed past me to the bedroom to do a last minute make-up check, but she didn't notice. As I was clearing the table, I heard a discreet little 'parp' from the road outside, and then I heard someone running up the steps, and a light tap on the door.

Loverboy had arrived.

I opened the door to him. He'd brought flowers. For Mrs Chester. What a total *creep*.

He was wearing a white shirt unbuttoned practically to the naval, which made him look even browner, and these baggy, Turkish looking trousers, like a dancer. And he oozed charm and sincerity. The Chesters were completely taken in by him. Mrs Chester cooed over the flowers and wheeled out the sparkling wine and cashew nuts once again. Mr Chester seemed fascinated by the fact that Alexander was half Greek – he kept asking him about his mother, and how long he'd lived on the island.

After ten ultra-charming minutes, during which I had difficulty keeping my dinner down, Alexander steered Zoë towards the door, promising to 'show her my beautiful island' and look after her.

'You look fabulous,' he murmured, as they escaped. 'My lady in red.'

'Oh, *please*,' I thought, in total revulsion. 'Ditch him *now*, Zoë – he'll start singing it in a minute!' But Zoë merely smiled moonily, and shut the door behind them. And then I heard, 'Shall I get the Scrabble board out?'

I had an extremely early night that night, which was just as well, because Zoë woke me up at 2am by landing on my bed.

'Brianna? Are you asleep?'

'Not any more,' I grumbled. 'Well – how was it?'

'He is *astounding*,' she announced, solemnly. 'He is just the most romantic, fabulous, gorgeous bloke I have ever met in my whole life.'

'So it wasn't too bad then?'

'We danced under the moon,' she chanted. 'We drank wine under the stars. He is just so *beautiful* to look at, and he's kind, and thoughtful – he bought me this flower.' And she thrust a rose into my face. *More* flowers, I thought sourly. Must have shares in a flower shop.

'We went to this tiny little bar and just talked for *hours*. I've never been able to be that open with a bloke before, never. It was like we'd known each other for years. Then this guitarist started up and we danced on this tiny dance floor, just the two of us, and Alexander kept asking him to play these wonderful, sad songs . . . Then we walked along the beach. It was so beautiful. He said if he ever had to live away from the sea, he thought he'd die. He loves the sea. He says he's only really complete by the sea. He had such a sad childhood.'

He would have, I thought, sourer still.

'He told me all about it. His father left when he was tiny. He told me it made it hard for him to trust people – to – to love anyone, to give himself to anyone. But he felt – he said – he thought it might be different with me.'

Oh, *spare us*. 'Zoë,' I snapped, 'didn't it occur to you that this was all a bit *deep* for a first date?'

She looked at me as though I'd punched her. 'What do you mean?'

'I mean going on about his sad past and how it might be different with you. I mean – isn't it all a bit *sudden*?'

Zoë studied my face, full of pity. 'You're such a cynic, Brianna. Don't you believe that two people can just know from the start that they're right for each other? Don't you believe in love at first sight?'

'Oh, for heaven's sake, Zoë. Yes, maybe. But you were the one going on about not taking holiday romances seriously, and now you're . . .'

Zoë got to her feet, frostily. 'I'm going outside,' she said. 'To look at the stars.'

Dear Pandora ✲ I think I'm in LOVE ! I have met the most amazing boy. Half Greek, half Australian. He is completely gorgeous, and he treats me as though I'm a princess. I feel fabulous when I'm with him it's unreal. Brianna is being a real cow about it. I suppose she's jealous, but I didn't expect her to be this mean. Wish you were here. Loads of LOVE ♡♡♡♡♡♡♡ xxx Zoë

Gooseberry Fool

I woke up the next morning determined to be more tolerant, and Zoë had obviously decided to be nice to me too, so we had a reasonable time getting breakfast together.

'When are you seeing Alexander again?' I made myself ask, as we spooned Greek cornflakes into our mouths.

'Well,' said Zoë, going all ingratiating, 'he'd like me – US – to go to *WATERWORLD* again today, and be – be with him while he works.'

'Oh, great. So I sit there like a big gooseberry, do I?'

'Oh, come on, Bri. It's a nice beach. You and I will be able to swim together and stuff, and he said he'd give us free rides and so on. I mean, he'll be *working*. It's not as though I'll be hanging round him the whole time.'

What's that irritating old saying? 'Famous last words'? As soon as we drew close to *WATERWORLD*, Zoë got that glazed, brain-dead expression she'd had last night, and fixed her eyes on the distant figure of Alexander as though no one else existed. Hanging round him? She looked like she wanted to achieve osmosis with him.

As soon as he spotted her he rushed over, grabbed her, and swung her right off her feet and into the air in greeting. Not a guy to do things by halves, obviously. Zoë was giggling delightedly, gazing down at him, while he looked up at her with an expression full of joy and passion. Then he set her back on her feet, treated her to one more super-smouldering expression, and they were off on this huge, saliva-swapping, five-hour snog. The Geordie practically had to prise them apart to get Alexander to start marshalling the queue of tourists that had formed on the deck.

'Stay here, angel,' Alexander whispered to Zoë, as he clambered into the boat. 'I won't be long.' Then he flashed his teeth at her, and disappeared over the side.

Zoë wrapped her arms round herself and gave a little whimper of joy, then wandered over to the edge of the landing stage. The bronzed cat-girls had disappeared. Zoë stretched out in their place. 'Come on, Bri,' she called. 'Let's do some sunbathing.'

I flumped down beside her. Try to be generous, I lectured myself. Just because you *are* totally and utterly left out doesn't mean you have to be all immature and *act* it.

I got out my suncream. 'Want me to oil your back?' I asked.

'Mmm,' she said.

'Which protection level d'you want?' We'd been dead scientific about staggering the protection levels. 'Eight or twelve?'

'Mmmm.'

I gave up. The thing is, Zoë wasn't really bothered if I was generous or not. She wasn't bothered if I talked to her or not. To be honest, she wouldn't have turned a hair if an alien spaceship had suddenly beamed me up on board. She'd wanted to get me along today because she'd have felt guilty about abandoning me, but that was the only reason. All she cared about now was waiting for Alexander. I slapped on some suncream, slipped off my straps and flopped down on my front to get my back brown. The landing stage was very hard and very uncomfortable to lie on.

By my side, Zoë lay propped up on one elbow, her eyes glued to the little speedboat as it shot around the bay. Soon, the boat got bigger, closer, then it roared up to the platform and stopped. Alexander sprang onto the landing stage, stretched out alongside an ecstatic Zoë and wrapped himself round her, and they were off on another marathon snogging session.

I'm not at all sure how much more of this I can take, I thought bitterly, trying to block my ears to all the dodgy necking sounds right next to me. I'd feel a lot less alone if I was *on* my own.

Soon, the Geordie was yelling about getting the next boatload organised, and Alexander very slowly disentangled himself from Zoë and stood up.

'There's room for you in the boat this time!' he beamed, doing a quick head count of punters. 'Coming for a spin?'

'Come on, Brianna,' said Zoë. 'You come too.'

It was all getting worse and worse. I had to go along

or I'd look like a real sour grapes merchant, but it meant sitting in the back next to two ten-year-old boys, while the two lovers practically ate each other in front of me.

'We're going parascending,' announced one of the little boys solemnly.

'Great,' I muttered.

'Are you?'

'No, not this time.'

'Why are you in the boat then?'

I fixed them with a wild stare. 'I really don't know,' I said.

'Look at those two!' said one of the boys, shocked, as Alexander and Zoë got even more entwined.

The other little boy was staring at me unblinkingly. 'Why haven't you got a boyfriend?' he asked.

I gazed hopelessly out to sea, and thought about diving over the edge and not coming up again. Come on, I muttered to myself, don't let things get out of perspective. It's worked out for Zoë, but not for you this time, that's all. No big deal.

Then the Geordie slowed the boat right down, and dug Alexander in the side. He did this casually, without even looking at him, almost as if it was a routine – as if he was used to his business partner being wrapped round a girl. I stared at Alexander as he buckled the first little boy into his harness. I bet you pick up someone new every week, I thought angrily. The reason you've got such an incredibly smooth, polished technique is because you practise it so often.

Alexander supervised the little boy's ascent into the sky, then went straight back to mauling Zoë. He was all over her like olive oil, and not the extra-virgin variety, either.

The boat roared along, and I glared at the back of Alexander's head as his mouth made contact with Zoë's. You oily git, I thought savagely.

After the two little boys had had their trip, we all returned to shore. This time there was a whole crowd waiting to go parascending, so Zoë and I had to sit on the landing stage again.

'Let's go and get a drink,' I suggested. 'Some of those beach cafés look good.'

'Oh, but the boat'll be back in a few minutes. And I promised Alexander I'd be here.'

'Zoë,' I exploded. 'Are you planning to be here *every* time his damn boat draws up at the side?'

She smiled endearingly at me. 'Can't you go and get some drinks and bring them back here?'

That did it. She was so obsessed it was sickening. I got to my feet and walked away without a word. I stomped across the blistering sand to the nearest café and ordered the most expensive fruit cocktail drink I could see on the menu. It had so many paper umbrellas and bits of pineapple sticking out of the top I could barely get my mouth round it, but it didn't make me feel better.

OK, I thought. This can't go on. Time to take stock and work things out. And I made up a sort of agenda in my head, chewing thoughtfully on bits of mango between each point.

Point 1. Through no fault of your own the holiday, which you were enjoying so enormously, has suddenly gone seriously downhill. Now you have to work out how to salvage it.

Point 2. Whatever you think about the creep, Zoë's gone on him. She wants to spend every waking moment with him, and probably some sleeping ones too.

Point 3. You can't stop that. If you try she'll hate you for it.

Point 4. She is TRYING not to leave you out. She's asked you to come along with her today. But tagging along makes you feel about as exciting as an old sock.

Point 5. You have no alternative. You have to leave them alone together, partly for their sakes, but mainly for YOURS.

Then I got wearily to my feet, and returned to the landing stage. I even bought Zoë an ice-cold can of Coke on the way back. Let no one say that I was being childish and vindictive about all this.

'Zoë,' I announced, as I sat down beside her and handed her the drink, 'I think I'm going to head back now. I really do feel three's a crowd right now.'

Zoë looked at me guiltily over the Coke can rim. 'Oh, Bri, are you sure? Alexander said he'd let us have a go on the banana, the first time there were some spaces free.'

'Oh – you want to go on the banana now, do you? You didn't fancy it yesterday.'

'Oh, Bri, come *on* – I'd just nearly been brained on the rocks when I said that . . .'

'OK, OK, forget it, I didn't mean it. No, I'm going to get the bus back. I don't really like this beach. I'll find some lunch at the apartment, and then go down to our beach for the rest of the day.'

Zoë tried unsuccessfully to repress the relief that played across her face. 'OK, then,' she said. 'You'll probably meet up with some people we know there, won't you?'

'Probably,' I said, stiffly. 'Anyway – see you.' And I left. When I'd got onto the boardwalk I turned back meaning to wave, but Alexander's boat had got in and the two were welded together in yet another all-out embrace. So I didn't bother.

Son Et Lumière

I was incredibly relieved to find the apartment empty when I finally got back, and I headed straight for the shower – a cold one. The island buses must be at their most uncomfortable in the middle of the day. I'd felt like a clay pot being fired in a kiln.

Then I grabbed a ragbag lunch and went and lay down on my cool bed to eat it. As I chewed on bits of cheese and fruit, I thought about how much fun it had been the last few days, just Zoë and I slamming around together, and then I thought about her with Alexander, and the very final way Karl had walked off the landing stage at *WATERWORLD*, and tears of chronic self-pity started to trickle down my nose.

'It's 'cos you don't have to put up a front any more,' I told myself dolefully. 'You're not that unhappy, just letting it out.' But the tears seemed to go on for quite a while, and then I found myself drifting into sleep. It was quite a relief, somehow.

I was woken by a cup of tea being rattled about two centimetres from my ear. 'Having a little siesta, are you?' beamed Mr Chester. 'And why not. This weather is absolutely punishing, if you ask me. Here's a cuppa for you.'

'Oh, thank you, that's lovely,' I said, struggling to a sitting position and hoping my eyes weren't too red.

'Where's Zoë?' asked Mr Chester, trying to seem unconcerned.

'Oh, she's still at the beach sports place – with Alexander.'

'Ah,' he replied, in a voice full of understanding and pity. 'They seem to have hit it off, don't they?'

'Yes,' I said weakly, taking a sip of my tea.

'Well look, Brianna, it's nearly four o'clock . . .' I gaped at him. I'd been asleep for over two hours! 'Mother and I are going to drive into Rhodes and see the *Son et Lumière* there. Did you know we'd hired a little car?'

I shook my head, feebly.

'It makes sightseeing so much more convenient. So why don't you put your togs on, and come with us?'

'Oh, but it's – that's very kind of you but I thought I'd go down to the local beach and . . .'

'But the sun'll be going down in a few hours. And you don't want to be heading off there on your own.'

Mrs Chester had appeared in the doorway. 'Not on your own, dear,' she echoed.

Being ON YOUR OWN was one of the Chesters' great taboos. They had this pathetic, parental belief that nothing could happen to a girl as long as she had a friend beside her. They didn't realise you usually got up to a lot more if you had a mate egging you on, and I suppose it wasn't in our interests to enlighten them.

'Come on,' said Mr Chester encouragingly. 'We

thought we'd treat ourselves to a spot of dinner first. There's some quite nice restaurants in the old part of Rhodes Town.'

What chance did I stand? They were being so kind it would have been churlish in the extreme to refuse. So five o'clock saw me 'with my togs on', waiting on the terrace as Mrs Chester wrote a note for Zoë. 'Goodness knows what time she'll be back,' she said, smiling at me indulgently, 'the naughty girl!'

I smiled back wanly. Then we headed down to the car-park and Mr Chester unlocked the hired car. We got in and sat in its broiling heat as he unwound a selection of tea-towels from the steering wheel. 'It gets too hot to hold in the heat of the day unless you take a few precautionary measures,' he explained, as he handed the tea-towels one by one to Mrs Chester, who folded them neatly.

Precautionary measures, I thought gloomily. They'll carve that on his gravestone.

Mr Chester drove at about five miles an hour, slowing down to even less than that whenever any other vehicle appeared on the same road as him. Most of the conversation on the way to Rhodes Town was take up with how hard it was to drive on the 'wrong' side, and how clever Mr Chester was to do it at all. At every junction, every turning, Mrs Chester would pat his hand and say, 'Remember to keep to the right, dear!' and laugh, and he'd laugh back and say, 'I will, dear, I will!'

I was ready to commit suicide by the time we got to the town and parked, I can tell you.

But when we walked into Old Rhodes, I was quite pleasantly surprised. It was far more lively than I expected it to be. There were crowds of people milling about, going in and out of restaurants and bars, and loads of interesting looking little shops, all spilling out onto the pavement and all open till late.

After a while, though, all the bustle and life just made me more depressed. If I could have been there with Zoë, or some gorgeous guy – someone like Karl – it would have been the most amazing fun. But I was there with the Chesters, and that was a bit like looking out from behind bars at everyone else's fun.

After a lot of walking about, expressing a lot of disapproval at all the anarchic little shops ('The thing is,' said Mrs Chester, 'with somewhere like Marks and Spencer, you know exactly where you are') they selected the most staid looking restaurant they could find. Mr Chester only changed his mind about where we should sit once, quite a record for him. Then he made me cringe by cross-examining the waiter on just about every item on the menu, and then ordering plain steak.

As the waiter cleared our plates, Mr Chester whispered something to him. I didn't think much of it – I was too busy jealously watching a besotted couple opposite. But then five minutes later the waiter came back and plonked before me a massive Knickerbocker Glory, complete with three flaring sparklers. Everyone – absolutely everyone – in the restaurant turned to admire it and stare at me, while Mrs Chester squealed and clapped her hands. Mr Chester raised his camera and called out, 'Let's have a smile, Brianna, while your face is so nicely lit up!'

I sat there baring my teeth, muttering 'thank you – it's lovely', and wanting to *die*. Everyone'll think it's my birthday, I thought, choked. I look like the sort of deeply sad person who spends her birthday on her own with two *parents*. Someone else's *parents*.

When the sparklers had finally fizzled out, I gagged down some synthetic cream and nutty goo, then said I really couldn't manage any more. Luckily, no one wanted coffee. Mr Chester paid the bill and I shot out of the restaurant, escaping thankfully into the anonymous darkness.

The *Son et Lumière* was being staged at an old castle near the city walls. Mr Chester laboriously explained to me that 'son et lumière' meant sound and light, and it was about the final Turkish invasion of Rhodes. Wow, I thought, big thrills. I was yawning before it even started, and when it did get going – well, sleep would have been a rave in comparison. The 'son' was a load of naff, warlike sound effects. And the 'lumière' was someone flicking lights on and off in different parts of the castle. For two hours.

Mr and Mrs Chester sat engrossed. At the height of the battle, a spotlight made a wall gradually turn red, and Mrs Chester nudged me, saying, 'I think that's meant to be the flow of blood.'

Just as well she put me right. There was me thinking it was supposed to be ketchup.

The only good thing about the whole event was a tribe of stray cats, who put on their own show at the same time, chasing each other in and out of the bushes. When the thing was finally over I went up to stroke one of the kittens, but Mrs Chester called out, 'Don't touch it, dear. These island cats are full of diseases.'

When we got back to the car, I thanked them as warmly as I could for the evening. They really had been very kind to me, and done everything they could think of to cheer me up. The fact that it had left me feeling twice as bad as before was absolutely not their fault.

There was no sign that Zoë had returned to the apartment. Mrs Chester's note was still there on the table, propped against a stone jar. It wasn't until I went into our room that I realised she had been back, and in a tearing hurry. Towels and her bikini were strewn across the floor, makeup lay scattered, topless, across the windowsill.

And when I opened the wardobe, I saw that my white dress was missing.

No Escape

I was woken up this time just before dawn by Zoë hissing into my ear, 'You're wrong about Alexander, Brianna. You're so wrong.'

I groaned and rolled over.

'I know you think he's coming on too strong too soon. But he is the most sensitive, caring guy I've ever met, and – look, Brianna – wake up! I have to talk to you.'

I groaned again, and rolled back to face her. 'What about?' I muttered.

'Look – I feel really bad about you being left on your own today—'

'I wasn't on my own. I was with your mum and dad.'

'Oh, God – well, that's worse then. But something's happened, Brianna – I mean, this is special – it's like nothing I've ever felt before.'

'OK, OK.'

'If you felt like I felt about someone – I'd be happy for you. I mean – I know it means you get left on your own and everything – but it's so *special* – and I can't . . .'

I rolled away again. 'It's OK, Zoë,' I muttered. 'Let me sleep.'

The whole Chester family were having breakfast on the terrace when I crawled out of bed later. From the way Zoë smiled innocently at me I had this strong feeling that she'd been engaged in some kind of damage limitation exercise with her parents. They'd been ticking her off for abandoning me, she'd been giving them *her* side, and they'd bought it.

'So,' said Mr Chester breezily as I sat down. 'What's on the agenda for today?'

'Well,' said Zoë, just as though she *hadn't* been telling him all about it three minutes earlier, 'Alexander's asked us both out on a big boat. He's doing a sort of excursion thing today round all the islands.'

'And he'll let you girls go, will he?' chipped in Mrs Chester. 'That's nice.'

Yes, but it's not 'you girls' is it? I thought savagely. It's Zoë – and her tagalong friend with no one to talk to.

'Or,' said Mr Chester firmly, watching my face, 'mother and I thought we'd drive back to Rhodes Town. It's the last day we've got the car for. I'd like to walk round the fortification walls on the outskirts of the city.'

Oh, *groovy*.

Everyone looked at me expectantly. I was obviously supposed to select one of these mouthwatering options. And all I really wanted to do was be left on my own.

'Well,' I began, 'if it's OK I might just go down to the beach for a swim and . . .'

412

'Oh, you can't stay here, dear,' said Mrs Chester firmly. 'Not *on your own*.'

Great. So Zoë's safe with that oversexed git but I'm in grave danger if I'm *on my own*. That's just great. But I knew when I was beaten. Their taboo about being solo was insurmountable. So I went for the Rhodes option. Anything was better than sitting at the back of a boat like some kind of sad voyeur as Zoë and Alexander got as close as they could without actually merging.

Zoë danced off to *WATERWORLD*, with lots of virtuous little 'Are you *sure* you won't come, Brianna?'s, and Mr and Mrs Chester and I walked to the car together.

On the way, I noticed a distinct briskening of attitude towards me. They obviously felt that I wasn't being left out – I was *choosing* to be left out. In their view, Zoë and Alexander had asked me on a nice trip, and I'd opted not to go. In their minds, Zoë and Alexander were still at the holding-hands stage, with the odd stolen kiss. Nor was there any way they'd learn the truth, either. After all, having her parents around wouldn't so much cramp Zoë's making-out style as crush it into total oblivion.

After the usual snail's pace journey, we arrived in Rhodes Town, parked, and set off along the barren route between the fortification walls. They were huge, towering, endless. It was like trekking along some great, hot gutter.

'What an amazing military conception,' enthused Mr Chester, gazing around him. 'You see how it

413

works? The enemy breach the outer wall and make it into the middle, here. Then the knights inside—' he pointed at the city wall '—have them TRAPPED.'

We passed a large pile of stone cannonballs. 'That's how they'd polish them off,' he went on. 'Cannon and burning pitch – brilliant, brilliant.'

Mrs Chester looked up at the walls nervously. 'It must have been fearful,' she piped.

'Absolutely,' he agreed, happily. 'And if the cannons didn't finish you off, the knights' swords would. Just imagine being trapped down here while HOARDS of the enemy swept down on you from above. Hundreds of men must have been butchered on this very spot. THOUSANDS!'

I was beginning to feel really claustrophobic and spooked. I thought about all the blood soaking into the ground we were walking on. I could almost hear the screams, ricochetting off the walls.

'Why don't we crack open the flask of tea now?' beamed Mr Chester. 'I could do with whetting my whistle.' He perched on a cannonball in the shade of a stunted tree, and Mrs Chester sat beside him.

'Come on, Brianna love,' she said, patting the cannonball next to her. 'D'you fancy a sandwich?'

They took fifteen minutes having their grisly picnic. Mr Chester read out details of some of the worst massacres from a little guide book as we ate. Then he stood up, and said, 'Come on ladies! Nearly half way!'

HALF WAY?! I couldn't believe we had to walk as far again.

We plodded on as the sadistic sun glared down on us, and the terrain got worse. Builders had been shoring up places where the walls had started to collapse, and their rubble was everywhere. As we clambered over a pile of planks and broken bricks, Mrs Chester asked, 'Are you sure we're meant to be here, dear?'

'Yes, of course we're meant to be here,' Mr Chester snapped. 'There are little signposts along the way.'

'But they stopped some time ago, dear,' ventured Mrs Chester. 'I noticed.'

Mr Chester harumphed and stalked on. Then we rounded a corner and faced a sheer drop into some sort of excavation site.

'Ah,' he admitted. 'Right. We'd better turn back.'

Mrs Chester looked panic stricken. 'What – *all* the way back?'

'Well, there's no other way out is there?' he snapped.

'But it's getting on for *midday*!' she wailed. 'You know I can't stand the midday sun!' Midday sun for Mrs Chester held the same fears as daybreak did for Dracula. She couldn't be out in it. She reckoned it would finish her off.

Mr Chester looked frantically about him. His role as protector was under threat. 'Look!' he suddenly exclaimed. 'The ground's much higher over the outer wall – look at those people!'

People were sailing along on the other side of the wall, visible from the waist up. Some of them looked down at us curiously.

'If we can just shin up that wall,' said Mr Chester, eagerly, 'we'll barely have a drop to the other side.'

'Shin up ... ? Drop ... ?' faltered Mrs Chester. 'Oh, Derek, I *can't*.'

'Yes you can, Marjorie,' said Mr Chester, looking over her head at me with a this-is-an-emergency-situation-help-me-out expression. 'Look at the rubble piled there – nearly to the top of the wall. No problem. Now, I'll climb over first, and then Brianna can help heave you up from below.'

Oh, great. Oh, terrific. Brianna can help heave you up from below. The three of us staggered up the rubble, and then with much straining and scrabbling for toeholds, Mr Chester clambered over the wall.

Then it was Marjorie's turn. I showed her where to put her hands, and moved her feet for her, while Mr Chester leaned over the wall, stretching out desperately to grab her arm. Finally, he got hold of her wrist. 'Now you PUSH, Brianna,' he yelled, 'and I'll PULL.'

I set my shoulder under her ample backside as it rose up the wall, and shoved with all my might. Finally, thankfully, with a wail and a scraping, slithering sound, she disappeared from view. Then they both looked down at me, over the wall. For one crazy moment I entertained the notion of saying 'See y'around, folks,' and making a bolt for it, back the way we'd come. But I knew I couldn't. I started to climb up the wall, and as soon as he could reach, Mr Chester grabbed my arm and heaved. Quite a little crowd had gathered to watch as I coasted over the top of the wall, only slightly grazing my knee. A couple of lads broke into slow, sarcastic clapping.

I looked neither to left nor right as we walked away, smoothing down our clothes. We were all very subdued as we headed into the first café we came across and ordered some drinks.

Mr Chester was the first to recover his composure. 'Well,' he said cheerily, 'that was a bit of an adventure, wasn't it?'

A long silence followed this remark. Then Mrs Chester said, 'I think I'd like to go back now, dear.'

'Oh, but it's still early! I thought we might take in The Grand Master's Palace, and have another look at the harbour where the Colossus is supposed to have stood. Do you know about the Colossus, Brianna? And then . . .'

Mrs Chester shook her head. 'I'd like to go back.'

Long years of cohabitation with his wife must have made Mr Chester know when it was useless to try to push things. He shut up, a bit tight-lipped, and soon we were crawling back to Lindos in the hired car, eating the rest of the sandwiches. It was barely two in the afternoon.

When we got to the apartment I felt hot and dusty, and in desperate need of a swim. 'Look,' I announced, 'I'd love a dip. I'm just going to go down to the beach and . . .'

'Good idea,' said Mr Chester. 'I'll come with you. And while we're gone, Marjorie, why don't you have a little nap. Then we can have a nice evening together.'

It was like a life sentence. I couldn't get away from

them. At the beach, Mr Chester did fifteen minutes of energetic crawl across the bay and back, then sat and *waited* for me. I mean *waiting* was very obviously all he was doing. So after I'd suggested a couple of times that I'd be *fine* on my own, why didn't he head off back and I'd see him later, and he'd said, 'No problem, I'll wait,' I gave up and said I was ready to go.

Back at the apartment I stretched out on the terrace in the one patch of sun I could find to try and improve my tan. The terrace was every bit as hard and unyielding as the landing stage at *WATERWORLD*. As I shifted about trying to get comfortable I worked out that there were only four days of the holiday left, and I felt very sorry for myself.

Pandora !!! Just dashing this off as I wait for Alexander to finish work. We're going to go into Kalimaros to tour the discos tonight. He's a fabulous dancer. And tomorrow he's got A DAY OFF!! Bliss! He said he'd take me out on his bike and show me the real Rhodes that the tourists never see. I can't believe I'm going to have a whole day with only him. It's TOO MUCH!! Can't wait to show you his photo! ♡
Love, love, love, Zoë xxx

418

Going Solo

I think being trapped between the fortification walls represented a bit of a turning point in the holiday as far as Mrs Chester was concerned. When she emerged from the master bedroom after her siesta she was quiet and peevish, as though she was tired of making an effort and wanted to let everyone know that this really wasn't her sort of holiday at all. It was late afternoon and a lovely, balmy breeze had sprung up, stirring all the plants on the terrace and making the vine canopy over the table sway wildly about. I leaned on the wall loving the feel of it on my face, but it didn't please Mrs Chester. She slammed back into her bedroom, and re-emerged with two bits of string. Then she got me to hold a chair for her while she caught up the hanging vines and tied them back in two bunches. Exactly like a pair of net curtains.

'Is there anything I can do, Mrs Chester?' I asked nervously, as she stamped into the kitchen.

She came out immediately with a little red plastic dustpan and brush and thrust it into my hands. 'Do you think you could give the terrace a sweep?' she asked. 'I do think all the leaves make it look so messy, don't you?'

I started crossing back and forth over the tiles in an uncomfortable, crouched position, scooping up all the leaves that had fallen. Meanwhile, Mr Chester had followed his wife into the kitchen and was arguing with her about going out that night. She wanted to stay in; he didn't.

'So a nice, simple spaghetti doesn't suit you, Derek?' she was saying, icily.

'I'm not saying that at all, Marjorie,' he replied. 'I just think you should take the night off after all that happened today. We could pop into Lindos and eat there.'

'With all those crowds and all those people getting drunk? I'd rather stay here, thank you.'

'Now, Marjorie. If we go in early, there won't be so many people about, will there?'

'There'll be enough.'

'Well, I just don't think you should cook tonight. You're on holiday, after all.'

'Yes, Derek. I *am* on holiday. I'm glad that fact hadn't escaped your notice,' she replied, in a voice throbbing with such fearful meaning that Mr Chester beat a hasty retreat and sat down heavily on one of the terrace chairs.

Bent double, I passed by him, still sweeping up leaves.

In the end, though, Mr Chester won and Mrs Chester agreed rather stiffly to a meal out that night. I had no option but to go out with them. When I desperately tried to say that I'd sooner stay here on my own, they were adamant.

'Not after dark, Brianna.'

'Not on your own.'

'That door has no real lock on it, Brianna.'

'Not on your own after dark.'

The three of us set off together at about seven. I'd almost forgotten Zoë had come on holiday with us by this stage. I felt as if I'd been in this threesome for eternity. The Chesters were sort of not speaking to each other, and the real reason for them insisting on me joining them dawned on me: I was needed as a sort of buffer zone between the two. Terrific.

As we got into the centre of Lindos, the little restaurants were just opening up and beginning to ply their trade. Mrs Chester wouldn't admit to liking the look of any of them. So we wandered round and round, and as it got later and later the streets began to fill up with people.

'You see?' she said, sniffily. 'I told you it would be crowded.'

Exhibiting masterful control, Mr Chester said nothing, but steered us into a back-street we'd not been down before. There was a tiny bistro right at the end, and on its doorstep sat an old woman, preparing something in a basin on her knee. She waved to us cheerfully and, as we drew closer, we could see what she was doing.

Shelling live snails.

Mrs Chester took one look at the black, splintered, squirming carnage and left, her hand pressed to her

421

mouth. It seemed to confirm absolutely, completely, and for all time that she had been right to want to stay at home and eat a simple spaghetti.

She didn't say another word for the next forty minutes. Mr Chester started in with a lecture about how we shouldn't judge the culinary customs of other lands, but it fell on entirely deaf ears.

No one seemed to have much of an appetite after that. I certainly didn't. We ended up slinking into a straight pizza place, choking down a large, plain Margherita, and heading back home at some speed. And there, on my pillow, was a note from Zoë, folded into a tiny square.

Hi Bri!!🕷
Going to be really late tonight.
PLEASE PLEASE cover for me. I know
you'll think of something. Just shout
through the door that I'm asleep or
something. LOADS 'O' LOVE 💗 Zoë x
P.S. DESTROY THIS NOTE!
P.P.S. DO THE SAME FOR YOU WHEN
YOU MEET SOMEONE!!! 🕷

I did manage to cover for Zoë that night, but I can't say I did it with a very good grace. I was cleaning my teeth at the basin after a midnight snack when Mr Chester tapped on the door and called softly, 'Zoë? Zoë? Was that you I heard moving about?'

'Yes, Daddy!' I carolled, through a mouthful of mint foam.

'You're back late, dear!'

'Shh, Daddy!' I gurgled. 'Brianna's asleep!'

And thankfully, that satisfied him.

I was beginning to forget what Zoë looked like. By the time I woke up the next day, she was dressed and shoving things in a little backpack, ready to go out again.

'Zoë?' I said sleepily. 'Zoë – you did come back last night, didn't you?'

'Yes, of course I did!' she squealed. 'What d'you take me for?'

'Someone who's gone brain-dead and obsessional,' I thought, as I asked, 'What time d'you get in?'

'Oh, about four.'

'*FOUR*! And you're going out already – it's only eight-thirty!'

'I don't need sleep,' she cried, bounding over and planting a kiss on the top of my head. 'I'm in love. We want to make the most of today. He's got the *day off*.' Then she stopped and looked at me. 'Bri, thanks for covering for me. I wish you could have met someone too.'

''S'OK,' I muttered. 'I just wish your parents would let me alone. I mean – they're being really kind and everything but . . .'

There was a *parp* from outside. Loverboy's motor-bike. 'Must dash!' squealed Zoë, and fled.

Not long after that, I got up too. There was no sound from the Chesters' bedroom. I let myself out and wandered through the tiny streets into the centre of Lindos, trying to decide whether to go into one of the cafés and order breakfast. But I didn't have the heart for it, not on my own. So I bought three fat, hot croissants and headed back to the apartment. The croissants were a bit of a peace offering. When I got back, I was going to put my foot down. It was a matter of basic survival.

As I opened the front door, I could smell coffee. Mr Chester seemed almost overcome with gratitude at the sight of the croissants.

'Brianna – what a LOVELY idea!' he said. 'I'll just take one in to Marjorie with her coffee – she'll be so pleased! She doesn't sleep very well in this heat, you know. I told her to have a lie in.'

When he re-emerged from the bedroom, I told him about my plans to go to the beach. He was quite acquiescent. I think he knew it was time to give me some space.

'Yes, I think a QUIET day's on the agenda today,' he said. 'Well, not Zoë's agenda, anyway, ha ha. She told me about her plans.'

I smiled mirthlessly back at him, and he continued, 'Fine, Brianna, you go on down to the beach, and we'll see you later. As long as you're careful. Your parents have entrusted your care to us, and I don't take that responsibility lightly. So . . .' and he ran through his A-Z of nags once more.

It was such a relief to be on the beach on my own that for the first couple of hours I felt really quite happy. I hired a sunbed and soaked up the sun for a while, then I swam, sluiced off under the beach shower and bought an ice-cream. I sat looking around me as I ate it. I couldn't see any of the people we'd got to know at the start of the holiday; they must have all flown home. Everyone seemed to be in couples or friendly groups – kissing, chatting, laughing, oiling each other – and suddenly I felt so alone it hurt.

I had the sun, the sea, the sand, but no one to share it with. I'd come to terms with the fact that a disastrous night with the beach vampires and a few disco-snogging sessions were going to be my lot as far as holiday romances went, but it would have been so good to spend some time with Zoë. With the *old* Zoë. When I wasn't feeling really angry with her for dumping me I could appreciate that she was smitten with Alexander, and almost understand why she was behaving like she was. But it didn't make it any easier to bear, or make me any less alone.

I was almost glad when Mr Chester appeared at my side to say he'd made a big salad for lunch, if I cared to join them. I really didn't think I could face eating solo at one of the beach restaurants.

The end of the holiday had been staring me in the face with the finality of death. Now it began to seem almost welcome. I realised, with some horror, that I *wanted* to go home.

Zoë and Alexander whirled back from their tour of the secret bits of Rhodes just as the sun was setting. They burst into the apartment, where the Chesters and I were sitting silently reading, radiating pleasure and happiness.

Zoë looks fantastic, I thought bitterly. I must look like an old cabbage in comparison. It's right what they say, about beauty coming from within. All I've got within me right now is resentment and depression. Whereas *she* . . .

'I've just come back to get changed for the evening!' carolled Zoë. 'Alexander wants to go to this special fish restaurant at Kalimaros . . .'

'Not many people know about it,' said Alexander, smugly. 'It's right on the quay; you watch the fishing boats come in by moonlight, then you eat the pick of the catch.'

'How wonderful,' enthused Mr Chester. 'Where did you say it was?'

Go on, Mr C., I thought cruelly, tell them you're going to go along too. But he didn't. He just listened as Alexander described it some more. And it all sounded so perfect I wanted to cry.

Soon afterwards, Zoë waved Alexander off, with lots of hand-kissing and promising to be back in an hour on his part. She wouldn't look at me as she rushed by to the bathroom. I was definitely in the role of someone you tried to avoid because you felt guilty about her. When she emerged from our bedroom half an hour later, looking stunning, Mrs Chester said quite firmly, 'Let's all have a little drink together, shall we?'

It was very wooden, sitting round the terrace table under the vine net curtains, sipping Pimms together. Zoë so much wanted to be somewhere else she seemed like a bird desperate to take flight. Her whole being was listening out for Alexander, though she did

426

manage to turn to me and invite me once more to WATERWORLD, tomorrow. I once more very firmly turned it down. 'Look,' I announced to the table at large, 'it's great Zoë's met someone she's having such a ball with. But there's no way I'm tagging along. I'm OK, honestly.'

Zoë looked massively relieved and Mrs Chester leaned over and patted my hand. 'That's very understanding of you, dear,' she murmured.

'And it's just as well, too,' beamed Mr Chester. 'The tour representative told me about a little coach trip tomorrow, out to the ruins of Kamiros. And I've already booked three tickets!'

The coach trip wasn't too bad, mainly because I'd sort of given up inside and become numb to everything. I'd decided that was the most restful thing to do.

Kamiros was on the opposite coast to Lindos, on a cliff at the end of a long, hot, dusty road, and the coach driver-cum-guide was in a bad mood. When we got there he did little more than stomp off to buy a group ticket, tell us all to be back at the coach at four sharp, lay back in the driver's seat and go to sleep.

Mr Chester wasn't fazed by this disgraceful copping-out. He bought a guidebook, and slowly began to tour the chess-board ruins of the ancient town, reading aloud as he went. Soon he had not only Mrs Chester and me but half the bus following him. He warmed to his theme, explaining which bit of the three-tiered city was for commerce, which for residential use, which had sacred significance. At one point, he actually asked the crowd if there were any questions.

The glare of the white ruins began to give me a headache. I wandered away, and walked right to the edge of the cliff. The sky was so blue it defied belief, the sea glinting and just as blue beneath it, and hanging there, always, the white hot sun. I felt I could understand why the stories about the old Greek gods had been so extreme, so excessive. The landscape and the climate demanded it.

How can *anywhere* be this hot, I thought. It was like being blow-torched. Everything looked hazy, my eyes couldn't focus properly. I had to get into some shade. Desperately, I looked around me. There were three parched little trees at the top of the hill, just beyond all that was left of the temple of Athena. They weren't exactly shady elms, but they'd give a bit of shelter. Panting with every step, I dragged myself up towards them.

As I drew closer, I swore silently to myself. Someone had got there before me. A boy was sprawled there, leaning up against one of the tree-trunks, with his back to me.

Well, too bad, I thought, as I carried on towards the trees. This is no time for holding back and respecting other people's space. I'm about to die from sunstroke. I stopped a short distance from the boy and coughed, hopefully. 'Would you mind if I . . . ?'

The boy turned round. It was Karl.

I'm No Princess

He looked at me, utterly gorgeous, totally unsmiling. 'Oh, it's you,' he said, unenthusiastically. 'Would I mind if you what?'

'If I shared your shade,' I said, heart pounding. 'Sorry, I didn't know it was *you*.'

'So you wouldn't have asked if you had known?'

'No, I didn't mean – oh *look*. I've got to get out of this *sun*.' And I threw myself down beside him. He hated me but I didn't care. I was too parched to care about anything.

'Don't get too near,' he said. 'I'm hot enough as it is.'

'Well, move over a bit then,' I snapped, and he did, very slightly.

'Better? It's not exactly cool under here.'

'Yes, better,' I murmured thankfully, as my eyes began to function again out of the glare. 'You don't know where you can get water round here, do you? I'm so thirsty I could . . .'

'God, any more requests? First she muscles in on my shade, then she wants my water.'

'I only asked where I could buy some . . .'

'There's no shop open. The last one closed down

two million years ago. Didn't you read the guide book?'

'Oh, ha ha.'

'Here,' he said, pulling a bottle out of his rucksack and handing it to me. 'Have some. If you don't mind drinking from the same bottle as me.'

Gratefully, I seized the bottle he held out, saying, 'I'm so thirsty I don't care *what*'s been drinking from – I mean . . .'

He smiled, wryly. 'That's all right then.'

'Thanks. This is great.' I took a long swig. 'Oooh, lovely.'

'Well, leave me a bit in the bottom.'

I screwed the top back on and handed the bottle back to him.

'So,' he said, 'all alone? Where's the princess?'

I gawped at him. 'How did *you* know she was called that?'

He laughed. 'I didn't. But the name does kind of spring to mind when you're around her.'

'She's not always that snotty,' I said loyally. 'Your mates were well out of order the other day, barging her off the landing stage like that.'

'That was an accident. And you knew it was, too.'

'Look, it wasn't me that got you banned!'

'No, but you didn't help!'

'Oh, knock it off. Look – I am really, really sorry you didn't get to have any more rides on that stupid banana. I realise it must have *ruined* your whole holiday and I *profoundly* apologise to you and all your friends. OK?'

430

There was a long silence. Then I sneaked a sideways look at him, and saw that he was trying not to grin. 'Where are your friends, anyway?' I said quickly. 'I thought you went round in a pack together?'

'Like jackels. No, not always. I've been spending some time on my own.'

'Why?'

'Why. Well, after a week or so of sinking ten pints of lager and then throwing up I just fancied bit of a break.'

For some reason, my insides had gone all warm. 'Why did you go on holiday with them,' I asked, 'if you didn't like their type of holiday?'

'What is this, an interrogation? Why did you go on holiday with the princess?'

'She's my good friend. And she asked me. I mean – I'd never get to go somewhere like this with my family.'

'Some friend,' he said. 'She's dumped you for that fascist water-sports guy, hasn't she?'

I gawped again. 'Have you been spying on us?'

He laughed. 'Come off it! I was out on the bike yesterday and I saw her in a bar – near Lardos Beach. She was with the guy from *WATERWORLD*. I bet he only banned us to impress her with how macho he is. The prat. Anyway, he seemed to fancy himself a lot more than he fancied her.'

I pulled a face. 'That figures. He's called Alexander, and he's Greek-Australian. Ego the size of – anyway, he's awful.'

'She didn't think so. She kept collapsing all over

431

him. Someone ought to tell her that if you act like a pushover you get treated like one.'

'She's in love!' I said indignantly.

'Oh, crap. He'll be off with another tourist next week. What a smarm merchant.'

There was a silence. Karl's views on Alexander matched mine so exactly I didn't know what to say. So I changed the subject. 'Why *did* you go on holiday with that lot?' I asked.

He turned towards me. 'Bit like you, I suppose. Opportunity. I play football with them, they're OK, we always have a laugh. I knew they had this holiday set up but I didn't want to be in on it. Then one of them dropped out – couldn't make the payments. They offered it to me cheap. I'm at college, I've got the whole summer off – so I did a bit of building site work and got the money together.'

'And now you're regretting it.'

'No. It's been OK. They're good mates. It's like I said – I just fancied some time on my own.'

'I don't blame you – that one with the stereo is brain dead,' I said, nastily.

'Oh, *cruel*! He really fancies you. He keeps going on about you, and what he'd like to – how much he likes you.'

Inside, I glowed. That kind of complement is always welcome, even from someone like Reg. 'He isn't exactly subtle, is he?' I said. 'Barging into Zoë. And he wouldn't let go of my arm for about ten minutes.'

'That's his pulling technique. He hasn't twigged yet

432

that it tends to send girls running in the other direction. He always goes for princess types, too, the poor sod, and he doesn't stand a chance.'

'Look – I'm not a princess,' I said, fervently. 'That's Zoë, and she only does it some of the time. I've got four brothers at home. You can't be a princess with four brothers.'

'Older or younger?'

'Both. Equal hell, both sides.'

He smiled at me, and I began to smile back. Then, somewhere at the edge of my consciousness, I heard a rumbling sound, and for some instinctive reason, it filled me with panic. I shot to my feet and peered down the hill towards the car park, shading my eyes. It was nearly empty – and heading off down the road, in a cloud of dust, I saw the rear end of our bus.

'Oh, no!' I wailed. 'Oh my *GOD!* That's the *BUS!* They've gone without me!'

The Ride Of A Lifetime

Karl stood up next to me. 'What were you on, some kind of tour?'

'Yes! With Zoë's parents! I can't believe they've just gone off without . . .' I broke off and peered at my watch. 'Oh, God. It's 4.15. They told me the bus went at four. But they might have *looked* for me – or at least *shouted*.'

'Well, you're some way off, up here. Maybe they did look, but not this far.'

I gazed at Karl, panic rising. I felt completely abandoned.

'Why don't you go down to the ticket office and ask there,' he said. 'They might have left a message for you.'

I started to run down the hill, heedless of the heat and the thorny little plants snatching at my ankles. Without saying a word, Karl had started to run beside me. Once, when I stumbled, he put out his hand and caught me by the arm.

I raced down the main street of the ruined town, and across the stretch of gravel in the entranceway. I came to a crash landing against the side of the wooden ticket office and shouted through the hatch,

'Excuse me! That bus that left – was there a couple on there who . . . ?'

'Ah,' said the ticket man importantly. 'You are Miss Brianna? Yes? From England?'

'Yes!' I wailed.

'Your guardian left message. He very angry, very worried, very anxious. His wife ill – heat-stroke. He take her back, and come back here with taxi for you. He say wait here.'

I heaved a sigh of relief. But I didn't like the sound of that 'very angry, very worried, very anxious'. I bet he was spitting teeth.

I turned to Karl. 'I,' I announced, 'am in *big* trouble,'

'I can give you a lift,' said Karl, shrugging. 'Get you back to Lindos before the bus gets there. Then at least the old man won't have to fork out for a taxi.'

'Oh – *could* you?' I'd come over totally trembly. And not with the thought of avoiding Mr Chester's wrath, either. 'That would be *brilliant*. You'd save my life – you'd—'

'OK,' he said. 'Don't overdo it. Come on.'

His bike was parked in the little car-park behind the ticket office. 'Here it is,' he said. 'These Greek bikes are pretty sad, really. Real slow. You should see what I've got at home.'

Love to, I thought. He straddled the bike, and kicked the engine into life. 'Come on,' he shouted to me over the engine roar. 'Get on.'

So, as elegantly as I could, I climbed on behind him.

435

'Now hold *on*,' he shouted, as he started to leg the bike forward. 'It's real bumpy here.'

I had no choice. The first lurch threw me right backwards, so I was forced to hold on to him really tightly. Then we were off.

It was on the bike ride that I became seriously smitten with Karl. I wrapped myself round him as close as I could get, pressing my face into his back, breathing in the smell of his sun-bleached shirt. My legs were against his legs, and my arms were around his chest. We roared along, faster and faster, just him and me in this wind tunnel on the edge of the white cliff tops, and I could feel every muscle move as he manoeuvred the bike.

I just about passed out with it all, I can tell you.

After a while, Karl turned sideways towards me, so that his mouth was like two centimetres away from mine, and started to say something. And the great thing was, I had to get even nearer to his mouth to hear what it was.

'Look – there's the bus. We've caught up with it already. I'll see if I can get the driver's attention – then we can get you on board.'

It was as if he'd hit me. The last thing I wanted to do was get on that stupid bus! I wanted to go on riding behind him for ever. But Karl had overtaken the bus, and was making vague 'stop' signs with his left arm. Then he slowed down until he was parallel to the bus driver's cabin, and made some more signs. Then all of a sudden he accelerated away, leaving the bus behind, his bike eating up the road as if it was ravenous.

After a while he slowed down again, turned his gorgeous profile to me again, and said, 'I couldn't get him to stop. The driver must think I'm a highwayman or something – he was swearing at me to clear off.' Then he faced the front and we accelerated off again.

I wrapped my arms tighter round his back, and let my face rest blissfully against his shoulder. This kind of glow was spreading all through me. Because I'd seen the driver's face too, and he hadn't been swearing at all. He hadn't needed to – he hadn't noticed Karl's signals. Because – I realised in delight – Karl hadn't been trying very hard to *get* noticed.

It's Better With Two

We drove off round the coast road, through a few straggling seaside resorts, and into the centre of a really pretty little village. When we reached the village square, all laid out with benches and well-watered trees, Karl slowed the bike and stopped.

'Look,' he said, turning back towards me, 'at this rate we'll be back hours before that bus. They always make loads of stops to drop all the punters off. And I could murder a drink, seeing as you finished off my water.'

'I'd love a drink,' I said, climbing off the bike. 'Where?'

'There,' he said, pointing. 'I've been to that bar before. It's good.'

Good? It was fantastic – the sort of Greek-atmospheric place I'd dreamed of finding. We climbed up the steps to the veranda and sat down opposite each other at an old wooden table. All along the veranda edge, lush, big-leaved plants tumbled out of white-painted oil drums; over our heads the vine sun-shade swayed in the breeze.

The friendly owner bought us bottles of beer and water, and we sat there savouring the cold drinks, chatting about this and that, and laughing over me being left behind by the bus. Karl had a wonderful laugh, sort of slow to get going, then really deep and warm. Laughing made his whole face come alive. I tried to seem dead relaxed as I chatted, but I felt like every particle in me was on full alert. All I wanted to do was watch him, but my eyes kept sliding away from his.

After a while, there was a stretch of silence. I looked over the top of my glass to see Karl staring at me, looking as though he was working something out.

'What?' I said, defensively.

'I was just thinking about that stuff your friend came out with, about how we were gits and pathetic and . . .'

'Look – you've got to realise how . . . threatening you lot seemed.'

'Did you feel threatened, too?'

'Well – a bit. I mean – there were seven of you. And two of us.'

'Two's enough, I can tell you! Just two is scary enough.'

'Oh, charming. What d'you mean?'

'I mean the way you look at people – and laugh together – like you're judging every bloke that walks past.'

Well, we are, I thought. 'Aren't you doing that to every girl?' I asked.

'I dunno – it's different.'

'Yeah? Why?'

'It just is. We don't do it – so seriously.'

439

There was a pause. He's shy, I thought in sudden delight. Someone this lush is actually a bit shy.

The sun was slowly going down in the sky; everything glowed red in its light. Then, as if at a signal, hundreds of cicadas began to chirp in a nearby tree. 'This is wonderful,' I sighed. 'When did you discover it? Not your mates' sort of hang-out, is it?'

He grinned at me. 'Look, Brianna, I am not joined to them by the hip. I told you, I've been spending some time on my own. I came here last night.'

'It's OK for blokes,' I said, 'they can go into bars on their own.'

'Yeah, but it's not as good as when you're . . .'

'With your mates?'

'With someone. Let's go.'

Back on the bike, I saw the approach of Lindos with a sinking heart. Now I had to face Mr Chester, and I had to say goodbye to Karl. Unless . . .

Karl locked his bike up when we got off it. 'I'll come in with you,' he said. 'Maybe it'll smooth things over if he sees someone's seen you right home.'

Somehow, I doubted it. What Mr Chester would see was one of the louts from the airport with a fast bike. Still, it kept Karl by my side for a bit longer. And that was beginning to matter more than any row with Zoë's dad.

I opened the door and called softly, 'Mr Chester? Hi? I'm back!'

Mr Chester came out of the main bedroom at speed,

a finger clamped to his lips. 'Don't wake her!' he hissed. 'She's been in a terrible state!'

'I'm back,' I repeated. I thought I should repeat it. Maybe he'd forgotten he'd abandoned me in a prehistoric town.

'Thank GOODNESS!' he said. 'We were SO worried, leaving you like that. I was just about to call a taxi to go back.'

'I'm really sorry about missing the bus.'

'After I'd TOLD you four o'clock latest! The driver refused to wait beyond 4.15. But how on earth did you get back so soon . . . ?'

Karl stepped forward. 'Hi,' he said. 'I gave Brianna a lift. We bumped into each other by the temple. I guess that's why she didn't hear you shout for her.'

'I shouted for AGES!' said Mr Chester, almost plaintively. 'And I went round all the streets again, and up to the temple – where were you?'

'In the shade, under some trees,' I explained. 'The heat had made me really . . .'

'Well, that's what happened to Marjorie,' he broke in. 'She was in such a state. Otherwise I wouldn't have dreamed of just going off without you and leaving you ON YOUR OWN . . .'

This was priceless. Mr Chester really felt the need to justify what he'd done.

'Marjorie gets very bad, sometimes,' he went on. 'I couldn't let her travel back on her own. I know it sound silly but – she needs me at those times.'

There was an awkward silence, and then Karl said, 'Well – Brianna didn't come to any harm. Luckily.'

441

'No,' said Mr Chester. 'Er – thank you.'

There was a muffled sort of wail from the main bedroom, like a seal being suffocated. 'There's Marjorie,' said Mr Chester weakly. 'I'd better go in to her – tell her you're safe.'

He disappeared, and Karl and I were left standing on the terrace alone. It was almost dark now, and a soft, warm wind had begun to blow, stirring the vine leaves.

'I love this weather,' said Karl. 'The nights are the best. Where does that wind come from?'

'I don't know,' I said, 'but it's magic.'

There was a pause, and then Karl muttered, 'Well – I'd better go.'

'Let me buy you a drink,' I said in a rush. 'To say thank you. Or dinner. To really say thank you. I mean – you saved my life, today. And I'm starving. Aren't you? We could walk into Lindos – there's lots of nice places to eat . . .'

'All right, all right,' he said, grinning. 'I'm convinced. Come on then.'

The Nights Are The Best

I tiptoed over to the Chesters' bedroom, and poked my head round the door.

'Mr Chester,' I whispered. He was sitting by Mrs Chester on the bed, mopping her forehead with a wet flannel. 'Is it OK if I go out for a few hours? Just into Lindos. To get something to eat with Karl.'

He looked round distractedly. 'To eat? Yes, of course. Here. . .' He drew something out of his pocket. 'On me.' And he handed me a little roll of bank notes.

I was stunned. 'Oh, you don't have to . . .' I began, but he'd put his finger to his lips again, smiling, so I just crept out.

Karl was standing on the terrace with his back to me, looking out to the shoreline over the low stone wall. I had this overwhelming urge to go and wrap my arms round him again and rest my face against his shoulders, just like on the bike.

'Karl!' I hissed. 'Look!' I waved the money at him. 'Courtesy of Mr Chester!'

'Great! He's got a guilty conscience, has he? Let's go.'

'Give me *three* minutes,' I said, and shot into my bedroom.

I grabbed my hairbrush and painfully began to put right the havoc from the bike ride. Then I zipped on some lippy and mascara, and a bit of damage-limitation aftersun cream. My tan is really beginning to look good, I thought, as I stood in front of the mirror. I turned, torn with indecision, to the wardrobe. God forbid that I should look as if I was *trying too hard* . . .

Oh, sod it. This was Greece. This was my holiday. And this was by far the best reason I'd had so far to wear my red dress. And if Zoë had chosen that night to borrow it I'd – well, she'd just better not have, that's all.

Five minutes later, I was at Karl's side again. In red.

'Blimey,' he said. 'You've changed – in three minutes. I didn't think that was possible for a girl.'

'Don't make sexist comments,' I retorted.

'OK. You look great. Is that sexist?'

I laughed. 'Let's go.'

We clattered down the worn stone steps together and off along the narrow street. Already the place was filling up with people planning to have a great night out. Swimsuits and shorts had been swapped for cutaway dresses and spiky heels, and there was a sense of excitement everywhere.

The lanes were crowded so we walked close together to let people get by. My hand was hanging by my side, swinging, awkward, unattached. What it wanted to do more than anything in the world was hold his.

'Let's go in here,' I said, stopping by a wide,

impressive doorway. 'My favourite bar.' It was the swankest place I could think of. Zoë and I had only been in it twice – we felt a bit intimidated by it.

We walked through all the potted palms and painted wooden parrots up to the bar. I studied Karl as he stood there, ordering drinks. He really was something special. Short, soft brown hair. And beautiful eyes. And long legs. And a wonderful mouth. And –

'Where d'you want to eat?' he said.

'On a rooftop,' I answered, without thinking.

'All right, princess! Where?'

'I am not a princess. There are loads of rooftop restaurants here. They're great. You're right near the sky and there's a terrific view and . . .'

'You've convinced me. Come on, let's find somewhere to sit.'

This bar was so posh it had sofas rather than stools to sit on. We found an empty one and sank into it. He sat close to me, but it might not have meant anything. It could have been just to leave room for someone to sit at the other end. He could just see me as a mate, someone he'd rescued. It's not as though we're on a date, I thought. But if this evening ends with him just saying 'Bye, thanks for the meal' and me saying 'Bye, thanks for the lift,' I think I'll kill myself.

We both took a few sips of our drinks in silence. I stared at his hand as he picked up his glass. I watched his throat as he swallowed. Come on, this is the age of sexual equality, I told myself. Launch yourself on him. But somehow, I couldn't.

We finished our drinks quickly, hardly talking, and

then went off to find a rooftop restaurant. The first two we tried were full, then the third said they could fit us in in ten minutes or so.

'Why don't have a drink while you wait, sir and madam?' said the waiter, indicating a tiny bar made of sherry barrels.

We bought drinks, and stood in the corner, under an indoor tree that twinkled with fairy lights. We were the only people waiting there. Waiting, waiting. I couldn't think of a thing to say. I couldn't even look at his face, so I stared at his chest. All I wanted to do was kiss him. It was getting unbearable.

He took a long swig of beer, and put his glass down. I put my drink on the bar too. Then I took a deep breath, moved closer to him, and laid one hand flat on his chest. 'Karl—' I began.

It was like I'd pulled a mains switch. He grabbed hold of my hand, wrapped his other arm round my back, and pulled me in close. Then we were kissing in a way that made all the other kissing I'd done in my life seem like kids' stuff.

After a while I drew back and looked up at him, and he looked back. Then I pulled his head down to mine again.

When we came up for air, the waiter was hovering nearby. 'I – er – had to give your table to someone else,' he said, a little stiffly. 'But there'll be another one free in a few minutes.'

Karl looked at me, hugging me tight, then we both started laughing.

Until Tomorrow

Once we were seated at our little table in the corner on the rooftop, we both moved in as close to each other as we could. He'd trapped one of my legs between his under the table, and on top I'd captured both his hands beneath mine. The magic wind was still blowing, making the candles stream sideways, bringing the scent of jasmine with it. And I was shaking. I couldn't believe what had just happened – what was still happening.

'Look at that sky,' I said. 'Wasn't I right to want a rooftop?'

'Yes. Are those really the same stars we see in the boring old UK?'

'No, special Greek ones.'

'Hey, Brianna,' he said, grinning. 'That was – I thought I was going to get a smack in the face back then. When I grabbed you.'

'Oh, for heaven's sake. Why d'you think I asked you out to eat?'

'To thank me, like you said. You'd've done it for anyone.'

'Oh no, I wouldn't. God, Karl, why are blokes so bad at body language? I haven't exactly been freezing you off since the bike ride, have I?'

He shook his head, happily. 'Maybe not – but after all that crap at Faliraki – I thought you thought we were all idiots.'

'Zoë thought that. I didn't. I just didn't have the guts to stand up to that greasy git Alexander. Anyway – what was I supposed to say? Don't ban the one in the green shorts, 'cos I fancy him?'

'Yeah! Why not?'

We laughed, and the waiter came and we ordered, garlic bread and steak and mushrooms and pasta – stuff that we liked, even if it didn't all go together. Then we settled to eating, stealing bits off each other's plates, and staring at one another across the table as we chewed.

'So,' Karl said, swallowing, 'Did you ever get to go on the banana?'

'No. And I don't want to.'

'Yeah, you do. We found somewhere else that has one. Stuff WATERWORLD. I could take you. Tomorrow.'

'Oh, great. So I have to face all your mates, do I, and have them bribe the boat driver to go extra fast to throw me off and . . .'

'Hang on, hang on, I didn't say anything about them coming along. We can hire it just for the two of us. That way it'll go even faster.'

'Oh, terrific. I've got a better idea. Let's just go to a beach – and do nothing.'

He smiled, widely. 'Almost nothing, maybe.'

We carried on eating, more slowly this time because we were holding hands and could only use our forks and fingers. 'Now let's go and get ice-cream on the beach,' Karl said, as we wiped our plates clean.

'You're mad! Nowhere will be open!'

'Yes it will. I know a really good . . .'

'Bar. You would. Let's go.'

This time we were so wrapped round each other as we went through the narrow stone streets we had difficulty walking. It was slow going, especially as we kept stopping to kiss. We made our way down to the shore, a way I'd never been before, and I began to hear music above the waves. And there, tucked beneath the cliff, was a fantastic café, full of welcoming, coloured lights and packed with people.

In no time we were nestled together at a little table, sharing Italian ice-cream.

'There's only two days of this holiday left,' I said mournfully.

'I know. Think of all the time we've wasted. If you hadn't been such a princess that day in Faliraki, we could've got it together then.'

'*ME?* It's *my* fault is it? You and your mates come on like some kind of rugby scrum – anyway, you were as bad. You looked at me like you hated me at Kamiros, when I tried to share your shade.'

'Tried to share? I don't remember getting a choice! And I only looked at you like that because I thought you hated me.'

'Well – I didn't.'

'And I didn't hate you.' He leaned over the table towards me, his mouth so close it gave me goosebumps. 'I fancied you something chronic. Nearly as much as I fancy you now.'

I sighed blissfully, and scooped the last of the fudge sauce from the bottom of the glass.

'In fact . . .' he went on, still halfway over the table, 'I fancied you from the plane.'

'Me too,' I said. 'Why didn't we do something about it *then*?'

'Well, it was all a bit crowded, remember? And besides, Reg really had something going for you. He – oh, God. I'd forgotten about Reg. He's going to go ballistic when he finds out I've got off with you.'

'So don't tell him.'

'No, I'll tell him he didn't stand a chance with you. Then it'll be all right.'

I shook my head over the male psyche. 'Why will that make it all right? I'd be gutted if someone said that to me.'

'Because if he didn't stand a chance, I didn't ruin anything for him.'

'I see. I think.'

We walked the long way back across the beach, stopping every now and then to kiss, then we lay down for a while in the sand, wound round each other, listening to the sighing of the waves. It occurred to me that with some other blokes, lying here so far away from anyone, I might feel a bit nervous. But somehow I didn't, with Karl. This time he could read my body language perfectly.

'I love the way your hair's all soft at the back of

your head,' I said, pushing my fingers into it. 'It looks spiky, but it's soft. Like a sea anemone.'

'A *sea anemone*? Is that meant to be a compliment?'

'Yes.'

'Well, yours looks like overdone candyfloss. What does it taste like?' And he caught a big strand of it between his teeth.

I laughed, and raised myself up on one elbow, so that I could stroke his hair and examine every inch of his face, before I kissed him again.

After a while he murmured, 'Brianna, I hate to bring this up. I'd like to lie here all night. But are you supposed to be back at any time?'

In panic, I looked at my watch. 'Oh, no. It's after *two*! Zoë's dad will go *spare*. That's twice in one day I've gone missing.'

He stood up and pulled me to my feet. 'Come on, we'll be back in ten minutes. And my bike's parked near your apartment, so he'll know you're still with me.'

'I'm not sure that'll reassure him,' I said. 'With any luck, Zoë will have covered for me. I've told enough lies about her and her precious Alexander this week. I even pretended to *be* her, once.'

Karl looked at me, amazed. 'How did you manage to do that?'

'I called out "Goodnight Daddy" while I was cleaning my teeth. He bought it.'

'God, girls are appalling. So . . . *devious*. How will I ever be sure you're telling me the truth?'

I laughed. 'Body language,' I said.

Too soon we were standing beside Karl's bike. 'Well, I'd better get back to Faliraki,' he said. 'Coming with me?'

I could tell he didn't mean it. Trying it on was kind of obligatory for a lad. 'No way,' I said. 'I bet you share a bedroom with at least two of the others, and you all snore.'

He laughed, and hugged me. 'So when can I see you tomorrow?' he asked.

Tomorrow. We had all of tomorrow. No school, no college, nothing to do but be together. 'As early as you like,' I said.

'Right. I'll pick you up for breakfast. If I have to watch Reg and the others eat one more full-fried-English, I'll go mental.'

'Fried breakfast,' I said. 'In this heat. How gross. I have cappuccino and croissants, and the occasional fresh fig.'

'OK, princess, whatever you say,' he grinned, and bent down to kiss me one last lovely time. Then he was on his bike and off into the night.

I watched him until he swerved round a corner and out of sight, then I floated up the stone steps and let myself through the main door. I tiptoed across the terrace. As I passed the vine net-curtains, I reached up and pulled the end of one of the bows. I just couldn't stop myself. The vine ropes tumbled down, chaotic and green and beautiful.

I crept into the bedroom. And there was Zoë, sitting up in bed, an indignant look on her face.

'It's *three o'clock*, Brianna! Where have you *been*? I got back early to *talk* to you.'

452

Well, excuse *me* for having my own *life*, I thought.

'I covered for you, anyway,' she went on. 'I said you were undressing.'

'Thanks, Zoë. I didn't realise it had got that late.' Actually, come to think of it, I didn't care.

'So – what were you up to?' she went on.

I told her, and I shall never forget the look on her face as I did.

Pandora 💋 You will not <u>BELIEVE</u> what's happened! Brianna has got off with one of the LADS FROM HELL!! I know she likes roughing it but this is ridiculous. He's one of a group of morons who THREW me of a pier into the sea! I'm sure she's not safe with him. Still, she's probably only doing this because I've spent so much time with Alexander. I feel really responsible. Love Zoë
xxxx

Simply The Best

I woke up the next morning early, absolutely shot through with happiness. I couldn't believe how well things had turned out. Karl and I might only have two days left together but I wasn't going to let that depress me. I resolved they'd be the best two days ever.

I left Zoë asleep and raced into the bathroom. If I was going out with Karl for breakfast I needed a bit of preparation. I had a quick shower, hair wash, and squirted on lots of body cream. Then I put on my favourite shorts and T-shirt, and packed my cozzie, makeup and money into my little backpack. I wasn't planning on returning to the apartment until nightfall at the earliest.

Zoë had just staggered out of bed onto the terrace when there was a 'parp' from outside. It was recognisably not from Alexander's bike. I rushed to the wall, leaned over, and saw Karl, looking completely gorgeous with his hair all blown back from the bike ride, smiling up at me. I melted, waved, and rushed for the door.

'Brianna!' Zoë wailed. 'Are you off already? Can't we *talk*?'

I turned to her. 'No, Zoë, we can't. I'm off out.

With Karl. Tell your mum and dad, will you?' And I left.

Karl was locking up the bike when I ran down the steps. He turned, and we faced each other for a minute, a bit uncertain, then I walked forward and put both my arms round his neck. He looked down at me, laughing, and said, 'You always this forthright?'

'Yup. Making up for lost time,' I replied.

'Good,' he said, and we had a long, long kiss.

Breakfast was beautiful. Hot croissants, hot coffee, even fresh figs, just as I'd said. Karl lowered the tone a bit by having scrambled eggs too, but he said he felt really hungry. There was this incredible feeling of excitement between us. We talked and joked – we were so open together, as though we'd known each other for ages. And as though we knew there was no time to waste in playing mind games.

Lindos seemed different now I was with Karl. Every little thing gave us a buzz. We wrapped our arms round each other and walked slowly through the tiny streets, stopping to laugh at some appalling postcards, or admire some beautiful silver jewellery, or stroke a thin stray cat.

We headed for the same beach we'd been to last night and hired sunbeds and an umbrella. Holidays kind of accelerate intimacy. I oiled Karl's back, slowly and enjoyably, then he did mine.

'You don't go in for this topless thing, then?' he asked casually, as two particularly well-endowed girls walked by.

I looked him straight in the eye. 'No,' I said. 'I burn easily.'

For the next few hours we were just like all the other besotted couples on the beach, the ones I'd spent the last week envying so much. We held hands across the gap between the sunbeds as we talked together, comparing notes on the most embarrassing bits of our holidays so far. I won, of course. No amount of crass laddish behaviour on the part of Karl's friends could come near making up a threesome with Ma and Pa Chester. Then he told me he knew a bit about reflexology and gave me a foot massage, from which it was obvious he knew nothing about reflexology or massage, but it was still nice. After that he came and squeezed on my sunbed with me for a while, and we necked shamelessly; then – when we both fell off the sunbed onto the sand – we went for a swim.

We played around in the shallows for a while, splashing and giving each other piggy backs and falling backwards. Then we swam out to sea. It was silent and beautiful far out in the bay. We hung there, treading water. You can kiss really well while you're treading water. Just your mouths touching.

After a while we swam to some deserted rocks, clambered out and sunbathed with the surf crashing about us, until our hunger and the burning heat told us it was time to find somewhere shady for lunch.

'What d'you want to do later on?' he said, as we broke bits of rough Greek bread at a shabby little beach café. 'Take the bike out somewhere?'

'Yes,' I said greedily. 'Where?' I wanted to do everything, I wanted to fit it all in today.

'Up into the hills – see the countryside. It's great by bike. We can watch the sun go down from a mountain top.'

We went and lounged on our sunbeds on the shoreline for a couple more hours, then we had one last, lazy swim. As the sun got lower in the sky, we grew restless and headed back to Lindos to get the bike.

'You don't need to go in for anything do you?' said Karl, reluctantly, as we got near to the apartment.

I laughed. 'You mean shower, change, curl my hair? You think I need it?'

'No. You look gorgeous.'

'Well, let's go then.' And as I climbed on the bike behind him, I *felt* gorgeous, too. After a day like I'd had, anyone would.

I wrapped my arms tight round him and snuggled my face into his shirt. 'Quick, get going,' I said into the back of his neck. 'Before the Chesters see us and force us to go up and join them for a drink.'

At that he accelerated away so fast I was nearly thrown off backwards. We raced higher and higher up into the hills, past parched looking fields and rocky outcrops. Half the time I was admiring the landscape, the other half I spent admiring the way the muscles in Karl's back worked as he manoeuvred the bike round the tight bends. I couldn't seem to keep my hands still on his shoulders.

After a while he pulled up next to a little roadside

457

stall and bought a bottle of water, and we both had a long drink. Then we kissed, mouths cold at first from the water we'd drunk, and roared off again.

After about an hour it seemed as if we'd gone as high as we could go. We were right at the edge of a cliff, with a spectacular view out over the sea. Karl stopped the bike and swivelled round, swinging both legs over on top of mine. I laughed as I ducked back to avoid him cracking me one with his knee then I moved in even closer to him, put my arms round his waist, and kissed him.

'This is an amazing place, Karl,' I said, looking around.

'I know.'

'That view is – stunning!'

'Sod the view,' he said, and started kissing me.

After a while we climbed off the bike and lay on the grass and talked and necked some more, totally engrossed in each other. We stayed there until it got quite dark. I began to feel I didn't want to see anyone else, or speak to anyone else. Only Karl.

'Where d'you come from?' he asked suddenly. 'I mean – back home?'

I told him, and he told me where he lived. He said it was very rural, hard to get to. There was a silence as we both took in quite how far apart we lived, and quite how difficult it would be to see each other once we got home.

'Well, I've got the bike,' he said, after a while. 'I travel huge distances on that thing. I mean, I do thirty miles a day just to get to college.'

'Which one d'you go to?' I asked.

'Rochester Tertiary. Near Bedford.'

I felt as though the air around me was suddenly fizzing with static. 'Rochester Tertiary – on Rochester Street?' I said, breathlessly. 'By the station? Near the hospital?'

He stared at me. 'Yes. Brianna? Which one are . . .'

'*THAT'S WHERE I'M GOING!!*' I screamed, and threw myself on top of him.

Unbelievable

It took us another five minutes before we really allowed ourselves to accept that we were going to the same college. Superstitiously, we checked the name of the principal, the number of dining rooms, the colour of the main building outside. Then we allowed ourselves to really celebrate.

'But won't you *mind?*' I squawked. 'I mean – are you sure you really *want* me there? You've probably got loads of girls in your class you fancy . . . you've probably . . .'

'Brianna, I'm doing an *engineering* course. There are only two other girls on it. And they're not my type.'

'Oh, this is brilliant. I'll be able to see *so much* of you . . .'

'Aren't you afraid I'll cramp *your* style? All those spunky new kids – all waiting to meet someone like you . . .'

I pulled a face at him. 'I've been to the college open day, remember. Studs were pretty thin on the ground, I can tell you.'

'That,' he said, stroking my hair back from my face, 'is great news. I don't want any competition. Not for you.'

I rolled over on to my back and stared up at all the impossibly bright stars and thought about the future. I'd put it out of my mind up until now, because it involved work, and effort, and change, all the things I didn't want to face until well after the holiday. But now the future had some kind of shape to it. It could be looked at, even looked forward to. The future had Karl in it.

So did the present.

Later, hunger and the desire for a drink made us mount the bike once more and head off into the night. We found a tiny, brightly lit restaurant, right off the beaten track, and peered in through the window. It was mostly full of locals but there were a few tourists round the edges, all looking superior because they'd found somewhere 'authentic'. Hungrily, I scanned the menu displayed at the front.

'Karl, let's go in – this looks great! All that mountain air has done me in – I'm famished.'

Karl looked worried. 'Er – Brianna – it's right at the end of the holiday and I'm, er . . .'

'Broke?'

'I'm afraid so.'

'Well I'm not. I'm loaded. The one good thing about being bored witless with the Chesters is you hardly spend any money. Come on.'

'Look – I can't let you pay for me.'

'Fine. Come in and watch me stuff my face and starve then. Come ON, Karl! You can buy me lunch at college!'

That convinced him. We ordered and ate slowly, in friendly silence, holding hands across the table. Then we drove back to Lindos. When Karl drew up outside the apartment, I was half asleep against his back.

'I'm nor gerring off,' I mumbled into his shirt.

'You what?'

'Can't move. Sleeping here.'

'OK, princess. Whatever you say,' he said, twisting round to rub his cheek against the top of my head. Then, after a few minutes, he said, 'Come on, Brianna. Move. It's our last day tomorrow, and I'm coming to pick you up at 6am.'

'OK,' I agreed happily, then I slid off, kissed him goodbye, and crawled up the steps to the apartment.

Zoë was fast asleep when I crept into our room. I was very, very careful not to wake her.

Dear Pandora ✠ It's past one o'clock and Brianna is still out with the git who threw me off the pier. I'm really worried. She wouldn't talk to me about him this morning – just raced off when she heard his bike. I just don't want her to get hurt. So much for keeping holiday romances in perspective! Not that I can talk!! See you soon ✠
xxx Zoë

Head For The Hills

I didn't really expect Karl at six the next day, but I did wake up early. Zoë, however, had beaten me to it. She'd even made me a cup of tea.

'So – how's Karl?' she said, perching beside me on the bed.

'Fabulous. Much better without his mates. How's Alexander?'

'OK.'

'Only OK? When are you seeing him?'

'Not till later today. Bri, he's –'

'What?'

'He's really been putting the pressure on. For me to – you know.'

'Oh God. Sleep with him.'

She nodded, eyes downcast, and there was a silence. Then she went on, 'He said if I really loved him I – oh, OK, Bri. I know what you're thinking. And don't worry, I'm not going to. But when we're together, and he's . . . oh, I don't know. At the start of the holiday, he kept saying how he'd come to England to see me – he has an uncle there and everything – but . . . but he hasn't been saying that so much, and he's . . .' She broke off, and sighed.

'This really isn't just a holiday romance for you, is it Zoë?'

She shook her head. 'What about Karl?'

'Well, I . . . I don't know.' I didn't want to tell her he'd be at college with me next term. I didn't think it would exactly cheer her up.

I knew she wanted to talk more, but I felt driven – as driven as she'd been those first days with Alexander. It was my last day in Greece with Karl. And no one was going to shorten it for me, not if I could help it. I got up and got dressed, and soon after that Karl drew up outside. As we walked into Lindos, hand in hand, I told him it looked like he'd been right about Alexander.

'I think Zoë knows it too,' I said, 'she seemed really down, she wanted to talk, but I . . .'

'She'll get over him,' said Karl. 'He's a loser.'

'I know. I still can't believe she swallowed all his *spiel*. I mean – single red roses and stuff. Really, a girl's a lot better off with someone totally unromantic and practical. Like you.'

He stopped dead, and looked at me. 'You,' he said impressively, 'are going to eat your words in a minute.' Then he pulled a little white box out of his back pocket, and handed it to me.

Intrigued, I opened it. Inside was one of the thin silver bracelets we'd been admiring yesterday. 'Oh, *Karl* . . .' I began.

'*And* I had to knock the shop up to buy it this morning. Romantic or *what*?'

'But you're *broke* . . .'

464

'Reg owed me some money. I got it back last night. I had to threaten to trash his CD collection, but it worked.'

'That,' I said, slipping the bracelet onto my wrist, 'is probably the most romantic thing I've ever heard. *Thank* you, Karl – it's lovely. Doesn't silver look good on brown?'

'Beautiful,' he answered, and we wandered down to the beach.

That day followed the same lovely pattern as the day before. Even knowing we had to fly home the next day couldn't spoil it – it only seemed to make the time more precious. As we lay on the shoreline, letting the waves lap at us, Karl said we should do something really good tonight, something to mark the last night.

'Great,' I answered. 'Like what?'

'Well – I'd like to drive out to the hills, like we did last night. I can't think of anything better.'

I smiled at him. 'Me neither.'

'And this time dinner's on me.'

I laughed. 'Reg owed you that much did he?'

'Yup. But first – would you – could you bear it if . . .' He took a deep breath. 'There's a disco tonight at the hotel block we're staying in. Sort of last night bash. They've been making a really big deal of it.'

'Oh.'

'The guys have been on at me to go. 'Cos it's the last night of our holiday. They said I should bring you too. I thought if we just went for an hour or so . . .'

I put my arms round. his neck and hugged him. 'Course we can go. I just – I was just thinking about Zoë. I wonder what's going to happen with Alexander tonight.'

'You could always bring her to the disco.'

'Somehow – *somehow* I think she'd turn that down. And Karl . . .'

'Yes?'

'If we're going to a disco, I need to go back to the flat. To change.'

'How long'll you take?'

'Just long enough for you to meet Ma and Pa Chester.'

'Oh, spare me,' he said. 'I'll sit outside on the bike.'

He did, too. I raced inside the apartment while he stretched out full length on the bike seats and shut his eyes. He needn't have worried, though. The place was empty. I think Ma and Pa Chester had given up checking up on us at this stage. And, as Zoë wasn't there, this time there was no contest for the white dress.

I showered and changed at top speed, then went wild with my eye-makeup, and rushed out to Karl. My hair was still dripping but I reckoned motorbikes make great hair dryers.

Karl smiled when he saw me. 'You look terrific,' he said. 'Go on – get on.'

I held on with one hand this time, and raked through

my hair with the other one as we sped along in the warm breeze. When we arrived, the hotel was already humming with life, and huge bundles of shiny balloons were tied all over the place.

'It's all part of their promotional budget,' Karl said. 'Send the punters off with a great night and they'll think the whole holiday was like that and come back for more.'

We met Karl's friends in the bar. I felt quite nervous walking over to them, but I needn't have worried. There were two other girls hanging out with them, so it wasn't like I was unique.

Reg took one look at me and groaned out loud. 'You look really gorgeous,' he said, sounding depressed. 'Karl, you're dead.'

And then the evening got going. Karl showed me round the pool and the gardens with their battered looking palm trees, and we found this old wooden bench behind some spiky bushes, really secluded. We stayed there for a while, arms round each other, just talking, then we started kissing. After a while we realised it had got quite dark and we thought we ought to go back to the room where the disco was held.

I was expecting it to be a bit sad, but the DJ was manic and it turned into quite a rave. All the lads seemed to have forgiven me for my part in the banana-ride ban, and they turned out to be pretty good dancers, too, even if they did have more energy than style.

Around ten o'clock, Karl got hold of my hand and said, 'Cool off outside?'

467

I nodded, smiling. I wanted to be on my own with him again. We went outside and stood by the pool. There were loads of other couples out there, too, wandering along under the palm trees and snogging on the sunbeds.

Karl looked at me. 'What d'you say, partner? Head for the hills?'

I nodded at him, again, grinning, and without another word we left.

A Friend In Need

It was unreal, packing early next morning to go back.
It felt like we were tearing everything down. I could
hardly bear the thought that we were leaving the heat
and the magic wind, the blue sea and the bluer sky.
There was a choking lump in my throat as I crammed
my clothes into my suitcase. The only thing that
stopped me bursting out crying was knowing Karl
would be on the same bus to the airport, and on the
same plane home.

Zoë told me she'd had a lovely night with Alexander,
and he hadn't pressured her at all. She was all full of
hope again. They'd exchanged addresses, and he'd
promised to come and visit, maybe at Christmas.
Christmas. It was so far away it felt like the millennium
after next.

Soon we'd handed back the keys and loaded the
cases onto the bus. Then we were on our way to
Faliraki. When Karl got on the bus I stood up, and
bravely walked down towards the front to sit next
to him. I was all tensed up, waiting for the lads
to start messing around or teasing me, but nothing
happened.

Relieved, I laced my fingers into Karl's, and we sat

looking out of the window in silence as the coach drove through Faliraki. Then we were onto a narrow track, with fields either side.

'It's going to be weird not seeing cacti growing everywhere,' I murmured.

'Or goats.'

'Or . . .' I broke off. Just ahead of us, on his bike, was the unmistakably glamorous form of Alexander. And behind him, hugged in close, was a girl with long dark hair. She was leaning up against his back, face pressed against his shirt, eyes closed in pleasure.

'Oh, no,' I murmured.

'It could be just a friend,' said Karl, doubtfully.

'No it couldn't,' I replied. I recognised that way of sitting on the back of a bike.

Slowly, I turned my head to Zoë, to see if she'd seen. She had. She looked stricken. She looked as though someone had dealt her a death blow.

The bus pulled out past Alexander and his new girl-friend, and overtook them. I didn't know what to do. I looked round again, but Zoë wouldn't meet my eyes. I got this feeling she didn't want me to join her. Her face was frozen; I knew she was fighting for self control.

At the airport, I had a real battle with myself. Zoë was going through the motions like an automaton, but I knew she needed me. And all I wanted to do was be with Karl.

'You didn't hesitate to drop me when Alexander came along, did you?' I muttered under my breath. 'And now you expect me to drop Karl to comfort you. Well, too bad.'

But as I looked at her stricken face, I knew I had no choice. Zoë had been totally smitten: she'd dropped me because she couldn't help herself. That was part of the problem. That was why she was suffering so much now.

Karl came up beside me and put a lovely, warm arm round my shoulders. 'I've checked with the steward,' he said. 'There's a free seat in our row.'

'Is there? Oh, Karl . . .'

'Come and sit with me,' he said, persuasively. 'Come on. It'll make leaving Greece not seem so bad if you're next to me.'

I twisted round and buried my face in his neck. I breathed in his scent; I looked up at his jaw, his mouth. Temptation wasn't in it. My finer self knew I should be with Zoë, while the rest of me just wanted to snuggle up with Karl. They fought an all-out battle for a few seconds and then – a bit to my surprise – my finer self won.

'Karl,' I said, looking straight at him. 'Zoë needs me right now. I mean she *really* needs me.'

And to his everlasting credit, he nodded in agreement. 'I guess she does,' he said, stroking my hair back. 'You're a great friend to her.'

'Reckon she appreciates it?' I said, a bit ruefully.

'I appreciate it,' he said.

Melt? You could have mopped me up with a J cloth.

When we got on the plane, I went and sat beside Zoë. After half an hour's choked silence and two glasses of white wine, the hurt began to pour out. I let her talk and talk. She sounded totally lost, totally betrayed – the way she saw it, she just hadn't been great enough to hold Alexander's interest. I couldn't bear the way she spoke, as though she was stupid, a dupe, a failure, and everything that had happened had just been a sham, fake, worthless.

'Look,' I said, drawing a deep breath, 'it wasn't all a sham. It *wasn't*. Nothing can take away from you that you *felt* that way, right? I mean, what you felt was *real*. And incredible. And if you have real feelings – you can't avoid hurt sometimes. That creep was just playing stupid games and cheating. He's obviously incapable of *real* feeling. You know something? I wouldn't want *his* emotional life. I feel quite sorry for him.'

Boy, was I inspired or what? Zoë was drinking in every word I said, as though I had a potion that would cure her.

'He's the real loser, Zoë, not you,' I went on, scornfully. 'What you felt was *real* – what he felt was just – I mean, he's fake. He's sad. You do know this wasn't about not sleeping with him, don't you? You know this would have happened even if you *had* slept with him? I mean – he's that type of guy. He makes the beach vampires look like beginners. He's a professional fake, and if you fake things, you end up with a fake life. Whereas *you* – you'll meet someone soon who'll feel as strongly about you as you did about him. You'll end up with something real. I know you will.'

Zoë gave a long shuddering sigh, and laid back on

472

the head rest. 'Oh, Bri,' she said. 'I was such a cow to you. I spoilt your holiday. I just went . . .'

'Mental,' I said soothingly. 'And it's OK.'

Then Zoë had another little cry and within five minutes, she'd fallen into an exhausted sleep.

I stood up and walked to the back of the plane, where Karl and the boys were spreadeagled. Mike, the blond guy, and Karl had a row to themselves. Mike was asleep in the outside seat. Beyond that, was Karl, sprawled and gorgeous. And on the other side of him, a space. My space. He'd saved me the window seat.

I didn't hang about. After all, I was an old hand at this seat-hopping lark. I climbed over Mike, balancing with incredible skill on the chair arms, and landed right in Karl's lap.

The rest of the flight was fantastic.

Not The End

Getting home was so strange. It felt alien, somehow. It was as though I'd been away for a lot, lot longer than two weeks. I gave everyone the presents I'd bought them and the two postcards I'd forgotten to post. Then I told them a bit about the holiday, how great it had been, while they admired my tan and the sun-bleached streaks in my hair. I didn't mention Karl. Not yet. Somehow, in the grey light of England, it didn't feel quite real.

After an hour or so I went upstairs and lay on my bed. I felt drained, and a bit wobbly – almost as if everything that had happened had been fantasy. I twisted the silver bracelet round and round on my wrist, and I missed Karl so badly it made my throat ache. After a while I fell asleep.

When I woke up it was getting dark, and Mum was tapping on my bedroom door. 'Brianna?' she called softly. 'Are you awake?'

'Yeah – yeah I am,' I said, yawning.

'There's a young man here to see you. He says he's ridden all the way from . . .' I heard her turn away and call down the stairs –

'*Where* did you say you'd come from?'

474